J.R. Ward lives in thportive husband
and her beloved golden retriever. After graduating from law school,
she began working in health care in Boston and spent many years
as chief of staff ~~~~ ~~~~ ~~~ ~~~~demic medical centres in
the n~~~~

Visit her online:

www.jrward.com
www.facebook.com/JRWardBooks

J. R. WARD

POSSESSION

piatkus

PIATKUS

First published in the United States in 2013 by New American Library,
A Division of Penguin Group (USA) Inc., New York
First published in Great Britain in 2013 by Piatkus

A CIP catalogue record for this book
is available from the British Library

ISBN 978-0-7499-5720-9

Printed and bound by CPI Group (UK) Ltd, Croydon CR0 4YY

Papers used by Piatkus are from well-managed forests
and other responsible sources.

MIX
Paper from
responsible sources
FSC® C104740

Piatkus
An imprint of
Little, Brown Book Group
100 Victoria Embankment
London EC4Y 0DY

An Hachette UK Company
www.hachette.co.uk

www.piatkus.co.uk

To Morris M. Weiss, M.D.,
a gentleman and true Renaissance man.

Acknowledgments

With so many thanks to all my readers!

Thank you also to Steve Axelrod, Kara Welsh, Leslie Gelbman and everyone at New American Library!

And with eternal love to my family, both those of blood and those of adoption, and to all of Team Waud—you know who you are.

Oh, and as always, I have to acknowledge the love and devotion of the better half of WriterDog.

POSSESSION

Chapter One

"Okay where am I? Where am I . . . where—"

Cait Douglass leaned into the steering wheel of her little Lexus SUV, like that was going to increase the odds of her finding the hair salon.

Tennis-matching it between the road ahead and the lineup of ritzy shops to the left, she shook her head. "The real question is, what the hell am I doing . . . ?"

As she trolled down an Epcot Center of luxury boutiques, she was out of her element. French bedding. Italian shoes. English stationery. Clearly this part of Caldwell, New York, was not only worldly, but capable of supporting these triple-H places: high-end, highbrow, high-cost.

Huh.

Might be worth a good gander sometime, just to know how the other half lived—not going to happen now, though. She was late, and more to the point, it was seven thirty at night, so everything was closed. Made sense. The rich were probably sitting down in their crystal-strewn dining rooms, doing whatever Bruce Wayne did when he was out of his Batman costume.

Plus the environs made her nervous. Yup, lesson learned: Next time she decided to get her hair done, she was not asking her cousin, the one who was married to a plastic surgeon, for a reference—

Cait hit the brakes. "Gotcha!"

Yanking an illegal U-turn, she parallel-parked at a meter that didn't require plugging, and got out.

"Brrr." With a shiver, she pulled her lapels in tight. Late April in upstate meant that it could still get cold enough to count as February in more reasonable places, and as usual, the winter was hanging in strong—like a houseguest with nowhere else to go.

"I've got to move somewhere. Georgia . . . Florida." Maybe relocating could be the crowning glory of her year of reclamation. "Tahiti."

The hair salon was the lone still-open standout on the block, its interior lit up bright as daylight—and yet there didn't appear to be anyone inside. Stepping through the glass door, the air was all sweet perfume with an undertow of chemicals, and the discordant, wavy music was way too sophisticated for her.

Whoa, fancy. Everything was black and white marble, the dozen or so stations spick-and-span, the row of sinks with their Liberace leather reclining chairs like some kind of napping center for grown-ups. On the walls there were framed, larger-than-life head shots of models rocking Zoolander's Blue Steel, and the floor was shiny as a plate.

As she walked up to the reception desk, her sensible shoes made a squeaking sound—like all that Carrara didn't approve of them.

"Hello?"

Rubbing her nose as it kept tickling, she thought, for the love of God, the thing needed to sneeze or get over itself.

Lot of mirrors—which made her truly uncomfortable. She'd never been much for looking at herself—not because she was ugly, but because where she came from, that kind of thing was frowned upon.

Thank God her parents lived out West when they weren't traveling. No reason they'd ever know she'd set foot in a place like this.

"Hello?" She went deeper into the interior, checking out the island in the middle that was obviously where they mixed the colors. So many tubes of various hues of blond, brunette, red . . . and some of a more Crayola spectrum. Blue hair? Pink?

Maybe she should blow this off . . .

The man who came out of the back was thin as a shadow, those shrink-wrapped black jeans clearly helping his toothpick legs keep him upright.

"Are you zee Cait Douglass?" he said in an accent that she couldn't place and could barely understand.

"Ah, yes, I am."

As his dark, dark stare narrowed and locked on her hair, it was like a doctor eyeballing a rheumatic patient—and though he hardly looked like a serial killer, something about him made her want to turn and bolt for the door. Her skin was literally itching for her to get out of here, and this time it didn't have anything to do with her family's fundamentalist value system.

"My chair, eez dis over here," he announced.

At least . . . she thought that was what he'd said—okay, yup, he was pointing at one of the stations.

Now or never, Cait thought, glancing around and hoping to borrow some courage from something, anything. But nobody else was with them, and that trippy electronic music bubbling overhead made her brain spin. Worse, rather than being inspired by those photographs, all she could think of was that people really didn't need to take what grew out of their head so seriously.

Wait, that was her mother talking.

"Yes, thank you," she said with a nod.

Following his lead, she sat down in an incredibly comfortable leather seat, and then she was spun around to face the glass. Ducking her eyes to her lap, she jumped as he burrowed his surprisingly strong hands into her hair.

"*So what are you thinking?*" he asked. Which came out as something close to, *Sue va troo zinking?*

This is a bad idea, is what she was *zinking*.

Cait forced herself to focus on her reflection. Same deep brown hair. Same blue eyes. Same fine features. But there was makeup on her pale skin now, something she'd just recently learned how to apply without feeling like she was going into Kardashian territory. The body was different, too. Eight months of working hard in the gym had leaned her out in ways that the scale didn't necessarily recognize, but her clothes sure did. And the handbag in her lap was bright red, the sort of thing she never would have worn a year ago.

Naturally, everything else was gray and black, stuff that had been in her closet since before this year of change. But the Sephora tips, like the pop of color, made her feel . . . well, not the way she used to.

"Zo . . . ?" the stylist prompted, as he came around and struck a pose against the mirror.

With his arms crossed and his chin dipped, he reminded her of someone, but she couldn't place it.

Cait fingered her hair like he had, hoping it would germinate an idea in her head. "I don't know. What do you think?"

As he pursed his mouth, she realized he had lip gloss on. "*Bloond.*"

Bloond? What the hell was—"You mean blond?"

When he nodded, Cait mostly sucked back the recoil. Red accessories were one thing. Lady Gaga was another: She was prepared to dip her toe in the salon waters. Not drown herself.

"I wasn't thinking that extreme."

He reached forward and did that fingers-through-the-locks thing again. *"No, deftly bloond—und viz the law lits as vell."*

Law lits? Like he wanted to go tort reform on her hair?

"I don't even know what those are."

"Tvust me."

Cait met her own eyes again, and for some reason thought of her closet, where everything was arranged by type—and she would have done color sorting among the blouses, pants, skirts and dresses, too, but there were only so many variations on shadow.

Photoshopping a blond wig on her head made her want to hit the door again. But she was sick of her mouse-brown, too.

Now is the time to live, she thought. Never any younger. Never any better. No guarantee that tomorrow would come for her.

"*Bloond,* huh," she whispered.

"*Bloond,*" the stylist said. "*And ve're lawyer up, tou. Ze changing vroom iz trough vere.*"

Cait looked over her shoulder. *Trough vere* was a little hallway that had four doors opening off of it. She didn't suppose which one you chose mattered. But not all decisions had such lack of consequences.

"All right," she heard herself say.

Getting to her feet, she squeaked her way across the shiny floor and felt as though she were walking on water—but not like Jesus did. This was not a miracle; this was a mortal woman feeling unsteady on an otherwise stable floor.

But she wasn't going to pull out. The recent tragedy that had struck the community in so many ways had woken her up on an even deeper level, and she wasn't going to waste time with any lack-of-courage bullcrap. She was alive, and that was a gift.

After a moment's hesitation, she went through the first door on the right.

⊢━━━━━━⊣

As Duke Phillips strode down the sidewalk, people got out of his way, even though this was a rough part of Caldie after dark. Probably had something to do with his size, which was a bene he leveraged in both his jobs: big and muscular. Maybe it was his temperament, too: In violation of the New York State code of avoidance, he met the other schmoes right in the eye, ready for anything.

Hell, even looking for something.

The full-on stare routine was a favor rarely returned. Most of the men, whether they were gang members, drug dealers, or partiers heading for the clubs, followed the rules, their peepers shifting away from him and staying gone.

Too bad. He liked fights.

As for the women? He didn't pay attention to them—although that was because he didn't want to fend off the inevitable "hey, daddys," not because they were a threat to him.

God knew females couldn't touch him on any level except physical, and he wasn't interested in sex at the moment.

What he was in search of was a purple door. An ugly-ass, stupidly painted purple door with a billboard-size handprint on it. And what do you know, about fifty yards later, the entrance he was looking for presented itself on the right. As he gripped the black handle, he wanted to snap the thing off, and the red neon outline of the word *Psychic* made him curse.

On so many levels, he couldn't believe he was coming here. Again. It just didn't—

A sudden fluttering in his chest made him wonder if he'd gone into atrial fib from annoyance—but it was just his phone on vibrate. Taking the thing out, he recognized the number.

"You need me?" he clipped, because he hated wasting time with any kind of "Hello, how are you, hasn't the weather been good/bad/rainy/snowy lately" shit.

Alex Hess's voice was deep for a woman, her words as direct as a man's. "Yeah, can you pick up an extra shift for me tonight?"

His boss was probably the only female he respected—then again, it was hard not to take seriously someone who'd snapped a grown man's tibia in front of you: As head of security for the Iron Mask, she didn't appreciate dealers on her turf, especially ones with short-term amnesia who she'd already warned not to sell in her club. You had one shot with Alex. After that? You were lucky if the damage was merely cosmetic and/or cast-related.

He checked his old watch. "I can be over in about forty-five, but I've got to be somewhere at ten tonight—that'll only take a half hour, though."

"Good deal, I appreciate it."

"No problem." Duke hung up, and faced off at the purple door again.

Compelled by a force that he had long detested and never understood, he threw the thing open, the old wood panels ricocheting off the wall. As he caught the thing in his fist on the rebound, he looked up the flight of stairs that double-backed on itself for five stories. He'd been coming here for how long?

Such bullshit.

And yet his heavy boots carried him up two steps at a time, his thigh muscles grabbing onto his leg bones, his hard hand gripping the iron railing like it was a throat, his body coiling for a fight.

When he got to the top, the sign on the door read, PLEASE

HAVE A SEAT AND WAIT TO BE GREETED. Like it was a shrink's office or something.

He didn't follow the directions, but paced back and forth on the cramped landing. The two chairs available for asses were mismatched and painted in a psychedelic array of bright-and-rainbow. The air smelled of the incense that was burned inside. And under his boots, a Tibetan rug was threadbare, but not because it had been made cheaply.

He hated waiting on a good day. Despised it in this context—frankly, he didn't know why the hell he kept coming back. It was like some unseen steel chain was linked around his chest and pulling him to this place. God knew he thought this was a waste of time, but he kept showing up—

"I've been waiting for you," came a female voice on the far side of the closed door.

She always did that. The woman always knew when he'd made an appearance—and it wasn't like she had video monitoring equipment mounted on the ceiling.

Then again, his pacing probably wasn't silent. Not with all the muttering, at any rate.

The knob on the door was old and brass, its face polished by the countless palms that had twisted it over time. Watching it turn, a warped sense of unreality crept into his body and laid claim to his mind. As the woman in draped robing revealed herself, he was the one who looked down and avoided confrontation.

"Come in," she said in a low voice.

Damn it, he hated this; he truly did.

As he stepped inside, a clock began to chime . . . eight times. In his ears, it sounded like a scream.

"You need to be cleansed. Your aura is black."

Duke shoved his hands into the pockets of his jeans and flexed his shoulders. "How's that different than normal."

"It isn't."

Exactly. Shit, for all he knew, she was making things worse instead of better, cursing him instead of healing him.

"Sit, sit, sit. . . ."

He glanced over at the round table with its central-casting crystal ball, and Tarot card deck, and white candles. Just like the heavily draped psychic herself, tapestries hung from the workspace to the floor, pooling in a swirl of every color imaginable. There were two chairs, one large enough to be considered a throne, the other more pedestrian, the sort of thing you could find at Office Depot.

He just wanted to leave.

He sat down instead.

Chapter Two

Six . . . seven . . .

Eight.

Sitting on the edge of his bed, Jim Heron waited to see if the grandfather clock on the landing had anything else to say. When all he got was an earful of silence, he took a draw on his Marlboro. He hated that goddamn timekeeper—the tone of it, the incessant gonging, and most especially the fact that from time to time, it let out a count of thirteen.

Not that he was superstitious.

Nah.

Okay, maybe just a little. Then again, events had recently shaken him out of his belief that reality was a single dimension based on what you could see, hear, and touch: Courtesy of accepting the position of savior of the friggin' world, he'd learned that the devil in fact existed—and liked Louboutins over Blahniks, long walks on the beach, and sex doggy style. He'd also met some angels, become one himself, and been to a version of Heaven that appeared to be based on *Downton Abbey*.

So yeah, clocks that didn't need to be wound, weren't plugged into an outlet, and couldn't count right? Not funny.

Taking a drag on his cigarette, he tilted his head back and blew out a steady stream. As the smoke rose, he looked around at his digs. Faded Victorian wallpaper. Ceiling with a stain in the corner. Leaded-glass windows in old sashes that were painted shut. Bed the size of a football field with a Gothic headboard that made him think of Vincent Price movies.

There were another thirty-three rooms like it.

Or was it thirty-four?

He'd been looking for inexpensive accommodations that were a little off the beaten path. He hadn't exactly planned for a decrepit ark that had iffy running water, spotty electricals, a stove that burped gas, and drafty walls that let plenty of chilly air in.

Perfect. Right out of *House Beautiful*.

The mansion's sole redeeming attribute, at least that he could figure, was the dour exterior: With dead vines crawling over its face and the cockeyed shutters and twelve kinds of glaring overhangs, the vibe suggested that whoever was inside might eat you alive. Plus the grounds were nothing but a couple of acres' worth of brambles, spiky underbrush, and soon-to-be poison ivy to fight through.

Wouldn't do a damn thing against Devina's minions, but would defo keep the idiot teenagers away.

"Where are you . . . ?" He stared up at the ceiling. "Come on, bitch."

His demon opponent was not known for being patient—and he'd been waiting for a response for how long?

As he stabbed out his butt, the colorful flag across the way was a glaring reminder of how his newest tactic might have gone sour.

In the game between good and evil, where he was the quarterback interacting with the seven souls on deck, and Devina, the whorish demon, and Nigel, the archangel with the stick up his ass, were "captains" of the teams, Jim was solidly ahead. Or rather, he'd put the good guys in front three to one. All it was going to take was one more victory—one more soul teased into choosing good over evil at a crossroads in his or her existence—and he had saved not just the world, but the afterlife, as well. And yeah, victory looked pretty much like you'd think it would: Not only could all the humans on the planet continue to go about their days, but the moral God-fearers who had passed Go, collected two hundred, and entered Heaven's Manse of Souls, were safe for eternity.

Like, for example, his own mother, who'd been raped and murdered—may she rest in peace—could stay right where she was.

All things considered, he should feel pretty damned good about where he and his remaining wingman, Adrian, were.

He did not.

Fucking Devina. That demon had something he wanted, something that didn't belong in her viscous prison of the damned. And thanks to all his military training and experience, the tactician in him had come up with a plan: Give him the innocent, and he would turn over one of his wins to the demon. Fair trade—and legal under the rules of the game. Those victory flags were his possessions—Nigel had told him that himself. And when it came to your possessions, you could do whatever you wanted with them.

Which was why eBay and frickin' craigslist existed. Duh.

He'd expected the demon to bitch and moan about things—but he'd been so damned certain that ultimately she'd jump at the chance. Yeah, sure, according to Adrian she was nutty about her stuff, but this was the war—and if she won? She got to take over everything; Hell would literally come unto the Earth.

Instead? After he'd made his offer, she'd told him she'd think about it.

Like it was a fucking pair of shoes or something? Come on. WTF.

Getting to his feet, Jim stalked around the room, disturbing the fine layer of dust that covered the floorboards. When the inevitable creaking got on his nerves, he headed into the bathroom out in the hall.

Talk about your bed & breakfast fantasies gone bad. The rose-patterned wallpaper had faded until there was nothing but a shadow of color left—probably better that way, considering all that estrogen-drenched-decor crap made him scratch. The ornate mirror over the sink was cracked and had liver spots across its reflective face, so when you looked at yourself, you got an eyeball full of where you were headed when you hit seventy. And the floor was a forget-about-it stretch of chipped marble.

But come on, he'd showered in so much worse.

Going over to the claw-footed tub, he supposed the thing might have been romantic if, one, he'd been into that shit, which he wasn't, and two, it hadn't been stained yellow on the inside from mineral deposits, and green on the outside from the copper feet. And then there was the noise. As he cranked the once-gold-leafed handles on, the cold side let out a scream, like the pipes were not happy about pulling chilly stuff in from the main line in the street.

The water that came out of the corroded showerhead was more a drool than any kind of spray, but over the last two days, it had proven capable of soaping him up and rinsing him off. Dropping trou, he stepped under the cold dribble and reached for the soap.

His body wasn't particularly bothered by the fact that there was no warmth. God knew, during his career in XOps, he'd done a hell of a lot worse to it. Sudsing himself up, he passed his palms over all kinds of scars, from old stab wounds, to bullet and shrapnel aftermath, to a couple of surgeries that had been performed in combat zones—except for that one that had been done in a bedroom in Paris.

"Where are you . . . Devina . . ." FFS, she was going to do his nut in.

Which was crazy. During his twenty-year career as a shadow assassin for the U.S. government, you'd think he'd be used to this: War had a rhythm that was counterintuitive. There were long stretches of inactivity and waiting—interspersed with great explosions of life-or-death, keep-it-tight-or-get-jacked drama.

Usually he handled the lulls better.

Not anymore, apparently.

Although, granted, the stakes were higher than anything ever wagered on his performance before. He won? Hell was nothing but a morality play that didn't have a stage anymore.

So maybe he should have just cooled his heels for one more round, taken a fourth win, and then the innocents would have been free, and everything would have game over'd in a good way.

The trouble was, he didn't know whether Sissy Barten would survive that. The girl was trapped down below in that wall—and if Hell was destroyed, wouldn't she go *poof!* with it? Or did she get a pass because her soul was clean?

He didn't know, and he couldn't take a chance on that . . . so he waited for Devina's response.

And had to wonder what the demon was cooking up—

Brilliant light exploded into the bathroom, blinding him so badly that he dropped the soap to cover his eyes with his hands.

He knew who it was—even before an aristocratic English voice cut through the anemic shower.

"Have you lost all your wits!" Nigel, the archangel, demanded.

Great. Just what he was looking for.

A confron with the boss.

Adrian's first clue that all was not well in Casa d'Angel was the illumination that cut in around the closed door to his bedroom. Bleeding through the jambs like the detonation flash of a car bomb, it could only be explained by a visit of the archangel variety.

Either that or that crap-ass stove downstairs in the kitchen had spontaneously combusted.

Getting off the bed, he limped to the door naked and opened things up so he could get a gander at the drama.

". . . not interested—so *fucking* not interested . . ."

As Jim marched out of the loo with a towel around his hips and water dripping off his hair, his voice was deep and low, like a rattlesnake giving a warning.

Nigel wasn't impressed. The boss man from Up Above was tight on the other angel's balls, the English-accented dandy looking like he was on his way to the symphony: White tie seemed a little formal for the ass kicking that was rolling out. Although it was after dark.

La-di-frickin'-daaaaa.

Neither of them seemed to notice as Ad leaned back on his doorjamb and Milk Dudded the show. Then again, any kind of third-wheel routine was way down on the list of their priorities.

". . . did you think you can just give away a win?" Nigel bit out as they went into Jim's room, his accent sharpening the syllables into knives. "You have no right— Dear God, is that the flag?!"

Adrian whistled under his breath. The last time he'd heard that tone come out of that otherwise proper mouth?

He and Eddie had spent a century or two in Purgatory.

Fun, fun.

Jim's gauge was still hitting high on the fuck-ya meter, however. "My possession, right? They're mine—you told me that yourself. So I can—"

The slap that resonated out of the open door made Ad wince.

"That's your free shot," Jim growled. "Next time you do that? I'm going to kill you."

"I'm not alive, you fool. And you are putting *everything* at risk."

"How do you know what I'm doing with the goddamn flag."

"You're giving it to her. For whatever reason I cannot discern. In fact, I cannot fathom what could possibly be as valuable as your being one win away from victory."

Adrian repositioned his weight off his bad leg and shook his head. Okaaaaay. Not aware that Jim was tampering with things on this kind of level. But he knew who it was about.

Sissy Barten.

"Fuck," Ad muttered as the math added up. "Fuuuuck."

"Nigel, welcome to reality," Jim spat, "you are *not* in control here."

"Have you no thought of your mother!"

There was a beat of silence. "You think that's your ace in the hole? My leash to bring me back to your yard?"

"Forgive me for making the assumption that you might care about her eternal salvation."

As the pair of them argued, swiping insults and getting angrier, the grandfather clock on the stairwell landing began to chime.

But hadn't it just gone off?

One, two, three . . .

That thing creeped him the fuck out.

. . . four, five, six . . .

Such hostile voices going back and forth, the pair of them like two wolves circling. And meanwhile, somewhere in Caldwell, a soul was in play—and Devina knew who it was.

But Jim did not.

Adrian rubbed his eyes and tried to refocus them. Getting used to having only half his vision was taking time, the flat plane of landscape screwing with his depth perception, his sense of where he was in space, the arrangement of his limbs.

. . . seven, eight, nine . . .

This stuff with the flag was bad juju: Jim takes a win down off the wall without telling Nigel? There was only one reason for that . . . the guy was going to try to trade it for Sissy's soul.

This was out of control. The whole goddamn thing.

. . . ten, eleven, twelve . . .

Adrian glared across the second-floor foyer, at that old clock on the staircase's landing. "Go on, do it, you fucking—"

The thirteenth chime that followed sure as hell felt as if the thing had flipped him off. And as the mournful sound faded, the argument raged on, Nigel and Jim locked into a rhythm where they were just emoting, neither of them listening to the other.

And as they wasted this energy? The game was continuing: Although there were parallels to football, there were no time-outs in this seven-round war between good and evil. And from the way things were just going in Jim's room? The savior wasn't giving in or seeing the light; he was just going to do whatever he damn well pleased.

His attention wasn't on the war. It was on Sissy—and it was going to stay that way.

And Nigel's focus? It was on wanting to beat the crap out of Jim.

Devina, however, was no doubt moving forward, circling around the soul even though she wasn't supposed to. . . .

The solution Ad came up with was radical and had a poor likelihood of success, but what else could he do?

The two bigger players on the team were at each other's throats—and there was no better predictor for an enemy's success than that kind of divided attention.

Going into his room, he pulled on some clothes, sat on his bed, and gripped his knees. As he closed his eyes, he sent out a request, the paranormal equiv of a page.

It took about two seconds to receive the summoning he was looking for.

Which meant Colin, the archangel, knew exactly why Nigel had gone earthbound—and was no happier about shit than Ad was.

Chapter Three

Victoria Beckham.

That's who the stylist reminded her of, Cait thought as Pablo shampooed the color out of her hair. And that wasn't an insult. It was the guy's black hair, sharp cheekbones, and the thin legs. And that posing/pouty thing he did with one hip out.

"Okay, sitz ups fer us."

Cait followed instructions, pulling her head out of the washing sink. Everything that was wet was immediately captured in a towel wrap, and then she was up on her feet, heading back to the chair.

"Noes oo lovf zis," Pablo announced as she sat down.

Guess he was saying that she was going to love it?

The strange thing about that accent was that it moved around, distorting different vowels and consonants in different ways, the lack of consistency suggesting he was either posing or had an intermittent speech impediment.

As for what her opinion was going to be . . .

He unfurled the towel, and everything flopped onto her shoulders.

It was impossible to tell what was what. Sure, there were some lighter parts, but considering all the foils he'd folded onto her head, she expected a hell of a lot more.

Pablo pulled open the top drawer of the stand-up cupboard by his mirror and took out a square brush the size of a cutting board. Palming his hair dryer, he began fanning things out and running the hot air underneath.

"*Ve dry frst und ten ve cut, cut, cut. . . .*"

Man, his eyes were dark as he worked. Not so much brown as black.

Looking into the mirror, she squirmed. This was such a dumb idea: Those three tubs of color with their separate paintbrushes? She could come out red, white, and blue for all she knew. And the hour it took for him to stripe down those tinfoil strips and origami them up against her scalp? Never getting that back. And the cost—four hundred dollars?

Maybe she was more like her parents than her chronic rebellion suggested. Because this excursion into vanity seemed like a waste on too many levels to count.

Plus she was going to have to keep it up—

"Oh . . . wow," she said slowly as she turned her head.

The section he'd been working on was . . . really beautiful. Now dry and straight, her hair was the color it had been during her childhood, what appeared to be a hundred different shades of blond weaving in and out of the thick, shiny strands.

"*Ive toll youz,*" Pablo said. Or something to that effect.

And the more her hair dried out, the better it got—except then there was a pair of scissors in his hand.

"Are you sure we have to do anything?" she asked, as the blades flashed in the overhead lighting.

"*Oh, chess.*"

Wow, she really couldn't place that accent of his.

Things started flying at that point, his hands spinning around her head, those sharp scissors slicing into her hair, pieces falling to the floor like feathers from a flushed bird. It looked as if she was getting layers—oh, God, bangs . . . she now had bangs. . . .

Cait closed her eyes. Color could be corrected with some Clairol back home. This stuff? It was going to take a year to grow out. The trouble was, she was on the ride—no getting off in the middle of the roller coaster.

What had she done to herself . . . ?

A tickle lit off on the back of her hand and she cracked an eyelid. A section of her hair had landed on her wrist, the three-inch length curling ever so slightly at the end. Taking it in between her fingers, she rubbed the smooth strands together.

Blond. Very blond.

When Pablo said something, she could only nod, her emotions bubbling up in her chest and distracting her from the outside world. The desperate edge to all this transformation business was not something she could ignore, not while she was busy getting turned into Veronica Lake. Not while she was paying so much for something that was entirely superficial.

Bottom line, unfortunately, was that it was so much easier to address defects in your appearance, and your car, and your apartment, than it was to dig deep and take a good hard look at your choices, your mistakes . . . your faults.

Like, for example, how playing it safe all your life had landed you in a prison of your own making.

The music track abruptly ended, as if the speakers had clocked out for the night, and in the silence, Pablo swapped the blades for something that looked like a curling iron, except it had two heated plates.

Straightener, she thought it was called. And the fact that she wasn't one hundred percent sure on that made her feel her isolation from the world even further.

A rhythmic tugging started up as Pablo pulled the wand down her hair, over and over again. And as he worked his way around her head, she had too much space to think, too much time to stare at the blond strand she held.

As tears speared into her eyes, she cleared her throat. At least authorities had found Sissy Barten's body . . . so those parents of hers had something to bury.

What a waste. What a further reminder that you have to live while you can—because you never knew when the ride was over.

"Look at vat vee haff."

Pablo spun her about to face the mirror, except for a moment she couldn't look away from what was in her hand. But then she lifted her eyes and . . .

"Oh . . . wow," she whispered.

Soft, shimmering waves fell from the crown of her head, the frizziness gone, the new highlights popping out, the length not much different at all.

Pablo's accent got rolling as he described the weight he'd taken off, and how that had freed her hair to express itself more completely. Blah, blah, blah—it was just vocabulary she let wash over her. What she paid attention to was how much younger she looked. Or maybe it was more . . . feminine? Vibrant?

This was some serious butterfly shit, as her brother would have called it.

She glanced down at the hair between her fingers, and let the strands fall to the ground. There was no rewind button you could punch, no going back . . . only ever forward. She had learned that when she was twelve, her first grown-up lesson at a very young age.

And Sissy's death had recently reminded her of that fact.

"My hair is . . . perfect," she heard herself say.

Cue the smiles from Pablo.

After he whipped the cape off her shoulders, she went back to the dressing room, put her clothes on, and got another load of *whoa*. Her hair elevated the black slacks and simple sweater to something that might have come from Saks. Even her red Coach bag took a step up, looking downright Italian all of a sudden.

As she walked out of the dressing room to pay, she felt like she had television-commercial hair, the kind that bounced with every step, and shined under even low lighting, and made men and women stop short.

At the reception desk, she got out her checkbook, and felt her eyes bulge even though she'd known how much this was going to cost.

"*Vuld yoo lick ta mayb yoo next abbointment?*"

Cait glanced up from the zeroes she was filling out. Right behind Pablo, there was a floor-to-ceiling mirror, and over his right shoulder, she caught sight of her new look.

Excellent marketing device, she thought, as she stared at herself and began to nod.

She left five minutes later with considerably less in her checking account, and an appointment card for a touch-up in six weeks in her purse.

As she walked out and went over to her Lexus, she couldn't believe she'd done it. But at least she was getting familiar with this feeling of buyer's shock. Heck, she still had it over her new car—well, the SUV was "new" to her. CarMax had given her a great deal on a used one, and she had to admit, it was the nicest thing she'd ever driven.

But she continued to have the head spins over the thing from time to time.

The second she got in her SUV, she cranked the rearview mirror down and fluffed her goldie locks. What good timing, she thought—considering that for the first time in God only knew how long, she was meeting a friend after hours.

Starting her engine, she pulled out onto the empty road and retraced her route away from the wealthy enclave. Her "date" was actually her old college roommate—

As the past began to bubble up, she turned on NPR to cut the quiet, and hit the brakes at a red light. Leaning in, she couldn't resist glancing into the rearview again—

"Oh, *crap* . . ."

Cait turned her head to the opposite side, even though that was silly. But at least she hadn't lost both her earrings.

The thing had probably come out in the dressing room. Her sweater had a tight neck, and those little gold shells had iffy backings. As the light turned green, she hit the gas and told herself to just leave it—

That didn't last long.

The earrings were solid fourteen-karat, but more than that, she'd bought them on her one Bahaman vacation right after graduation.

Wrenching the wheel left, she executed an illegal turn and headed back to reclaim what was hers.

As Adrian manifested himself in Heaven, he hummed that Eric Clapton song—in tune, because there was no one around to annoy with his fake tone-deaf routine.

". . . would you know my name . . ."

The lawn was a bright spring green, and the sky as brilliant and resonant a blue as a cathedral's stained glass. To the left, the protective walls of the Manse of Souls stood sturdy and tall as a mountain range, the drawbridge down over a moat that shimmered in sunlight that had no obvious source.

Up on the parapet at the top of the wall, only two victory flags waved in a lazy way—one colorful banner was missing.

What the *hell* was Jim thinking?

Adrian kept walking. Off to the right, next to a croquet setup, there was a table set for tea, four chairs surrounding all kinds of damask and porcelain and silver. No one was sitting at it. In fact, as he looked around, he got the distinct impression he was alone.

Made no sense—Colin had summoned him here, so the archangel had to be—

The whistle was high-pitched and distant, floating across the landscape to his ear. Pivoting around, he looked toward the river, and then started marching over in the uneven gait he was still adjusting to. Funny, he hadn't noticed before how much grass there really was—but with his bum leg, he'd been learning new things about what distance really meant.

The archangel Colin was down at the tree line, by the old-fashioned British campaign tent that was his private quarters. Standing in the stream that wound around his little slice of Heaven, he was buck-ass naked, the rushing water teeming up to his hips.

"Moving a bit slower now, mate?" the guy said as Ad got in range.

Whatever—his gimp routine was not the reason he'd come. "We have a big fucking problem."

Typically, Colin was good for a wisecrack or two—not tonight, evidently. The archangel emerged from the river, his powerful body glistening, his strong legs leading him over to where he'd hung his white towel on a tree branch.

"How bad is it down there?" he asked as he covered up.

Ad grunted while he lowered himself onto a rock, its warm face feeling good on his sorry ass. "So you know where Nigel is."

"But of course."

"Then you also know why I'm not going to waste time here." Ad held up his palms to cut the oh-no-I-couldn't-possibly's. "Jim's just taken a left-hand turn off the road and into the weeds. No one down there is in the game—except for Devina, and you know what? If Jim's distracted now? That ain't nothin' compared to what'll happen if the demon gives him that girl."

Colin's response was just a shake of the head. And that was *so* not good enough.

Ad cursed. "Seriously. Before we lose this whole goddamn thing, you need to step up. I already know I can't go to Nigel about anything—he and I are oil and water and then some."

Colin pushed his dark wet hair out of his harsh face. "I had hoped . . ."

When that was as far as the guy got, Ad shrugged. "Hoped what? That Jim slipped in the shower and hit his head hard enough to wake the fuck up? Hell, if there was any chance of that, I'd cock him upside with a two-by-four myself. But let's not kid ourselves. The savior's no longer in this game, and I don't think he's coming back—even if Nigel threatens to rip him a new one."

Colin curled his hands into fists, like he wanted to do a little swinging himself. "Jim is the *sine qua non*. There is nothing we can do to turn him over, if that's what you're suggesting."

"Like I want the job?" Ad laughed harshly. "Are you fucking me."

"That is not why you came?"

"I want to win. That's the only reason I'm here."

Colin lifted an aristocratic brow. "You are actually engaged in the war. Quite a shift for you, is it not."

"We can't lose this."

"Because of Eddie?" When he didn't reply, the archangel frowned. "One need not apologize for loyalty to the dead, and in truth, if it makes you focus, I shan't complain."

"Give me the name of the soul. That's all I need."

Colin didn't seem surprised, but then again, he wasn't an idiot. Unfortunately, he also wasn't prepared to break the rules: "You know I can't do that."

"We'll keep it between the two of us."

"Don't be daft. And no, it's not Nigel I'm concerned with. I have some sway over him. It's the Maker, dear boy."

"Then get down to Earth and intercede with the soul yourself. Jim isn't going to—and this obsession he's got going on is gonna kill us all. Who the fuck gives a win away?"

"Were you unaware of his intentions with the flag?"

"Of course I wasn't! I'd have done something to stop him—my buddy's soul is on the line."

"I'd wondered."

Colin plugged his palms into his waist and walked around, his bare feet leaving a pattern in the silt by the river's edge.

"Tell me who it is," Ad prompted, "and I'll take care of it."

"You cannot intercede, any more than I'm allowed to."

"Okay, fine, give me the soul and I'll figure out a way to put Heron in front of him."

The old Adrian would have push-push-pushed into the silence, but the logic was sound, and spoke for itself—and Colin was the rational one in the group. Always had been.

"I can't get involved," Colin said under his breath.

"Then let me."

"That isn't done either, I'm afraid."

Great. "So what's our goddamn option? Sit around and watch Jim blow this whole cocksucking thing?"

When nothing but silence came back to him, he began to get really worried. "Colin, you gotta help us. Not to go *Star Wars* on your ass, but you're our only hope."

"*Star Wars?*"

"Forget about it. Just . . . fucking do something, would you?"

The archangel was silent for a very long time. "I can't take you all the way."

"You don't have to. Point me in the right direction—that's the only thing I need. But know this. You boys up here keep doing the hands-off shit? We're going to lose this. I'll put what's left of my balls on it."

Chapter Four

Alex Hess's office at the Iron Mask was just like the woman herself—stripped down to its most functional components, with a lot of hard corners. As Duke waited for his knock to be answered, he jacked up his jeans.

The door opened inward, and the guy on the other side was the only thing Duke would ever take a step back for: Alex's husband was tall as a basketball player, built like a boxer, and had the kind of physical confidence only trained killers had.

Mortal combat wasn't just a video game to him.

As they passed, Duke nodded, and John Matthew, as he was called, did the same—and that was the extent of it. No one had ever heard the SOB say a word, but by the same token, anyone built like that didn't have to talk.

"Sorry to bug you," Duke said as Alex sat down in the chair behind her desk. Her eyes were on the departing hubs, lingering at a level that suggested she was checking out his ass. "Where do you want me? Can't find Big Rob."

"Out front."

That was where they usually put him, although God only knew why. He was more barbed wire than velvet rope.

"Any special instructions?"

Now she looked at him, that dark gray stare narrowing. "Nope. Just do you."

Lucky him. That was the only thing in his repertoire.

Striding back out into the hall, he pushed through the staff-only door into the club proper, and on the far side, the Goth clientele was a total snore for him. He'd long ago lost interest in women who wanted people to be interested in them: After so many push-up bras, bustiers, and sprayed-on leather pants, the ready-for-anythings formed a composite identity that just spelled desperate and easy.

They liked him, though, their eyes locking onto him like Alex's had to her man—and wasn't that the eternal conundrum of sex: Chicks who needed attention only got hot and bothered over men who didn't notice them. The good news, he supposed, was that when he did want sex, there were always volunteers.

Outside, he took position next to a guy named Ivan who was built like an SUV, and faced off at the line that had already formed. The rule was two of them at all times—because you never knew what could—

". . . fucked my sister! You did! You fucked my sister, you cock-sucker!"

Exactly.

"I got this," Duke said, breaking rank and striding down all the antsy, stamping, pre-drunk, ante-stoned, chilled-to-the-bone people.

". . . did not fuck her! I let her blow me—"

Crack!

Apparently the brother didn't appreciate the fine line between a suck off and coitus.

And then it was a case of cue the hysterics. The woman in question, a lovely little beaut with Marilyn Manson features, mime makeup, and your friendly neighborhood stripper's version of a wardrobe, got right in between the men.

"Danny, listen to me! I—"

Before Duke could reach them, the pair of men locked onto each other—and the sister got shoved right into the road, her high-heeled boots failing to find purchase on the sidewalk, the curb, then the payment.

Duke let her go. One of two things was going to happen—she was going to land on her ass and rip that skirt, or she was going to get mowed down by a car. In either event, it was off club property, and not his business.

What was part of his job was the fact that her boyfriend or fuck buddy or whatever he was to her was all about the payback—so what you now had were two guys in New Rocks shoving each other in a china shop of other people who were jonesing for their fix of drugs, alcohol, or sex.

And therefore likely to hit back.

Given that humans one-on-one were dumb enough, but in a group they could be truly stupid, he knew he had to take control. Jumping in between the two, he strong-armed both at the collarbone.

Before he could start his speech about pulling their shit together, the four men behind the fight decided to get involved.

Fists flew around him, one of them clipping him in the head.

No more talking.

Duke dominated the situation, grabbing lapels and throwing men bodily onto the concrete, elbowing others in the chest, cold-cocking whoever tried to step to him. The entire time, as hands latched onto him and he ducked punches and dodged a knife, he was utterly calm, totally detached.

He honestly didn't care whether he got arrested for violence, or stabbed, or shot. And he didn't give a damn whether he did permanent damage to the people he was submitting—or whether that chick got turned into a hood ornament or not.

"Nah, let him go," he heard Big Rob say over the din. "He needs the exercise."

The sound of flapping clothes and the grunted curses from the crowd he was controlling cut through the night as the line tried to re-form around the drama and all kinds of cell phones broke out. Fortunately, the club's front entrance was not well lit, and this was going to be over soon.

Which it was.

There weren't a lot of MMA fighters waiting to get in line to hang out at the Iron Mask, so the men who had volunteered for a beat-down didn't have a lot of staying power. One punch was usually enough to wipe their slate clean—which was a pity. He enjoyed hitting them, feeling his knuckles connect with flesh, watching them go down or trip over their own feet.

He was not interested in being on the news, however.

Wrapping things up, he went over to the two primary aggressors, who had parked it at the curb and were in recovery mode, grimacing as they rubbed their jaws, their heads, their shoulders. The sister in high-heeled boots had tottered back into their orbit, her mascara-stained face and crazy hair pretty much the way they had been before the argument over familial relations had broken out.

Both men gave Duke the hairy eyeball as he loomed over them.

In a quiet voice, he said, "Don't stand in my line again. Or I'll follow you home. Clear?"

"You can't threaten us!" the lady of the hour hollered, going all stampity-stamp-stamp with her size sixes. "We have rights."

Duke leaned in, putting his face into hers. "You won't know I'm there. You won't see or hear a thing. But I'll come after you— you can bet your life on it. And know this—I like scaring people. It's fun for me."

Whether it was his dead eyes, or the hiss in his voice, or the words he spoke, she went quiet. And moved closer to the man who she'd put her knee pads on for.

Duke looked down at the two dummies, giving them a chance to speak up if they were so inclined. Total silence. And then the pair of them stood up and escorted the girl away.

Turning back to the club, he found that the line had reestablished itself and was back to inching its way inside. Keeping his head down, so that any pictures wouldn't show him clearly, he regained his post.

"Shit, man," Ivan said, "You're not even breathing heavy."

Duke just shrugged. When you worked road crews for a living, shoveling hot asphalt in the summer and road salt in the winter, your heart was quickly turned into an efficient machine, its atria and ventricles, its myocardium, its three hundred or so grams, pumping with total coordination to supply oxygenated blood to the body.

No big deal. Just an issue of training.

The real miracle was that he was somehow able to live without one. Oh, he had that hollow muscle posterior to his sternum, sure. But in the metaphysical sense? He'd lost his heart years ago—and he wouldn't change a thing about that.

Nope.

Duke lifted his arm to check the time— "Fuck."

"What's up?"

"I lost my fucking watch." He leaned out and looked down the sidewalk to where the fight had taken place. Naturally, there was nothing on the ground that appeared even vaguely metallic.

Then again, if that clasp had broken, and the thing had slipped off his wrist and been seen by any one of the, oh, say, hundred or so kibitzers? It would've been snatched. Vintage Rolexes were desirable, even to morons.

It was the only nice thing he owned, a relic from the past.

Had owned, that was.

Whatever. He'd lost more than that along the way, and he was still upright and walking.

"I gotta leave a little before ten," he told Ivan. "But I'll flipside in thirty minutes."

"That's what Big Rob said. I think he's going to cover."

"Cool."

Back at the hair salon, Cait knocked on the glass door and leaned in, trying to tea-leaf whether Pablo was still inside. The lights had been dimmed, which was not a good sign, but come on, it had taken her less than five minutes to—

The stylist walked out from the rear, in the process of pulling a black jacket on. "*Vev closed,*" he called out.

"I know," she shouted back, her breath condensing on the glass. "I lost my earring? I just want to check the dressing room floor?"

She tugged at her earlobe, like that would help in translation.

Pablo was a little huffy as he unlocked things and let her in. "*Lovt und fond behd desk?*"

"I think it's probably in there." She pointed to the hallway.

"*Wen yoo in here?*"

Cait frowned. "I'm sorry?"

He waved his hand with impatience. "*Yoo go thur. I get out box.*"

Wow, she thought as he turned away. Maybe he had short-term amnesia from all the peroxide in the hair color? Too much aerosol from the sprays? Mousse-induced dementia?

Cait went back to where she'd done her disrobing and got down on her knees, patting under the built-in bench, looking around on the carpet. She even pulled her sweater out at the neck to see if the shell had gotten stuck in the weave.

"Damn it . . ."

Heading back out, she went over to Pablo, who was clearly tapping his boots to go home. The "*lovt und fond*" was in fact a Stuart Weitzman shoe box, and in it there were two pairs of sunglasses, a stringy scarf, a couple of chunky, fake-gold necklaces, and . . .

A hoop earring that was big enough to double as a choker.

No dainty seashells. But she hadn't really expected it to be there—Pablo didn't seem like the type to rock a vacuum around his business before he left for the night.

"Okay, thanks," she said. "It's a little seashell, a gold shell!"

"*Do ve haf number for oo?*"

"Ah . . . your assistant called it yesterday to confirm my appointment with you?"

He seemed confused. "*Vell, wee call if fond.*"

"Thanks."

Outside, she shook her head. Weird, weird, weird. But lost accessory be damned—the guy did great hair, and that's what she was paying him for.

He must have one really short Christmas list, though.

Back in her Lexus, she gave the whole head-to-Old Caldwell thing another go, and about fifteen minutes later, she made it to the part of town where an entire twelve-block section of multi-colored Victorian mansions had been turned into condo associations, cafés and shops—although the latter were nothing like where she'd just been. Here they were folk-art galleries, organic spice sellers, hemp clothiers, that kind of thing.

"Four seventy-two . . . four seventy-two . . . where are you . . . ?"

Seemed like this was the theme for the night, her out in the dark, searching for—

"Got it," she said as she hit the directional signal.

The café was called the Black Crow, but its exterior was all about the friendly: the gabled details, the overhang above the door, and the curlicues under the eaves were painted pink and yellow and pale blue. Matter of fact, the facade looked like a cartoon face, its two plate-glass windows like oversize eyes, with the rafters as the brows and the slate roof like a bowl haircut.

Following the arrows around behind, she rode out the potholes in the dirt lane between buildings and parked in the shallow lot.

Grabbing her bag, she got out—

Over by a door marked "Staff Only," a man was getting off a vintage motorcycle . . . and as he removed his helmet, long dark hair swung free across a broad back. His leather jacket was beaten up, but it seemed weathered from age, not some kind of designer distressing stuff, and his long legs were covered with the sort of jeans that were very un-Victoria Beckam.

With a smooth movement, he bent down and took something from the back of the bike—a guitar case?

She couldn't see the front of him because he was facing away from her, but the way he strode into the back of the café would have made her notice him even more than that dark rush of hair: He moved with total confidence. Maybe he was an owner? Or . . . the talent, given that case?

Whatever his role, he was in charge.

As that door clamped shut behind him, Cait shook herself, feeling strange that she'd just eyeballed some man. Then again, maybe the blond had gone to her head?

Har-har, hardy har-har.

Shaking herself back to reality, she walked around to the café's front entrance and pulled open the door.

In a rush of air, she got hit with a hot blast of coffee, vanilla and patchouli—like a latte had been splashed in her face by a member of the Grateful Dead. Rubbing her finicky nose, she eyed the thick crowd and wondered how she was going to find anyone in the place: the café was long and thin as a cattle chute, with a bar that ran down one side, little tables lined up along the opposite wall, and about two hundred people squeezed between the two.

At least she was in the right place to hear music, though. At the far end, there was a raised stage big enough for a quartet, and all around the exposed brick walls, folk instruments hanging from wires alternated with fairly serious-looking speakers—

"Cait! Over here!" came a holler from down in front.

"Hey!" With a wave, she started to work her way toward the stage, squeezing between vertical waiters in sherbet-colored T-shirts, and seated patrons who struck her as disproportionately female.

"What the *hell* did you do to your hair?" Teresa Goldman said as she got to her feet for a hug.

Teresa had been a good friend in high school and a great roommate in college, the kind of girl who could be depended upon to give you a straight answer whether you needed it or not. In short, she was awesome—and a little frightening.

Especially when you'd gone from blond to brunette without any warning.

"Is it awful?" Cait fussed with her bangs. "Is it—"

"Fuck, no! It's fantastic! Are you kidding me? And, Christ, have you lost more weight?"

Cait shuffled into a wooden chair that squeaked. "I haven't lost any, I swear."

"Bullshit."

"Does your mother know you talk like that?"

"Who do you think taught me to curse?"

As they went through the back-and-forth they'd coined in their freshman year, a server brought Cait a menu printed on cardboard.

Cait stopped laughing as she looked things over. "Wait a minute—what's all this stuff? Kombucha? Tulsi? Yerba mate?"

"You are *so* behind the times—"

"These people ever heard of Salada?"

"What a plebe—"

"No Earl Grey—?"

"You are *not* cool enough for your hair."

Just like the good ol' days, Cait thought with a smile. And see, this was exactly what she needed: a break from her work routine, a good distraction from her mourning, an opportunity to put her money where her mouth was—and live a little.

Teresa leaned forward. "Fine, forget the libations—I didn't bring you here for the drinks."

"Good." Cait frowned. "Because I'm going to pass on all this. Call me common, but I'm proud of my simple Midwestern roots— Dunkin' Donuts coffee is as exotic as I get."

"The singer. It's all about the singer."

That man on the motorcycle? she wondered. "I didn't know you were into music played in a place like this. Not exactly Aerosmith or Van Halen."

"Ah, but the good news is Katy Perry isn't showing up, either."

"Hey, I like to work out to her stuff."

"I can't help that."

"You know, you should really try to past eighties metal. How old were you when it came out? Three?"

"Have some kombucha with that judgment, would you?" Teresa grinned. "Anyway, his name's G.B. and he comes here the last Monday of the month. As well as Hot Spot on Wednesdays at eight, the Hut on alternative Tuesdays, and the—"

"Are you a fan or his tour manager?"

"Wait'll you see him. He's incredible."

The waiter in the raspberry shirt came back. "What can I getcha?"

"I'll just have water."

"We have tap, Pellegrino, Rain Forest—"

Too much choice around here, she thought. "Just tap."

"With or without cubes?"

"Ah . . . with?"

"In a mug or a glass?"

"No preference."

"Infused with—"

"Honestly, just plain tap would be great, thanks." She smiled up at him as she handed the menu back.

As he left, she exhaled. "I don't know how you handle it."

"Again, not here for the drinks. Although I've tried the strawberry infusion and it's awesome." Teresa eased back in her chair. "So what's new? I feel like it's been a month since I saw you over the holidays."

"That would be five months ago, I think."

"Is it almost May? Wow." Teresa shrugged. "I don't pay much attention to time."

"Which was why you gave me your schedule of classes each semester."

"You always were a great sheepherder. Wish my assistant was as good as you were."

"How's work?"

"Same shit, different day. But I knew that tax law wasn't going to be glamorous."

"It's clearly lucrative, though. What kind of bag is that? Prada?"

"Aw, you noticed, how sweet."

As Teresa settled into a pause that grew much, much longer, Cait stiffened. Silence was antithetical to her old roommate. "Okay, what's up. And tell me now, before the waiter comes back and interviews me for five years over whether or not I want a cinnamon bun."

"Their croissants are better."

"Spill it, Goldman."

The hesitation lasted through the delivery of a tall mug full of ice cubes and H_2O.

When they were alone again, Cait said grimly, "You're scaring me, Teresa, and no offense, after the last couple of weeks, I don't need any more of that."

"Yeah, I'd heard that Barten girl went to Union."

Cait ducked her eyes. "She was in my drawing class."

"Shit, Cait . . . I didn't know you knew her."

"I did. And she was a lovely girl—I had her for my intro to sculpting seminar, too."

"You going to the funeral?"

"I wouldn't miss it." Cait looked up. "Now tell me what you don't want to tell me."

"There's a sentence and a half."

"Talk, Goldman."

Her old friend cleared her throat. "Did you hear about Thom and the girlfriend?"

Cait looked away again. Yes, she thought. "No," she said.

"They're pregnant. Due this month, as a matter of fact. I ran into him downtown at the courthouse. I guess one of his colleagues was brought up on embezzlement charges and he was there to testify, and I was there for . . . shit, what does it matter. I just . . . yeah, I figured you'd want to know."

Cait forced a smile onto her face, and didn't know why she bothered. Teresa knew better than to be fooled by a fake show of teeth. "I'm happy for him. For them, I mean."

"Look, I don't mean to be a bitch, but it had to have been a mistake. I can't picture Thom with his nitpick all covered in spit-up, while he changes diapers and fills bottles with formula. That man used to vacuum his dorm room. Who does that?"

"In his defense, we did."

"We're *girls*."

"Traditional sex roles much?"

"Whatever. You know what I mean."

Cait nursed her water, feeling a cold tingle in that molar with the iffy filling she needed to take care of.

The truth was, Thom had told her the news six months ago. As soon as they told their families. And to his credit, it had been in a kind way—because he didn't want her to hear it from anyone else, and his GF was shouting it from the rooftop, evidently. Cait had been shocked to the core, but she'd said all the right congratulatory things . . . then hung up the phone and burst into tears.

The woman who was about to give birth to his baby was the one he'd cheated on her with.

Margot. Her name was Margot. Like she was a French movie actress or something.

Hell, maybe it was even spelled Margeaux.

At least they'd been together for a while now. How many years had it been? Almost as long as Cait had been with him. No, wait . . . longer. So why the pregnancy had been such a shock to the system, she hadn't a clue. But it had thrown her into a tailspin that had landed her here, in this hard little chair, with new hair, and an improved body . . . and a sense that she was through hiding from life, and ready to . . .

Okay, she didn't know the answer to the "what" on that one.

"Hey, did you know you're missing an earring," Teresa said.

"Oh, yeah. I think it happened at the hair salon—"

"Here he is," Teresa hissed as she sat up straighter.

Cait glanced over her shoulder. And did a little spine stretching of her own.

Yup, it was the one she'd just seen by the bike . . . and if the guy had been an eye-catcher from the back, the front view was even better: His face was a stunning composite of strong lines, enhanced not only by that holy-crap hair of his, but a goatee and a pair of hooded eyes that had bedroom all over them. Long and lean, he was wearing just a muscle shirt now, his arms covered in flowing black and gray tattoos marked with lettering in a foreign language.

As he sat down on a pine stool, he drew a hand through that hair, pushing it over his shoulder—and it refused to stay put, copper highlights flashing in the stage illumination as it rebelled back into place.

His smile was easy as a summer breeze, and as he tapped the mic to make sure it was working, Cait found herself wondering what his voice sounded like—

"Hey," he said, deeply, softly. "How you doin' tonight?"

The line was anything but cheesy coming from him, especially as the tenor of the words floated down from the ceiling like a caress.

"So I wanted to share a new song with you, something I just wrote." He looked around as he spoke, and even though Cait was sure he didn't focus on her, it felt like he was speaking to her and only her.

"It's about living forever," he intoned. "And I wish I could use my guitar, but there's been a technical difficulty there—so you're just going to have to put up with my voice all by itself."

The clapping was quick and fervent, suggesting that there were a whole lot of Teresas in the crowd. In fact . . . this was why there were just women here tonight, wasn't it.

He was even waving at a couple of them, like they were friends.

As he cleared his throat and took a deep breath, Cait found herself turning her chair around to face the stage.

"Told you," she heard Teresa say with satisfaction.

Chapter Five

The demon Devina took form in front of the nondescript, almost-modern headquarters of Integrated Human Resources, Inc. Located in one of Caldwell's countless professional services complexes, the "firm" had no clients, no employees and was neither a resource for humans, integrated, or incorporated. It was, however, the perfect, protective shell for her collections, and the name was a nice play on what she did.

She was good at integrating herself into humans.

Had just come out of a rather accommodating vessel, as a matter of fact.

Loved those black jeans.

Striding to the door, she passed through the locked steel panels and emerged into the empty, shadowy interior. Inside, there were no desks, no phones, no computers, no coffee machines or watercoolers—and even M-F, eight a.m. to five p.m., there were no meetings being held, interviews set up, or business being conducted. If she had to, however, she could conjure that illusion out of the air at the drop of a hat.

After her last hideout had been infiltrated by Jim and his angel buddies, she'd had to relocate, and so far, so good.

"Hi, honey, I'm home," she said to the newest sacrificial virgin who was hanging upside down over a tin tub by the elevator.

He didn't answer her, natch.

In his previous life, before he'd become something important, he'd been a computer geek—God, with the chronic shortage of virgins in contemporary America, she'd never been so grateful for technology; all she had to do was search the yellow pages under IT.

And yet, even with him serving as a metaphysical ADT system, creeping tension made her walk faster and faster toward the elevator doors. There were two choices for other floors: "2" and "LL," and when she got inside, she hit the latter. Silence accompanied the drop in height as she proceeded down to the windowless, open space of the basement. Her breath trapped in her lungs as the doors parted. . . .

"Oh, thank fuck," she said with a laugh.

Everything was there. All her clocks, which responded to her presence by resuming their count of minutes and hours; her many bureaus full of things that had just re-lined themselves up, their pulls still clapping from the return to proper position; her countless knives that were now once again facing point-first to the south; and her most important possession—the most priceless thing of all, in spite of its ugly state of decay—her mirror, was right where she had left it in the far corner.

Well, and then there was also the fun stuff in her "bedroom" area, the king-size bed, the vanity with all her makeup, her racks and racks of clothes, her shelves of shoes, her cupboards of bags.

Whenever she left, her possessions discorded, the orientation of the vast space becoming jumbled and confused. When she returned? Order was reestablished.

The same way a magnet would pull metal shavings together.

And just as her objects orbited around her, she too was drawn to them. Her greatest fear, at least on Earth, was that someday she would come back here and something would be gone. Or all of it would be. Or just a part.

As her heart rate regulated and she took off her fur coat, she walked down the aisles created by the bureaus. Stopping randomly, she pulled open the top drawer of a Hepplewhite she'd purchased from its maker back in 1801. Inside, there were eyeglasses from the period, thin wires curling around, circles of aged glass glinting. As she touched them, the energy of their past owners surged into her fingertips and connected her with the souls she had claimed and now held in her prison.

She knew each and every one of the sinners, her children, the beloved chosen who she nurtured through eternal pain and humiliation in her wall down below.

Fucking Jim Heron.

That goddamn "savior" might well be the death of her—literally. And that was not supposed to be the way shit went. In the beginning of this seven-round war, she'd had such hope for him, had been convinced that his bad side, cultivated in his professional pursuits for so long, would serve her well. Instead? That cocksucker was playing for the other team.

And *winning*.

If he pulled off one more victory?

Overwhelmed, Devina surveyed her collections, tears spearing into her eyes.

If that savior won for Team Angel, all of this was gone, all of her things no longer existed—worse, all of her souls were history as well. Everything she had spent eons amassing? Up in smoke.

Her, too.

Fucking Jim Heron.

Marching over to her vanity, she tossed the mink onto the bed, pulled out the dainty chair, and sat down. As she stared at herself in the oval mirror, she approved of the way she looked— and hated the way she felt.

First off, she despised the fact that there was a female who Jim wanted badly enough to give a win up for. And then there was her personal rock and a hard place—give up something she owned?

When was the last time she'd let anything go?

Well . . . hell, she'd have to go Taylor Swift on that one: never, ever, *ever*. . . .

Man, OCD sucked on a good day. Faced with losing all the shit in this basement? It was enough to give her a fucking heart attack—

Bracing herself on the vanity, she had to open her mouth to breathe. "You're immortal . . . you're immortal. . . . you don't have to call nine-one-one . . ."

'Cuz for fuck's sake, you couldn't resuscitate someone who didn't exist in the crash-cart kind of way.

Good logic. Except as high-octane panic roared through her veins, and knocked out her higher reasoning, that little slice of rational got kicked in the can. With a trembling hand, she brushed her dark hair out of her face and tried to remember the cognitive behaviorial therapy she'd been doing.

Not going to kill her. Just physical sensations. Not about the things, Devina—it's about trying to exert control over . . .

Bullshit it wasn't about the things. And even immortals could in fact die—she'd proved that when she'd killed Adrian's precious little buddy Eddie in the round before last.

"Oh, God," she moaned as a sense of disconnection separated her from her environment, her eyesight going funhouse, her balance destabilizing.

Winning the war meant that she had dominion over the Earth and all the souls on it. Awesome. Totally. But losing?

Just the thought made her want to throw up.

The stakes could not be higher.

Fucking Jim Heron—

"Can't . . . breathe . . ."

Great. Looked like this was going to be another three-appointment week with her therapist. Maybe four.

Forcing herself to focus, she tried breathing in deep with her belly. Tightened her thigh muscles repeatedly. Told herself she'd been in this pounding place of adrenaline overload a million times before and survived it every single time. Thought about the new season at LV and what she was going to buy in New York at the mother ship on Fifth. . . .

In the end, what brought her back was an earring she wouldn't have worn even if there'd been a crystal knife at her throat.

Seashell? Really. How fucking Cape Cod.

The woman who'd worn it had probably gotten the damn thing from some boyfriend or another after a long weekend spent walking on the beach, holding hands, and doing it missionary position in a B & B.

Snore.

Taking the pathetic fourteen-karat trinket out, Devina bypassed a lineup of five bottles of Coco by Chanel and pulled forward a shallow plate made of a shiny silver composite. The earring bounced as she dropped it, and for a split second, she wanted to crush the thing to dust . . . just because she could. Instead, she began to speak in her mother tongue, her voice distorting, the Ss prolonging like a snake's hiss. When it was time, she closed her eyes and extended her palm, the spell gathering in intensity, heat brewing up.

Images began to lift from the object, the movie of its owner channeling into her, the narrative and visuals locking into Devina's CPU for future use. Oh, yes, metal objects were so handy, the energy of their possessors forever trapped in between the molecules, just waiting to be absorbed by something else.

Before she ended the session, she gave in to temptation and added a little something else to the mix, a minor chaser, just an itty-bitty push in her own direction. Nothing like she had done in previous rounds, nothing even close.

Just a little artificially manufactured law of attraction.

That was all.

Cracking her lids, she stared into the white-hot maelstrom that was spinning like a tornado above the flat plane of the plate—and then it was done, the energy exchange complete, the interaction between objects over.

No big deal. And if the Maker wanted to split hairs to this degree? He needed her therapist, too.

Devina sat back, the presence of her objects something she felt, the essences of the souls down below intermixing, and yet retaining their individual characteristics.

Just as things were in her wall.

Fuck Jim Heron.

And fuck the game, too, by the way. The Maker needed her. She was the balance in His world—without her? Heaven would lose its significance altogether; no need for it if Earth was a utopia.

Evil was required.

Unfortunately . . . however true that was, this war was going to determine the future.

She was down by so much: four rounds, and she had only won one.

Grabbing her iPhone, she went into her contacts, hit a number, and while the call was going through, she deliberately stared out over her things, reminding herself of how much she had—and how much there was to lose.

"You've reached the voice mail of Veronica Sibling-Crout, licensed social worker. Please leave your name and message, as well as a number where I can reach you, repeated twice. Have a lovely day."

Beep.

"Hi, Veronica, this is Devina. I'm wondering if you have any sessions available ASAP? I'm going—" Her voice cracked. "I'm going to make a difficult decision right now, and I need some support. My number is . . ."

After she rattled off the digits, repeating them twice even though the woman no doubt had her on speed dial at this point, she hung up, closed her eyes and gathered her strength.

This was going to be the hardest thing she had ever done.

Other than fucking Jim Heron, of course.

Because like the war and the position she was in, it was difficult to admit . . . that she truly had fallen in love with him.

And that was another reason this hurt so badly.

At nine fifty-one, Duke left the Iron Mask's front door, getting in his truck and hitting the Northway. Two exits later, he got off at a cluster of apartment developments that were conveniently located right off the highway. With names like Lantern Village, which had an old Colonial theme, and Swisse Chalets, which was some Albany architect's version of Gsaatd, these were well maintained but densely packed stables for young professionals just starting their double-income, no-kids lives.

He should know. He'd lived here once.

Turning in at the signage marked Hunterbred Farms, he was on autopilot as his truck wound around the various horse breed–referenced streets, passing identical stacked buildings that were painted dark green and gold and had central staircases open to the air.

Eleven-oh-one Appaloosa Way.

There were two spaces allotted to each two- or three-bedroom apartment, and he pulled in next to a five-year-old Ford Taurus. He didn't bother to lock up as he got out and strode up the walkway. Two at a time for the stairs. Down to the far end. Last door on the left.

He knocked once and loudly.

The woman who opened up was still in surgical scrubs, her dark hair loose on her shoulders, her eyes exhausted after what had undoubtedly been a very long day. As she shoved her bangs back, he caught a whiff of a chloroxylenol-based antimicrobial soap.

"Hi," she said, stepping back. "You want to come in?"

He shrugged, but entered. The truth was, he didn't want to be here at all.

"You eat tonight?" she asked.

Nope. "Yeah."

"I was just sitting down to Lean Cuisine."

As she headed through the sparse living room, he took the envelope he'd filled with five hundred dollars in cash out of his pocket. There was nowhere to put the damn thing—no table by the door, no side stand by the wilted leather couch, not even an ottoman to lay up aching feet on after a day running meds to ICU patients.

Damn it, he thought as he followed her to the linoleum-floored eating area, with its round table and four chairs.

From out of the galley kitchen, she emerged with a black

plastic tray filled with something that was steaming, and a glass of pale white wine.

She sat down and arranged the stainless-steel fork and a paper towel to the left of her "plate."

No eating, though. And she couldn't look at him—which was nothing new.

"Here," he said, bending forward and putting the money on the chipped tabletop.

As she stared at the envelope, she looked like she was going to cry. But that was also not a news flash—and another thing that was none of his business.

"I'm going to take off—"

"He's getting into trouble," she mumbled as she took her fork and stabbed at whatever creamed thing was fresh from the freezer and the microwave. "It's bad."

"At school?" Duke said remotely.

She nodded. "He was caught stealing a laptop from the computer lab."

"Suspension?"

"Three days—and mandated counseling. He's been at Mom's until I can pick him up after work—I'm due over there right now." She shook her head. "I don't know how to talk to him. He doesn't listen to me . . . it's like he can't even hear me."

Duke put his hands in the pockets of his jeans and lounged against the wall. If she was waiting for him to tell her everything was going to be all right, she shouldn't hold her breath. He wasn't in that line of work.

She put the fork down. "Listen, I hate to ask you to do this . . ."

Duke closed his eyes and shook his head. "Then stop right there."

". . . but could you sit down with him? The older he gets . . . the harder this is becoming."

"What makes you think he'll give a shit about anything I say."

As his old lover glanced up at him, her dark eyes were hollow as empty closets. "Because he's afraid of you."

"And you're okay using scare tactics," he muttered.

"I just don't know what else to do."

"I've got to go back to work."

As he turned away, she said, "Duke. Please. Someone's got to get through to him."

Looking over his shoulder, he traced her hair, her face, the hunch of her shoulders as she sat over that cooling plastic dinner of hers.

In the silence, the years melted away, the recession making it feel like he was walking toward her, getting closer even though physically he didn't move.

He saw Nicole in memories from so very long ago, sitting across a lecture hall at Union College. Biochem, with that professor who was bald but had had brows like salt-and-pepper tumbleweeds. Duke was in the back; she was down in front. A fire alarm went off and she twisted around like most of the other students, looking up to the rear exits as if she were planning her escape should it be the real thing instead of a drill or a malfunction.

Dark hair. Dark eyes. Small build but long legs shown off by shorts, because it was a warm one in the middle of September.

Instant attraction on his side, the kind of thing that had turned all the other women in that whole fucking school into cardboard cutouts. Later, he'd learned that she hadn't even noticed him that day. But once she did?

Best three years of his life.

Followed by a nightmare he was still in.

"Why are you looking at me like that?" she said. Even though she knew.

He was staring at her because now she was over thirty and so was he, and they were as far away from that pair back on that fire alarm day as two strangers: She was a nurse instead of the ob-gyn she'd been planning on becoming. She was also middle-aged before her time, raising a kid on her own because the father was . . .

He couldn't finish that sentence. Not even to himself. It cut too deep.

And on Duke's side? He wasn't a cardiac surgeon. Nope. Not even close—all he had left of the education he'd been so committed to was some useless vocabulary and a catalog of heart-related fun facts that meant he could occasionally get *Jeopardy!* answers right.

He was nothing but a bouncer and a road worker, his brain locked in neutral as his body took the pole position in his work.

The pair of them were proof positive that tragedy didn't have to be traumatic in the car-accident sense. Sometimes, it was as no big deal/commonplace as a single night of unprotected sex.

As he remembered where they'd once been, the vault in his chest creaked open, and for once, it released a burp of emotion that was something other than anger or bitterness: Picturing those two eighteen-year-olds and their grand plans for life, he felt . . . sorry for them. So damned pathetic, all that yearning and optimism, that ignorant conception that you could go through a list of majors and classes and actually pick what the rest of your life was going to be.

Like destiny was an à la carte menu.

Assuming that youth was indeed wasted on the young—and shit, yeah, it was—aging was the payment for that period of blissful stupidity, and frankly, the exchange wasn't worth it. Better to come out of the gate knowing that nothing was planable except death and taxes. No illusions meant you were never surprised when you got shanked.

Back in Biochem, if he'd had a more realistic vision of

things . . . after she'd looked to the back exits, he'd have banged her for a week straight to get the burn out of his gut and then he'd have walked away free and clear. He wouldn't have wasted all that time with her—and certainly wouldn't have been side-tracked so badly when the wheels had come off.

Instead? No M.D. after his name, and there was never going to be. And she was one of those single, harried moms who'd last had a date back before she'd been pregnant.

"Please," Nicole said. "I know it's not something you want to do, but—"

"I'll see you next month," he said, walking away from her and the kid he "took care of."

As he left his old apartment, he closed the door firmly.

The financial contribution he made was all he was willing to give to her—and he hand-delivered it every thirty days because he liked to make her suffer: He enjoyed standing in front of her and putting those envelopes down, and seeing the exhaustion and defeat in her once-pretty face.

It was like bloodletting, he supposed, a painful cutting that offered a release. He always hated coming, but leaving made him feel . . . powerful, cleansed.

And yeah, that wasn't fair.

But neither was life.

Chapter Six

Sitting in her hard little seat at the café, Cait started clapping, and it was a case of join the crowd. Everyone in the whole place was applauding the singer up on the stage, and he was so gracious about it, nothing arrogant in his bowing. If anything, he seemed sheepish.

"What'd I say," Teresa spoke up over the din. "What *did* I say."

"You were right. He's . . ." When she hesitated over the wording, her old roommate got really superior looking. "Oh, come on, I was an art major, not an English one."

"Speechless is speechless."

The singer waved to someone in the back, and laughed like there was an inside joke between him and whoever it was. Then he took another bend at the waist and waved to somebody else. More bowing.

How many songs had he done? Seven? All from memory—

hell, she didn't know if she could do more than "Jingle Bells" and "Happy Birthday" without sheet music. And that "Live Forever" song he'd composed? Truly incredible.

"You know, he writes his own material." Teresa's eyes stuck to the guy as he came down off the stage and chatted with a couple of women across the way. "And I mean, no Auto-Tune or anything like that for him. He's the real deal."

Cait nodded, and really wished she wasn't gawking like everyone else, but her eyes were where they were. When he'd been performing, it had been like watching TV—no stumbles, no amateurish high notes that barely made the pitch, no trite-and-sappy Hallmark verses; he was, in fact, the real deal, and that made him unreal, in a way. So the idea that he was just walking in and out of the tables, gabbing with the regulars, laughing like a normal person? Almost more captivating than him up onstage—

Without any warning, the man looked over at her, their eyes meeting, her body jerking from embarrassment . . . and a shot of heat that was a shock.

Cait looked away fast, paying all kinds of attention to her mug of water. When she figured the coast had to be clear, she glanced over again.

He was still staring at her, even though there was another woman standing in front of him, making gestures big enough for a cheerleader.

"Well, well, well," Teresa said, "looks like someone else's noticed your new hair."

Cait went back to her water, tracing triangles on the smooth, thick flanks of the mug. "I don't know what you're talking about."

"Oh, my God, he's coming over."

"What?"

"He's coming—"

"Hi," a deep voice said.

"—over."

Not looking, Cait told herself. Nope. There wasn't enough of her water left to douse her when she spontaneously combusted.

"Hi," Teresa replied in an octave higher than normal. "Great set. Songs, I mean. Fabulous."

"Thanks, that's really cool of you. I think I've seen you before?"

"Oh, you know, I'm kind of into the music scene."

News to me, Cait thought with a grin.

Another pause.

Shoot, she was going to have to make eye contact. It was either that or Teresa was going to kick her shin under the table like it was a football. God knew the woman had done that before—

Okay, wow. He was even better-looking up close.

"I'm G.B.," he said, putting out his hand.

"Cait. Cait Douglass."

As she shook what he offered, he smiled as if he liked the feel of the contact—and then he held on to her palm for a split second longer than was polite.

"Is that with a C or a K?" he asked.

"It's C-A-I-T as in Caitlyn."

"That is a beautiful name."

Cait grimaced. "I've always hated it. Too girlie— Ow."

As she glared at Teresa, G.B. laughed. "I'm a Gordon Benjamin, so I know how that goes. G.B. is as close to my real name as I can stand to get. So, are you into music, too?"

"No." She shot a don't-you-dare at Teresa. "But I'm glad I was invited out tonight. You really are something."

"Thanks, but the set felt rough on my end."

He was cut off by the arrival of a trio of women, all of them crowding in and talking fast—saying pretty much what she and Teresa had, and wasn't that embarrassing. As the din got louder and more fervent, Cait fully expected him to peace out and pay attention to his fans. Not how it went. Five minutes later, Gordon Benjamin, a.k.a. G.B. of the golden pipes and Fabio-without-the-cheese hair, had parked it at their table, ordered a chai latte, and was leaning back in his chair, apparently ready to stay the night.

"So what do you do for a living?" he asked Cait.

"I'm an artist. I teach at Union College and I illustrate children's books."

He nodded as his bowl-size mug arrived. "So you're like me, making a living off your passion."

"It must be hard to be in the music business. Things have changed so much, haven't they? I mean, file sharing, piracy, all that."

"Actually, that's just the business side. Creatively? So much worse. The overuse of Auto-Tune, singers functioning as marketing concepts, everything so totally packaged." He pushed his hair back, and she was momentarily distracted by how beautiful it was. "There are very few of us left who write our own material—and I'm not a twenty-year-old girl writing about famous boyfriends who treat me like crap. I want to convey truer emotions than puppy love gone bad, you know?"

"Teresa told me you write your own lyrics." She nodded across the way to make sure her friend was included. "That song about eternal life was . . . inspirational."

Like he was reading her mind, G.B. smiled at Teresa. "And that's what everybody wants, right? The time we have here is so damned short—and we need to leave something behind."

"So you'd be immortal if you could be, huh?" Cait said.

"In a heartbeat. Come on, life is great—I don't want to lose all this. I don't want to get old. I certainly don't want to die."

"With the way you sing," Teresa cut in, "everybody's better off with you on the planet."

"Does that mean you'll vote for me on *American Idol?*"

Teresa clapped her hands. "Hell, yeah! Are you trying out?"

"Maybe. Will you vote for me, too?" he asked Cait.

"I don't watch that kind of TV, but if you're on it? I'd be there every night."

"You guys are the best." He pushed that amazing hair back again, and Cait lingered on the way the stuff gleamed. "But I haven't pursued that one yet. I don't know . . . I hate to go that route. It feels like a copout in some ways, but the reality is—it's time for me to break out on a national scale, and I need a platform. I mean, I do okay money-wise, like, singing backup for people on tour, and doing voice-over work down in Manhattan. And I've just gotten a part in the local production of *Rent.*"

"Have you sent any tracks in to record companies?" Cait asked, like she knew anything about "tracks" or "record companies."

"I have, but again, it's hard to get noticed. That's the only reason I'd do *Idol.* If I could get on there—"

"You would," Teresa said.

"And you'd do well," Cait echoed. Star quality, it was called. And he had it.

"Thanks. That really means a lot." G.B.'s smile was so genuine, Cait found it hard to believe the three of them hadn't been friends for years. "It's not about the fame thing, by the way. I just . . . you know, I want to leave behind something important, something that lasts. And that's not a bad thing, is it?"

Cait thought of recent events . . . and upcoming funerals. Shaking her head, she said grimly, "Not at all."

"So how about you?"

"Me?"

"If you could be ageless, would you?"

She took a drink of her water and grimaced. The ice cubes had all melted and there was a tinny aftertaste now. "I don't know. I suppose if everyone I loved could be along for the ride with me? Well, then the losses wouldn't be that bad and I'd say yes—because the thing is, it's not only you. What good is having forever if you just have to watch your friends and family die? That would be hell, not heaven." She shrugged. "Personally, I think it's better to just focus on the here and now. Immortality is not going to happen, so why not learn how to live the best life we can in this moment?"

When G.B. fell silent, she winced. "I sound like Oprah, right? I don't mean to get preachy—"

"You are a deep thinker. And I like that—a lot."

Flushing, Cait looked away. She didn't know what to do with comments like that, and the fact that Teresa was with them made her feel even more awkward.

When another couple of women came by to chat with him, she checked her watch. As much as she was enjoying this—

"So, you look like you're getting ready to head off." As she glanced over, G.B. smiled at her—and wow, his dark eyes were pretty. Were they brown? Blue? "Do you have anyone waiting at home for you?"

Cait's brows rose. He wasn't suggesting that—

"She doesn't even have a cat," Teresa interjected. "Or a goldfish."

"Oh?" G.B. smiled again. "So no one, huh."

Cait started to feel truly antsy. "Well, I'm allergic to cats."

"Me, too." G.B. took a long drink of his tea and then resettled with the base of the mug balanced on his knee. "Is it okay for me to ask for your number?"

As G.B. waited for Cait as in C-A-I-T to respond, he was more than happy to pass the time looking over at her.

The blond hair was hella 'tractive, and that smooth skin—his hands just wanted to touch her again. That shake of theirs had been way too short, and he'd been racking his brain ever since to find another socially acceptable reason to make some sustainable contact. Not that this was Regency England, but come on—he didn't want her to think he was a letch.

He really wanted to go out with her.

The second he'd gotten on the stage, he'd seen her in the crowd, sure as if she had been sitting under a spotlight: long and tall, simply dressed, really good hair. Nothing bar harlot about her, and she was listening to him like she was interested—but not with that rapt thing that most of the women sported.

This one was going to be different. He could feel it.

"I promise to be a perfect gentleman," he tacked on, since she seemed to be on the fence about the whole phone call thing.

"I—ah . . ." Cait jerked upright in her seat and then shot a hard look at her friend.

"Of course you can call her," the dark-haired woman said. "Here's her number."

As the buddy took out a pen and scribbled on a napkin, he was more than happy to take what was offered. But he looked first to Cait—he wasn't touching those digits unless she was okay with it.

"You sure about this?" he asked her.

The fact that she seemed shocked that he'd call her made him want to get on his knees and beg her—just so she would feel like a queen.

Abruptly, she straightened her shoulders like she'd given herself a pep talk, and met him right in the eye. "I'd love to hear from you."

Yes, he thought with triumph. The day hadn't started off all that well—what with someone messing with his guitar while he'd been voicing a commercial for Petco, and then him fighting a northbound traffic jam coming out of Manhattan. But this blond woman with her even-toned voice and her expressive hands and that delicious reserve had turned it all around.

"Well, I think I'd better get going," she said as she bent to the side and picked up her purse.

"It's Friday night," her friend pointed out.

"I'm under deadline."

"What are you working on?" G.B. asked, hoping to keep her around a little longer.

"It's a book for five- to eight-year-olds—about a chocolate Lab who worries about things. I have to admit, it's been one of my favorite projects. The puppy's adorable, if I do say so myself."

"I'd love to see your work sometime. Seems only fair after you've heard me sing."

She got to her feet, and she was even taller than he'd thought—and that was just more good news. "I can't imagine you'd be interested in that kind of stuff."

"Oh, I'm interested." His eyes drifted down to her mouth . . . and then went farther, to the pale column of her throat. "I'm sure you do beautiful lines."

God knew she was made of them—at least according to his peripheral vision, which was working just fine, thank you very much. And he knew better than to go any farther with the gawking than that. Whereas some women might be flattered by him going all obvi with the check-out stuff, she was not one of them.

And yup, that was a really nice change of pace.

Although . . . that being said, he wasn't exactly sure he was looking for a long-term relationship with anything other than his singing. Then again, he'd been "dating" the same kind of groupie for how many years? Maybe it was time for quality instead of quantity.

As Cait smiled at him, he felt a shot of lust go right through him. Yes, he really did want her . . .

"You're a charmer, you know that?" she drawled.

"That's been mentioned before—maybe once or twice. Is it such a bad thing, in your opinion?"

"Of course not."

Liar, he thought.

Leaning forward, he wanted to take her hand, but didn't. "Just so you know, it is possible to be both charming and honest."

"Of course it is."

She was still lying. And didn't that make him want to prove her wrong. "I *will* call you, by the way."

"Of course you will."

G.B. smiled again as she put the strap of her purse up on her shoulder. "You've made my night, you know," he told her.

Cait actually rolled her eyes—and though her friend looked mortified, he *loved* it. This was not your average woman, easily seduced by a song and a stare.

"I'm serious about that," he said. "You really did."

"Well." There was a pause. "You've cheered me up also, how about that."

"Answer my call and I'll see if I can keep the trend going."

"It's a deal."

And a date, he thought.

With a couple of words to her friend and a casual wave over her shoulder, she was gone, weaving in and out of the little tables, passing by the bar, disappearing through the front door.

G.B. carefully folded up the napkin and put it in the front pocket of his shirt. Then he smiled at her friend. "She's pretty special."

The dark-haired woman nodded. "Yeah, she is. And this is really good timing for her."

He stared at the exit she'd used. After a moment, he murmured, "Me, too."

Chapter
Seven

"—godforsaken, miserable piece of shit!"

As Jim faced off at the stove from hell, he thought about giving the cast-iron nightmare a swift kick in the oven door—but with the way things were going, he'd either break that little glass window or his foot.

Which would be the perfect fucking nightcap to an absolutely magical fucking evening.

All he wanted was a couple of eggs—scrambled, over easy, fried, he didn't give a good goddamn. He couldn't remember the last time or thing he'd eaten, and when Ad had made a food run to Hannaford earlier in the day, the guy had had the brains to pick up some Eggland's Best.

It wasn't like he was after truffles or twelve kinds of fancy, culinary crap.

Eggs. Just eggs.

Except like everything else, he couldn't make it frickin' happen:

The only thing the burners on the cooktop seemed to do was burp gas; the pan he found looked like it had been forged by hand in the Middle Ages; and he wasn't sure, but he thought that the refrigerator was doing the death rattle of something about to meet its maker.

Which in this case was . . . General Electric, going by the logo on its off-kilter door.

Giving up, he sat down at the table and lit a cigarette, figuring the nicotine might perk his immortal ass up. At the very least, holding the Marlboro would give his right hand something to do other than make a fist and test the structural integrity of the walls.

"What a dump," he muttered as he looked around at the ancient appliances, the pitted countertops, the cracked floor, the stained ceiling.

Last time he ever took a rental without seeing it first.

But, really, resolutions about his real estate accommodations were pretty far down his list of priorities.

You are endangering the outcome of the entire war.

Exhaling, he watched the smoke rise through the cold air and curl up around the ancient light fixture hanging above him. The chandelier dangled at the end of a corroded black chain and had five arms, although only three of the bulbs were working. Probably a good thing. Bright illumination would only make the kitchen look worse—like hitting a ninety-year-old with headlights.

"Devina, where are you," he gritted before taking another drag. "Where the fuck are you . . ."

He tapped his ash into an ashtray.

Waiting . . . waiting . . .

He wasted more time glancing around, like maybe something had changed in the point-three seconds since his last observation.

In his previous life, before he'd been electrocuted on a job site and recruited for this dumb-ass, thankless job, he'd have loved to have tackled a place like this. It was the carpenter in him. Room by room, he would have gone through and replaced floors and re-plastered walls and sealed and repainted ceilings. Stripped mold-ings back down to the original wood and revarnished. Swapped out 1940s appliances and fixtures for things that had been made in the current century, but looked old and weren't fire hazards. Made the cabinets and cupboards himself.

For a moment, his blood pressure dropped as he entertained the fantasy, the smell of pine being cut on a circular saw filling his nose, the sound of nails being hammered home ringing in his ears, the rhythmic scratching of sandpaper tightening his arm muscles.

So much more satisfying than anything else he could do with his life: What was great about home renovation was that the im-provement was immediate and lasting—and absolutely measur-able, no backsliding, no double standards. You had a toilet that ran all night? Take it out, get a new one, do an install. Heating didn't work? Run some fresh ductwork and get yourself the right unit. Upstairs drafty? R-19 insulation, baby.

It is utterly reckless to give away—

I'm not giving dick away, Nigel! For fuck's sake, I've got to get her out of there.

One girl cannot be more important than the victory.

She didn't deserve what she got.

You simpering fool! The exigencies of fate are not always just—surely you are not so naive as to believe otherwise. And your role is not to balance the scales. You are here to win.

Fuck you, Nigel. You don't need to remind me what my job is—and I'm done talking about this. Those flags are my possessions. You told me so yourself. What I do with them is my business, not yours.

Yup, that had been a fun conversation. Productive, too—they'd both been even more worked up and angry at the end of it.

"So you gave up on the eggs?" Adrian said from behind him.

Jim shut his eyes. "I don't want to talk about Nigel."

"I thought I was asking about breakfast protein?"

"And I'm not interested in your opinion."

"Well, you already heard it—because I agree with Nigel."

Jim took a long drag. "Do us both a favor and back out of this room—"

The bomb went off in the front of the house, the thunderous noise rattling the shelves in the cupboards and rocking that light fixture.

Jim was out of his chair before the noise faded, shooting through the dining room, pounding into the foyer . . .

The fact that the door was still intact was a shocker, but there were cracks in the leaded glass windows on either side of it. As he yanked open the heavy oak panels, he had a crystal knife in hand—that shit had not been made by a human, and that meant he'd do better with something that had a little more kick to it—

Jim stopped dead.

Lying on the weathered floorboards of the front porch, a female form was tucked in on itself, a dirty shift covering pale skin, thin legs pulled in to the belly as if to protect against a beating.

Long blond hair fanned out, the strands catching the light that flowed from the open doorway.

Jim fell to his knees, his body weight slamming down on itself. He felt no pain from the impact, a stunning numbness taking him over.

His hands were shaking as he reached out and touched the ends of the blond strands. Between one blink and the next, he saw a drain, a pool of blood, a red stain on the golden waves.

"Sissy?" he croaked in a voice he'd never heard come out of his mouth before.

"Where's my fucking flag."

Jim jacked his head up.

The demon Devina was standing over them, hands on her

hips, Sofia Vergara body filling out something black and leather-ish. Her eyes were gleaming, but not with satisfaction.

Jim ignored her. "Sissy . . . ?"

That bitchy voice came from above, sharp and demanding: "Excuuuuuuse me. Leave that stupid-ass little girl alone and give me what I'm—"

Wrong tone. Wrong attitude. Wrong motherfucking words.

Jim attacked before he was aware of moving, his body exploding up, his left hand locking on the demon's throat, his massive strength throwing Devina back against the side of the house so hard he didn't just break the shutter behind her back; he shattered it into splinters.

Devina just purred. "How nice to have your full attention."

Jamming his face into hers, he put the tip of that crystal knife right to her temple. And then for a moment, all he could do was pant, his brain jammed up with what she had done to Sissy, what she had forced that innocent to see down in Hell . . . what he wanted to do to the demon in payback.

Instead of her fighting to get free, her thigh inched in between his braced legs. "Maybe we can seal this deal properly—"

Jim shoved his palm against her mouth, pushing it in so hard, he distorted her fake beauty into an echo of how ugly she really was.

As she began to struggle, he bared his teeth and thought about biting her somewhere, anywhere.

"Adrian," he growled in an inhuman way. "Get the flag."

When uneven footfalls began to retreat, it was clear that the other angel was on the case.

Devina began to fight in earnest, wrenching her head, clawing at his arms. Except as she got her mouth free, she just whispered, "Someone's watching you."

Jim frowned.

Oh, fuck, Sissy.

He dropped his hold and leaped out of the demon's range.

Sissy had pushed herself up and was cowering in the far corner of the porch, her knees drawn in against her chest, her arms locked around them. From behind a veil of tangled blond hair, she stared out with horrified eyes.

And she was looking at him that way. Not Devina.

Jim dragged a hand through his hair. "Shit."

In his peripheral vision, Devina yanked her clothes back into position and stamped her heels like her panties had gotten into a wad and she was hoping gravity would do the work.

Tossing her hair, she addressed Sissy. "Are you scared of him? You should be—"

Jim put his body in the way. "Don't talk to her."

"What. Like you fucking own—"

Ad picked that perfect moment to reappear with the flag. "Take it and get the hell out of here," the angel said in an exhausted voice.

For a split second, Devina's real face showed through the skin she wore, the decaying flesh and glowing bone surging through the lie.

That hideous spectacle cranked over in Jim's direction. "We're not through. Not by a long shot."

As Jim's chest pumped up and down, he didn't trust himself to reply—he just prayed that for once in her horrible life, the bitch took someone else's advice and disappeared without another syllable leaving her mouth.

After all, the last thing he wanted was for Sissy to be exposed to more trauma. And yet even with that hanging over him . . . he wasn't sure it was enough to keep him from ripping that demon limb from limb.

The cold, clear air felt good on Cait's face, her sinuses tingling, her mind clearing. It had been hot in the café—and not just because of the body heat from the crowd.

You've made my night.

She shook her head. "Stop it."

Unfortunately, the command was oh, so easy to follow: In the work of a moment, thanks to all kinds of heavily forged neuropathways, her mother's religious narrative took over, mowing down the nice fact that a very attractive man had asked for her number—not because she'd dressed inappropriately or said anything provocative or behaved badly. Not even necessarily for sex. It was just two adults who might get to know each other better and see where things took them.

Cait struggled against the tide, but she was tired . . . and yes, ma'am, being guilty for no good reason at all was a custom-made hair shirt. Fit her just perfectly.

Then again, across town, a family was in mourning. And her response? Go out and get her hair done, and cap the night off flirting with a stranger.

Real classy.

As she hoofed it down the shallow alley and entered the rear parking lot, other stragglers were also going for their rides, the women talking in quick bursts, like the afterburn of those songs and that singer was still revving them up. In contrast, Cait felt totally apart from them, in spite of the fact that they'd all seen the same performance and been in the same mind-set inside the café.

She spent a lot of years walking this stretch of isolation.

By the time she came up to her car, the temperature had gone from refreshing to chilly, and she made fast work of the unlock-

and-open thing. Getting in, she shivered as she shut the door, and immediately hit the *start* button. Heat, heat would be good, but . . . shoot, it was going to be a while coming: Three other cars had their white reverse lights on and were inching around, trying to navigate the cramped space. All at the same time.

She was going to be stuck in place for a while . . .

Later, she would wonder what exactly had made her turn her head to the left. Not a sound, no. Or a flash of movement. Or anything of outward significance.

But sure as if someone had called her name, her head swiveled and her eyes searched the darkness.

There was a truck parked next to her, a rough, rangy vehicle that seemed like it belonged more in farm and forest territory than at a city-dweller café. And behind its wheel, sitting with eerie stillness, was a man. A big man.

She could not see his face, but his sharp profile cut through the ambient glow of the lot's security lights, carving a black path through the illumination. His head was nearly shaved, his brow heavy, as if he were frowning, his hard chin giving the clear impression that "uncompromising" was probably not just something he was familiar with, but an operating principle.

The other thing she noticed? His shoulders were tremendous, although that was likely some kind of coat or something against the cold.

Without warning, his head whipped around.

She could see nothing of his eyes, but oh, God . . . she felt them crossing the distance, doing away with the car doors, melting through the glass, tearing down any and every barrier between them.

Cait told herself to look away. Pointed out that the idea there was any kind of connection was ridiculous. Made a list of all the reasons that women who lived alone should never, ever encourage strange men—especially ones who were built like that.

Wait, she wasn't encouraging anything—

Oh, really? Then why hadn't she looked away, backed away, driven off? 'Cause those other cars had left and the lot was clear.

The man went for his door.

Before she knew what was happening, he got out of his truck and prowled around the front of it, his huge body moving like . . .

Maybe the word was . . . erotic.

Take out the "maybe."

Cait did not look away. Couldn't. In the sweeping headlights of one more car that had a more sensible driver than her, she got a clear shot at him—much taller than she'd thought, and the body was . . . even stronger than it had looked through the glass. And that heft? Not a jacket or a coat, nope. It was just muscles in a T-shirt.

As for the face? His was completely in shadow, the light shining from behind him.

So she couldn't tell.

Her heart pounded as he came up to her car, except it was not from fear. Probably should have been. As things stood, it was more as if an electrical charge was coursing through her rib cage.

Her window went down. Sure as if something other than her mind controlled her arm, her hands, her fingertips.

It was as if she were possessed.

Looking up, her first thought was that she recognized him from somewhere. Maybe it was another case like Pablo and Victoria Beckham? Or, God, had he been on the front page of the newspaper for some horrible crime?

No . . . something else.

"Do I know you?" he asked in a low voice.

Before she could reply, a car horn went off and his head shot to the left—and that was how she saw his face properly. Holy Mary, mother of—

He was . . . breathtaking. Absolutely stunning.

He had the looks of a fighter, and not as in the puffy distortion of a boxer, but the shrewd, hawkish features of a man who might have been in the military. Eyes were blue, brows were dark as his hair, and that hard, heavy jaw was, yup, a very clear indicator that you tangled with him at your own risk.

On that note, when he turned back, she said, "No, you don't— and I'm sorry. I didn't mean to stare."

Even though she couldn't see, she felt his eyes narrow, as if he were testing the statement for truth.

"It's okay," he murmured.

"I have to go." Except she didn't have any impulse of the sort. She just kept staring up at him. To fill the silence, she blurted, "I really just came to hear the singer. With my friend."

"And did you like him."

Not a question. It was as if he already knew the answer.

"Yes. Very much."

"You're missing an earring."

So he was staring at her as much as she thought.

"I lost it earlier tonight. At the hair salon." Okay, maybe she'd better put the SUV in reverse before she told him her life's story. "I went back, but . . . it wasn't in lost and found or anything."

Shut it, Cait.

"It was gone," he filled in.

"Yes."

"That happens."

"Did you come here to listen to G.B., too?"

"No."

She nodded. "I can imagine that's not your kind of music."

"Quick read on me, huh."

"Yes. I have to go."

"But you're still here, aren't you."

"I don't want to run over your feet."

He shrugged. "Steel-toed boots. Wouldn't feel a thing."

FFS, that probably would have been true even if he'd been in flip-flops. Not that he'd wear that kind of thing.

"I could swear I know you," she whispered.

"I don't get that a lot." He leaned in. "Tell me something."

"What . . ."

"Do you like what you see?"

Cait's mouth parted so she could breathe.

"Do you," he repeated. When she didn't reply, he said in that very, very deep voice, "Cat got your tongue?"

"Okay. Well . . . good-bye."

He laughed, the sound a rumble through his chest. "You're still not leaving."

"I need to go."

She put up her window more to cut herself off than anything else, and she was relieved that as she began to back out, he did step back. It didn't stay that way. As she put things in drive, he came forward, her headlights making a stage for him, illuminating him as he stood with his legs locked, his head up, his hands on his hips.

A challenge directed to her, even though they were strangers.

And God help her, her body responded: Lust, unrestrained and unrepentant, went through her, waking her up in places that were not just dormant but previously nonexistent.

Run, some inner voice told her. Run fast and far—and pray that he doesn't choose to follow you.

There was no saying "no" to a man like that. Not at all. Not even if he wasn't good for you. Not even if your parents would insist you'd be a sinner.

Cait hit the gas so hard her tires scrubbed out, but he didn't jump out of the way. He took a single step away so that she all but struck him.

Probably would have left a dent in her car before he got hurt.

Shooting through the narrow slot between the café and the art gallery, she had to slam on the brakes when she came out to the main road.

It wasn't until she was on the highway, heading for her residential neighborhood, that her heart began to slow down.

Leaning into the front windshield, she looked up at the night sky. Naturally, she caught nothing of the stars, not even a faint glow. But sure as she knew where she lived, and how to drive her car, and what she was going to be doing in the morning, she was convinced someone up there was weaving out a destiny for her.

Too many strange things in one night—

When her phone went off, she let out a bark and grabbed for her heart. Had G.B. called her so fast?

Nope. According to her nav screen, Bluetooth had Teresa on the line.

Cait was too rattled to be let down. "Hey."

"I want the name of your hairdresser. Right now. And yes, I'm thinking about going blond, too."

As Cait started to laugh, some of the tension bled out of her—but not all of it. In the back of her mind . . . that man lingered.

And not the singer . . .

. . . the other one.

Chapter Eight

Talk about shock and awe.

As Devina poofed out with her prize, Jim stared down at Sissy, his brain totally and completely blank. The girl was shaking as she held on to herself, her eyes wide and terrified as she looked between him and Adrian.

Poor goddamn girl.

Christ, now what.

"Go inside," Jim said softly to Adrian, "and find Dog."

Ad beat feet once again, disappearing in that uneven gait of his.

Left alone with the girl, Jim crouched down, both his knees popping. Putting his palms forward, he tried to make his voice nonthreatening. "I'm not going to hurt you."

"Is she gone?"

The three words were so rough, he wasn't sure what he'd heard. But then it computed. "Yeah. She—"

Sissy lunged for him, her body flopping forward in spastic discombobulation, tripping all over itself. He barely had time to catch her as she flailed in his direction, his hands slipping on her torso before finding purchase, his arms easily holding her up off the porch's cold floorboards.

Up against him, she was soft and painfully light—although she held on to his shoulders like a cat trying with every claw to stay out of a deluge.

"I got you," he said hoarsely. "I've got you. . . ."

For a brief moment, he dipped his head, putting his face into that blond hair. Then he felt her shivering, and knew he had to get her somewhere warm. As he stood up, he had the clear sense that he could have let go of her completely and she would have remained Velcroed to his chest.

"I know you . . ." she said into his neck. "You came . . . you told me . . ."

"I would get you out."

Going in through the front door, he kicked the thing shut—and ran out of gas. He wanted something clean and fresh for her, a hotel room with sheets that smelled like lemon, and room service that would bring her a hamburger, or a piece of chicken . . . or frickin' nachos with melted cheese if that's what she was into. His options?

Bedrooms that were out of a *Hoarders* episode, a limp-along kitchen, and a whole lot of draft and dust.

After glaring at the stairs, like maybe that would change the composition of the second story, he picked the sofa in the parlor. For whatever reason, maybe because that room was over the boiler in the basement, it was always warmest in there. Except . . . when he got to the couch, he took one look at the white sheeting that covered the damn thing and thought, Nope. He wasn't about to put her on that filthy mess—and removing the draping would only create a dust bowl.

"I'm going to . . ." Shit. "Take you upstairs."

"Where am I?"

"Out," he said as he backtracked and went for the barely car-peted steps. "You're out of there, and you're never going back."

"Promise?"

He stopped and pulled her away from him. Staring down into her eyes, he said, "Never. I don't care what I have to do or where I have to go, she's never getting her hands on you again."

Sissy blinked. And then she nodded, the agreement rendered upon nothing more substantial than breath and voice, and yet forged in stone between them.

As she collapsed back into his chest, he took the staircase two at a time, and snarled at the grandfather clock as he passed it by—if that thing let out even one gong, he was going to take a chain saw to it and light the pieces on fire in the back-fucking-yard.

It would be the single most satisfying way to blow a security deposit.

When he got to the second-story foyer, he carried her right into his bedroom—the sheets were tangled, but at least they'd been laundered in the last two days.

The instant he put her on the mattress, he went to step back—and found himself locked in.

"You can let go now," he told her.

In the end, he had to reach up and gently pry her hands free, her nails scratching at his skin even through his shirt.

He made sure he went way back, not stopping until his shoul-ders hit some kind of plaster. Across the room, she tucked into her-self again, looking minuscule on the king-size bed, her wide eyes jumping around like she expected the walls to give way and reveal where she really was.

"You're out," he repeated—and wondered which of the two of them he was talking to. "And you're never going back there."

"Where was I."

Jim exhaled, and unconsciously went for his pack of cigarettes. Except he wasn't going to smoke around her. "Not a good place."

"Was it really . . ."

The idea that she'd been thrown in with Devina's tormented masses made his chest burn. "Yeah. It was Hell."

Sissy's eyes locked on him. "How many years was I there?"

"Ah . . . it wasn't years. Not by a long shot."

She shuddered, and seemed to brace herself. "So how many . . . decades. Or . . . was it centuries?"

Jim recoiled. "It was only a matter of weeks."

She shook her head. "No, that can't be right. I was there for . . . an eternity."

Some kind of warning tickled its way up the back of his neck, and he followed an instinct that told him not to argue with her. Fucking Devina.

"You know I'm never going to hurt you," he said. "You don't have to worry about me like that."

Sissy refocused on him, her eyes seeming so old, he wondered if maybe she was right. Maybe it had been forever for her in that wall.

"I know," she said.

Such simple words, but the relief they gave him was worth a million cigarette drags—

The clipping of little feet across bare floors brought his head around to the open doorway. As Dog made his appearance, Jim vowed to give the little guy roast turkey for the next month and a half.

"Your dog!" Sissy cried out.

Dog took that as the cue to do what he did best: get in someone's lap and stay there. As he jumped awkwardly up onto the bed, Sissy opened her arms and the two became one, the girl holding all that scruffy fur to her heart, the animal burrowing in as if she were a living, breathing quilt whose sole purpose was to make him warm and comfortable.

"Actually—" Jim had to clear his throat. "He's everybody's."

She didn't hear him, though, and that was okay. She was murmuring to Dog, soothing him—and likely, by extension, herself.

Jim scrubbed his face. In his negotiating with Devina, he'd never thought beyond the deal—hadn't considered what would happen if Sissy actually was sent back.

"Do you want some food?" he asked.

She didn't answer him, her attention solely on the animal.

"I'll go get you some . . ." Well, probably not eggs, no. But maybe he could get something delivered—it was before midnight. "I'll be right back."

Ducking out, he—

Ran right into Adrian. The other angel was standing in the second-story foyer, his face grim, his eyes sharp.

The rise of one of his brows was all the comment that had to be made: *Your bedroom. Really.*

"It's not that," Jim growled. "For fuck's sake, she's a goddamn child."

All that got him was the second brow hitting that dark hairline: *Uh-huh. Right.*

"Fuck you, Adrian, for real."

If that angel wanted to make up shit in his head, there was nothing Jim could do about it. He knew where he stood with Sissy—he'd rescued her, and now he was going to take care of her until the war was over. After that? Hopefully he won, and she could go live in the Manse of Souls, where she belonged.

That was all there was to it. He might have murdered for a living, might have violated a thousand different laws in the process, might have had sex with whores and prostitutes and women who were capable of cracking skulls and killing blindfolded . . . but he'd never been with a virgin, and he sure as hell was not starting now.

And certainly not ever with Sissy.

God knew, she had already been through enough—

Dimly, he wondered why he was lecturing himself on the topic. Like any of that sort of thing could ever be a reality.

"Do you want food?" Jim asked the other angel. When all Ad did was shake his head, Jim shrugged and headed down for the kitchen, where he'd left his phone.

As he jogged along, it dawned on him that Sissy was going to have a lot of questions.

If he were smart, he'd start working on the answers now.

Shit. This was going to be another long night.

Chapter Nine

Mornings were always the best for working.

As Cait sat in the sunshine, the light fell across her drafting table from over on the left, the illumination so much better than anything that came from a lamp. In its crystal-clear glow, the red of the little chocolate Lab's collar was ruby brilliant, and his brown coat seemed made of velvet, and the happy green of the blades of grass under his paws was bright as an emerald.

No more seasonal affective disorder for her—no matter how bad or long the upstate winter got, since she'd moved in here, she'd been free of the January blues.

And the light meant warmth, too. Although it was just before seven a.m., and the morning temperature itself was in the mid-forties, the all-season porch she worked out of was tropical-toasty, the three sides of floor-to-ceiling windows giving her a nice view of her shallow backyard with its bushes and budding trees.

Reaching out blindly, her palm found her stainless-steel mug, and she took yet another deep drink of her coffee. She hadn't slept much over the course of the night, those two men circling in her head, images of what they'd looked like, and sound bites of what they'd spoken, and close-ups of the way they'd stared at her, going around and around and around. She'd finally given up hope of anything REM-ish at five, and had gotten out of bed to make the first of two pots of coffee. Fortunately, solace had come as soon as she had sat in her padded chair.

Leaning back into the paper, she completed the finishing, colored ink touches on the puppy's eye, giving him a lift to his cocoa brow, and tiny dark lashes that flared, and a little flash of silvery white around the edge of his iris.

Done.

But she double-checked anyway, capping the pen and returning it to its set before reviewing every inch of the two-foot-by-one-foot drawing. The puppy was in the process of sniffing at a bird, his tail in the air, his triangle ears pricked, his chubby legs ready to rear backward if the robin in front of him turned out to be foe rather than friend. The text was going to be mounted above his back, so she'd left a six-inch square blank space in the pale blue sky for the words.

"Good," she said, as if she were her own student.

Unfastening the four corners, she carefully took the sheet and carried it over to the six-foot-long portable tables she'd set up on the solid-wall side of the room. This was page twelve of the book, and she put it at the end of the lineup.

Yup, this layout thing was a critical part of her process, she thought. It gave her a far more complete vision of the work— inevitably, she unconsciously reverted back to certain poses, spatial orientations, expressions, nuances. This way of measuring the project as a whole, all at once, helped her avoid repetitions that probably only she noticed, but which were defects nonetheless.

God . . . she loved children's books. The simplicity of the lessons, the clarity of the colors, the rhythms of the words . . . there was something to be said for a child's binary grasp of the world. Good was good. Bad was bad. Things that were dangerous were stoves, open flames, and light sockets—all easily avoided. And the bogeyman in your closet was always your summer camp sleeping bag wedged into a corner—never, ever something that could really hurt you.

From out of the corner of her eye, the messed-up copy of today's *Caldwell Courier Journal* loomed even though it was lying flat on her coffee table. She hadn't gone very far into it to find the information she'd been looking for—the article on Sissy Barten's funeral was below the fold on the first page. Services were at St. Patrick's Cathedral, with burial at Pine Grove Cemetery immediately following.

She'd be there at the mass, of course.

Pushing her hair behind her ears, she turned back to her workspace . . . and took a moment to mourn the fact that Sissy would never enjoy another morning like this—and if her parents and family ever did again? It was a good decade away. At least.

She'd met the mother and father at parents' weekend back in the fall, when Sissy had brought them to the art department's facility and showed them her wonderful pencil drawings.

It was so eerie to think back to when Cait had shaken those hands and smiled and offered sincere praise. In that moment, if someone had told her the girl would be dead six months later? Inconceivable.

But it had happened.

When she'd gotten the call, it had been from the department head. He'd told her that Sissy had gone missing the night before, not returning from a quick errand out. Her parents had called her roommates on campus in case she'd gone there instead, and then the police had been brought in. They'd found the car she'd taken to the supermarket, but no trace of her.

Vanished.

Until she'd been found in the quarry.

Cait had been the one to clean out her things from the locker and storage compartments Sissy had used in the art building. The duty had been done after hours, when the only people in the department had been the cleaners and the security guard.

She had cried so hard that she'd needed to go to the bathroom for paper towels.

After packing up all the supplies, drawings, and paintings, and then boxing up the sculptural pieces, Cait had taken everything to her own house and called the emergency contact number listed in Sissy's files—but she'd gotten voice mail and, after leaving a message, had never heard back.

Then again, that family had so much more to worry about.

She supposed at some point she was going to have to mail everything to the home address. She'd prefer to hand-deliver it all, but she didn't want to intrude—and knew for sure she wouldn't be able to hold herself together if she saw those parents again.

She couldn't imagine what they were feeling. Having lost her brother at an early age, she knew something of the pain, but she had to imagine if it was your own child, it would be so much worse.

Sitting back down at her drafting table, she rearranged her Prismacolor markers, and double-checked the points on her lead pencils, and made sure her watercolor brushes were super-clean.

Such fragile things, all snappable, the tips easily ruined. In her hand, though, they were powerful instruments, capable of making something out of nothing. Without her guidance? Just inanimate objects collecting dust.

That was the beauty of life, though. It created purpose and meaning in that which was otherwise void. In its absence, however . . .

So strange, the thoughts that occurred to her now. Her knack for making three dimensions out of two had been parlayed into a very nice living for herself. But she had never thought further than paying for her mortgage and her heat and food, had never considered the real implications of not having children . . . had not, until this instant, confronted the idea that what she left behind on paper might be the extent of her contribution, such as it was, to the human race.

Not exactly a groundbreaker, was it. Not very lasting, either—because without a doubt, people would eventually stop reading the books she'd illustrated, and her drawings would fade or fall apart, and she would be, as we all were, forgotten by the living and breathing.

Children were the only immortality mortals got—and even then, two generations later, three at the most, no one knew you in person anymore.

Strains of that song from last night at the café wound through her mind.

G.B. might have a point about wanting to live forever.

It certainly seemed more meaningful than the short time and game-over you got otherwise. And P.S., a seventy-five- or eighty-year-old situation was the best-case scenario.

It wasn't what the Bartens were dealing with. It wasn't the violent, out of sequence, senselessly horrible death of a daughter—who'd been stolen from them by a madman—

Cait stopped and pulled herself back from the depressing rabbit hole.

She was going to feel badly about Sissy for a long time, and that was appropriate. But she still had to get her work done.

Bringing over the next blank sheet, she tacked the drawing paper in place, checked the notes and text the author had provided . . . and once again put pencil to page in the lovely morning sunlight.

It was so much better than thinking; it truly was.

Sissy Barten sat on the porch she'd woken up on the evening before. In front of her, rising through the still-spiny trees of spring, the sun was coming up, its rays gold and peach and potentially warm.

She'd never expected to see this again.

Pulling the blanket she'd brought down with her more tightly around her shoulders, she blinked as the light intensified. Behind her, the house was silent, those two men no doubt asleep in whatever beds they'd finally fallen onto. Through the course of the night, she'd heard them walking the floors for hours—either that or there were ghosts in the old place.

It was when the pair had finally stopped, when there had been no more creaking, no more muttering, no further scent of cigarette smoke, that she had come out of the room she'd been given.

The only thing on her mind had been seeing her family. And that was still true.

She just wanted to go home, be home, stay home.

The trouble was, she didn't know if she could trust this version of reality—and what if all this was just a cruel joke, a further facet of where she had been for an eternity, an illusion created specifically to increase suffering when it was stripped from her?

Then screw that. She'd rather not go back to her parents' house.

She wasn't going to give that woman, demon, whatever she was, the satisfaction—

Sissy glanced over her shoulder. Standing in the open doorway, the man who had rescued her filled the jambs, looking like a harbinger of doom rather than anyone who'd protect somebody. His dark blond hair was standing straight up, as if he'd been pulling at it, and his brows were down so far, she couldn't see his eyes beneath the overhangs.

Under other circumstances, she probably would have steered clear of him. But not now. Not here.

It was a relief to see him.

"You okay?" he asked.

She looked back to the sun. "Is this real?" To emphasize the question, she knocked on the floorboards she was sitting on—then had to brush the paint chips off her knuckles. "Is any of this real?"

"Yeah."

"How much of it?"

"All."

For a moment, she wasn't sure she could trust him. But then images came to mind, the vivid horror of them giving him a credibility that no words or pledges could have ever done.

"What am I?" she blurted.

"You're . . . you."

She shook her head. "I need a better definition than that."

There was a long silence. Then she heard his footfalls.

He sat down beside her, his big, bare arms bunching up as he put his elbows on his knees. "I don't know what to tell you beyond that."

"Am I a ghost?"

"No."

"Are you?"

"No. Do you need a coat? It's cold out here."

"I have my blanket. Or . . . yours, I suppose. That's your bedroom, isn't it?" When he didn't answer, she shrugged. "It smells like you. Cigarette smoke and shaving cream."

It was a nice scent, actually. The only thing she'd liked about the room.

Sissy pushed her hair over her shoulder, feeling it shift across the baggy button-down shirt he'd given her. "Is she the devil?"

When he didn't answer, she glanced over. His eyes had a killing light in them as he stared out at her sunrise. "Is she?"

"Yeah."

"So that makes you . . . an angel?"

"Don't know about that sometimes. But it's part of the job description."

"You don't have wings." When he just shrugged, she felt her eyes well up with tears. "If you're an angel, you can't lie, right?"

"Not to you, at least."

"So if this is real, and not an illusion . . . I want to see my family. Can you take me to them?"

Without hesitation, he looked at her and nodded. Almost as if that had been part of the plan—get her out, take her home.

He reached over and brushed a tear from her cheek. "Whenever you want, we go. Besides, I promised your mother I would bring you back to her."

"You've seen her?" she whispered.

"I went to her, yeah."

"Is she . . . all right?" Dumb question. None of them were okay. "I mean . . . so I can live with them? I can go back and—"

"That I don't know."

Bullshit, she thought. She could tell by the set of those massive shoulders, and the fact that he wasn't meeting her in the eye anymore—there was no going home in the conventional sense.

Sissy resumed watching the sunrise, her brief flare of optimism snuffing out. "I feel like I'm losing my mind."

"Been there. Done that. This is . . . hard."

The idea that there was somebody who understood a fraction of what she was dealing with helped. But . . . "Are you sure the devil can't come after me and take me back."

"Over my dead body." His eyes shot to hers. "You got that?"

God, she hoped he was as tough as he looked, because that demon from Hell was a nightmare. "If you're an angel, doesn't that mean you've already died?"

"You don't need to worry about that. Just remember—she's not going to get you."

Sissy frowned and rubbed her forehead, wishing, not for the first time, that she hadn't ended up where she was, sitting on this porch, halfway between the living and the dead, with an enemy she didn't understand and a savior who clearly wasn't happy about his job.

"I can't remember what happened," she muttered. "I don't remember how I got stuck in the down below. Do you know?"

When he remained quiet, she turned to face him. "Please."

Before he could answer, a ten-year-old Honda drove up to the front of the house. From out of the open window, a bagged newspaper went flying—but the aim was off. Instead of landing anywhere near Sissy, it went right into the bushes by the side of the house.

The car screeched to a halt, and as the driver's-side door got shoved wide, the man beside her stiffened and shifted subtly, one of his hands going to the small of his back.

There was a weapon there, she thought.

Except as a sixteen-year-old got out of the car and trudged up the front lawn, Jim relaxed—

"Chillie!" Sissy jumped up. "Oh, my God, Chillie!"

Chillie, a.k.a. Charles Brownary, didn't look over. Or stop in shock. Or . . . show any response at all. Her best friend's little brother just kept going over to the scrubby bushes, cursing under his breath, shrugging into his Red Wings hoodie like he was beyond done with winter.

"Chillie," she said dully, as he picked up the *CCJ* and turned to the porch.

The second attempt worked like a charm. The paper flew right past Sissy, nearly clipping her in the arm.

"Chillie . . . ?"

As he turned away and headed back to the car, everything hit her hard: the terror from down below, the confusion and fear up here, the pain of losing her family, the horrible amnesia. . . .

Sissy opened her mouth and screamed as loud as she could— and she kept screaming, the sound exploding in her head, rising to a concert level, flushing the birds from the trees at both ends of the house.

Chillie's feet slowed, then stopped. With a twist of his upper body, he looked behind him—but his eyes were focused on the house, roaming around the windows as if he were expecting to find someone staring out of them. Shuddering like the place had Norman Bates'd him, he scurried for his car and hit the gas as if chased.

A strong hand grabbed her arm, and that was her only clue that she was listing forward. As her legs buckled out from underneath her, the last thing she remembered was the way Chillie had looked, silhouetted against the gathering light, his short hair pushed back by the cold wind as he had stared right through her.

And then she lost consciousness.

Chapter Ten

G.B. rolled over in bed and patted around the cardboard box he used as a table for his phone. He found the TV remote, the base of his garage sale lamp, that dust-covered Nietzsche book—

Bingo.

Fumbling to light the cell up, he groaned when he saw the time. Eleven o'clock. Considering he went to bed at five a.m., this might as well be the middle of the night—not that he could see daylight. Thanks to his blackout drapes and the fact that he'd put a washcloth over the front of his cable box, there was no illumination around him at all.

It was like he was floating in air, and he loved the weightless feeling as he reclined against his pillows and stared up at a ceiling he couldn't see.

His erection was of the pleasant variety, nothing that demanded attention—more like a suggestion in the event his right palm was bored. He was a little hungover—not bad, though. After he'd left the café, he'd met up with a couple of buddies and they'd ended the night talking about songwriting in the back of a friend's dive of a sports bar.

G.B. glanced at his phone's digital readout again.

That children's book illustrator had to be up by now. She'd gone home early so she could work in the morning.

Should he wait until the afternoon, though? Look less desperate?

As he considered his options, he smiled. Usually with women, he was a real straight shooter—no games, no overthinking, no drama. Then again, he couldn't remember the last time he'd gotten turned down by one, so it wasn't as if he needed game.

Like, last night hadn't exactly ended at the sports bar—which was why his cock was a little less than insistent at the moment. The sex hadn't meant a thing to him, though.

On that note, he pulled up Cait's contact.

He'd put her into his phone by her first name, because he still didn't know what her last one was, and he hesitated before hitting her number with his thumb. The fact that he was naked under his sheets and in the dark and already aroused made this a little tacky—in contrast to the chick he'd done at four a.m., who'd had her tits out and all but put up a billboard that she wanted some grind, Cait was no doubt working quietly.

His illustrator was . . . well, it sounded trite to put it like this, but she was a good girl.

He let the pad of his thumb go down to the screen and initiate the call. Then he put the iPhone to his ear and listened to the ringing. If it went to voice mail, he was going to keep it short and—

"Hello?"

He smiled so wide his front teeth felt a chill. "Hi. Do you know who this is?"

God, he hoped so. It would suck to be any less unforgettable than he thought he was.

"You called," she said with a laugh. "You actually called."

"I told you I would." Pulling the covers up higher on his chest, he put one arm behind his head. "I keep my promises."

Man, that throaty laugh of hers made him flex his pelvis. But he put a lockdown on that motion.

"How are you?" she asked.

He made no bones about trying to hide his yawn. "I'm still in bed, can you believe it?"

Actually, he wanted her to know where he was, wanted her to wonder what, if anything, he had on.

"Musicians probably don't keep bankers' hours, do they."

"Definitely not. I went out after you left—nothing crazy, though." For some reason, he got off on the fact that reassuring her felt right. "Just with some colleagues, I guess you'd call them. Did you go straight home?"

"I did. And got right into bed."

Mmmm. "Did you sleep well or were you distracted by dreams of a soulful singer who managed to get your digits?"

Yup, her laugh was the goal to reach for—he loved the sound of it. "Yes, that was what kept me up. How did you know?"

"Maybe he was dreaming of you, too." He followed that up with a quick, "How's work going? Your puppy and you having a good time of it?"

"Actually, I've done three pages, which is awesome."

As a text came through to him, he winced at the beeping notification in his ear. "How long do you have until the book's due?"

"I've got another week, but you don't want to take any

chances. Better to finish early than find yourself squeezed for time and rushing things. The good news is I'm on track—I have about eight more pages to go, and I got lucky today. Sometimes the flow is just right there, you know?"

"Inspired, maybe?"

"Are you trying to sell that singer again?"

"I am. He comes with a good warranty, not a lot of wear and tear." Kind of a lie, but come on. . . . "He's functional, reliable . . . and attractive in so many settings."

"Is this a lamp or a man we're talking about?"

"He's bright, too—did I mention that?" As she laughed again, he smiled. "And he's eco-friendly."

"How so?"

"He eats organic."

"A lamp with a hearty appetite?"

"Oh, sorry—I mean he only accepts those curlicue bulbs."

"Do they sell these things at Target?"

"No, someone has to give him to you."

Even he heard the purr in his voice at the end of that one—and she obviously got the drift, because there was a quick pause.

She cleared her throat. "Sounds . . . pretty magical."

He lowered his voice and dropped the riff. "Will you come to see me sing tonight? It's just backup, but I'd love to have you in the audience as my guest."

Before she could answer, he jumped in. "You can come backstage, hang out with somebody famous—your Facebook status would be awesome. It's a Millicent Jayson concert—you must have heard of her?"

Say yes, he thought. Say yes. . . .

As he waited on pins and needles, he couldn't remember the

last time he'd felt this way. For some strange reason, all he wanted was to be inside this woman—it didn't make sense, but that was destiny for you.

The powerful wasn't necessarily the comprehensible.

Duke walked out of his bedroom into a haze of pot smoke. Coughing, he went over to the cabin's front door and ripped it open, letting the cool spring air in.

"Man, you gotta put up that damn bong," he muttered at the couch.

Naturally, his star boarder, Rolly—short for Roland—was out like a light, the guy's roasty-toasty pea brain taking yet another THC-induced breather.

"Freeloader." Duke kicked the back foot of the sofa on his way to the galley kitchen. "Wake up!"

"Mom?" came a muffled reply.

"No, I'm not your mom. And you're thirty-two—that should *not* be the first thing coming out of your mouth in the morning anymore."

No response. Well, not verbally, at any rate. There was a shift of position—that led to a throw pillow falling off the far end.

Maybe the cold would wake the guy up.

Or the smell of coffee.

Worse came to worst, Duke had a claw hammer in his toolbox.

At the three-foot-long counter by the stove, Duke made a pot of nonfussy coffee—i.e., no measuring to exactitude, no flavorings, just caffeine and water, add heat and a mug. He poured himself some before things had finished brewing, and he drank the first dose at the window, staring out at the farmland that surrounded the place he rented. For the second dose, he faced in, leaning his ass against the lip of the stainless-steel bucket sink.

One story. A thousand square feet. One bed, one bath, plenty of privacy, and the cost was cut in half because he did the mowing in the summer and the snowplowing in the winter for the owners who lived down the lane.

No Warren County muni services on the roads in and out of these three hundred acres. Frankly, the family was lucky to have city water and cable.

As a familiar snoring lit off from the couch, he poured himself mugful number three. Fucking Rolly. What a pain in the ass.

"You need to get a job," he barked when he finally put his mug in the sink.

It was like having a sixteen-year-old in the house. The good news was that on a regular basis the guy somehow found some chippie to pick up the slack. The relationships never lasted longer than a couple of months, but at least they gave Duke a break.

Would miracles please never cease.

In truth, he really needed to throw the guy out. But Rolly had him over a barrel: Old friends, like bad habits, died hard—so there was nothing he could do. Well, nothing except pray that soon, very soon, on one of the bastard's pot buys, or a bar crawl, or for shit's sake a trip to a Frito-Lay aisle in the local Qwikie Mart, some new version of tits-'n'-ass looked at that handsome baby face and *fuelll in uuuuuuuuuuuvvve.*

As nauseating as that was.

Matter of fact, rumor had it there was a female on the horizon at this very moment—would that she would get her ass in gear. He was so ready to reduce the secondhand emissions in his house and get his sofa back.

Ten minutes later, he was going out the open doorway. The temperature of the "living room," such as it was, had dropped fifteen degrees and was still falling—and Rolly hadn't even noticed.

Kinda. The guy had pulled the back cushions over his body and was doing a fetal.

Duke was of half a mind to just leave shit open, but he didn't relish the idea of coming home to a pothead Popsicle who had to be nursed out of pneumonia.

No locking things up behind him. He didn't have anything to steal, and he wasn't giving Rolly a key in the event that someday he booted the guy for good.

This week he was only working twelve to five for the county, because it was a little early for the real spring cleanup and a little late for any snow removal. Soon enough, though, the backbreaking would start, and he was ready for it—the Caldwell city parks needed upkeep, and he was exactly the kind of thug to get into the brambles for ripping and tearing.

So much more satisfying than babysitting the wait line at the Iron Mask.

Getting into his truck, he started the engine, hit the gas and took the back roads to what the crews called "the Shed." The facility was located on twenty-five acres waaaaaay outside of town—so his commute, even to an eight-hour shift that started in the morning, was just him and his truck and the farmland roads. Period. The only time he stopped was for deer crossings.

As he drove along, his eyes didn't stray from the pavement ahead. There was no looking around and measuring the weather, or the progress of spring, or diddling with some radio station or another.

There was, however, something on his mind.

That woman from the night before.

He'd still been thinking about her as the sun had come up. Hard to explain why she'd stuck with him—yeah, sure, she was good-looking, but on a regular basis he saw that—hell, he saw a lot more, given the undress code at the club. But something about her was different . . . important, even.

Man, he didn't like the whole thing. Not the fact that she was like a ghost who wouldn't stop haunting him, or his ridiculous, overblown reaction to her—but especially the reason she'd been to that café, the man who she'd gone to see.

Fucking G.B. That bastard—

As his phone went off, he dug it out of his jacket and didn't bother checking to see who it was. "Yeah."

"Duncan?"

Oh, for fuck's sake. No one called him that—and what the hell was that psychic doing on his phone. "Yeah."

"I had to call you."

"Yeah." Not a question; he didn't want to encourage her—and frankly, this was a good reminder that he really needed to quit going to see her.

"I had a dream about you last night."

Not interested, honey—although he didn't think it was a sexual thing. He'd never gotten that vibe from her. "Yeah, so."

"I see a crisis coming. A crossroads." The urgency in her voice made him roll his eyes. "This is unlike . . . anything I've ever been shown before."

At that moment, he came up to one of only three traffic lights on his route into work. It was glowing orange.

"Duncan, I see a brunette—she's the nexus around which this spins, she's the focal point. And this will change everything."

He punched the gas, speeding through the four-way intersection. Just as he went under the light, it turned red.

"Thanks for calling," he muttered. "I'll be sure to date blondes and redheads, how 'bout that."

"Duncan, you've got to listen to me. The brunette . . . she's a game changer for you, and the consequences are dire, Duncan. Please—"

"I gotta go, I'm pulling into work." Or rather, he would be about five minutes from now. "Thanks."

"You must heed this. If you don't engage with her, there's a possibility it can all be avoided—"

"Bye."

"*Duncan.* What I saw was a warning. The consequences are going to hurt you—"

Duke hung up on her—and turned his ringer off.

So not doing that. No more engaging with that fruitcake. And while he was at it, no more thinking about the woman or . . . the past.

Or the future.

Man, he was so done with the whole life thing, he really was . . .

As the thought occurred to him, he eyed the tree line and wondered what it would feel like to unclip his seat belt, turn the wheel and run his truck directly into a thick oak, just hit the accelerator and slam himself right into oblivion.

Fucking air bags. He'd probably end up with nothing more than a pillow in his face and a monster deductible bill to fix shit.

About five miles later, he took a right onto the two-lane road that led in and out of the Shed, and when he got to the gate in the chain-link fencing, he stopped and showed his ID. His supervisor had given him his marching orders the day before, so he proceeded to the parking lot, dumped his truck, and picked up the keys to a county version of same at the front office. For the next five hours, he was going to scout and prioritize park projects. It was the kind of thing that someone higher up should be doing—but his boss preferred hanging out in a climate-controlled environment, kicking back and watching sports commentary on his iPad.

The mayor's brother-in-law really didn't like getting his hands dirty in the field.

Whatever, Duke thought as he entered the Shed proper and strode by row after row of heavy-duty dump trucks, and snow-plows the size of houses, and various other kinds of John Deere–ish vehicles. The air inside the aviation hangar-size space was cool and smelled like gas and oil, and high above, in the steel rafters, birds flew around and squawked as they crapped all over the county's collection of big-boy toys.

Tossing the keys up and catching them, tossing and catching them, he knew things could be worse. He was going to be out-doors and on his own, and the Ford F-350 pickup truck he'd been assigned, number thirteen, was a newer one, with a seat that hadn't been worn out.

The day was looking up—

"Hey—I'm supposed to ride with you."

As a deep voice echoed through the vast space, Duke stopped and looked over his shoulder. A man had entered behind him, a large body cutting a shadow through the daylight that poured in from the open bay. Whoever it was seemed dressed right, with jeans and a heavy jacket, and those were boots on his feet. All you had to do was swap that baseball cap for a hard hat, slap an orange reflective county vest on him and he'd fit right in.

Except something was off. Duke couldn't put his finger on it . . . but something was wrong about this.

"Who are you looking for?" he asked the guy. He hadn't been told about this, although that wasn't unusual.

"I'm supposed to come in here and find you. You're Duke, right?"

Shit.

Duke started walking again, zeroing in on the truck he'd been assigned. "If you want shotgun, you'd better get over here. I'm leaving now."

As he got the key fob ready, he left the guy to do whatever he wanted. But damn, he wished he'd gotten in five minutes earlier; then he could have missed—

He froze as he gripped the door handle. Across the interior of the truck, through the windows . . . the man was waiting for Duke to unlock things, having somehow traveled the distance of the fifty-five-foot-long garage in the blink of an eye.

Duke looked back at the open bay. Maybe it was sixty-five feet.

Had he just had a TIA?

Shaking his head, he unlocked the vehicle and climbed in. Beside him, Mr. Speedy did likewise, the guy settling in the seat and turning away to pull the belt across his heavy chest.

At least he looked like he could handle a little physical labor.

As Duke cranked the engine over, he supposed he should ask what his shadow's name was, but he didn't care and wasn't going to waste any breath on it.

"Where we heading?" the man asked.

Duke reversed out into the Shed's open lane and K-turned. Putting the engine in gear, he glanced over at his new buddy.

And found himself frowning. From underneath the brim of that ball cap, the eyes that met his own seemed . . . odd. And not just because one was cloudy.

For some reason, he thought of the psychic.

But she had been talking about a brunette woman, right?

"Out into the parks," he heard himself say as he looked away and hit the gas.

He was losing his mind. Totally. Completely.

Bye-bye, birdie.

Chapter Eleven

At six p.m. that evening, Jim ran out of cigarettes.

He'd started his vigil outside of Sissy's bedroom with a full pack, but that had been hours and hours ago—although he couldn't say he'd actually smoked all that much. Sitting across from her closed door, ass on the Oriental runner, back against the lath and plaster, he'd mostly just lit them and let them burn out.

Exhaling a curse, he ground his last one in the ashtray; then he braced his palms on the threadbare carpet. Punching upward, he hefted his weight up on his arms and let some fresh blood get down into his lower body.

She couldn't be dead, he told himself. She was just asleep . . . resting . . . chilling in the room they'd moved her into.

She'd already died.

From out of nowhere, a *Seinfeld* episode came to mind: *You can't overdie; you can't overdry.*

He'd heard the line while flying over some ocean, heading

somewhere dry and hot to kill someone—and he held on to the foggy memory because it was so much better than the other direction his mind wanted to head in . . . namely, the image of the girl hanging upside down over that white porcelain tub of Devina's.

Rubbing his eyes, he refocused on the corroded brass doorknob across from him. Like that would wake Sissy up and make her put the thing to use.

After she'd had lights-outed on the front porch, he'd picked her up and carried her to the second floor. He'd thought about giving her his room again, but that was wrong. Sooner or later he was going to have to change clothes—or hell, have a lie-down. The last thing he wanted was for her to get creeped out, and shit knew she had enough to worry about right now—sleeping in some man's bed even though he wasn't in it? So not it.

In the end, he'd walked down the hall with her in his arms, kicking open doors, trying to pick the best of the bunch. Talk about splitting hairs. Each room was a different version of the dusty last, the beds all cratered in the center, the drapes hanging moth-eaten and limp, the wallpaper faded or falling off at the corners—or both.

He picked the one on the far side that had the most sun exposure—that way, if she woke up, she would see that she was not in the wall. She would see the sunlight.

Or at least, that had been the plan. But the afternoon had come and gone, and so had the sunset. Now it was dark all around the house, and inside, too . . . so if she—

When she got up, he corrected himself.

"For Godsake . . ." He supposed he should go and turn on some lamps, but he didn't want to leave now. What if Sissy finally got—

Illumination flared over on the right—and considering that

the last time he'd seen a burst of light, Nigel had come to rip him a new one, his head whipped around.

The sound of a heavy person walking with a limp told him who it was—and reminded him that he hadn't seen Adrian all day long. Or Dog, for that matter.

The latter was a good thing, though. Jim was pretty sure that the little guy wasn't alive in the conventional sense, any more than the rest of them were, but he still felt uncomfortable smoking around the "animal"—and there had been no way he wasn't lighting up over the course of this day.

As Adrian made an appearance at the head of the stairs, the angel took a breather after all those steps, leaning on the balustrade.

For a split second, Jim got pissed that the guy had sacrificed his physical well-being just so Matthias could get laid in the previous round. But come on. It wasn't like Jim had a leg to stand on when it came to making questionable calls about personnel.

Adrian looked at Jim's door, and in the overhead light his face registered all kinds of, Whatever, dude.

"I'm down here," Jim muttered. "And so is she."

Ad glanced over. Limped over. Didn't sit down—then again, getting him back up from the floor would be a thing.

"I'm glad you moved her," Ad said gruffly.

Exactly when had the guy grown a sense of propriety? "She's still asleep."

At least . . . that was the theory.

"I'm going to bed," Ad said. "There's leftover Pizza Hut in the fridge."

"Where you been?"

"Out. I've been out."

On that note, the guy shuffled away with his cane—and went

past the door to his own room. He just kept going, heading for the staircase, and then going by that, too.

Clearly, he was crashing in a linen closet in the hall. And didn't that make as much sense as anything did lately.

A moment later, Jim looked up at the high ceiling above his head. Footfalls in the attic sent dust down like a mist, making him sneeze once. Twice. And then there was a series of thumps, as if a box had been overturned and whatever encyclopedias had been in it were scattering across the floor.

Silence.

Ad was clearly seeking solace with Eddie.

God, if that angel had been with them right now? Jim could just imagine those red eyes staring at him like he'd lost his ever-loving mind.

Nearly made him relieved the guy was gone.

With a groan, Jim got to his feet. Lifting his arms up over his head, he pulled his spine back into alignment, and as his verte-brae resettled, he went across to Sissy's door.

As logical as he wanted to be, his adrenal gland got the better of him. He knocked quietly, his waiting game over.

No answer. He knocked a little louder.

In the end, he cracked the door, but didn't look in. "Sissy?"

When there was no answer, he wished he had even one care-taking gene in his body. That girl in there deserved her mother's TLC after all she'd been through—or at least someone's compas-sionate hand stroking her hair, rubbing her back, bringing her food, drink . . . whatever she wanted.

To have died and gone to Hell . . . only to be brought back in a kind of limbo?

"Sissy . . . ?"

He put his shoulder through the opening, pushing it wider. Then he leaned inside.

There wasn't much light to see anything, but he heard the covers shuffling as if she were moving around. "Sissy?"

He took a step into the room, and opened the door all the way, weak illumination falling on her curled-up form.

She was definitely breathing. Whether she was asleep or just pretending to be? He didn't know. What he was clear on was that she didn't acknowledge him.

After a moment, Jim closed the door. Sat back down. And kept waiting.

"Actually . . . I'm meeting him now."

As Cait hit her turn signal, she tried to figure out exactly where the cut-through to the Palace Theatre's parking garage was.

"Okay," Teresa said over the phone, "I'm not going to lie. I am so jealous I can barely speak."

"Well, it's not like we're dating. Don't get ahead of things."

"You are going on 'a' date. One more after this? You are 'dating.'"

"Finally!" Cait slammed on the brakes and yanked her car into the two-inch-wide slot to hit the ticket kiosk. "Why don't they mark these things better?"

"You're deflecting."

She put down her window and took what the little machine spit out. "No, I'm trying to park."

"So you have to tell me how this happened."

Cait frowned as she hit the gas and began her ascent, looking left and right for an opening in the lineup of cars. "I departed from my house, got on the Northway, and took the exit for—"

"No, let's try, 'I was sitting by the phone and it rang and—'"

"He asked me to come to this show." She shrugged even though her friend couldn't see her. "It was that simple."

Well, kind of. She was *not* mentioning that he'd called her while he was still in bed, and that there was a strong possibility that he'd been naked. No confirmation, and maybe it was just her imagination—but that tone in his voice?

It had said *naked*.

"He's singing backup," she tacked on in the unlikely event Teresa could read her mind over the phone. "For Millicent Jayson."

"Well, I've heard of her. But what a waste for him."

"Agreed."

"So how's it going to work? Do you have a backstage pass? Or is he meeting you?"

"I'm supposed to go wait by will-call. Honestly, I don't know."

"What are you wearing? Tell me you have some cleavage showing."

"Aha!" Cait pulled into a spot between a Kia and a Mini—two cars with small profiles that probably wouldn't door her—plus as a bonus, it was only two floors up and right under a security light. "And as for cleavage? Come on, you know I don't have a lot to show."

"Quality over quantity, baby."

"Uh-huh. Right. 'Cuz that's how Pamela Anderson made her money." Cait snagged her phone, locked up, and walked fast for the open-air stairwell. There was an elevator, but in her new workout-world mentality, stairs were king. "Okay, I'm going to go—and yes, before you ask, I'll call you as soon as it's over."

"I hope I don't hear from you until tomorrow morning."

Cait was quiet for a moment, nothing but the *clip-clomp* of her loafers ringing out around the cold, concrete garage. "You're a really good friend, you know that."

"Yeah, yeah, what can I say. I'm also a sucker for romance—and if it can't be me, there's no one I'd rather it be than you. It's beyond time for you to get out there again, Cait."

The latter was said as gently as Teresa could put anything—and it had to be about Thom and his soon-to-be-here baby.

Damn it, that whole thing still stung, Cait thought. Even though it had been years, and was now totally and completely not her business.

Teresa cleared her throat. "Call me later, even if it's two in the morning—in fact, especially if it's after midnight."

"Okay, I will."

"And try to kiss him, will ya? I'm dying to know what it's like! Oh, and if it sucks? Lie to me so I can keep my fantasy going. Thank you. Good-bye."

Cait was laughing as she hung up and disappeared the phone into her purse.

A couple flights of stairs later, she emerged out onto the sidewalk, looked to the right and there it was in the distance: the iconic Palace Theatre vertical sign that ran up the corner of the building. Long the staple of Caldwell postcards and T-shirts, the forty-foot-high, spotlit jewel was exactly as it had been in the forties, the bright red, gold, and white swirls spelling out the name . . . and the fantasy of the stage.

The theater was the best kind of throwback, a gold-leafed, crystal-hung, red-carpeted palace that rebuffed the relentless fleece-and-sweatpants nature of modern life, and made you feel like a schmuck for not wearing a belle cloche and gloves when you stepped out.

Total Bette Davis fabulous.

Beneath the sign, she fell into line with a processional of other pedestrians, all of whom were walking over a mosaic'd stretch of pavement that also spelled out the theater's name. And then inside the front receiving foyer, the iconic pattern of reds, golds, and whites was further repeated in the tile floor and the papered walls.

As the crowd filed in like cards getting shuffled into an orderly deck, she noticed that she was surrounded by couples, and wasn't that yet another reminder of how long she'd been single. In fact, she could barely remember what it was like to go paired up somewhere, whether it was a party or a movie or the park on a nice day.

The last date she'd been on . . . ?

Oh, jeez, it had to have been that setup her parents had arranged long-distance. What a nightmare—her mother and father's theology had shown up at an Olive Garden in a suit and a tie, proceeded to order for her, and then stepped up on a soapbox to hold forth for two hours of her life that she was never going to get back.

Before that high point? It might . . . yes, it might even have been something with Thom. Back in college.

But she was breaking that dry spell tonight.

Rising up on her tiptoes, she peered over the sea of heads, hoping to find G.B. standing by the will-call—nope. Well, at least not that she could see. Maybe he was somewhere else in the lobby—

"Oh . . . my God."

There was someone she recognized.

Over against the wall by the interior sets of doors that led into the lobby.

Standing alone, looking like he didn't belong and didn't care.

Slowing to a halt, she was knocked into from behind, someone's elbow digging into her shoulder. The bump didn't restart her in the slightest. Especially as he swung his eyes up and around—right at her.

It was the man from the truck last night, the one who had been parked next to her at the café.

The big, powerful man who had come up to her window and spoken in a voice that had made it impossible for her to fall asleep.

As her body flushed, she expected him to register a flash of recognition and then look away for whoever he was waiting for. He didn't refocus elsewhere, however. He just stared at her.

Cait shook herself and got with the program, telling her feet to get going so she didn't plug up the flow of people. Rising onto her toes again, she searched for G.B.

Nope.

And when she looked back at the other man, he was still staring at her.

Maybe he knew Teresa's favorite singer?

When all he did was continue to meet her eyes, she wondered if he hadn't been sent for her—and didn't that seem somehow . . . inevitable—

Okaaaaaaay, she told herself as she made her way over to him. Let's not go all Cupid on this, shall we?

Then again . . . wow. He was wearing black jeans and a black leather jacket, and that body of his did all the work and then some when it came to giving the clothes structure. Between his incredible eyes and that jawline, the only thing she could think of was that he should be photographed or drawn—someone needed to capture what he looked like permanently.

And on that note, she so wasn't the only one who noticed him. Every woman glanced in his direction and did a double take.

He, however, was only looking at her.

"Hi," she said as she came up to him. "I, ah, I don't suppose you're waiting for me?"

"Yeah, I am."

Cait cleared her throat. "Oh, good. Okay. Well, this makes sense then."

She waited for him to say something. Instead, his eyes slowly went down her body.

Holy . . . crap. She felt like someone had put her on a hot

plate. And even though there were a hundred people around her? Instantly, it was just the two of them, and God help her, she liked it that way—as well as how he was looking at her: He was a stranger who was radiating sex, and rather than being offended, all she could think of was what it would be like to have him doing that while she was naked.

While he was naked—

Yeah, okay, time to step away from the ledge. Any fantasy of that was absolutely insane. She was a lights-out, under-the-covers, missionary kind of girl. Or at least, she had been . . . back when she'd had a sex life.

A decade ago.

When her lips had to part so she could grab enough oxygen, his eyes locked on her mouth—and he might as well have been kissing her. Pure, animal attraction flared out of his stare, his stance, his body . . . and she responded to it, her skin, her core warming even further.

Live now, a voice said in her head. Live while you have the chance.

As if he knew what she was thinking, he said, "I get off work at three thirty. Meet me."

Not a question. Not even an invitation. A demand—like maybe he'd spent time thinking about them hooking up, and whereas it had never dawned on her to follow through on the chance intersection from the night before, he had made a point of crossing her path again.

"I don't do one-night stands," she blurted.

"Who says one will be enough."

Right. Okay. Those words, framed by that deep growl? Talk about a carnal promise.

"I don't know you." Damn, her voice was husky.

"Does that matter."

"Yes."

He stuck out his hand. "Duke Phillips."

Walk away, Cait told herself. This is not the seventies. No one has casual sex anymore—

Abruptly, scenes from *Girls* flashed through her mind. With him in the picture, naturally. Great.

"I'm here to meet G.B." Wow, didn't that sound like a protest.

He dropped his unshaken hand. "What's that got to do with me?"

"Wait, I thought he asked you to get me and take me back-stage?"

"When I said I came for you, I can assure you, it was not on anybody else's behalf."

Cait's mouth nearly fell open, but she caught it in time. Although come on, it wasn't like she was sporting any swagger over here, what with the blushing routine and the self-talk about her very non-*Girls* existence.

"Three thirty," he repeated.

"I'm sorry, I already have . . . plans."

"I work at the Iron Mask. Use the staff entrance in from the back parking lot. Ask for me."

Cait frowned. "Quick question here. Does this approach actually work for you?"

"I've never used it before. So you tell me."

"I don't like cavemen. And I do not sleep with strangers."

"I gave you my name. I'm the one at the disadvantage on that."

Bullshit he had any disadvantage. But at least he didn't deny that this was just about sex.

He leaned in. "Don't tell me you didn't think about me last night."

"Are you always this arrogant?"

"I don't worry about what other people think."

"And what if that kind of attitude doesn't get you where you want to go."

He shrugged and resettled against the wall. "You want this, too. Don't deny it."

"I cannot believe . . ." She looked around, expecting G.B. to make an appearance at any moment. ". . . you."

The surreal sense that this couldn't possibly be happening resurged, making her feel a little dizzy. Then again, she wasn't breathing right and her heart was pounding.

If she fake-fainted, maybe he would catch her and then she could get a real feel for him.

Oh, there was a plan.

"Excuse me?"

Great, she'd said that out loud—

Abruptly, she narrowed her eyes. "How did you know I was going to be here?"

His shrug was casual. "You told me you went to that café for the singer. It's not that tough to extrapolate you might want to see him again. And he put on his Facebook page that he's doing backup here tonight. I took a gamble—and you walked through that door. I didn't know you were meeting up with him."

Interesting. He expressed himself like he had an education, and he enunciated his words without any accent at all. But the Iron Mask was a hard-core club of some kind—she'd seen its ads in the *CCJ*. So he had to be a bartender or . . . given his build, a bouncer?

That really shouldn't have made him even hotter.

Really.

Like, not at all.

"And that doesn't bother you," she said absently.

"What? That you've got a date with some singer? Christ, no. I don't care if you were here to meet . . . Channing Fate-um or whoever that stripper dude is. The only thing that would stop me would be a husband, and you don't wear a wedding band."

"What if I told you I had a boyfriend? A partner?"

"Then why are you going out with the singer."

"I'm not meeting you in the middle of the night. I don't know you—and the fact that you gave me two random names and offered your palm doesn't change that."

"Google me."

"Not helpful."

The man, Duke, whoever he was, leaned in again. "Bank on this. If you come over after my shift, I'll tell you anything you want to know about me. And then I'll show you the more important stuff."

Cait licked her lips. "And what would that be."

"You'll find out. If you think you can handle it."

With the smooth move of an all-man type, he walked around her, his body shifting with barely reined-in power. As he passed, he didn't touch her, brush her arm, lay a hand on her. But he didn't have to.

He'd already left his mark.

"Damn it," she whispered as she stared over her shoulder and watched him leave.

Chapter
Twelve

"There you are, Cait!"

As Cait heard her name, she turned around. G.B. was weaving in and out of the crowd, waving his hand at her, making progress even as he was recognized and stopped by people.

Forcing a smile, she struggled with a ridiculous sense of guilt as she waved back at him and met him halfway.

"I'm a hugger," he announced, holding his arms wide.

She went in for the clinch out of reflex. In reality, she could barely concentrate—but as their bodies came together, the woodsy scent of his cologne and the feel of his chest cleared out some of the cobwebs.

Boy, did he smell good.

And close up? He was even more handsome . . . and that hair was softer than it looked as it brushed against her cheek.

"Hey! G.B.!"

Someone broke up the embrace, and that was all right with her. As she pulled away, she needed a minute.

With a vague thumper starting up behind her eyes, Cait went to rub them—and stopped herself just in time. She had makeup on, so unless she wanted to do this date thing raccoon-style, she'd better chill with the scrubby-scrubby. And it was hard to keep still as G.B. chatted with some woman, her hands fiddling with her purse, the collar of her coat, her hair as she played by-stander.

The idea that another man had just come on to her, and that she'd been seriously attracted to him . . . seemed like something she had to confess—but come on. That was bullcrap. Number one, she was not in a relationship with G.B. Number two, she hadn't asked tall, dark and wow-are-those-pecs-real? to show up. And number three, even if she decided to meet a stranger at a public place and get to know him in a very "personal" way? That was her choice as an unattached, adult woman.

She wasn't living under her parents' roof—or their closed-minded value system—anymore. And she and G.B. had a long way to go before they knew whether there was a future ahead of them.

In fact, if she wanted a chance with Teresa's favorite singer? The one guaranteed way to screw it up was to start babbling about what was essentially a nothing-at-all.

"So come on back," G.B. said, taking her arm. "I've got you a pass to the green room. We just have to pick it up in the of-fice."

"Oh, that's wonderful, but really, you didn't have to go to any trouble—"

"And listen, forget about the penguin suit, okay?"

She glanced over at him. She'd been so rattled, she hadn't

even noticed he was wearing a tuxedo. "Very nice . . . and you have nothing to be embarrassed by. Trust me."

"Is that a compliment?" he asked as he punched open a door marked, STAFF ONLY.

"It is."

G.B. looked across his shoulder as he led the way into a concrete corridor. Lids dropping low on his eyes, he murmured, "Well, thank you. I'm glad you like me in it."

"But you also look good in jeans."

"Really? Tell me more." As they laughed, he offered her his arm. "Will you let me be a gentleman?"

"Yes," she said, tucking a hold on to him. "I will."

As they walked along, they passed by a placard that read, THE-ATER OFFICE, with an arrow underneath pointing in the direction they were headed.

He pulled her even closer. "I haven't told you how good you look tonight."

As his voice deepened some, she was reminded of the way he'd sounded from his bed this morning.

"Do you sleep in the nude?" she blurted out.

"Yes . . ." His eyes shifted to hers . . . and they were intense, a deep blue that seemed to offer both a soaring height and a safe place to land. "I do."

In that moment, it didn't take much imagination to picture him lying back in some sheets, head on a pillow, arms stretched out, tattoos glowing on his skin.

"Oh . . ."

"Good or bad," he prompted.

"What?"

"Is that 'oh' a good or bad one?"

"It's . . . good."

"Then can I ask you the same question?"

She hesitated, wishing she had more sophistication going for her. "Well, I hate to be a buzzkill, but I'm not a birthday suit kind of gal."

"Silk is good on a woman."

As he wagged his brows—like he was trying to put her at ease, Cait laughed. "Yeah, no, not that."

"Satin, maybe?"

"Try flannel."

He nodded sagely, like he was performing a complex analysis in his head. "Hmm, soft. Warm. Can come in patterns other than plaid. Total winner—on you, that is."

Cait grinned. "You're being charming again."

"Still only honest." He put his hand over his heart. "Just keeping it real over here in tuxedo-land."

As she laughed again, they rounded a corner, approaching a glass-enclosed reception and office area. "Figure you might as well know up front that I'm not a lingerie girl."

"Guess what?" Coming up to the see-through door, he opened the way in and dropped his voice to a whisper. "That's even hotter than anything from La Perla."

"What's La Perla?"

G.B. laughed so hard, he threw his head back, and the deep rumble attracted the attention of the young woman sitting behind the receiving desk. As she looked up, he put his arm around Cait's waist and led her over.

"Hey, Jennifer, I'm here to pick up the backstage pass for my friend here."

"Jennifer" focused on Cait, and yeah, wow, time to take a step back. Talk about an unwelcome mat—the receptionist or office manager or whoever she was clearly did not appreciate some part of this. Like maybe that whole arm/waist thing?

"I don't have the credentials," Miss Thang snapped. "I gave 'em to Erik."

G.B. cleared his throat and moved in front of Cait, as if he were attempting to shield her from those death rays. "Do you know where he is?"

"He left for the day."

There was a beat of silence. Then G.B. turned around. "Cait, I'm so sorry, could you excuse me for a minute?"

"Oh, yes, absolutely. But please—don't worry about me. We can just meet up afterward?"

G.B. shook his head and took her back through the door. In a quiet voice, he said, "Give me a sec to deal with this."

As he disappeared back inside, Cait pivoted away so that she wasn't eavesdropping—except although that meant she couldn't see them, it didn't do a thing to drown out the rising voice of that woman as it promptly got higher. Louder. More shrill.

And the arguing went on forever.

From time to time, someone would walk by and she'd give them an awkward smile—even though they were never looking at her. Nope, they were craning for a peek into that office, seeing what sure as hell sounded like a grudge match—at least on the girl's side. G.B., when he was able to get a word in edgewise, kept things much, much quieter and more reasonable.

It was impossible not to get the gist. G.B. had taken the girl out and that had led to certain expectations on her part. When those hadn't been met, as evidenced by G.B. showing up on a date, looking for the backstage pass? Cue the drama.

When he finally emerged, he helped the door ease shut behind him, and nodded in the direction they'd come from. "Ah, listen, can we . . ."

Considering Cait could feel the woman's stare all the way out here in the corridor? "Sure, absolutely."

He led her back around the corner, stopping when they were

out of eyeshot. "I'm so sorry. You need credentials to go backstage—and they've . . . disappeared."

Cait touched his sleeve. "It's okay."

"No, see, it really isn't." He pushed a hand through his hair, those luxurious waves shining even in the dull fluorescent ceiling lights. "Look, I want to be honest about what's going on. I hooked up with her—it was totally casual. We were out with friends, and it just happened. She thought it was a start to something. On my side, I wasn't thinking like that. I probably could have handled things better. It just didn't dawn on me that she'd take it so seriously."

"Don't apologize. It's none of my business."

G.B. gripped her shoulders. "But it is. I didn't ask her on a date—it's nothing like . . . well, this stuff between you and me is different, okay? I just don't want you to think I go around banging random chicks and then treating them like hell because I can."

She so could not doubt him. Not with the steady way he was meeting her in the eye. "I appreciate your saying something. And I could kind of tell that the problem was on her side."

"I swear it." He looked around. "Now, about the rest of tonight. I've got to go warm up, and there's still a ticket waiting for you at will-call—we probably should have picked it up first, actually." He cursed under his breath. "I'm really sorry. . . ."

"So you mean the worst has happened"—she smiled up at him—"and all I get to do is listen to you perform with an incredible singer and watch you do something you love. Oh, the horror."

He seemed momentarily nonplussed. "I can't believe . . . you."

"Good or bad."

G.B. laughed tightly. "Good . . . very, very good. You're just being really cool about this."

"It's not your fault."

"No," he said with an edge. "I can assure you it's not. And I better get going. I'll just walk you back to will-call—"

"It's only down at the end here, right? Don't worry about me, I can take care of myself."

G.B. paused again, his eyes roaming around her face. Then in a quick move, he dropped down and kissed her on the cheek.

"Thank you so much. The ticket's under your name. Just give them your driver's license."

Man, he smelled good. "I'll see you afterward?"

"Go to the lobby and wait—I'll find you. After the event, they sometimes loosen things up and I might be able to sneak you back then. It depends on how cool her staff is."

"I'll be there, and take your time. I don't mind people watching."

"And then we'll have drinks, yes?"

"You can bet on it."

For a split second, she was convinced he was going to kiss her again—this time on the mouth: He focused on her lips and tilted toward her. But then at the last minute, he pulled away and blew out an exhale.

"I gotta go," he said ruefully.

"Break a leg—or is that only for actors?"

"Coming from you, it works for me, and that's all that matters."

On an impulse, she reached out and squeezed his hands. "See you in a bit."

As she turned away, he said, "Cait."

She glanced back at him. "Yes?"

"That woman in there . . . she's not you, all right? I don't want to scare you off."

"You haven't."

He smiled a little. And then he lifted his hand in a wave and strode away, rounding that corner with his hands in the pockets of his tuxedo pants and his head down like he had no intention of engaging with Jennifer again.

Making her own way, Cait went back to the lobby, his last

words lingering with her. As she got out her driver's license and stood in line in front of will-call, she thought . . . he wasn't the type who was going to scare her off.

That other man was.

The two were opposite ends of the spectrum, for sure—and it was so much healthier to focus on the latter instead of the former . . .

When it was her turn up at the Plexiglas window, she put her ID in the sliding drawer and leaned into the microphone that was mounted in the glass.

"Cait Douglass," she said. "I believe there's a ticket for me?"

The man on the far side nodded, his voice tinny through the little speaker. "Sure thing, Miss Douglass."

Cait glanced behind her, searching the faces of the late arrivals who were rushing to get to the ushers.

"What was the name again?"

She refocused. "Cait? With a C? The Douglass has two Ss?"

The guy went back to a box that held a lineup of envelopes, leafing through with deft fingers that had clearly gone through that motion a number of times. "Nope. Nothing by that name."

She put her purse on the marble ledge. "G.B. was supposed to leave it for me?"

All she got was a shaking head. "I'm really sorry. There's nothing in your name."

"Are there any tickets I can buy?"

"The event's sold out, I'm sorry."

Cait opened her mouth. But what could she do? There were people who were waiting behind her, and it wasn't like she could negotiate with No Vacancy.

As he pushed the sliding drawer back to her, she took her license and moved free of the line.

Stalling out, she thought . . . okay, not what she had planned.

Chapter Thirteen

"Take me to my parents. Please."

At the sound of Sissy's voice, Jim came awake like a rubber band, consciousness snapping his neurons alive, his body jerking out of its slump on the floor. From habit, he checked his watch. Ten o'clock.

Sissy was standing in the doorway of her bedroom, dressed in the jury-rigged outfit he'd laid out for her, nothing but a button-down shirt of his, and a rolled-up pair of his sweatpants to cover her up and keep her warm. Her hair was smoother than it had been, probably because she'd brushed it with her fingers. Her feet were in the pair of tennis shoes he'd found in the back of a closet downstairs.

Damn him, he thought for the hundredth time. What had he brought her back to?

And she'd asked him a question, hadn't she. . . .

"Yeah, I'll run you over there." Jumping to his feet, he was ready to go even though he'd been out like a light a moment ago. "Give me five."

"I'll meet you downstairs."

As she walked by him, the calm that surrounded her was disturbing. Too expressionless. Too removed. Too opaque.

A zombie without the limp-and-snarl routine.

"Fuck," he muttered as he went to his room, grabbed a change of clothes, and hit the shower out in the hall.

By his watch, he still had twenty-five seconds to go as he jogged down to the foyer. Sissy was by the front door as promised, her slender form bent over so she could pet Dog, that hair of hers falling down and veiling her face. As she straightened and looked Jim in the eye, her stare was that of an adult.

She might be going "home" to her parents', but she was not a child.

"Do you want a coat?" he asked, wondering what he could give her if she said yes.

"I'm fine. I don't feel anything."

He could believe that—and he was the same way. "We'll take my truck. It's parked around back by the garage."

That was the extent of the conversating as they left Dog behind to guard Adrian, Eddie and the house. Outside, the night was not all that old, but it was utterly dominant, no trace of the sun left, what little warmth there had been during the day having faded into another forty-degree chill.

Was spring never coming this year, he wondered.

Maybe it was waiting to see who won the war.

As they approached the F-150, he wanted to help her with her door, but she got there first and took care of herself, shutting things up, yanking her seat belt into place. Left with nothing to do for her, he went around to the driver's side, got in, drove off.

"They go to bed early," she said as she stared out the window next to her. "My parents. They always . . . went to bed early."

"It's after ten o'clock."

"They'll be asleep."

"You want to go in the morning?"

"No."

When she fell silent, he let her stay that way—even though the silence made him want to curse on every exhale.

"You know where I live?" she said after a while.

Looking over at her, he measured the way the headlights of oncoming cars illuminated her face in brief flashes. "Yeah, I do."

And he got them there in record time, cutting crosswise out of the old estate section of town, speeding through darkened suburban shopping areas, heading into a more modest neighborhood of houses that were set back among big trees.

As he drove them down the correct street, and then came to a stop in front of her house, he felt like he had kept his promise to her mother—but only in theory. What had he brought back for the family, really? It wasn't like their daughter was going to slip into her old role, filling the horrific void, reversing the agony and the grieving.

Turning off the engine, he glanced across the seat. Sissy was staring out of the side window, her chest pumping up and down under his shirt. As she lifted her hand up to the glass, her thin fingers shook so badly they skipped across the surface.

"You sure you're ready to do this?" he said gruffly.

"Yes."

But she didn't move.

At least now he could help her.

Exiting, he went around behind the truck and remembered what a bitch his own postmortem check-in had been like—namely, him waking up in the morgue at St. Francis and enjoying the truly bizarre experience of looking at his own dead body. This had to be the same for her, consciousness and reality colliding in a way that just shouldn't ever happen.

Man, even after all the atrocities he'd seen and done, that shit had stopped him short. He couldn't imagine what it was like for her.

As he opened her door, she dropped her arm. "Do you want to know why I didn't come out all day long?"

Desperately. Anything to give him a clue where she was. "Yeah."

"The thing that bothers me most is their pain. I don't care what happens to me—that's a whatever. But to see their suffering? That's a hell I will not survive . . . so I wanted to make sure they were sleeping." She got out and faced off at the house as if it were an opponent. "Guess I'm a coward."

Measuring her set shoulders, he shook his head slowly. "Not what I'm thinking. Not in the slightest."

Sissy didn't seem to hear him as she hit the walkway, her feet carrying her haltingly up to the front door. Before she opened the way in, he had an impulse to stop her, thinking of how he'd found her mother sitting in that chair in the living room, the woman's grief as tangible as a black shawl covering her whole body.

But maybe Mrs. Barten could go to bed now that Sissy's remains had been found.

As he stepped forward too, more memories came back to him, making him rub his eyes, like that might stop the videos from streaming. He hated thinking of how he'd found Sissy in that cave at the quarry, everything that had made her a living, breathing entity left to rot in the damp earth, discarded as if she had been nothing but garbage.

Goddamn Devina.

"How do I get inside?" she said, as if she were thinking to herself.

Shaking himself back into focus, he cleared his throat. "Walk right in."

After a hesitation, she gripped the doorknob and turned. "It's locked."

"I didn't mean that way." Taking her arm, he urged her forward. "Just trust me."

A bright flare of pain in his forearm told him she was gripping him hard, but he didn't mind—her reliance on him as she got scared made him feel strong in a way that had nothing to do with his body, and everything to do with his soul.

It helped him deal with the sense that he'd failed her back in the beginning.

"Wait," she cut in, pulling away. "I can't . . . just go through."

"I think you will." After all, that newspaper kid hadn't seen her—so there was a chance that "solid" objects were not all they were cracked up to be for her. "Trust me."

This time she followed as he stepped forward . . . and she let out a strangled sound as they passed through the panels of the door, the sensation of buffering only the briefest interference; then they were out the other side, breathing the warm air of the house, taking up space along with the living room furniture.

Sissy looked down at herself, flaring her hands, flipping them over and checking out her palms. "I . . ."

She didn't finish as she looked up and seemed to realize where they were.

No mother in that chair across the way. But yeah . . . you only kept vigil for someone you hoped would come home, not if you had a coffin to bury.

"Oh . . . God," Sissy whispered, putting both hands up to her mouth.

Jim let her go, watching from just inside the door as she walked into the room beyond. He couldn't see her face, but he didn't need to. The horror was in the way she moved: her shoulders shrugged in, her head going all around, her breathing forced. And then she turned around. In the dull light coming from the one lamp left on in the hall, there were tears rolling down her face.

"I'm dead," she choked out. "I'm dead. . . ."

"I'm so sorry," he said roughly.

"Oh . . . God . . ."

In spite of the fact that he was awkward with compassion on a good day, he walked over to her. "I'm . . . so damned fucking sorry."

He was unaware of his arms reaching out to her, but a split second later, she was up against his chest. And as Sissy clung to him, he found himself cupping the back of her head, urging her onto his heart, holding her even closer. Syllables were leaving his lips, but goddamned if he had a clue what he was saying.

"I'm dead," she sobbed. "I'm . . . gone."

"I know. I know. . . ."

As he held her, his eyes lifted to the bookcase that stood next to the bay window. Photographs of the family were lined up on its glass shelves, the frames all different sizes and shapes, the pictures taken in various eras starting when the children were really young, and then later as gangly preteens, and finally as near-grown-ups.

There were going to be no more images with Sissy in them, and this crying right now? No matter how concerned she was for those she had left behind, in this moment, he had a feeling she was experiencing her own loss for the first time.

And Devina had done this to her. To all of them.

The bitch had to go down.

Chapter Fourteen

When Cait headed back into downtown a little after ten o'clock, there was no traffic getting in her way, no messenger bikes weaving in and out in front of her, no buses crowding the four-lane surface road route. Nothing but a couple of red lights, and a cop car that went screaming by her.

It was as she pulled over to the side to let the CPD unit pass that she realized she was on Trade Street. And what do you know . . . she was right in the midst of all the clubs.

Not far from one specific club, as a matter of fact.

As she hit the accelerator and got back in her lane, she told herself there was no reason to slow down in front of the Iron Mask. But a couple of blocks later, she found herself letting up on the gas and coasting into her second pullover.

No cops going like a bat out of hell this time.

Just Duke's supposed workplace.

With her foot on the brake and staying there, she checked out the scene. She'd never been to the club before. For one, it had opened up after she was out of college and past her barhopping days. For another, going by the black facade and the Gothic lettering? Didn't exactly look like her kind of venue.

And yup, the long wait line at the double doors confirmed the extrapolation.

Right, the last time she'd seen that much drippy black hair and clothing? A Nick at Nite *Munsters* marathon. In fact, it was like her vision had gone fifties monochrome on her.

Strange to think that somewhere inside the low, windowless building, that man was working—at least in theory.

She had Googled him.

As soon as she'd gotten back to her house, she'd gone to her laptop, fired up Internet Explorer, and typed in "Duke Phillips, Caldwell, NY." The good news? No articles about him murdering or stalking anyone, no mug shots, no crime-blotter mentions— and there was a picture from an old Union College yearbook that indicated he had at one point been premed. No address or phone number, but he could be a renter and only have a cell phone. No LinkedIn profile. Nothing on wife or children or parents.

She'd even gone on Facebook and searched under the name. No profile that matched him.

G. B. Holde on the other hand? After doing a search on him, she found that the guy had nearly nine thousand followers on Facebook—almost ten thousand on Twitter. No college profile for him, but plenty of articles on his singing, shows, and fans.

Cait frowned. The club's entrance was being manned by two guys, and as one of them walked over to address somebody, she realized . . . it was him.

Her mystery man.

Okay, not *hers*.

And yeah, big surprise—he was not taking any lip from the

Goth aggressor who'd stepped out of line, literally. He marched right up to the vampire wannabe, his arms hanging loose, his jaw clenched, his height acerbated by the ass kicking he was clearly prepared to dish if that was the way things went.

Except what do you know. Mr. Darkness Personified with the walking cane and the pseudo-Victorian leather duster backed down, his eyes dropping away as Duke got up into his face and stayed there.

Cait braced herself for a fight, but there wasn't one coming— once Duke had established his dominance, the drama was over. He went back to his post, and the guy with the mouth turned into a pussycat with an anachronistic collar.

Pulling herself out of stalker mode, she got back on the right path, heading down Trade and navigating Caldie's grid pattern of one-ways. Her second foray through the Palace's parking garage wasn't quite as successful as her first. The only vacant spot she could find was waaaaaay up on the top floor that was open to the elements, and when she got out, a stiff, cold wind shaved her head. Burrowing into her coat, she hurried for cover, jogging around to the way she'd just come up because that was closer than the stairwell.

Sure, the ramp was for cars, but she was not going to ruin her blowout by staying in that stiff breeze any longer than she absolutely had to—

Shoot. She was turning into a chick.

As she emerged onto the level below, she was at the far end, the red Exit sign to the stairs and elevator glowing in the distance. But at least the wind-tunnel effect wasn't happening down here.

With any luck, she'd gotten back in plenty of time. She'd be waiting for G.B. in the lobby if she could get inside, or the outer foyer if she couldn't—

A second set of footsteps joined her own.

Cait frowned and looked over her shoulder. Someone had come down the ramp also, the dark figure about ten yards behind her.

She could not make out the face . . . or much of anything else. It was almost as if a haze had settled in and thickened the air between them.

Cait picked up her pace, the sound of the hard soles of her loafers like a heart beating faster and faster. Glancing around, she realized there was no one else in the vicinity—and there wasn't going to be for a while. The concert didn't end for a half hour, and no one was going to be parking or unparking a car anytime soon.

The person behind her sped up, walking more briskly. Keeping up. No, zeroing in.

As she broke into a jog, she felt a little paranoid—she'd probably been dwelling too much on Sissy Barten's story. But then she looked back again. . . .

They were coming even quicker.

Panic surged, and as she wrenched back around, she locked eyes on that Exit sign like it was a safety hatch—except if she got into the stairwell, what then? Would they chase her down it?

Even faster. She went even faster, her shoes smacking into the concrete, her arms pumping—and right behind her, whoever it was sped up, too. Terrified, she took her purse off her shoulder, and held it in front of herself because it was the only "weapon" she had—wait, she should go for the eyes, right? The groin of the head—

Was she really channeling Dwight Schrute at a time like this?

Just as she came up to the heavy steel door of the stairwell, the elevator next to it binged and opened. No one was in it. No one had punched the down button, either.

Who the hell cared?

Cait tripped as she jumped inside, and threw herself at the

lineup of buttons on the panel to the right. Punching the number "1" over and over again, she looked out of the open doors. The dark figure was running, closing in on her—

"Please, please . . . *please* . . ." she gasped.

Cait hit that lit numbered button with both hands, her purse smacking against the elevator's wall, her breath exploding out of her mouth.

". . . please . . . shut . . . oh, God . . ."

Her eyes shot to the row of numbers that glowed up above. The number "4" was lit—

Abruptly the wind shifted direction, hitting her in the face even harder than it had up top—as if that figure, racing for her, coming at a dead run, was a menace from the Old Testament, its presence marshalling the elements, and sucking the illumination from the fluorescent lamps that glowed on the columns—

The lights flickered over her head, strobing everything as the parking lot ahead of her abruptly went dark.

Evil was coming for her.

Blinded by the blinking lights above, she couldn't see its form, but vision was unnecessary. Her bones, her very soul recognized the threat as time slowed to a crawl and reality twisted into a nightmare.

Was this how it went down for people? When a victim was struck, did they all feel this careening terror, this tunnel vision, this sense of, *No, not me, not now, how is this happening?*

As if her brain were retreating to safety, flashbacks of earlier in the night flickered through her consciousness, images of her in her car, of her at a stoplight, of her in front of the Iron Mask . . . of her turning into the parking garage one hundred and twenty seconds ago . . . tantalized her with the false idea that she could somehow go back in time.

If only that ticket had been waiting for her at will-call, this would not be her destiny. She'd be safe in the theater, listening to music along with five thousand other people who didn't have a clue about what she was actually facing.

Tragedy was about to happen.

If only she had not stopped to look at that man at the club. Or if she had decided to try to park on the street. Or if—

"Please, God . . . close—"

The doors abruptly got with the program, shutting so fast it was as if they were spring-loaded. *Thump. Ding.*

Whoosh.

The elevator began its descent.

Backing up against the poster-size ad for the theater's new season, she focused upward on those numbers overhead, praying that the lift didn't misfire again and stop at the floor below. One flight down the stairs was no big distance to cover. . . .

Every creak of the car was magnified until her ears burned like she was at a concert. Each foot down was like a mile at walking speed. Moments stretched into hours, days. Hands cramping up, fingers cranked into claws, her body was in full fight-or-flight—

The phone, she needed to get her goddamn phone. With a jolt of action, Cait fumbled in her purse, things falling out; she didn't care what—

Ding.

Bump. Halt.

Cait's head jerked up to the doors as the "3" lit up, and the descent stopped. "No . . . no . . . !"

Lunging forward at the panel, she hit the bright red stop button. As a ringing alarm exploded into the enclosed space, she had no idea whether she'd shut down the opening mechanism.

Phone—where was her phone! Shoving her hand back into her purse—with enough force to break one of the straps—she rummaged around until her fingers ran into the thing. But she couldn't keep hold. As she brought the cell out, it slipped away from her, bouncing across the floor, sending her on a goose chase as she fell to her knees to catch the—

Are you sure you would like to make an emergency call? the screen asked her as she got it and began working the screen.

"Hell, yes!" She nailed the green button and put the phone up to her ear, staying frozen in that crouch, her eyes locked on the double doors as she prayed they'd stay shut—

"Yes!" she shouted over the din as she plugged her free ear. "I'm in an elevator in the Palace Theatre's parking garage." What was the address? What the hell was the— "Yes! On Trade! Help me—there's someone trying to—"

Above her head, the inset lights in the ceiling started to flicker again.

"I'm alone, yes—I'm in the elevator!" She kept shouting, because the alarm was still going off loud as a jet plane—and because being scared shitless really wasn't conducive to library whispers. "I've stopped it at the third floor—what? That's the alarm, ringing—no! It wasn't a malfunction—I stopped the elevator! There was someone chasing me and I ran into—excuse me?" She actually took the phone away from her cheek and glared at it. "Are you kidding me—lady, no offense, but he would have just followed me down the stair—no! My car was on another level."

Was this woman on the other end actually critiquing her choice of escape?

"Thank you—yes, I would like the police!" Much preferred over an embalmer at the end of all this. "Thank you!"

As they went around in circles for what felt like an eternity, Cait told herself to try to reel in the frustration. Not a good idea to fight with the source of the cops. But for godsakes . . .

"No, there's no telephone—wait, there is a call button, yes." Why hadn't she noticed it on the panel? "Yes, I'm hitting it now."

A buzzer cut in through the alarm. And then . . . a whole lot of nothing but that screaming, ringing sound. Maybe the security guard was on break?

"No, no, answer—oh, God, please just send someone—"

Pounding on the double doors made her scream.

Chapter Fifteen

As Sissy stood in the center of her parents' living room, she held on to the only thing that seemed solid in the world.

The man who had returned her home.

And it was strange. Even through her hysteria, she had some vague thought that he was hard all over: His back was as unforgiving as stone, his arms like bridge cables, his chest a table to rest her head on. He was strong, so very strong; she could sense it in the way he held her to him. If she fainted again? He was going to do what he'd done before with ease.

Pick her up. Carry her somewhere safe.

But was there any true safety to be had anymore?

Probably not. And that was another reason she'd locked herself away all day long.

She hadn't been sleeping; that was for sure. Nope. She'd been reliving the past—and not as in distant history, not the happy or sad or poignant stuff she could recall from her real life. No, she'd passed those solitary hours mourning the prosaic trip out of the house that she'd made however many evenings ago: She'd replayed in her head everything she could remember about the night she had been abducted . . . in the kitchen, going to the fridge, looking for ice cream. None. Calling out to her mother, who was in the family room, watching TV and cross-stitching.

I want to go to the store—can I have the keys?

Her mother's reply: *They're in my purse. Take some money, too. And can you pick up some . . .*

She couldn't remember what her mom had asked her for. Broccoli? Bath soap . . . ? Something that began with B.

The next thing she remembered was going out the front door and getting in the car . . . and thinking that as usual, it smelled like Wrigley's Juicy Fruit gum and coffee—which might have been nasty, but was actually wonderful. Talk about straight out of childhood. Her mom had always taken a travel mug with her whenever she was in the car in the mornings, and in the afternoons, she was all about the gum. When Sissy had been in middle school and the seasonal rotation of field hockey/swimming/dance, etc., had required a nearly constant juggling of rides, the sweet, earthy smell in that Subaru had been all about home.

God, that hurt to think of right now. . . .

And strange that on the night everything had changed she had noticed it one last time—and had smiled to herself as she'd backed out and gone at the speed limit down the road they lived on. She had been saving up for her own car, and looking forward to the summer break when she could pull big hours at Martha's, an ice-cream place across from the Great Escape theme park near Lake George. If she bunked in with a couple of friends and worked pretty much around the clock, by the time September rolled around, she would have been able to buy her own beater and go back and forth more easily from school.

The drive had been less than four miles and taken maybe eight minutes, tops.

After pulling into the parking lot at Hannaford, she'd left the car about five spaces up from the handicap reserves, and walked quickly to the entrance with its shopping carts centipeding in rows. Inside . . . she had lingered over picking out the ice cream. In the end, it had been all about the Rocky Road—because she liked the crunch of the nuts and the chocolate chips and the smooth, super-sweet veins of marshmallow.

Rocky Road. How fitting.

At the self-checkout, she'd scanned the two things in her basket, the ice cream and the B whatever it had been that her mother had wanted. She'd paused to check out the new issue of *Cosmopolitan*, but she hadn't gotten permission for it, and it felt wrong to buy the trashy magazine without having asked first. At that point, she'd gone for her cell to call and see if it was okay, but no-go. Having been in a rush, she'd only taken her wallet and the twenty-dollar bill her mom had let her have.

No way to phone home—or for help either, although she hadn't been thinking about that at the time.

She could remember putting the ice cream in one of the plastic bags that was held open by struts on a Ferris-wheel scale.

Out toward the automatic doors. Into the parking lot.

Everything after that was hazy. Someone had stopped her? Someone who'd needed a . . .

She'd tried throughout the day to get her brain to cough up the goods, give her what she wanted, show her the steps that had led . . . to Hell.

All it had gotten her was a migraine.

Turning her head to the other side, she saw the curtains that hung by the bay window. Her mom had picked out the material about two years ago and made the panels herself. She'd needed help putting them up, and she and Sissy's father had gotten a stepladder out and worked together for an hour, changing the hardware that was screwed into the walls, anchoring the rod, clipping the tops of the drapes into the hooks.

Sissy and her sister hadn't paid any real attention to the efforts or the result—Sissy had been on her way out to a friend's house and had offered only a passing, "It's great!" as she'd run out the door.

Now she wished she'd been a part of the whole process.

Taking a deep breath, she pushed herself back from the warmth she'd taken advantage of. And then she stepped away from her savior. Like the relentless searching of her empty data banks, getting stuck in neutral in the middle of this room was going to get her nowhere. She had come to see her parents in their slumber, and that was exactly what she was going to do.

Except first she looked around again. Inhaled deeply. Went over to the bookcase with all the family photographs on it.

She had to blink away the tears, but she made herself stare at each of the images: If she couldn't handle two-dimensional photographs, how the hell was she going to get through standing over her family?

"This is easier than that."

"What?" came a deep rumble from behind her.

Okay, guess she'd said that out loud. "The wall. However hard this is, it's got nothing on that prison. I have to . . . remember that."

After a moment, Sissy squared her shoulders and walked over to the base of the stairs. Gripping the handrail, she felt the smooth wood and leaned to the side. Down at the base of the balustrade's footer, there was the dipsy-doo, as her father had called it, the little ring around where the fixture curved into a circle. At the center of it, there was a space on the floor that was uncarpeted and hidden unless you looked down from this angle.

Every year, her parents had insisted on doing an Easter-egg hunt in the house for her and her sister—and that tradition, which had started in their toddlerhood, had continued even as they'd gotten older. It was always done inside—after all, in upstate New York, outdoors was usually not an option, assuming you didn't want to wear a parka with your Sunday best. And her father had always used "live eggs" as opposed to those hollow plastic casings that you could fill with stuff. Didn't seem right otherwise, he'd maintained.

Everything had usually gone well . . . except for that one year. Within a day or two of the hunt, an incredible stench had lit off in the house, the nose-curling horror worsening by the hour and permeating throughout—talk about your once-more-with-feeling on the hunt thing.

It had been to no avail, however. No one had been able to find the egg.

They'd had to have the place fumigated and were about to start knocking through the Sheetrock to see if some critter had taken one of her father's "live ones" into the walls of the living room when an unlikely solution had presented itself.

On four legs.

The neighbor's dog had discovered the dead body. Brought in as a Hail Mary, with no hope anything would help, the terrier had zeroed in on the offending item immediately—and found it in that two-square-inch space at the base of the dipsy-doo.

They'd had a good laugh about that for years.

Sissy looked over her shoulder. Her savior was standing pretty much where she'd left him—except that he'd turned to face her.

"They can't hear us, right," she said.

"I don't think so, no."

Yeah, probably not given the whole Chillie situation from this morning.

Sissy walked up the center of the stairwell, listening for the creaks that always happened when she'd done that before. The fact that there were none made her grab the shirt she was wearing and twist the fabric over her heart.

None of the living could hear her voice . . . and she didn't leave footsteps in any tangible sense . . .

Never before had the division between the quick and the dead seemed so real.

At the head of the stairs, she looked left. Right. Straight ahead.

She went into her parents' room first, seeping through the closed door on the left in a way that creeped her out.

The first thing that registered was her father's snoring. Rhythmic. Low. Like an engine revving.

And then she saw her mother's hair, messy on the pillow, highlighted by the illumination from the security lights outside.

"Mom . . . ?" she heard come out of her mouth.

Her mother stirred in her sleep, head rotating back and forth, matting things further.

Sissy had to cover her mouth and look away.

On the nightstand, in front of the alarm clock that her mom set every night and turned off every morning, there was a book, a Bible . . . and a picture frame facedown.

Sissy went over and, without thinking of all the reasons she might not be able to move the thing . . . picked it up. The face that stared back at her was her own, and she remembered just where and when the picture had been taken—at a field hockey game while she'd been on the bench, thanks to a sprained ankle. She was staring at the action, her brows down, her profile sharp, one hand up by her chin.

It was hard to imagine now getting that jazzed over some dumb-ass high school game. In fact, she couldn't access those feelings at all, failing utterly in the attempt to step back into that old, familiar laser focus about a ball being paddled around by a bunch of chicks with sticks. Such a silly pastime, running around on the grass for no good reason, squads of teenage girls getting hyped over their score, their plays, their team's progress in their division and the rival they'd just had to beat . . .

All those sleepless nights before big games, the rampant joy after a win, the stinging, lingering burn of a loss.

Such bullshit, she thought as she put the frame back as it had been. Such manufactured drama to exercise the emotions of people whose lives were steady and secure enough to require artificial tension and stress and "big deal" moments.

Starting in the center of her chest, anger curled up inside of her, ushering out the sense of loss and replacing it with . . . something that was foreign to her, but oh, so very vivid.

In the flush of that new sensation, Sissy stood over her parents for the longest time, hands on hips, head down, eyes tracing the pattern of flowers on the bedspread.

She knew why the image of her was facedown. It wasn't because she had been forgotten. Just the opposite, in fact.

"God . . . damn this whole thing," she whispered.

Eventually, she knew she should go, and gave her mother and father a last look. They were aware that she was here, she thought. Just in the same way Chillie had stopped short when she'd screamed, her mother was getting more and more agitated in her sleep, and her father had stopped snoring, his brows cranking down hard over his closed eyes, his head, too, tossing back and forth.

No reason to torture them by sticking around. Besides, she wasn't sure it was healthy for her, either. She was just getting more and more pissed off.

Leaving the room the way she'd come in, she found that her savior had come up the stairs and was waiting just outside the door. Too jazzed up, she stepped past him without a word and went across the way to her own room.

Her door was shut as well.

On the far side of it, Sissy stood stock-still, hands on her hips, anger surging even further. Just as in her parents' room, light penetrated the thin draping over the windows, bringing out of the darkness her twin bed, her desk, her bookcases, the posters on her walls, a bluish hue tingeing everything, thanks to the color scheme.

How strange, she thought.

Instead of feeling some huge overload of emotion, some visceral connection to herself . . . all she did was remember her senior class trip to Italy. She'd gone on it because her friends were going and her parents had told her this was one of the most important opportunities of her life . . . yada, yada, yada. When she'd gotten there, she'd liked the architecture, sure, and the food had been nice, yes, but the museums? God, the museums. Endless corridors and high-ceilinged rooms filled with statues and paintings and artifacts, the lot of it all populated with people so reverent. It was like they were in church.

Those tour guides and the docents and the chaperones from school had spoken names like da Vinci and Rembrandt and Van-something-or-another like they were quoting the prophets.

Sissy had made an effort to get into it all, but hadn't been able to go much further than noting that, yup, it was a painting. Or, yup, that was another marble sculpture that was missing an arm.

Her prevailing sense had been that none of it related to her life—and the same thing was happening now. The big difference, of course, was that these were her things, not relics of a vast past lived by strangers.

Had been her things, she corrected.

She went over and opened her closet door.

The waft of flowery perfume and body lotion made her recoil as if it were a bad smell. And as the overhead light came on automatically, the shirts and dresses and pants that hung in an orderly row off the dowel were like items in a retail store, not anything that she'd ever worn.

She couldn't take any of these, she thought as she rifled through her old wardrobe—and in retrospect, it had been ridiculous to think she could. If she raided this closet, someone would notice what was missing—and that was a theft, wasn't it.

No, these were not her things. Not anymore.

Pivoting away, she thought, no, not her bed, her desk, her room, her clothes.

Still her family . . . but she didn't belong with them, either.

She left without a second glance, and out in the hall, she met the eyes of the silent man who was clearly guarding her. "I want to say good-bye to my sister."

As he nodded, she thought, wow . . . was this really good-bye?

Was she never returning here again?

Sure felt like it.

Going to the door that was cracked open, she pushed the wood panels with her hand. Her sister's room was on the back side of the house, and as such, there wasn't as much light. So dark inside. Too dark.

Choking back a feeling of panic, Sissy crossed the soft carpet and stopped at the base of the bed.

Shit, she thought. All this stuff with her death? What was it going to leave her sister—

"Sissy?"

Sissy jumped in her own skin, hands flying up to her mouth.

"Sissy? Is that you?"

Her sister rolled over, the slice of light from the hall falling on her face. Her eyes were closed, but like their father, those brows were down tight—and agitation was sending her legs back and forth, as if she were running under the covers.

"Answer her," that deep male voice said behind her.

"Sissy?"

Sissy opened her mouth. Croaked. Cleared her throat. "Yes, it's me."

Instantly, her sister settled down, the tension releasing, a breath exhaling as if she'd let go of a great weight.

"I knew you'd come back," her sister mumbled as she turned to the door and rubbed her face with a floppy hand. "I knew it."

Sissy wiped her eyes as tears came. "I'm . . . here. But I can't stay."

More with the frowning. "Why not?"

"I just can't. But I wanted you to know . . . I'm okay."

"Don't sound okay."

"I am." She looked at her shaking hands, and told them to be still. "I am going to be fine. Tell Mom and Dad that, all right? I want you to tell them that I came to you, and we talked, and I want you to remember this. Promise me, Dell. You remember this."

Her sister's tone went into little-girl territory. "Don't go."

"I don't belong here anymore, I'm so sorry."

"Sissy—please, no—"

Without thinking, she placed her hand on her sister's foot. "Shhhh . . . rest now. Shh . . ."

Instantly, her sister eased.

"Dell, you will remember this. You will hear this in your mind when you are worried about me, you will tell this to Mom and

Dad when you see that look in their eyes. Promise me? I am . . . okay."

"Only if you come back."

Always a negotiator, her sister was. "Dell—"

"Only if I see you again."

"Fine. I promise."

"When?"

"I don't know."

"At your funeral?"

At her . . . oh, God. "No, not then. But I promise. Go back to sleep. And remember that I will always love you, Dell."

Sissy all but stumbled out of her sister's room. And in the hall she was caught once again by the man who had brought her here and had witnessed the temporary return to a life she didn't—couldn't—be a part of any longer.

As he led her down the stairs and out through—literally—the front door, Sissy held herself, her arms straining around her own rib cage. So hard to come here, so hard to leave. The emotions were too big to name, too heavy to bear.

Out at the street, the truck's door magically opened for her—oh, wait, it was her savior doing the duty.

Getting up into the seat, she focused on the house as the door was shut. The people under its roof were not like her clothes or her bed or her books. They were still a part of her, even though the tether felt so weak and strained.

"Put your seat belt on."

Sissy jumped. "Oh, right."

"You want to eat something?"

Food . . . food? Was she hungry?

"McDonald's," he announced as he started the truck's engine and hit the gas.

Sissy just kept an eye on that house until it wasn't possible to see it anymore. Then she wrenched herself back around and stared through the front windshield.

The loudest thing inside the vehicle, apart from the muffled growl of the engine, was the tick-tock of the directional signal as he took lefts and rights to get them out of the neighborhood.

She supposed she should thank him.

Turning to him, she could only stare.

"Why are you looking at me like that," he asked abruptly.

"I don't know."

Funny, that halo that glowed around his head wasn't something she'd noticed before—but it made sense that as an angel he'd have one.

Guess all the depictions in church had been accurate.

"I just . . . can't believe this," she mumbled.

Covering her face with her hands, all she could do was shake her head back and forth.

"Look, I know where you're at," he said roughly. "I've been there. The only thing I can tell you, and it's not going to help . . . is that just because you can't believe it, doesn't mean the shit's not real." There was a long pause. "Unfortunately."

Chapter Sixteen

"Blah-blah, blah, blah!"

As Cait stopped screaming, she had to struggle to make her hearing work over the din of the alarm—and her adrenaline gland. Too much input in too tiny a space with too little air to breathe.

And maybe that was her brain along with the elevator.

"Police!" came a holler on the other side of the closed doors.

"Ms. Douglass? What's happening?"

Oh, right, and the 911 call was still live in her ear.

"Ah—the police say that they're here—but I'm not opening these doors until I know for sure."

"Hold one moment." Like this was a catalog call and they were verifying her credit card. "Ms. Douglass? The officer's name should be Hoffman. Peter Hoffman. Ask the individual who they are."

"What's your name!" she yelled over the alarm.

"Hoffman! Pete Hoffman—badge number ten forty-one!"

She addressed the phone. "Ten forty-one? The badge?"

"That checks out, ma'am. Open the doors."

"I'm staying on with you if I do."

"I'm right here."

Cait watched as her hand went forward and her fingers tripped the red switch downward. Instantly the alarm was extinguished, but the ringing continued, her ears struggling with the sudden silence.

She did hear another ding, however, like the elevator was clearing its throat and preparing for a redo. Then the doors slid to the left, stacking in on top of each other.

The navy blue uniform and the shiny badge on the other side? Best. Thing. Ever.

She nearly launched herself at the guy. Wait—actually she did. "Oh, thank God."

"Ma'am?" The cop grabbed her arm and hoisted her up. "Let's sit down."

Yes, let's, shall we?

The shaking was pretty unparalleled, as if her insides had come to a rolling boil. And nothing much registered, not whatever Peter Hoffman, badge 1041, was saying to her, not the cold, hard concrete her butt was on, not the words she was apparently speaking in response to questions. The largest part of her was still in that elevator, lunging for the alarm, praying that the locking mechanism of the doors held, wondering how the evening had mutated into nightmare.

". . . didn't see them clearly," she heard herself say. "Someone was rushing toward me. They were coming from the ramp, walking quickly—then breaking into a run."

"And then what happened?"

"I raced into the elevator and hit the button." Every time she blinked, she saw her fingers in the strobe lighting, punching, punching, punching. "I just . . . and then I called nine-one-one. Oh . . . God . . . I can't stop this shaking."

"You're in shock, ma'am."

Guess so. The thing was, talking about it to law enforcement made everything concrete, any vague fantasy that this was just a bad dream concocted while she was asleep in her own bed dissipating into the cold air.

The good news was that the officer was calm and even-toned, and that—along with the gun holstered on his hip—made her feel a lot safer. "Backup has just arrived and they're going to search the perimeter and the floors. But whoever it was? They're probably gone. I hate to say this, but a woman alone in this part of town? We get a lot of these calls—and unfortunately, the aggressors are very good at disappearing."

She was inclined to agree with the get-gone theory. Seemed only logical. Trouble was, the lack of closure was a black hole for her—and now that the primary wave of anxiety had passed and she couldn't see her attacker, she was stuck wondering whether she had overreacted.

Or had she just saved her own life?

Pickpocket or violent mugger?

Rapist or just someone trying to tell her she had toilet paper stuck to her shoe?

No, she decided. As she remembered the wave of menace, she knew the answer—and had to wonder yet again how God made the choice between who survived and who didn't. Who was granted a lickety-split save . . . and who ended up in a living hell.

Strangely, the prospect of that decision making made her feel bad for whoever was up there in the clouds watching all the drama on Earth. If you went on the theory that God was a beneficent creator of all things? You had to assume He felt the pain of victims as they didn't so much cross into the afterlife, but were thrown over in pieces.

Horrible . . .

As two other officers appeared and reported that there was nobody in the parking facility, things took a turn for the paperwork, the whole event downshifting sharply into procedural territory— confirming her statement, receiving a case number, a business card, an escort back to her car.

Normal. So amazingly normal that she was nearly as rattled as she had been while in full panic mode.

After she had belted herself in and started her SUV, the police officers, all three of them, watched her back out of her space— and their expressions were like those of parents watching a six-teen-year-old go off alone for the first time.

Fragile optimism backed up by a whole lot of hope-she-calls-if-she-needs-us.

Cait barely remembered the drive home, but the one clear part was checking and rechecking that she'd locked the Lexus's doors. Then, when she parked in her garage, she waited for the panels to come back down before she got out—and she threw the dead bolt as soon as she was in the house.

Shower was the first and only goal—after she initiated her ADT alarm. And when she got into her bathroom? She turned the lock on her loo as well.

Wonder how long that habit was going to last.

Cranking the shower on, she undressed, and for the first time in recorded history, left her clothes where they lay: shirt in the sink, loafers and socks kicked off around the base of the toilet, pants sloughed onto the bath mat in front of the tub. Usually she stripped in her closet by her three wicker laundry baskets, one each for whites, darks, and delicates/colors—the last a twofer because she had few colors. Oh, and her dry-cleaning bag was in there, too.

Amazing how fearing for your life could prioritize things.

As she got under the spray, she wrapped her arms around herself and hung her head. The water was a balm inside and out, as solid and warm as a blanket over her shoulders and back, as calming as an ocean breeze as the steam rose up and went down deep into her lungs.

It wasn't until she had dried off, gotten into her robe, and gone downstairs to make herself some tea that she realized . . .

"Shit."

Going over to the counter by the stove, she did another dive into her mangled purse. Pulling out her phone, she called up G.B.'s number out of her Received List and hit *send*. As it rang, she ran through her apology in her head.

I'm so sorry, but I was nearly . . . mugged?

Not really accurate.

I'm so sorry. I . . . was chased in the parking garage, and ended up trapping myself in an elevator and calling 911 and having a chat-up with the police—such nice guys, by the way . . . .

Flustered, she ended the call before he picked up.

Pacing around in her bare feet—which, P.S., kind of grossed her out even though she'd cleaned the floor on her hands and knees the day before—she tried to pull things together.

Cursing again, and thinking that it was a rare night for her to have dropped so many R-rated words at all, much less in the matter of an hour, she tried to get her brain working.

What a no-go that was. It was like she had a hangover, everything clogging up, moving slow, making little sense.

But that was no excuse to leave G.B. hanging. How long had he waited for her in that lobby?

Feeling awful about so much, she brought up her phone, and—

She had a voice mail. From G.B.

It had just come in, but she'd put her phone on mute because she'd assumed she'd be in the theater all night long.

Bracing herself to feel even worse than she did, she initiated the recording, putting the phone up to her ear.

His voice sounded so rich and deep. "Cait? Oh, my God, I'm so sorry—I hope you didn't wait very long for me? I got tied up backstage, and I couldn't get free forever—they were doing publicity shots, and interviews, and I tried to send someone out there for you, but everyone who was affiliated with the show was running around like crazy. Please . . . give me another chance? I blew it. I know I did." As he exhaled in frustration, she pictured him dragging his hands through that long hair of his. "I'm really, totally sorry. I'm going to finish up with the other folks now, and then . . . I guess I'll go home. Call me if you feel like it, okay? Again, I'm so sorry."

Cait put the phone facedown on the table. Curled up a fist and rested her chin on it.

As she stared across the linoleum, she felt weird. Not exactly depressed—because that would be ridiculous. In the first place, she was alive. And secondly, as it turned out, she hadn't been the one to let things down with G.B.: If she hadn't been chatting with the uniforms, she'd have just been cooling her heels in the foyer of the theater, stewing on whether or not to call him and when she should leave.

The evening had turned out to be a total bust.

Glancing down at her feet, she flexed her toes.

Her lack of footwear, at least, was an issue she could do something about.

Getting up, she hit the stairs in search of fresh white socks and her UGG slippers. And as she went, that odd off-kilter feeling followed her to the second floor, staying on her close as a second skin.

Maybe it would help if she put a label on whatever it was . . . but she was too afraid to.

As she came back into her room, she thought about Sissy again, and prayed that the afterlife was easier than the stuff that went down on the earth.

At least if you were a ghost, or an angel, or whatever you turned into, you didn't have to deal with being chased in parking garages. Or talking to the police.

As Jim sat behind the wheel of his truck, making turns like he knew where he was taking him and Sissy, he felt pretty damn castrated. Even though there was a lot about this situation that wasn't his fault? Didn't matter. Someone had to take responsibility for the unfairness and there was no one else in line with him.

Plus, he didn't like the way she was just sitting there. Especially as she put the visor down and looked at herself in the credit card–size mirror. When she flipped it back up, he wasn't sure whether she'd seen what she wanted. Probably not.

"McDonald's," he repeated, in case she'd been too distracted. "Okay?"

When he didn't get a response, he let her be. A Big Mac, large fries, and a Coke were probably not first on her mind right now, but if he didn't get some food in him, he was going to—

"Fuck!"

Wrenching the wheel to the right, he narrowly missed a black cat that ran right out in front of them. Which was the good news. The bad? As the damn thing shot off in the opposite direction, the truck beelined for an oak tree big enough to be in a Harry Potter movie.

Without thinking about it, Jim threw an arm bar across the seat, catching Sissy at chest level, as if that would somehow work out better for her than her goddamn seat belt. At the same time, he tried to course-correct by yanking a hard left and slamming on the brakes.

As time slowed, he watched the tree rush for the front grille, all defensive lineman and then some.

Wasn't this perfect timing—a car accident right in the middle of—

Boom!

Okay, really getting tired of explosions at this point. And the impact certainly sounded like the discharge of a small-bore can-non—or at the very least a bazooka. But he had more important problems than pegging a decibel match.

Unlike Sissy, he'd forgotten to put his seat belt on.

And also unlike her, his air bag failed to deploy.

He caught the steering wheel in the pecs and the windshield right in the face, a brilliant flash of light making him feel like someone had hit his good self in the puss with a roman candle.

Man, there had been waaaaaaaaaaaaay too many light shows and loud noises . . .

. . . lately.

"What the fuck!" he yelled as someone came at him.

Instead of waiting for an answer, Jim grabbed whatever was in front of him and hauled the weight to the side, rolling with it and mounting up with every intention of beating the ever-living—

"Stop! Stop! I'm a paramedic! I'm here to help you!"

As his "attacker" cringed into the pavement, Jim frowned and noticed that there was a stethoscope around the man's neck. And the guy was wearing a uniform with patches. And there were red and blue strobe lights going off everywhere.

He looked around, still keeping one hand locked hard on that throat, and the other curled into a fist and held high over his shoulder.

Over to the right, like something out of an ad for insurance policies, his truck was wrapped around a tree trunk—

The tackle came from the other direction, the one he wasn't looking in, and whoever it was had some experience knocking people down. Jim bowling-pinned it to the ground, the force sliding him across the asphalt, ripping a hole in his arm, driving the breath out of his chest.

Unlike him, however, his wrecking ball was not prepared to beat the shit out of his target.

As Jim was all but bolted face-first to the ground, a sensible voice said in his ear, "You've been in a motor vehicle accident. You were unresponsive when we arrived on scene. The EMTs are in the middle of their medical assessment, and with your consent, they would like to continue."

Jim strained the one eyeball he had with any upward trajectory. The mountain heap on top of him was an African-American CPDer with a goatee and a bald head. And the heavy bastard seemed perfectly content to take a TO on Jim's backside for however long the situation required it.

Sissy! Where was—

"What's that, sir?" the cop said. "Sissy? You were alone when we found you, sir."

"No! Sissy was with me!" Oh, great. He had the enunciation of a three-year-old, the words coming out with all kinds of *ths* where they shouldn't be.

"Look, how about we take this one thing at a time. Do you consent to be treated?"

"I need to find her."

The EMT Jim had welcome-matted came over, walking with a limp. "I think he's got a head injury—"

"Sir, I'm going to have to cite you for—"

As they both started yammering at him, Jim figured he'd change his tactic. "Fine, treat me," he spat.

The main issue was that he had to find out where Sissy was—so he needed his booty-sitter up and off of him.

God, please let Devina not have shown up with her normal fucking impeccable timing.

The cop dismounted slowly. "You're going to have to lie still. Your head went through a lot of glass, and we're also worried about your spinal column."

Roger that, occifer.

Jim immediately flipped over onto his back with every intention of getting to his feet. But the instant he tried to do the upward-mobility thing, his body went weak on him.

"Nah," the cop said, "you don't need to be doing that—"

"I'm right here."

Jim wrenched his head to the female voice. And as he did, a sharp shooter rode up right into his brain, making him wince.

"Let me get a collar on him," another medic said.

"Can you tell me your name?" the cop asked.

But Jim wasn't tracking, and he didn't care what they did to him. Sissy was standing under a streetlamp just on the periphery of the action, watching over the drama, her arms wrapped around herself.

Talk about an angel.

Maybe it was his injury . . . but man, all he could think of was how beautiful she was—and not in the ways of a girl, but as a woman. That illumination she was under cast a beckoning thrall around her, her long, straight blond hair teased by the wind, her eyes grave and serious, not wide and scared: In spite of the accident, she stood tall and strong, even though there had been way too many traumas tonight.

"Thank God," Jim breathed.

"Really," the cop said as the EMTs crowded around and various medical devices were taken out of carry-ons and attached to him. "Didn't think parents went with Thank anymore as a first name. And God's pretty unusual."

Wha—oh, the name question. "No, I found her," Jim muttered.

"Who?"

"Sissy." Jim tried to lift his head again. "I'm okay," he called out to her.

"Have you had anything to drink, sir?" the cop asked.

"Are you sure you're all right?" Sissy said.

"Yes," Jim replied. "I'm sure."

"We've got a confirm on the alcohol," the cop interjected.

Another uniformed somebody or other came over. "Have you found a wallet on him?"

"Sir, do you have a driver's license?"

"Don't worry," he told Sissy.

"Well, I'm supposed to be concerned about this," his cop said. "It's my job."

"Give the man your license," she interjected.

Shit. He probably still had his old one with him, but if they searched the name and photo? "I'm dead," he mumbled.

The paramedic who he'd clotheslined laughed. "If so, you're the first stiff I've ever met who has blood pressure."

Wait for it, Jim thought.

"I'll put a spell on them," Jim said as a cuff was put around his neck. "It'll take care of everything."

"Bring over the stretcher," a voice shouted.

"I'm not going to the hospital."

The cop leaned in and smiled at him. "A spell, huh? You're just going to blink and this is all going to go away?"

Jim met the man right in the eye, locking on, locking in. "That's right."

With a force of will, he sent energy outward, pushing it through the air molecules between them, assuming control of the man's mind, and through it, all of his thoughts and actions. The solution out of this mess was to do the same thing one by one with the others, and then he and Sissy were free.

Hell, he could even get this uniform to give them a ride home—

"You guys get your board?" the cop asked as he turned and looked over his shoulder. "Time to get him into transport."

Jim blinked in confusion. *What the hell?*

The EMT who'd been checking the blood pressure shrugged. "There's little flight risk, if that's what you're worried about. His leg's probably broken. He's going nowhere."

"He managed to jump you pretty good," the police officer pointed out.

Wait, wait, wait, this was not how it was supposed to—

"Here's the board. Okay, sir, we're going to move you. On three. . . . One . . . two . . . three—"

As pain barged in and took over, shorting his brain out, Jim's last thought was that it should have worked. Ever since Eddie had shown him the tricks of the angel trade, he'd been able to influence things and people like magic.

Apparently, playing sledgehammer with your own face cut those benes short.

Damn it.

Chapter Seventeen

Hours after Cait put herself to bed . . . she was suffocating.

In spite of all the cool, clean air in her bedroom, she was chok-ing, a band of constriction tightening on her ribs, making it impos-sible to take a deep breath. In fact, it was almost as if she were underwater and being held there, the surface something she could only see in the distance through a wavy, blurry death sentence.

For the one millionth time since she'd gotten into bed, she looked over at her alarm clock. The Bahama-blue digital number glowed 2:34.

Oh, the irony. Even freaked-out in the dark, her mind still somehow knew when to check the time so that the numbers were in sequence.

Her eyes had long ago adjusted to the dimness of the room, and as her house gently snored, its familiar creaks and buckles like the rhythms of a sleeping dog, she measured the order that sur-rounded her, defined her.

Across the way, all the books on the shelves on either side of the window seat were arranged alphabetically. The throw blanket was precisely folded over the carefully arranged down pillows in the alcove. The pictures on the walls were set in identical frames that had been hung not by eyeballing it, but through a torturous process involving two tape measures and four hours with a pink hammer and slippery little nails. Her desk up here was for bills and documents, not drafting or drawing, and everything was where it needed to be, the pens locked away in a tray in the middle drawer, her to-be-paids filed in a vertical holder with beginning-, middle-, and end-of-the-month slots, the paperwork she was in the process of dealing with set aside in a manila folder.

No clutter. Nothing out of place—ever. And the same was true with her bureau, her closet, her whole life.

Rubbing her face, she wanted to scream.

Her insides felt radioactive, like the experience in that parking garage had contaminated her, and the after-effects were going to have a sizable half-life. And goddamn it if being around all of her obsessive need for control wasn't making that itchy-twitchy burn so much worse.

Don't tell me you didn't think about me last night.

Are you always this arrogant?

I don't worry about what other people think.

And what if that kind of attitude doesn't get you where you want to go.

You want this, too. Don't deny it—

Okay, she was *not* thinking of that man. She was absolutely, positively not thinking about that man—

Shoot. Maybe she was. And maybe . . . just maybe she kept picturing where she'd left her car keys, downstairs by her purse.

But come on, it wasn't like she was actually going to go down to the Iron Mask and meet him. Not possible. Not ever—

especially considering what she'd been through earlier . . . because that would be like having a fire in your living room, and deciding, after the men with the trucks and hoses had left, that maybe you should arson up the rest of your house just so things matched.

If you come over after my shift, I'll tell you anything you want to know about me. And then I'll show you the more important things.

And what would they be.

You'll find out. If you think you can handle it.

Cait rolled away from the clock, hoping that if she didn't look at those numbers, she'd forget that she had enough time, provided she left now, to get dressed and make it downtown right when he'd told her to be there.

Live now, a voice said. It's the only chance you have.

Punching at her pillow to fatten it up, she threw her head back down on it and deflated the thing. This was just so crazy. Except if Heaven didn't exist, and all you got was a dirt nap at the end of your life, how stupid would she feel if she stayed in this cold bed alone . . . when there was something hot and powerful waiting for her across town?

Safe sex worked if you did it right. All it took was a condom put on correctly.

Besides, the born-again-virgin routine she'd been rocking since college was getting depressing. . . .

"No. Absolutely no."

More pillow fluffing. And cursing.

It was two forty-six when she exploded out of bed. Put jeans on that she rarely wore. Chose the only lace bra she owned. Pulled on a turtleneck that could be trampled underfoot.

Behind the wheel of her SUV, heading out of her neighborhood, she did not look back. Didn't think, either. The decision made, she wasn't going to dwell on it or the fact that there was a high probability she was still in shock from what had happened earlier. There would be time tomorrow morning for doubts and recriminations—right here and now? There was only her destination.

Her phone went off just as she was getting on the Northway. Without thinking, she snagged it and checked who it was.

Teresa. No doubt calling because the interminable insomniac hadn't gotten an update as promised.

Cait let the call go to voice mail. She didn't want anyone else's opinion on this bright idea, and didn't trust herself to keep things on the DL. Besides, her old roommate was half in love with G.B., in that way people got hooked on TV or movie stars. Knowing how Teresa was hardwired, she was likely to get offended on the singer's behalf.

Cait was too practiced at being guilty not to spot that trap.

Not when this collision she was about to cause was only an exit ramp and a couple of traffic lights away.

And she had no interest in saving herself.

"Don't ask me to clear your head for you," Duke growled. "Because I'm going to use that bathroom stall you're hiding in to do it."

Every night around two a.m., the Iron Mask's entrance line got shut down, and that meant that he had a good hour to deal with a dwindling number of ever more intoxicated and compromised brilliant thinkers—like this wiry guy who'd decided he was going to be cool and do coke out in the open on one of the tables. Confronted, he'd dodge-balled around the security staff and locked himself in here.

The sound of a giant inhale through a deviated septum suggested that Einstein with the powder fixation was going for some more nose courage.

Maybe he'd do another line and end up levitating right up and out.

Of course, it could be worse. At least Fleet-foot hadn't picked one of the private bathrooms—because then Duke would have had to hard-shoulder through a locked door in front of the patrons. As it was, the guy had gunned for a public facility, and picked the middle of the three bays that were opposite the urinals.

Out of the corner of his eye, Duke caught sight of his reflection in the mirrors over the lineup of sinks. Jacked forward on his hips, he was unaware of having curled up a pair of fists, but there they were.

"On the count of three," he barked. "You come out, or I'm coming in after you. One—"

"Duke."

The sound of his boss's voice cut through his aggression. Slightly.

Twisting on his hips, he looked over his shoulder at Alex Hess. "I'm handling this."

"No, you're not." She jerked a thumb at the door she'd come through. "Out."

"I got this." He turned back around. "Give me—"

Alex materialized in front of him, moving impossibly fast, and the force of her presence was like getting popped in the face with a crowbar. In a quiet voice, she hissed, "Here's the deal. You've been walking that line tonight, and if you go any further with this? You're going to hurt him." As he opened his mouth, she put her palm up. "My turf, my rules. Don't make me escort you the fuck out of here, because I will. If you kill someone on this job? I've got the CPD so far up my ass, I'm stirring my coffee with their badges."

In all her buck-stops-here anger, her gray eyes seemed to glow, and it wasn't like he doubted that she'd physically relocate him if she had to. The boss lady was usually right and always in control—of herself, and of others.

But come *on*.

Duke shook his head. "This is no different than any other night."

"And the fact that you don't recognize where you're at proves my point. Now back off."

Abruptly, the room became preternaturally clear, everything from the bright shine of the black tile on the walls, to the white veins in the black marble floor, to the sound of the wheezing coming from that middle stall.

"You're going to kill someone," Alex said roughly. "I can see it in your eyes. And you've got to trust me on this before you do something both of us are going to regret."

"Fucking hell," he muttered.

When she just cocked an eyebrow, he peeled off, stalked to the door, and punched his way through—

Hello, peanut gallery of meatheads.

Immediately outside the loo, a crowd of security staff had gathered, the bunch of them standing in a half-moon orientation, like they were ready to catch the fallout of either him or the blowhead or the boss coming out of the enclosed space.

Cursing under his breath, Duke ignored them all, and marched to the back of the club, shoving through the staff-only door and then pacing up and down the empty corridor between the offices and the locker room.

The air was cooler here, and he took some deep breaths, the lingering perfume and body oils from the working girls doing some kind of aromatherapy on him.

He was on his second round trip down and back when Alex came through the door he'd put to use. "My office. Right now."

Ah, shit.

Duke walked over with her, but didn't sit down once they

were shut in together. Picking the far wall, he leaned up against the concrete and crossed his arms in front of his chest.

Alex parked it behind her desk. "Here's what we're going to do."

Great. He couldn't wait to hear this.

"We're giving you a couple of nights off."

He looked up. "That's ridiculous. I'm—"

Alex cupped her hand by her ear. "Not going to argue with me? Fantastic. Good choice."

Duke scrubbed his face so he didn't start yelling and thereby prove her damn point. "I don't need—"

"To waste either of our time trying to convince me otherwise? Man, you are getting *so* smart. I really respect where you're at."

As he resumed glaring at the floor, he could feel her staring at him across the desk.

Abruptly, she picked up the one living thing in the room: a small plant in a green-colored plastic pot.

"You see this?" she said. "You know who gave it to me? A nice guy named Detective de la Cruz. He paid me a visit here a little while ago, and you wanna know whose health plan he's on? The CPD's. Again, nice guy. But I didn't want this fucking plant, and I reallllly don't want him to come back—most certainly not because we had bodily damage of a permanent variety happen in one of my fucking bathrooms by one of my cocksucking bouncers."

"I can keep it together."

She put the pathetic ivy or fern or whatever it was back down. "It's my own damned fault. I didn't realize this, but you've worked the last twenty-five nights that we've been open in a row—I shouldn't have asked you to come in last evening. You're just too dependable, and frankly, too good at your dumb-ass job. Unfortunately, you're also getting burned out. It happens. Those idiots out there will drive you demented."

He opened his mouth, but she cut him off. "This is not subject to compromise or discussion. At all. You either do what I say, or, as much as it pains me to say this, I'm going to fire you."

Duke felt his temper flare even higher . . . but he knew better than to argue. She was holding all his cards, and she probably wasn't being all that unfair. Damn her.

"Can I finish out tonight?"

"As long as you relax? Yeah. But then it's two shifts off." Duke turned to go. "I didn't say I was done with you."

"What," he asked the closed door.

"You have a visitor. I put her down the hall in the interrogation room."

Duke cranked around. "Visitor?"

Alex offered a sly smile. "Blond. Five-eight. Looks out of place here—which I can't help but think recommends her. In fact, maybe if you spend a little time with the female? You'll get in a better mood."

Duke blew out of the boss lady's office and strode down that corridor. When he got to the door of the room they "talked" to people in, he didn't knock, just opened wide.

And there she was, standing in her sensible shoes, hands in the pockets of her jeans, eyes shooting over like she was out of her element, her comfort zone . . . and her mind.

At least in her opinion.

Duke would beg to differ, however.

Dropping his lids, a sense of purpose calmed him out so much better than the chain-yanking of his boss.

As he shut the door, she lifted her hand awkwardly. "Hi. I . . ."

He put his finger to his lips and *shhh*'d her. Then he went over to the monitoring equipment in the far corner and reached waaaaaay up, disconnecting the unit that was mounted on the ceiling.

Facing off at her, he drawled, "I'm assuming you don't want this recorded."

"Ah . . ."

As she clearly searched for words, it was obvious she hadn't been playing when she'd said she didn't do shit like this.

No problem. He was going to take care of everything.

Closing in, he already had her naked in his mind, naked and up on the table in the middle of the room, her legs spread for him as he kissed her so hard, she fell back on the scratched surface.

He didn't say anything as he reached for her, slipping a hand around the base of her neck and pulling her forward by the throat.

She put her palms out to his chest and held him off. "Don't you want to . . ."

"What? Talk?" His eyes locked on her mouth. "That's not why you came. That's not why I asked you here."

In the recesses of his mind, he found it strange that he was so sexed up over this female. But he wasn't wasting time on that one. She was here. She was not going to say no. And he needed this with a desperation he not only didn't understand, but knew better than to question.

He wanted her willing, however.

And that meant he was going to have to seduce her into the fucking.

He moved his hand up so that it plowed into her hair, and then took her by the waist. "I saw your car earlier. You came by the front of the club, didn't you."

She swallowed hard. "I wanted to see . . ."

"Me." He leaned in, putting his chest against her breasts and his mouth next to her ear. "You wanted to see me again, because you couldn't believe you were thinking about meeting me here. You couldn't believe that while you were watching that singer . . . I was the man on your mind."

He moved his hips in, brushing his erection against her before he backed off to measure her reaction.

Oh, yeaaaah. That's what he wanted: Her lids closed briefly and her lips parted—so she'd definitely felt what he'd wanted her to.

"I knew you were going to come," he said, "for me."

That was when he kissed her, shifting fast and taking over, gathering her hard and bringing her in tight to his body as his mouth found hers. She was stiff against him, but that didn't last. As he licked his way into her, she went loose all over, and man, that was good—just as good as the way she tasted.

Talk about transformation. All that pent-up frustration he'd been riding got rechanneled into lust for her, and the heady surge of erotic power was his first clue that this casual hookup was going to be different. But then he didn't think of anything much else. She was the perfect receptacle for his burn, her tongue meeting his, her spine arching her forward, her arms shooting around his shoulders to hold him in return.

When she pulled away briefly, he knew what she was worried about.

"No lock on the door," he told her. Because the last thing the club needed was an accusation of false imprisonment. "But the thing opens inward, so if you want privacy, I can fuck you up against it."

Her eyes widened, as if she were trying to figure out whether the coarse language offended her or turned her on even more.

When she brought his mouth back down to hers, he took that as a "wow, what a great idea to body-block everyone out of our little piece of privacy."

Roger that. Duke maneuvered her against the panels and went for her turtleneck, yanking it free of her waistband so he could slip his palms onto the smooth, warm skin of her torso. In response, she put her arms up, and he didn't wait for further instruction; he swept the shirt up and over her head, tossing it aside.

Nice bra.

Little girlie for his tastes, but he so didn't mind that lace on her in the slightest—through the peekaboo weave, he could see her tight pink nipples, and as much as he was enjoying what was going on with her lips, he wanted at all that, too.

No reason to bother removing those fragile cups. He nuzzled his way south, kissing her throat, her collarbones, the smooth plane of her sternum—and then going on to her breast. Extending his tongue, he went for that nipple, licking at the tip of it, sucking it in, running his lips back and forth against the combination of lace and flesh. And she liked the attention he was paying her. Her hands dug into his hair and tugged at his head—not to push him away, though. Hell, no. She was holding him to her.

He didn't need the encouragement.

Man, he loved the way she smelled—as well as the fact that she'd showered before she came to him: The undercarriage of her hair was just a little damp, and on her skin, a faint fragrance lingered. No heavy lotions and stuff for her, not like the working girls here at the club. Delicate soap, something natural and clean.

Looks out of place here—which I can't help but think recommends her.

At least he and his boss could agree on one thing tonight.

Easing back, Duke hooked both of the straps at her shoulders and braced himself to see her properly. Pulling downward and caressing her upper arms as he went, he revealed what he had been attending to.

"Fuck . . . " he breathed.

Talk about perfect. Nothing but creamy skin and those tight little nipples he could now get to without anything in his way.

With every inhale she took, her breasts swayed ever so slightly . . .

The groan that boiled up out of him sounded like the growl of a beast—and wasn't that pretty damn accurate. At the moment, he was feeling about as civilized as a panther.

And this sweet-smelling female who was now half naked in front of him?

She was going to be his meal.

Chapter Eighteen

Cait was out of her mind, and she wasn't going to do one damned thing about it. The man who had just kissed her like no one else ever had was now taking off her bra—and for once in her life, she wasn't freaking out over the mole on the breast on the right, or the fact that maybe she wasn't precisely symmetrical, or . . . all those other real or imagined things that had previously come to mind when she'd been getting naked in other circumstances.

The only thing she cared about was getting his mouth on her without any barriers—

"Fuuuuck," he said deeply.

Well, now. Wasn't that an entire thesaurus worth of compliments— a you-are-so-beautiful-totally-hot-freaking-awesome-blowing-my-mind all rolled up together.

And then he growled. Like, actually let out that sound she'd only read about men making.

She didn't have any time to dwell on it, though.

With a surge of his powerful body, Duke dropped down and licked at one of her nipples, his attention turning to a suckling as he snaked a hold around her waist and bent her backward. As he went for the other one, her body got torqued into a completely unnatural position, but she didn't care. Not with those lips tugging at her, not with his soft hair once again in her grip, not with that erection of his pushing into her hip.

His free hand went between her legs.

No preamble. No sweep up a thigh or sneak downward. No I'm-going-to-touch-you-now.

He took what he wanted.

And she orgasmed.

As if he knew exactly where he'd taken her, his lips broke contact with her breast and he moved upward, retaking control of her mouth, swallowing the harsh sounds she made, muting her as he worked her sex through her jeans. And it was funny, she wasn't worried in the slightest that someone might hear her—especially as his fingers pressed in and rubbed the hard knot of the seam against her core. If she screamed the place down? Fine. Whatever. He was helping her ride out the release even as he kept the pleasure going, and her body wanted it all—wanted everything he could give her.

He didn't stop. With another release riding hard on the heels of her first, her nails clawed into his shoulders, and she bent her knees, opening her legs farther to give him more access—which was a good idea, but there was a problem. With her thighs as weak as they were, her balance went off-kilter—

Duke was on it. With a quick move, he picked her up like she didn't weigh a thing.

Aloft in his arms, she had a brief, striking impression of . . . pure masculine power. He was built all over, as if his body had been carved, not born, the muscles clenching under his clothes and his skin as he held her off the floor. This was not Thom, a lanky, soft-bellied college boy. This was a man in his physical prime, a male who was sexually aroused and had every intention of doing something about it.

A second later, she was sprawled on the floor.

"Gotta make sure the door stays closed," he purred against her breast.

And then he was on top of her, his weight pushing her into the linoleum, threatening to crush her—which was just all the more erotic.

As his mouth found her nipples again, she felt a tugging at her hips. Her jeans. He was attacking her zipper, then dragging the denim and her panties down her legs. Cool air hit the heat between her thighs, but that didn't last long.

His hand went immediately back to where it had been, only this time with nothing between her slick core and his fingers. When he entered her, he recaptured her mouth, thrusting his tongue in against her as he dominated her sex down below—

Cait came even harder, biting her lip, arching up into his chest, the whirlwind both taking her out of her body and locking her in her skin as the sensations poured through her flesh.

And then there was a brief lull, when the pressure on top of her relented.

A jangling sound. His belt. He was taking off his—

"Condom," she said hoarsely.

"Got one."

Thank God, because she didn't. In truth, she'd thought through so little about this. Although even if she'd sketched it out? She wouldn't have come close to the real experience. So much hotter and more raw—

Duke reared up on his knees and gave her a shock.

He'd shoved his jeans down low on his hips and his sex was

tremendous, so thick and long, standing out straight from his body.

This was going to get . . . even more intense.

The condom was a Trojan, and he tore off the corner of the blue square with his sharp white teeth, the foil ripping open with obliging ease. And then, as she watched him sheathe himself, she had to bite her lower lip again, especially as his blunt fingers took care of business over the heavy head and that thick shaft.

A split second later, he was on top of her again.

Cait took over from there. When she gripped him, he bore down on his teeth and cursed, his head rearing back on his neck, the cords of muscle popping out on either side.

"Jesus . . ." he groaned.

She felt the exact same way. Except as she guided him to her, she braced herself. It had been a long time for her, and given the way he was built?

She had no interest in stopping this, however. If anything, each level of this improbable, out-of-control hookup just incinerated her even further—and she relished the inferno precisely for its burn: in the midst of it, nothing else existed, her terror in the parking garage seared away, her weeks of worrying about Sissy obliterated, her years of loneliness and her sadness even still about Thom gone, gone, gone.

She was beyond ready for this. Had been for a while, and not in the several-hours sense.

With Duke poised to enter her, he thrust his arm underneath her shoulders and brought her face close to his. His eyes held hers—

Just before he surged forward, he looked away.

Someone like him being shy? Impossible—

Pain lanced through her, stiffening her body, snuffing out the heat in a split second. And as Duke froze, those eyes shot back to hers in something close to alarm.

"No," she muttered. "It's just been a while for me. Don't you dare stop."

To prove the point, she thrust her hands down his powerful torso to the small of his back—where she went even lower, pushing under the loose seat of his pants to his totally tight ass. Jacking her hips up and pushing him to her, she joined them properly, from tip to base, deep within her core.

The stretching, the filling, the electric shock of pleasure, it brought back the fire—and that was even before he started pumping.

Stranger or not, he was careful with her, moving slowly at first, giving her a chance to adjust. And oh, God, adjust she did. Her sex reloosened as the friction increased, that great body above her own thrusting with growing urgency, another crest building deep inside of her until he was clapping against her, holding her roughly in place . . . fucking her.

This was not making love. There was nothing polite about where they were now or where they were headed—and she wanted it just like this, hard, fast, brutal.

It was a shock to realize that she was having the sex of her life, right here on the floor of this bald room, in almost-public. But holy hell was it *good*.

With a jerk, she brought his mouth back to hers and he was right on it, kissing her as his hips pistoned over and over again until there was no way to keep their lips together anymore.

Breaking off, he groaned again. "You're so tight. *Fuck* . . ."

His head dropped into her neck, and the idea that he was struggling to keep it together made her feel even more sexual, more liberated.

Oh, God, he smelled so good. And his hair was incredibly soft. And his beard scratched against her cheek . . .

In the back of her mind, she took notes on as much as she could absorb, well aware that she needed to remember each part of this, the whole thing. Because even though she was out of her mind, she wasn't kidding herself. This was a one-time-only—and it was so totally worth—

Her third orgasm was the most powerful of the bunch, making the others seem like just warm-ups, the rhythmic pulses contracting through her, her eyes clamping shut so hard she saw stars— and he followed along with her, his erection stabbing in and kicking inside of her over and over again. . . .

And then it was done.

So still.

They both went so still except for their breathing, which remained haggard.

In the aftermath, her body glowed from the exertion, her heart rate slowing gradually, the heat rolling out of her muscles and her skin until she began to feel the cool floor beneath her.

So good. The whole thing was exactly what she needed.

Except . . . as the silence began to sink into her addled brain, she thought, Now what? She had no clue how this was supposed to work—

"Duke?" a male voice said on the other side of the door. "You in there?"

Oh. Crap. Talk about a reality injection.

Her . . . lover, she supposed was the word for it, lifted his head and shot a glare upward. He also cranked his leg around and shoved his knee into the steel panel to make sure it wasn't opened—and in the process, reminded her that they were still very much joined.

Dear Lord, what had she gotten herself into?

"No, I'm not," he said in a guttural snarl.

Pause. "Duke, my man, you got someone in there with you?"

"No."

"Because the visual and the audio are off and we're concerned that you're—"

"He's not alone," Cait said sharply. "Okay?"

Pause. Longer this time. "Oh, Jesus, sorry . . . I, ah, shit, man, we never thought that you would be with a— I mean, you don't usually do that with the females, or, I mean, anyone, so, ah—"

"Later, Ivan," Duke snapped.

"Oh, yeah. Sure . . . absolutely, my man . . ."

The volume on the commentary drained out, like whoever it was, was walking off the apology. Or tripping over it, as was the case.

Duke focused on her, his expression utterly unreadable. "What he means is, I don't bang women at work."

"Then why'd you ask me here?"

"Because I couldn't wait any longer and you already had a date for tonight."

"What if I hadn't gone to the theater?"

"I'd have been stuck having to stalk that idiot singer until I ran into you again." This was said as if he'd rather have teeth pulled out of his head by a tractor.

Cait had to laugh. "G.B.'s music really not to your liking?"

For a moment, something cold flared in his face. "No. Not at all. You, however"—he brushed his lips across hers—"would be worth the audio suicide."

She brushed her hand though his short hair, and studied his face, memorizing it.

"I should go," she said eventually, even though in her heart of hearts she didn't want to. She just didn't know what the other option was—the sex had made him anything but a stranger. Unfortunately, that had only lasted while they were doing the deed.

His lids lowered. "I'm not finished with you."

Instantly, her heart started to pound again. She should probably try to play it cool, but she wanted more of him. In whatever form the sex took. Life was too damned short not to be transported to heaven at least one more time.

"Good," she said.

"Tell me your number."

After she recited the digits, she frowned. "Don't you want to write it down?"

"You're not that forgettable—trust me."

As if to prove the point, he took her mouth again and kissed her thoroughly, even as he reached between them to the base of his erection and held the condom in place while he withdrew.

Chilly air hit her most sensitive skin, and yup, that reminded her that her breasts were everywhere and so were her clothes.

A sudden image of the other set she'd left on her bathroom floor flashed before her eyes.

Maybe this was a trend?

Okaaaay . . . he was up and dressed so much faster than she was. Then he turned away, as if he knew she wanted a little privacy.

Getting to her feet, Cait pulled her jeans back on and then fumbled with her bra, the straps confounding her, the hitch in the middle of her back refusing to cooperate. The turtleneck was the same, going on messily over her head, her arms getting stuck.

"All right," she said.

As Duke pivoted back around, he seemed so remote, so tall, so removed.

Had they really just done that?

He opened the door without another word and the air that

rushed in smelled kind of like the salon's had, all kinds of shampoos and hair sprays mixing together. Which was strange. Maybe they had dancers somewhere in the club—

Oh, look, a group of big guys with black shirts that had STAFF printed on them. And they were allllll staring at her from their vantage point of about ten feet away.

Fantastic.

As Duke started to walk forward, she hid behind his shoulder to avoid meeting his colleagues in the eye—and what do you know, that was when reality set in.

Yup, that had actually happened. On the floor. Behind an unlocked door at his place of employment.

Shit. Maybe she couldn't handle being a blond, after all.

As Duke led the way over to the rear exit, he avoided the wide stares of his coworkers and did his best to block their sight of his lady friend. Not sure how successful he was at the latter. Damn it.

It wasn't that he was ashamed of what they'd done. She had come here for exactly what they had both wanted, and it had been awesome. But he wasn't going to have her gawked at.

The door opened outward, so he turned himself to the side, his broad body shielding her. And as she shuffled by him, her arm brushed across his chest, reminding him of all the different kinds of contact they'd just had on the floor of the interrogation room.

Mmmmmm.

Outside, she went over to a Lexus SUV of some sort—and he followed, tracking every move she made: Those hips were swaying, not in the hyper-extended way some women threw it, but in the natural fashion of a woman who'd been properly serviced. And the curve of her ass? He wanted to put his hands all over that—

His cock started to thicken, the sexual urge coming back to him like he hadn't been laid in weeks. Months. Maybe years.

She'd been . . . really fucking hot. Nervous, uncomfortable in the beginning . . . and then nothing but high-octane, full-bore with it during the sex, her nails ripping into his shoulders as she opened herself wide on the floor, uncaring about anything except the two of them coming together.

Not what he'd expected, to be honest.

This whole thing had started as a way to stake a claim against a man he hated. But the actual experience had shifted his goals. Now, this wasn't about a vendetta rooted in the past anymore—in fact, he'd meant exactly what he'd said to her. They weren't finished, and no, he most certainly did not need to write her number down. It was in his brain like those orgasms he'd given her were: indelibly.

As she hit her key fob and disengaged the Lexus's alarm, he jumped ahead, opening her door. And just as with the start, she didn't seem to know how to end things.

He did.

Stepping out of the way, he let her get into her seat and do up her belt and start her engine. Then, when she turned and looked up at him—

"We're not done yet," he said, the statement a bald demand more than anything romantic.

With a lunge, he went in for a dominating kiss, capturing the sides of her face in his palms, penetrating her mouth the same way he had back when she'd been naked and sprawled out underneath him.

She responded instantly. And as generously and openly as she had before.

She was like a well with no bottom.

To the point where he eyed her backseat. Pretty big. He didn't know much 'bout these fancy cars, but if she sat on his lap . . .

A shrill round of sirens brought his head up and out of the car. On the far side of the parking lot, a pair of cop cars were whistling down the back lane at a dead run—and they reminded him that as tough as he was, the boss lady didn't let her security guards pack, and the later it was, the more likely anybody was to get jumped in this part of town.

This woman might well be safe with him right now, but she still had a drive to get out of here.

"You'd better go," he said, refocusing on her face. Her hair was all messed up, and he liked the fact that his hands had been the cause.

Especially considering who the other option had been.

"Yes . . ." she whispered.

"Go now." Before he stopped thinking straight and started getting her into that backseat.

Duke shut the door before she could say anything else. And then for some reason, as he stepped away, he was suddenly totally and completely anxious—something he did not have much experience with.

He was better with aggressive. Much better.

And he really didn't want to look at the fear too closely.

As she reversed out of her spot, he walked forward, staying in her headlights, staring through the bright illumination, meeting her in the eyes even though he couldn't see them.

And then she was gone.

Duke took some deep breaths and pulled it together. A moment later, he went to look at his watch—and was reminded that his Rolex had disappeared. Taking his phone out of the back pocket of his jeans, he checked the time that way.

Damn it. Too early to leave so he had to go back in and face the music.

And gee, what do you know. Big Rob, Silent Tom, and Ivan were still kibitzing, now by Alex's door.

Duke headed in the opposite direction, back to the interrogation room. Which proved to be a dumb idea. As he went over to that far corner and started to reattach the wires to the monitoring units, the three of them took the opportunity to line up like they were at a zoo and had taken an interest in one of the tigers.

"Don't ask," Duke said. "Not one of you ask a single frickin' thing."

When he finally had to turn back around to them, he thought, Fucking hell, even Silent Tom, who never took much of an interest in anything, was focused on him.

"She's not from here," one of the three—not Tom—said.

Done with his little tech job, Duke pushed his way through the other bouncers. With any luck, there'd be a couple of stragglers in the bar area who he could muscle out the front door—preferably when it was closed and locked.

One thing he was *not* going to do was discuss with the old ladies on his tail the woman, the hookup, or any future plans.

Out in the club proper, he was bummed. The lights had been cranked up, the chaos of a busy night showing in all the wet places on the floor, and the cockeyed furniture, and the dropped napkins—and the condom wrappers.

How romantic.

As he started to do a sweep, the brigade of boots following behind him proved that gossip wasn't just for sixteen-year-old girls with Hello Kitty fetishes. Apparently, yoked-up muscleheads could be into it, too.

Duke spun around. "No. No. And no."

One for each of the nosy bastards.

"You were out of sight for a while," Big Rob drawled. "So there was a 'yes' in there somewhere."

So not doing this.

As he turned away, Ivan said, "Come on, man, it's just, you haven't—"

The voice that cut the guy off wasn't one he recognized. Then again, Silent Tom hadn't gotten his nickname for no good reason: "Okay, boys, let's back off."

That was all it took.

Maybe the other two hadn't ever heard him speak either, and were too shocked to keep bloodhounding their other colleague.

Whatever it was, Duke thanked God as he was left in peace—

Stopping in his tracks, he realized . . . his woman had never given him her name.

At least he had those digits, though.

Chapter
Nineteen

When Jim came awake in a hospital bed, all he could think was, Maybe it had been a dream. Maybe . . . the whole thing, from meeting Nigel and the other archangels, to the Devina nightmare, to the game itself . . . had just been a product of the electrocution at the job site.

A fiction created by an overload of neurological stimulation.

And assuming that were true? Well, then, Adrian was fiction, and so was Eddie and the fact that the guy had died. There were also no souls to be saved. No Heaven and Hell, either—at least not that he had to be concerned with.

He had nothing to worry about other than simple problems like paying monthly bills and whether his truck was running sound under the hood.

Shiiiiiiit, whoever didn't think normal was bliss? Hadn't lived very hard.

Closing his eyes, he reached over his head and pulled himself into a glorious, full-body stretch, the relief pouring through him. He was free for the first time in his adult life. Free of his shady work as a member of XOps. No longer the puppet of a cruel mastermind. And not now or ever a "savior" tasked with rescuing humanity from a bored Creator and a super-bitch demon—

"You're finally awake."

Jim jacked up off the pillows.

Across the room, sitting in a chair, Sissy Barten was alive and well.

Which meant they were both dead. And his reality hadn't really changed.

"Fuck," he breathed, easing back down and shutting his eyes again. Wonder how many hours he'd been out? Hard to know. Felt like a while.

"Are you okay?"

Bringing his hands to his face, he rubbed, hard—at least until every pain receptor in his entire body told him to CUT THAT OUT RIGHT THIS SECOND.

Ah, yes. His face had in fact gone through the windshield.

And that meant his truck was wrapped around a tree, his head had sustained a trauma, and his leg was fucked-up. It also meant that somewhere, at this very moment, if not sooner, a police officer was running the plates on the F-150 and discovering that the vehicle was registered to a dead man . . . who looked exactly like Jim.

"We've got to get out of here." With a groan, he sat up, swung his legs around, and saw, oh, joy, that he had a cast on his left calf.

Nothing he could do about that at the moment.

Redirecting, he started to go to work on the inside of his arm, taking out the IV with practiced efficiency. "Come on—"

As alarms started going off behind the bed, Sissy shook her head. "Oh, no, I'm not going anywhere. The doctor came in with the nurse. You've got a concussion and . . ."

Jim let her keep talking as he got on his feet and tested out his left leg. Sore. Very sore. But thanks to the cast, it held his weight well enough that he could hobble around and look for some clothes. Rifling through the mostly empty closet, all he could think of was the last time he'd done this, in this hospital. That nurse had been a battle-ax, but—

Sissy stepped in front of him. "Get back in that bed. You're not leaving."

"Oh, really." He leaned down so they were eye-to-eye. "Let me clue you in on something. I don't actually exist in this world, and I've learned from experience, you can't have a foot in both places. It fucks with their heads."

"Your leg is broken."

"Doesn't bother me at all."

"Then why are you limping."

"I'm not."

She glared right into his face. "Do you know the definition of the word?"

"Do you know how fast we gotta get going here?"

Moving around her, he started opening drawers in a shallow, fake-wood cabinet. Nothing. No pants, shirt, boots. "Don't worry about me. I've had much worse and lived."

"Except for that one time when you died, right." Sissy went back and sat in the chair. "Whatever, I'm staying. Where you go off to is your problem, not mine."

Jim cranked around and blinked away his double vision— okay, clearly, he was in a lot of pain, but he was backseating the sensation so completely, he was unaware of anything other than his internal directive to get-the-fuck-out-of-here. "You're crazy."

"All things considered, I'd say that's your diagnosis, not mine—"

"Much as I loathe to agree with him, the fool has got a point."

The dry English tones brought both their heads around.

"Colin," Jim muttered. "Nice to see you."

Not.

The archangel was dressed in whites, but it was his version of same, not Nigel's—white track pants, white T-shirt, white Converse All Stars. He looked like a Beastie Boy. Or . . . a hot guy who most women would enjoy looking at.

And for some reason, that cranked Jim out—especially as Sissy slowly got to her feet and came forward. For shit's sake, it would have been so much better if the guy had been decrepit or sported a stick up the ass, like Nigel did. But nooooo, he was nothing but tall, dark and haloed. In short, not Sissy's type.

At least, not if Jim had anything to do with—

Wait a minute. Was he actually getting jealous here? In a hospital room. When Sissy was doing nothing but simply stare at the slick bastard?

Guess the concussion thing was right enough—and apparently, the sector in his brain responsible for having any fucking sense at all had been shut down by the swelling.

Jim kicked shut the drawer with his bad foot and nearly passed out. "I got this, Colin," he muttered.

When neither of them paid any attention to him, he put his body in between the two. "I. Got. This."

Colin cocked a dark eyebrow. "Actually, mate, there's considerable uncertainty about that—which presents us all with a problem, doesn't it. You've got a lot riding on you."

"Thanks for the recap. But I'm tight."

"Then why would you be here on a ward with your head in bandages and your leg—"

"Because shit happens, Colin, okay? Now will you leave—"

"You must take care of your business." Colin's stare narrowed. "Before you compound your bad decisions."

Jim leaned in, even though he was in no shape to fight about things. "I *am* taking care of—"

"Not that business—"

"Sir?"

Annnnd here was another interruption, this time by a nurse who had thrown the door open. "Sir? Please get back in bed—"

Ignoring her, he focused on Colin. "I can handle—"

"Who are you talking to? And, sir—your IV! You took it out?"

Cue the chaos. Suddenly there were people in white coats and scrubs all over the place, all of them talking at him—while Sissy backed up into the wall, and Colin looked on with a bored expression.

Jim shoved the medical staff away, at least until a six-footer got up into his personal space and announced, "There's no AMA checkout for you. You're going nowhere until the police take you down to book you."

Jim rolled his eyes. "You actually think I'm going to get arrested?"

"It's called reckless driving. Misappropriation of identity. Assault—remember when you tackled that paramedic? We had to treat him for lacerations, by the way."

With a curse, Jim tried to collect his shit, to concentrate, to throw out some kind of magic, anything that would help him control this mess. And it should have worked, goddamn it. Ever since Eddie had taught him the how-to's, he'd been able to take care of things the *I Dream of Jeannie* way.

Except . . . fuck, it hadn't worked back on that street. And as he tried again . . . and again . . . and again . . . and nothing happened . . . he knew it wasn't working now.

"Get back in that bed, sir," the orderly said. "Or I'm going to put you there myself."

Through his haze of pain and frustration, Jim figured there were two obvious options: Lie down like a good boy and wait for the CPD to crawl up his ass . . . or let Colin take care of things.

He picked door number three.

Wheeling around, he grabbed the chair Sissy had been sitting in and hauled it at the plate-glass window across the way. Just as contact was made, he took one last go at the magic routine—and things must have come together somehow, at least slightly: The four-by-five-foot section blew outward, exploding into the night and letting the cold air plow into the room.

Jim traded places with the dark breeze.

Diving through the opening, he went into a tuck as he hit a brief free fall. Then he rolled out on the gravel-topped roof of the building that was one story down from where he'd been.

Man, thank God for the jigsaw-puzzle architecture of most medical centers—he'd only guessed there would be a roof to catch him; he hadn't known for sure.

As he took off at a sloppy run, he had a momentary communion with Adrian and everything that other angel had to deal with. What a painful pain in the ass this broken leg was, the shocks of incredible agony making his heart thunder in his chest and his head go fuzzy. But he refused to let the physical stuff matter. In fact, it felt like old home week as he put aside the problems within his body and gunned hard for the far edge of the building.

He prayed there was something at that end that he could use to get to the ground.

He also prayed that Sissy understood he wasn't deserting her. Not for long, at any rate. The bottom line, however, was that Colin was with her, and Jim knew that Devina wouldn't go anywhere near the archangel. He also knew that for all the angel's annoyance? He wouldn't leave an innocent to fend for herself; he just wouldn't.

All Jim needed was enough time to regain some of his power

because shit knew he was useless in that sea of humans in his current condition—

Off in the distance, shouts broke out behind him, echoing down from that hole he'd made in the building.

Sorry, fellas. But look on the bright side, that window was one last thing for the cleaning staff to disinfect.

Shuffling along, he headed past some industrial fans and was, thank you, baby Jesus, provided with a way down: Over at the corner, dull security lights illuminated the curled arms of a ladder.

As soon as he got over to the thing, he swung himself up and around and then slid down like he was on a pair of ropes. Landing in a heap, he had to catch his breath, his leg hurting way more than his head, his eyes sweeping around, looking for an opportunity through an irritating haze.

He knew he didn't have a lot of time. Hospital this size? It was going to have a big security force that was jacked into a central command.

Dragging himself up to his feet, he cut through a rear delivery courtyard, navigating thanks to halogen lamps set up high on the concrete-block walls—

As sirens began to wail, he was willing to bet they weren't ambulances. Try the real police coming to look for him, too.

Fucking hell, why couldn't he find a car to break into?

Coming around a corner, a set of squealing tires had him skidding to a halt—just before the heavy steel body of a Mercedes wiped him out.

The passenger-side window went down, and the one female on the face of the planet that he never wanted to see again smiled at him.

"Trouble in paradise?" the demon drawled as she leaned across the leather seats.

"Fuck me . . ."

"Get in and I will," she told him with an evil smile. "Otherwise, guess you'll take your chances with the CPD."

As Sissy's hobbling, pissed-off savior launched himself out of the window he'd busted, she bolted forward like maybe she could catch him and pull him bodily back into the hospital room—and she wasn't the only one with that crazy idea.

Unfortunately, the hospital staff got there first, crowding the view, blocking her out.

Oh, God, if he couldn't survive a car accident without ending up here? Falling five floors down to the ground was probably going to kill him—

Okay, so maybe he was already dead, but whatever. Angels in the real world could obviously still sustain broken bones and injuries that were more than cosmetic. And maybe there was something she could do to help him—

Frantic, she pushed into the knot of nurses and doctors who were shouting and arguing in front of the gaping hole, forgetting that she wasn't really there, that she was no longer "human," that she was—

It was hard to say what happened exactly.

One moment, she was shoving against someone, and the next . . . she could see out of the window, visualizing the one-story, not five, drop to the roof below.

And that was what she'd been after. The trouble was, it was from a different height. And her sense of color was off. And her body felt really weird.

Bringing up a hand to rub her eyes, she froze . . .

And then screamed.

Instantly, everyone turned to her. "Mary? What's wrong?" somebody said.

"Move her to the bed. Get her on the bed! For God's sake, this is how her brother died—"

"I don't have a brother," Sissy mumbled.

"Shh," one of the nurses soothed. "Come here. Sit."

Sissy lifted that hand again and found that it was still . . . not her own. Pudgy, wrinkly, with a set of wedding rings that needed to be cleaned, the thing was under her control—she was able to flex the fingers and turn it over to see the palm—but it was not hers.

Looking down, she saw that she was no longer in the loose baggy shirt and rolled-up sweats Jim had given her. Instead, she was wearing a set of blue scrubs and had a pair of laminated IDs on a lanyard around her neck. Picking them off a chest that was about eight sizes bigger than her own, she stared at a picture of a fifty-year-old woman named Mary T. Santiago.

Wheeling around, she confronted the other angel, the one who had come in before Jim had gone out the window. "What am I?"

The Englishman's haughty, hard face registered a momentary shock. "You are . . . not supposed to be able to do that."

"What did I do?"

One of the male orderlies stepped in front of her and there was real fear on his face. "Mary, you're okay. You're all right . . ."

"What did I do!" she shouted around him.

The first of the female nurses addressed her. "Mary, you didn't do anything. You weren't even there when he jumped. Mary, oh, Mary . . ."

As Sissy was encased in a hug, she smelled a faded perfume, and some kind of astringent, and felt . . . well, mostly an incredible sense of support. Out of reflex, she put her arms—or Mary's arms, as it were—around the other woman, her mind scrambling to understand how this was possible.

"Just step out of her," the Englishman said crisply. "That's the way it works—or so I've heard."

"Step . . . out . . . ?" she mumbled.

"Shh, Mary, it's okay." The nurse started in with some soothing strokes of Mary's hair—which Sissy felt as clearly as if it were
her own. "Just breathe with me."

For some reason, maybe because she needed a hug and the
nurse was damned good at giving them, Sissy closed the eyes that
were not her own and gave herself up to the comfort.

"That's it. I know this is hard. . . ."

Dimly, Sissy was aware of some others arriving in the hospital
room—blue-uniformed officers who had security badges on their
sleeves. She then felt herself get inched away so that she wasn't
anywhere near the black hole in the room.

As she breathed a little easier, she became aware of a psyche
other than her own. It was in the background, thoughts and feelings and memories of another person, suppressed by God only
knew what.

Step out? she thought. How was that going to work? If she had
any impulse to move, the other woman's body responded.

"Will yourself free," the Englishman said. "Just decide to separate."

Sissy listened to the command like she had the ones her
coaches had given her in field hockey, ordering herself into an action that was more interior than exterior.

As she broke away from the nurse, she watched as the shorter,
older woman she had just inhabited went down like a stone, fainting dead away. Immediately, Sissy lunged forward to catch her, but
her arms had no substance, and Mary Santiago slid onto the linoleum floor, going through Sissy's attempt at throwing out a hold
like water through thin air.

Sissy backed away until she felt the far wall come up against
her back.

"I don't understand any of this," she said, panic twitching her face, shaking her hands. "I don't . . . know where I was. How I got in there. Why I got out."

She looked at the man in white. "I need answers."

It was an accusation—as if he knew, and was deliberately keeping her in the dark just to piss her off.

The man—angel, whatever—drew a hand through his black hair. "Bugger. Fucking . . . bugger."

"I'm not sure what that means exactly, but if you think this all sucks? Then I'm right with you—and while we're bonding? Do you have any idea where Jim went?"

The Englishman crossed his arms over his sizable chest and glared at the broken window. "Don't get me started on him right now."

As he stayed silent in the midst of the chaos, anger boiled deep inside of her again, sharpening her tone. "Okay, well, how about you help me with myself, then."

When he transferred that narrowed stare to her, she noticed that his eyes were a color she'd never seen before—and wasn't that a good reminder that she was dealing with something way outside of normal. Maybe something dangerous.

For a split second, she thought about backing down—except then she reminded herself that she had nothing to lose: She'd already been in Hell, and her life as she'd known it here on Earth was over.

So what the good goddamn could he do to her.

"I'm waiting," she snapped.

Chapter
Twenty

"You know, I'm more than willing to nurse you back to health."

When Jim didn't reply, Devina glanced across the seat. The angel was steaming pissed, big-time banged-up, and in the most pathetic excuse for a hospital johnny she'd ever seen—and he was still captivating in a way that made her think of her OCD.

She wanted him that badly.

"You could come and stay with me for a while," she said.

He glared over at her, the glow from the strips of blue lights that ran down the Mercedes's doors making him seem deliciously evil. "I already have roommates. You killed one of them, remember?"

She batted that stupidity away. "Please. Eddie should have seen that coming, and because he didn't, he got what he deserved. How is the dear boy, by the way? Still smelling like a rose?"

Jim just looked out the front windshield, that jaw clenching, his hand curling into a tight fist.

Yummy.

Coming up to a stoplight, she began to get excited. They were together again, alone at last, and how could all kinds of dating scenarios not go through her mind? Maybe they could head back to the dirty part of town, park the car, and go see some after-hours porn? The strip clubs were closed, which was a bummer—then again, she wasn't sure she wanted to be around him while he was looking at naked women. She was liable to kill the bitches.

Yeah, seeing porn movies in public sounded like a great idea— with some live action between the pair of them as a chaser. With that annoying vestal virgin around, she wanted to filthy him up. Get him nice and nasty so that when he went home and little Sissy-Two-shoes looked up at him with those big blue eyes, he felt ashamed of where he'd been and what he'd done.

On that note, maybe she should just pull over and blow him?

When he kept quiet, she checked him out. The angel was still sitting there, looking incredibly bangable—as well as hostile. And wasn't that the perfect combination. For her, aggression and hatred were Molly and oysters, baby.

And she wasn't the only one who was into that shit. Jim liked it, too—in fact, she thought fondly of their last private time, down by the river, in that boathouse. The two of them had been so pissed off and sexed up. So hot. So fucking hot . . .

Try giving him some of *that*, Sissy Barten.

"I'm surprised you got in the car," Devina said in a moment of weakness.

"This way I know where you are."

The demon put a hand to her collarbone. "I'm touched."

"Don't be."

Oh, wasn't that his way, she thought with a smile. Fighting the inevitable with everything he had—even though he had to know he was going to give in, in the end, and let them have what they both wanted.

At least . . . she had to believe that he would, even with that girl in his possession.

Surely that wasn't going to change things.

Right?

Abruptly unsettled, Devina drove around the junkie part of town, passing by abandoned houses, and storefronts that were boarded up. Her Benz got noticed, the humans who were lying against the buildings and propped up at the bases of cracked stairwells looking over as she went by—and not just because hers was the only car on the street.

Jim still wasn't saying anything.

And that made her feel unstable.

"There's a knife in my purse." She nodded at the Gucci sack between them. "If you're feeling like you have to let something out."

Some hard-core foreplay was probably just what the doctor ordered for the pair of them—oh, yeah, she was getting hot just thinking about it—

"I'm not going to kill myself over you."

She glanced back over. "I was thinking you might like to come at me—or in me, even better."

"Never going to happen."

Devina bore down on the steering wheel. "You know, you don't treat me very well."

The laugh he let out was a curse if she'd ever heard one. "You're fucking incredible."

Devina smiled. "Why, thank you."

"Not a compliment."

"I'll take it any way I choose."

She stopped at a traffic light and thought, Hmmm, maybe if they went classy, she'd have more success.

Hitting the directional signal, she doubled back and headed for the world-famous Freidmont Hotel. Located in the heart of

Caldwell's business district, it was the grande dame of downtown, a place where the old ways were still preserved: the doormen wore white gloves, the concierge was available at his desk in the lobby twenty-four hours a day, and the tub in your suite's bathroom was deep as an Olympic swimming pool.

Romance. She could use some romance. And she'd still have her knife with her if they wanted to get a little kinky.

Ten minutes later, she pulled up to the regal facade.

Jim looked over. "What's this for?"

"I thought we could get a room."

"For what."

Devina frowned. "What do you mean?"

"You don't actually think I'm going to fuck you."

Feeling like she'd been slapped across the face, Devina had to blink her vision clear. "I don't understand what the problem is."

"You *actually* think I'm going to spend the night with you—"

"I just want us to be together—"

"Then you are totally delusional, bitch."

Losing her temper, she spat, "I'm trying to make this work, Jim. Even after everything you've done to me!"

"What exactly have *I* done to *you*? Other than save your sorry ass with that trade we just did."

Devina was vaguely aware that she was breathing heavily, and that, tragically, Jim was not focused on her heaving breasts.

Talk about criminal. Her bustier was red as blood and fit more perfectly than the skin she was in. How could he not look?

At that moment, a uniformed doorman came around to her.

Not wanting to be rude, and hoping that there was still a date possibility open somehow, she put her window down. "We'll just be a second."

The guy seemed confused—oh, right, Jim wasn't showing himself.

Devina smiled. "I mean, I'll be a moment."

"Of course, ma'am."

As the doorman went back to his station just inside the entrance, Jim leaned into her, but not for a kiss. "Listen up, sweetheart. You and me? We don't have a relationship, and we're not fucking anymore. Ever. No matter what you do, or where you take shit, or how this cocksucking game shakes out? I'm not tapping that again."

Devina recoiled. She'd seen him in a lot of moods over the last four rounds, but never like this. He wasn't being pissy or showing off or playing hard to get.

Bedrock. In his eyes, there was nothing but granite.

He went for the door handle before she could hit the locks, and then he was out of her car, limping along with that cast, his hospital johnny opening from the back and flashing his ass.

The motherfucker didn't look back. And he was going home to . . .

The demon's stiletto slammed on the accelerator without her being consciously aware of it, and she aimed the Mercedes right at him, her headlights becoming gun sights, her car a bullet.

Her target, seen only by her.

As Jim wrenched around, his face showed nothing. It was as if he were already dead—duh.

In the instant before impact, he closed his eyes, but not in a bracing kind of way: He was trying to concentrate himself out of there.

It worked. Tragically.

Just before he disappeared, there was a bump, like she'd hit a pothole—but then he was out of her sight . . . ghosting away to his other life, the one that pitted him against her.

Devina hit the brakes, and her car behaved perfectly, coming to a complete stop just before she hit the curb. Yanking at the handle, she shoved the door open and got out. Someone whistled at her—and God help them, literally, if they decided to follow through on any of that goddamn shit right now. She was liable to eat them alive.

Coming around to the front of the Mercedes, she checked out the grille. Not a mark. Both headlights were totally intact and functioning. No dents in the hood.

She'd hit him, though. Surely, she'd—

Yes, she had. The iconic circular symbol of the carmaker was ever so slightly crooked . . . and when she snapped the thing free and examined it in the bright white glow of her high beams, she saw there was a red stain on the stainless steel—but it was simply a surface imperfection, nothing more.

So she hadn't hurt him.

Infuriated, she hauled back to throw—

Devina stopped. Retracted her arm. Focused on what she held.

The symbol was heavy in her hand, heavier than it would have been if she'd weighed it—because the angel had left something behind in the metal . . .

Thanks to the hood ornament having clipped some part of his body, probably his leg.

Well, well, well . . . wasn't this a bright spot on the horizon.

Objects, particularly metal objects, retained part of their possessors, and even though there had only been a split second of connection, the pain the impact had caused Jim, the raw mental state he had been in, the weakness of his corporeal form . . . all of that meant that something of him had been fused into what was now a very, very valuable commodity to her.

Extending her tongue, she licked his blood off the outer rim and smiled.

Inadvertently, he had given her the key to his castle.

Chapter
Twenty-one

When Sissy opened the door to Jim's house, it was a cliché that the thing creaked. And as she shut herself in and looked around, shades of seventies horror movies, the kind she'd watched with her sister on Sundays, came back to her.

Stalling out in the front receiving hall, she didn't know what to do. The Englishman had dropped her off here in the same way Chillie had tossed the paper onto the porch—except the angel's aim had been better. She'd made it to the front door on the first try.

And now, left to her own devices, her anger, her sense that destiny was for shit and fate just another word for "screwed," made her feel as though someone had their hands around her throat and was squeezing.

What was she going to do now? She had no idea where Jim or his roommate were, and no clue what she could do, if anything, to help them . . .

Surrounded by the colossal old mansion, with all of its decayed luxury, her mind retreated from the present and sought shelter in memory, her thoughts going back to happier days, when the week had had a reliable rhythm of work and time off, when her family had been something she'd had the luxury of taking advantage of, when her goals had been things like graduating from Union and finding a job . . . and maybe meeting a guy she could marry.

Sundays had been all about Vincent Price for her and Dell.

Those horror movies she and her sister had been into had been the "safe" sort of scary-scaries. Nothing gruesome, like the *Saw* series, but old-fashioned stalwarts like *The Abominable Dr. Phibes* and *The House of Usher* and *The Innocents*. It had been an arguably strange tradition, she and Dell impatiently waiting until family dinner was finished and their homework done before raiding their father's DVD collection and snuggling up in the basement in the dark. They had watched one or two before bed every week during school.

It had been the best way to chill out and get ready for the six-thirty alarm clocks of Monday and the pressure of the M-T-W-R-F ahead.

Mom had maintained that they were sick in the head. Dad had been so proud that he was raising the next generation of movie appreciators. She and Dell had just liked being together.

Haunted by the past, Sissy walked into the parlor and turned on one of the glass lamps. Its shade was probably a single season in the sun away from total disintegration, the creamy yellow a function of age-staining rather than any decor choice.

Boy, her sister would love this place, the furniture all a mystery because it was shrouded, the faded Oriental rug big as a lawn, the dark wood molding carved so deeply it was like a horizontal statue running around the high ceiling.

From what she'd seen, the entire house just offered more of the same.

It was the kind of fancy living that people wrote books about, but this version had been distilled through the grinder of a reversal of fortunes, a case of history not translating well into the present thanks to a lack of funds.

Pity.

Crossing over, she lifted up one of the sheets. Underneath, a faded green velvet sofa with all kinds of curlicues looked orphaned.

She ripped the covering off. Went on to the wing chair next to it and did the same. Kept going around the parlor, moving faster and more violently, until dust hung thick in the air and a pile of dirty laundry took up most of the middle of the room.

At least she'd gotten to the bottom of something.

Not her issues, though. Not in the slightest.

The angel who'd escorted her here from the hospital had magically transported her across town, but it had been without explanations—he'd told her nothing about herself, her situation, or exactly how he'd pulled off the relocation. He'd also left alone things like how he was tied to Jim, and why he'd come to them, and what his role was.

Just more black holes to add to her collection.

Pacing around, she followed the oval pattern on the carpet because it seemed like the only clear path open to her. That anger that had taken root earlier was rising again, making her feel trapped in spite of the fact that the door she'd come through was not locked, the house had dozens and dozens of rooms, and unlike in her previous life, she had no one she had to answer to—no parents, no teachers, no roommates at Union.

She was free.

So why the hell did she want to scream.

Hard to know what exactly started it, but before she knew what she was doing, she was frantically searching the fireplace's mantel, going up high on her tiptoes in those borrowed sneakers, patting the cobwebbed shelf around the candelabra and the—

The little box rattled as she brought it down, and yup, there were matches inside.

Moving in a jerky frenzy, she ripped a sheet off the pile, shoved it into the fireplace, and struck up a flame.

Holding the teardrop-shaped glow to eye level, she stared into the yellow heat, and the fury in her expanded even further, flowing through her body, changing the shape of her, growing deep within—sure as if it were cultivating in her soul, finding crevices to root among and take over from.

Dropping to her knees, the cold marble bit into her skin through the sweatpants, but she didn't care—she brought the tiny fire to the tangled wad and held it there. Smoke rose first, a tendril forming and then quickly thickening into a rolling river.

Proper flames appeared, flaring up, licking at the sheeting, consuming the cotton fibers with increasing greed.

Unable to look away, Sissy reached behind herself, stretching out until she connected with the soft pile she had made. Dragging more forward, she fed the heat, pushing the sheets into the blaze, feeling the burn on her hands, her wrists, her arms, her face.

In her head, a string of curses was like the fire she was creating, flaring to life, consuming—

"What the fuck!"

Sissy ignored whoever it was, utterly focused on her inferno as she wondered what else she could put in it. The drapes. She could rip down the—

Hard hands grabbed onto her shoulders and yanked her back—and that was when she lost it. Just f'in lost it.

As if detonated, she went crazy, screaming, kicking, biting at whatever she could get access to. And as she attacked, her vision whited out, nothing registering except the need to hurt someone, anyone—

With the inner explosion came a freakish strength.

Which was how she ended up twisting around and kneeing her captor right in the balls.

"Fucking hell—*fuck*!"

For a split second, the hold on her loosened, and she took advantage of the release, bolting out from the smoke-filled parlor and tearing for the front door. Grabbing the handle, she ripped things open and launched herself off the steps, landing in a messy sprawl on the wide sidewalk. Shoving her hair out of her face, she—

Headlights.

Down the lane on the left, coming toward her.

Jumping up to her feet, she ran for the car or truck or SUV, streaking out into the road, facing off, thinking of how Jim had gotten hurt. She wanted to feel the impact, wanted to be solid enough to sustain the strike, to have at least one of the old rules of life apply to her: Don't play in traffic because you will get hit.

"Sissy! Shit!"

"See me!" she screamed at the approaching lights. "*See me!*"

"Sissy, goddamn it!"

Her prayers were answered for once. Just when she thought she'd be denied, the car's horn blared loud enough to get through the fury that was driving her. Then she had a brief impression of the driver looking right at her in terror, some inside light in the sedan illuminating his pale face with eyes stretched wide and a mouth open as if he were yelling—

She was bodily removed from the path, a far greater weight

muscling her out of the way as brakes squealed and the world spun.

She landed on the grass strip on the far side of the road, her savior's body crushing her, pain both clearing her head and scrambling it in a different way. Instantly, she was spun onto her back, her arms pinned over her head, her legs trapped in between two heavy thighs.

Above her, Jim looked as pissed off as she felt—

"Where did she go?"

Dimly, she turned her head. A man was getting out of the BMW that had almost hit her and looking around frantically. "She was right there in the middle of the road."

A woman emerged from the other side of the sedan. "I saw her, too. She came out of nowhere."

Just like that cat, Sissy thought numbly as her anger dissipated. The one that had jumped in front of Jim's truck earlier.

"I'm over here," she called out weakly. "God . . . I'm over here. . . ."

The two of them focused in her direction. "Did you hear that?" the man asked.

"Hear what?" the woman said.

The man approached, but it was clear he couldn't really see her anymore. And as she opened her mouth to yell again, Jim clamped his hand on her mouth, silencing her.

"Don't you think we have enough problems," he hissed.

She tried to fight against him, but without her fury, there was no contest: He was way stronger, and stilled her without any real effort. And as expected, shortly thereafter, the couple got back in their luxury car and drove off.

As their red taillights flared, her frustration rekindled.

This was it? After all the good deeds she'd done in her life, after everything she'd unfairly been through down below, her eternity was getting stuck in the halfway-house version of an afterlife? Neither here nor there, Heaven nor Hell—nothing but a shadow that could take shape on rare occasions and maybe make car drivers hit their brakes in passing?

Fucking *bullshit*.

"I'm going to let you up," Jim said. "Okay?"

Sissy nodded and waited for him to pull back, giving him all the time in the world to misjudge how calm she was . . . and when he finally did—

She went back at him, flailing with her fists and kicking with her legs until the pair of them were rolling around on the sidewalk, the concrete scratching her forearms, her calves, her cheeks. She didn't care—she was crazed again, her fire finding another corner of her emotions that had yet to be immolated.

And maybe Jim knew that. Because instead of sitting on her again, he let her go while still controlling her, fending off her attack with moves so practiced, it was as if he anticipated her strikes before she even thought of them.

Which naturally just pissed her off even more.

Eventually, even though she felt at her core that she could go on for ages, she ran out of gas, her body getting sloppy, her strength ebbing: The anger didn't disappear; there was just no more physical energy left to provide an outlet for it—

Sissy ended up collapsing against his chest, breathing in ragged bursts, unable to lift her head, much less her fists.

Closing her eyes, she cursed long and hard inside her head . . . because, God knew, she still couldn't get enough air down into her lungs.

When she finally found her voice, she said hoarsely, "Why me . . ."

And then abruptly, she shoved herself away from him. "And why do you care so much about me—I don't know you—"

"Sissy, look, I know you've been through a lot—"

"Just leave me alone, okay? If I want to get hit by a car, let me do it—"

"Sorry, but I can't."

"Then actually help me! Tell me where I am—"

"I wish I could—"

"Whatever," she derided. "You want to keep your day job as an angel? There're another two hundred and fifty million people in this country—go save them. But as of this moment, I'm not your problem, and you are not mine."

Getting to her feet and brushing herself off, Sissy stared into the street and felt cheated. But at least they had seen her; they really had—

A rough hand clamped onto her arm and snapped her around.

Her savior didn't look like anything close to a saint. His eyes were narrowed into slits, his upper lip had curled off his teeth, and the rage radiating out of him was probably the only thing that could have gotten through to her.

His voice, when he spoke, was a snarl. "I saw you dead, how 'bout that. I broke through a door and found you bled the fuck out. I was too late to save you then, so call me stupid for trying to do right by you now." He stuck his finger in her face. "You want to get all frustrated and shit because you don't know who you are? Fine. But don't burn down my fucking house, and don't resent me because I don't fucking know what your deal is." He jabbed his finger at his own chest. "You think I know myself in this mess? I don't. I don't have a goddamn clue about so much of it all. Jesus Christ."

With that, he was the one who spun off and went back for the house, all the while dragging that injured leg behind him like it hurt like hell.

How he was walking on that cast, she had no idea. . . .

As she watched him go back across the road, she regretted the whole evening. And yet even as she calmed down, under her surface . . . the anger was still there, simmering along.

To think she'd assumed that Hell would be the worst thing that happened to her.

This . . . seemed so much harder.

Chapter
Twenty-two

Jim locked himself in his bedroom. And it wasn't because he was sulking.

He didn't trust himself at the moment. He was beat to shit, partially starved, and angry as hell—not exactly a trifecta of healthy relating.

Rifling through his stuff, he found, through the grace of God, a pack of unopened Marlboros in his winter parka. As he lit one up and sat down on his bed, he ran through what he was going to need to cut the cast off his leg. Some kind of saw?

Underneath the plaster or whatever the hell it was, he knew damn well the bone was probably still broken, but similar to the way the scratches on the backs of his hands were healing in front of his eyes, the leg had to be doing the same. Guess it made sense. What kind of savior would he be if he was sidelined by injury?

Wonder if he cut off his arm, would it grow back?

Exhaling, he watched the smoke curl up toward the ceiling.

Then he put the cig in between his teeth and went for his crystal knife—the one he had left. 'Cuz the other was in the cab of his truck—or in the CPD's evidence room, more likely.

The weapon was as beautiful as it was deadly, the ultimate lights-out switch for minions and harpies alike—two subspecies of demon he had had the joy of coming into contact with lately. It was also handy-dandy when it came to exorcisms, as he'd learned in the first round.

Shit, that felt like forever ago.

As he turned the blade over in his palm, the prism caught the illumination from the lamp on the bureau, a rainbow of colors flashing and making him think of Eddie.

That angel wouldn't have approved of any of this. Not the trade. Not Sissy here on this side. Not the distractions.

Jim took another drag and angled the tip onto the cast, right in front, below his knee. As he pushed down, there was some initial resistance, but then the plaster gave way, the blade cleaving a path down, down, down along his shinbone. Jim was careful to go slowly—and as he progressed, all kinds of in-the-field injuries came back to him, times when he'd been cut or wounded and had had no medical anything to fall back on.

Just like the good ol' days. Except he wasn't getting shot at while he was treating himself.

Things were looking up.

Although, meh . . . if he were honest, he felt like he'd been popped in the sternum by a forty. As long as he lived, in any sense of the word, he was never going to forget the sight of Sissy rushing into the path of that car.

Seeing her dead once had been more than enough—and then he'd had the chaser of her being in Hell. Yup, more than plenty, thanks.

Just leave me alone, okay?

Refocusing, he finished the cutting job at his foot and laid the blade aside on the messy sheets. After taking a drag on his cigarette, he turned his fingers into claws and penetrated the fault line he'd created in the plaster, prying the cast apart until it cracked free and fell off.

His leg looked just the same. So not a compound fracture, obviously.

Rubbing his calf to get rid of the itchies, he finished his coffin nail and ground the thing out. Then he stood up and put some weight on his leg as a test. Held like a dream. Achy? Yes. But it worked—and with the help of its twin, took him out and to the bathroom, where he ditched the johnny, showered, shaved, and brushed his teeth.

His stomach was hungry. The rest of him was not. In fact, as he went back to his room with a towel around his hips, all his brain wanted him to do was get drunk. Really hammered, seeing-double drunk. Tragically, he didn't think there was any alcohol in the house—at least not that had been made after Prohibition.

Throwing the towel into the dirty pile, he collapsed on his bed, sprawling out on his back like da Vinci's *Vitruvian Man*—

The lamp across the way flickered as if the bulb was fritzing out—or maybe the electricity was failing.

Then everything went dark.

"Annnd something else breaks in this house."

Crap, he really should go back out there and get Sissy. Bring her in from the proverbial rain. Apologize for biting her head off.

And he intended to do all that—just after he rested his heavy eyes for five minutes. Besides, she probably needed a little more time to cool off. What a temper—and bizarrely, that made her even more attractive.

Suggested there might be passion—

Like a cop facing off at an armed suspect, he ordered, "Stop it. Right there."

Put down the inappropriate thoughts and step away with your hands on your head, not on your cock.

Huh. Wonder what Miranda rights would look like under that scenario. . . . You have the right to remain erect, but anything you do to yourself will be used against you in a court of conscience—

Okay, he was losing it. And it was time to take everyone's advice and pull it together. He was going to have a five-minute TO followed by clean clothes and a good solid attempt to try to talk to Sissy again.

Taking deep, easy breaths, he chilled himself out, willing his emotions back into the closet that they'd jumped free of—

Knock. Knock.

Jim lifted his head. "Yeah?"

As the door opened a crack, light sliced through all the pitch-black. "Can I come in?"

At the sound of Sissy's voice, Jim grabbed the covers and yanked them over his crotch. "Now's not a good time."

"I just want to apologize."

"Can I meet you in the kitchen?"

"I'm really sorry, Jim," she said hoarsely.

"Shit. Me, too."

With a graceful shift, she peered around the door, and God, in that illumination streaming in from behind her, her blond hair looked like a halo. Momentarily struck by her presence, he rubbed his eyes, thinking maybe this was a dream. Maybe he'd fallen asleep quick, and his subconscious had presented this chance to make up.

"I'm cold," she said in a small voice.

"I'll give you a sweatshirt." He went to get up, and remembered the whole naked thing. "Actually . . . ah, it's over there."

As he gestured to the corner where the clean-clothes pile was, Sissy stepped inside and stayed where she was. "I wasn't . . ."

She cleared her throat.

Oh, right. This actually wasn't about any kind of body-heat issue. She didn't know how to properly take back what had happened out there—and yeah, he knew what that felt like.

"You don't have to say it," he murmured.

"Really?"

"Nah."

"Oh, good." She shut the door. "I'm glad."

Jim frowned as he heard her closing in on the bed . . . and then the mattress dipped under her slight weight. "What are you—"

"I'm cold. I'm so . . . cold, Jim. I just need . . . to be warm."

Jim felt his eyes bulge, but there was no time to react beyond that: Before he knew what was happening, she had stretched out next to him and curled up into his chest.

"Just . . . put your arms around me for a little bit. I need it so badly."

Her voice was tortured, sadness and exhaustion cracking it. But this was a serious no-go.

Holding his arms out to the sides as far as he could stretch them, he shook his head even though she couldn't see him. "Sissy . . ." His voice was rough to his own ears. "You can't . . . no, this isn't right."

"Why?" Her voice deepened, reminding him yet again that she was not who she had been. "I'm not asking for sex."

Jim recoiled, shocked by the candor. But he believed her on that one. The issue was him. Plus, oh, heeeeeey, he was naked.

"Please," she said. "I feel lost. So lost, like I'm going to float away. And there's nothing holding me here . . . just let me stay the night. I promise I won't bother you."

Not likely on that one, he thought.

Except he wasn't going to turn her away. He couldn't.

Pushing himself to the far edge of the mattress, he mummied himself in the sheeting. "I'll . . ."

What, he thought. Tell her he was going to keep his hands off of her? He didn't want her to know he'd even gone *there* for a second.

"Come here," he muttered.

Sissy came in close again, once more snuggling up against his chest, but this time she took it even further—she tucked her arms in between them, and put her head under his chin.

The rough sigh she let out was such a commentary on where she was that he wanted to kick his own ass for getting tangled in the head for even a second about any attraction bullcrap.

She was lost, and he was, for the time being, her imperfect anchor.

Made him wish he were a better man; it really did.

With some stiff herky-jerky, he adjusted himself to her position, but he didn't touch her and kept his hips way back. There was still a lot of skin exposed on his part, but she didn't seem to notice.

He was all too aware of it.

God, she was so small against him—not because she was short, but rather because he had, what, almost a hundred pounds on her?

She smelled so good. Not fake perfume-y, just lovely, beautiful, fragile woman. And the fit with her was perfect, as if their bodies had been made for each other.

"Thank you," she whispered.

Jim squeezed his eyes shut. Then he gently put an arm around her, holding her very loosely. As she shuddered and inched in still closer, he realized that she wasn't the only one who needed warmth. He did, too.

Had for a long time, actually.

After a while, Sissy's breathing became deep and even, and with her safe, he let himself follow her lead. The war was still going on; Devina was out there and so was the soul; time was passing.

But in this room . . . there was peace—and he was hard-pressed to say that he and Sissy didn't deserve it, at least for a little while.

Chapter
Twenty-three

Talk about your one-eighties.

As Cait sat at her desk and stared out at the overcast, gloomy morning, she was a shadow of yesterday's productive artist: She'd been sitting here, staring at a blank page for well over an hour. And this was after she'd slept through her alarm, and then wasted another twenty minutes just lying in bed and enjoying the aching stiffness that lingered in her legs . . . and various other places—

Riiiiiing. Riiiiing.

Cait slammed her hand over her cell phone, grabbing it and turning the thing over. Local area code. Local exchange. This could be—

"Hello?" she said breathlessly.

"Hi, this is Cindy over at . . ."

As Cindy from Cindy's Alterations and More informed her that the suit, pants, and two skirts she'd had taken in were ready, Cait wanted to scream. Instead, she led with, "Oh, thank you. Yes, I'll be over to pick them up today, or tomorrow at the latest."

Hanging up, she knew that waiting for a maybe-never phone call from Duke was not helping her workload. But it was impossible not to jump anytime that phone rang—which had been, like, twelve times. For whatever reason, anyone she'd dialed recently or contracted for work was getting back to her this morning.

Not Duke, though.

And perhaps it was a good idea to point out to herself that he might never call. Given that she'd only left him, what, seven hours ago, it was way too early to give up hope, but still. He wouldn't have been the first man to take a number in postcoital bliss, only to have his head clear later and realize the woman wasn't his type.

He hadn't even written her digits down.

Riiiiiing. Riiiiinnng.

This time Cait didn't bother to check her screen. It was probably her accountant calling about taxes. Or a neighbor telling her they were putting on a back porch and going to be working right next to her office for the next twelve weeks. Or Flo from Progressive. The frickin' gecko from GEICO.

"Hello."

"I thought about you all night long."

Bolting to attention, Cait gripped her phone as the rough male voice shot into her ear and went right through her body.

"Hello?" Duke said.

Oh, right, she was supposed to purr something in exchange. "Ah, hi."

Wow. She was a real Angelina Jolie over here.

"I want to see you."

Boom. No preamble, no sweet talk, and no awkwardness: Clearly the man talked in the same way he had sex. And what do you know, she responded the same way she had at the club: Instant. Arousal.

"Where?" Two could play the straight-up game.

"I have the night off. Dinner—the Riverside Diner. Six."

Cait started to smile so wide her cheeks hurt. "Dinner, huh?"

"I have fairly good table manners. And I figure, since what we're doing isn't your style, it might make you feel more comfortable."

The words were gruff, and the thoughtfulness a surprise—and probably because of both, she was especially touched.

"I'd love that."

"Good." There was a pause. "Don't wear a bra."

"Why," she breathed.

"Why do you think."

Cait closed her eyes and swayed, images of his head down at her breasts, his mouth sucking and licking, hitting her hard. "Okay."

"I want you under me again," he growled.

That was his good-bye.

As she hung up on her end, she actually fanned herself with her hand, something she'd assumed people only did in TV commercials and bad sitcoms. And then she couldn't hold it in. Bursting up from her workstation, she ran around her house like a crazy person, making a bizarre kind of *eeeee* noise as she completed the circuit back to her desk.

At which point there might have been some pirouetting.

Putting her hands over her mouth, she immediately started wondering what she should wear. She needed to go to the dry cleaner's—there was a low-cut blouse that she could throw on. And maybe she could hit Talbots at the mall and see if they were having a sale. A new pair of slacks would be nice. . . .

A quick check of the clock had her cursing. Ten o'clock.

Damn it. She was already out of time for the morning—

God, the way he'd moved inside of her, those massive shoulders bunching up above her, his body surging, his eyes glowing.

And that voice of his.

Sitting back down, she put her head in her hands. She couldn't believe she was going to get to have that again in, what, eight hours. Well, maybe nine and a half, depending on how long dinner took.

Made fast food really damned appealing.

Arby's, anyone?

As her phone went off again, she accepted the call immediately, hoping it was him dialing back just so they could have the same conversation all over again. "Hello?"

"Are you still speaking to me?"

Cait winced. "Oh, G.B., hi."

As the first half of the night came back to her, the guilt rolled in along with a shiver of the fear, as if her insides were switching railroad tracks.

"I'm so sorry, Cait. Oh, my God, I couldn't believe I got tied up like that. . . ."

With his heartfelt explanation of everything washing over her, she scrambled for what she was going to say when he asked her out again. Originally, she'd been really happy that he'd invited her to the theater, but now? It was as if the road in front of her had a curve in it, and her new direction was away from him, not toward him.

". . . lunch?"

"What?" she said, coming back to attention.

"I just wanted to know if you'd be free for lunch downtown? I'm back at the theater today, rehearsing for *Rent*—and I really want to make it up to you."

"Well, I have a class to teach at eleven." And if she didn't get her butt in gear, she was going to be late. "It gets out at one. I could be downtown by one thirty—I'm not sure if that fits into your schedule?"

"I'll make it work. Come to the theater—and this time I can get you back no problem, because it's just a rehearsal, not a performance."

"Okay, thanks. I'll see you then—"

"Cait. I can hear the hesitation in your voice. I swear, last night was a fluke. That's not who I am—I didn't flake out on you on purpose."

Well . . . he was right about the pause, but way off-track on the "why" behind it. Dear Lord, how did this work? Did she tell him that she'd seen someone else last night?

"Seen" as in "had sex on the floor in the back of a club with him."

At what juncture did she tell G.B. she was seeing somebody else? Was she even dating Duke? Maybe it was just a two-nighter.

What a mess.

"I know," G.B. muttered. "It's not at all how I thought the night was going to go."

Shoot, she'd spoken out loud. "No, no, I meant . . ." Better to do this in person, she thought. "I'd love to have lunch with you, and I really do understand about last evening. I'll see you after class?"

The relief in his voice was palpable. "See you then, Cait. And thanks again for being so cool."

Jim woke up alone.

As his eyes opened, the first thing he did was look for Sissy, but she was gone as if she had never been. Rolling over, he could still smell her in the sheets, however, just the faintest hint of sweet female skin lingering where she had lain next to him.

Getting out of bed, he pulled on some clothes, took a pit stop in the bathroom, and then went down to her room. The door was ajar, but he knocked on the jamb anyway. When there was no answer, he put his head in. The bed was made, with no sign of her having been in there.

He hit the stairs, descending quickly—

Jim stopped dead on the grandfather clock's landing. Food. He smelled . . . real food. Like the homemade stuff his mother had made all those years ago.

"What the hell?" Adrian said from the top of the stairs. "Is that . . . breakfast?"

"I think so. I certainly didn't make it."

"Duh." The other angel limped around the balustrade and joined him to finish the trip down. "When I smelled smoke last night, I figured you were trying to bake."

Yeah, not hardly.

The pair of them strode for the kitchen, and the closer they got, the more the nuances came out. Cinnamon. Eggs. Coffee.

"Wow," Adrian said as they came into the room.

Sissy was working over the stove like she knew what she was doing, whisking something that looked like scrambled eggs in a bowl and then pouring the mix into a pan that sizzled. Three plates had been set out on the little table in the middle of the room, mismatched silverware was lined up, and mugs sat like flags at the upper right corners of the settings.

"Oh, my God, toast," Adrian said as he barged ahead and parked it in one of the chairs. Without waiting for an invitation, he reached for the stack of what had been bread, but was now golden brown crunch just waiting for butter. "I didn't know we had a toaster—how the hell did you pull this off?"

Sissy glanced over her shoulder, meeting Jim's eyes only briefly before looking away. "The oven. Under the broiler. That's how we did it at summer camp."

"Can I help myself?" the other angel said, in the process of buttering things up.

"Please do. I like mine with cinnamon sugar on top." Sissy turned around with the pan. "I hope this is okay? I'm not a sunny-side-up person. Uncooked yolks are nasty."

There was a pause, as if she were waiting for Jim to sit down.

He wanted a cigarette more than he needed breakfast, but he wasn't going to be rude. "This is great. Thanks."

A second later, she served Ad first, using a wooden spoon to shuffle some fluffy onto the angel's plate. Then she was close by, doing the same for Jim.

She'd had a shower; he could smell the shampoo he himself used, and the ends of her hair were damp. And the fact that she was in the same clothes she'd worn the day before made him decide they needed to take care of her wardrobe today.

"Thanks," he said again as he picked up his fork.

Light. Hot. Delicious. A real break from the crap he'd been throwing down his gut lately. And yet even as he ate like the starved man he was, it was impossible not to think of how they'd spent the night, lying together in that bed of his. He knew she had to be remembering it, too—she was stiff and awkward as she moved over to her own plate and then put the pan in the sink.

Lot of clinking as silverware met china, the sounds of the meal loud in his ears, making the silence between the three of them a tangible fourth party.

Adrian ate most of the toast, all of his eggs, and drank two cups of coffee along the way. And then he folded his napkin and hefted himself to his feet. "I'm going to shower and then head out."

Jim frowned. "Where you going?"

"Out."

"Where?"

"Out."

As the guy turned away, Jim's first impulse was to throw out a shitload of hell-no-you-pull-that-with-me, but then he caught sight of the way Sissy was fidgeting in her chair.

Was it possible Adrian had actually grown some tact and was giving them a little space?

"I was hoping to talk," Sissy said softly as they were left alone.

Will miracles never cease.

"Excuse me?"

"Sorry. Just thinking about my roommate—the one with the hollow leg."

"Is that why he limps?"

Jim lifted his brows. "You've never heard that expression before?"

"It's a saying?"

"He's just really hungry."

"Oh."

Sissy got up and went back for the coffee machine, pouring more of the strong java she'd made for them all. And as she moved around, he found his eyes running up and down her, measuring her shoulders, her hips, her legs. Hard to see anything underneath those baggy clothes of his, but he'd felt enough of it that he could extrapolate—

Rubbing his temples, he thought . . . man, he had to stop this shit.

"More coffee for you?" As she pivoted around to him, her mug in one hand, the pot in the other, he pulled it together.

"Yeah. Thanks."

He held out his mug and watched the steam rise as she topped him off. Then she was back in her chair.

Lot of silence.

"So, I didn't think this kitchen worked at all." He nodded as he glanced around, noticing that the countertops didn't look quite so dingy, and neither did the floor. Clearly, she'd tidied up a little as well. "I thought it was nothing but a dust-catching relic. Like the rest of this place."

"I went through the cupboards and the drawers. I found pretty much everything anyone would need."

"Where'd you get all the food stuff?"

"I borrowed a motorcycle out back—"

Jim coughed coffee all over the place. "Wha—?"

"Oh, shoot, sorry," Sissy said, bolting up for—oh, hey, they had paper towels, too. "Here, I got it."

"No, it's okay."

Taking control of the Bounty picker-upper, he tried to get her to stop patting him down: She was so close to his chest, to his body, her scent getting in his nose, his brain, all kinds of wires being crossed. Especially as he thought of her on one of their Harleys.

"I didn't know the bikes were off-limits."

He cleared his throat. "They aren't. I'm just, you know, surprised."

She lowered herself back into her chair. "I wasn't sure what else to do. I came down here, and there was nothing to eat . . . and I was going to take the Explorer, but I couldn't find the keys. The Harley had its in the ignition."

Jim blinked, trying to imagine her scrubbing out on one of those huge bikes they'd parked around back. Then something else occurred to him. "Wait a minute, how did you—"

"Turns out people can see me. If I concentrate hard enough." She shrugged. "But I need to borrow fifteen dollars and seventy-two cents. I've never stolen anything before, and I'd rather be in debt to you than keep this petty theft on my conscience. It really isn't sitting well."

When he just stared at her, she flushed. "Look, all I did was go to the closest Qwikie Mart and disappear myself when I was in the store. I wasn't sure what do to, but then I discovered that whatever I was holding disappeared with me. I took only bread, butter, coffee, and more eggs—that's it. Oh, and the paper towels—which double as filters for the pot. And the cinnamon." Abruptly, she leaned in. "You do have cash, right? I mean, your truck and the bikes all have gas in them, so I figure you must have some currency in your pockets."

"Yeah, we do." They were living off his savings, which were substantial, thanks to XOps paying well for hazardous duty and his having had no life outside of the military for twenty years. "That's not a problem. And I don't care that you took a bike, I'm just a little shocked that you could . . ."

"Handle it?"

"Well, yeah. Those things weigh a ton."

"My dad taught me how to ride a long time ago. He had a Harley, too—has, I mean." She stared down into her mug. "So, yeah, the breakfast is a peace offering. I'm really sorry about how I behaved last night. I just . . . it came over me. Everything exploded in my head—I shouldn't have gone at you like that. You didn't deserve it, and I am grateful for everything you've done for me."

He looked into her eyes. "You don't have to apologize. And I don't blame you. This is not easy shit you're dealing with."

"It's just hard to be so . in the dark about, like, everything."

"You don't remember?"

"How I ended up down there? Not really. I mean, I've got details up until I walked into the supermarket. After that? It's a fog."

Mixed blessing, he supposed. And he hoped it was the same for when she'd been in Devina's—

"But I remember everything about that wall," she said hoarsely. "Everything. I still swear I was stuck in that black prison for centuries."

Damn it.

She helped herself to the last piece of toast, but then only took one bite before putting it aside. "I think that's part of why I'm struggling. It's all I've got, that . . . experience . . . with those others who were suffering. I close my eyes and it's what I see and hear and smell—the stench and the twisting agony, the years of time passing." As her voice cracked, she brushed under one eye as if clearing a tear. "It's eating me up—and I thought that going to my parents' would reconnect me, but it just reminded me of everything that I'm not anymore. I've got to have something con- crete to put my feet on, but there's nothing, is there."

Basically what she'd said to him last night in the dark.

Jim took a page from her book and stared into his coffee. "Are you sure you want to know." As she went utterly still, he looked over at her again. "Before you answer, think about it carefully. Some kinds of knowledge you can't get rid of." Abruptly, he thought of all the men he'd killed, some of whom up close. "Once it's in your mind? It's like a tattoo on your brain. It's a permanent thing and you can't go back."

"Tell me," she whispered without hesitation. "Even if it's horrible . . . I have to know. I'm still a prisoner even though I'm out here—I'm still trapped, but it's the ignorance now. There's no context to anything, no structure, nothing but questions no one is answering. My mind . . . is eating itself alive."

Shit, she was too young to feel like that. And he knew exactly where she was; he'd walked miles in those shoes, and not only was it hard, it had hardened him. Set his emotions in concrete.

He didn't want that for her. "Do you mind if I smoke?"

"Not at all. It's not like it's going to give me cancer, and I kind of like the smell."

He leaned to the side and took his lighter out of his back

pocket. A second later, he had a Red between his lips and was taking a drag.

On the exhale, he noticed that his hands were stilling. Funny, he hadn't been aware they were shaking.

"I don't know everything." He reached behind him to the counter, snagging an ashtray and putting it by his empty plate. "You need to be clear on that. I'm in the dark about a lot of shit."

Which was a reminder, like he needed one, that he didn't have much free time here. Still, he felt compelled to get her on as even a keel as he could. It was only fair—and she hadn't gotten a lot of fair lately.

The war would have to wait just a little longer.

"So tell me," she said, arms tightening around herself.

Jim opened his mouth, searched for words . . . and had no luck. There was another way, though. More dangerous, but it would more likely get her what she was looking for than any conversation they could have.

Jim got up abruptly. "I gotta go talk to my boy for a minute. I'll be right back."

He stalked out of the kitchen and hit the stairs. Up on the second floor, he rapped his knuckles on the bathroom's closed door. "Yo, Adrian."

From the other side, the response was something along the lines of, "What do you think this is, a *Rocky* movie?"

"I need you to do something for me."

"I gotta leave."

"You're kidding me." He should have known better than to think Adrian's departure had been about the polite. "And where the hell are you going?"

The door opened. Adrian was fully dressed, with wet hair. "I gotta go."

Jim took the guy's arm in a strong grip. "Where."

Ad narrowed his eyes. "While you're with your girlfriend down there? Worrying about her? I'm taking care of business. And that's all you need to know—unless you're planning on getting back in the game?"

"Oh come on, that's bullshit."

"Is it. Really." Adrian ripped free and limped in the direction of his room. "I'm thinking it's not."

"So where are we?" Jim demanded as he followed the guy into his private space. "What's going on?"

Adrian just shook his head as he went over to his bureau and shrugged into a holster. "You ready to play ball? Because, again, until you are, there's no point in wasting my breath, is there."

With a curse, Jim thought of Sissy, sitting in that kitchen, relying on him to be the compass in her fucked-up world. She had no one else. "Look, I just need to get her up and rolling. This has been a shocker, okay—"

Adrian wheeled around as he popped a forty in under his arm. "Fuck you, Jim. I've lost my best friend, and some other pretty heavy shit. Permanently. So first off, do *not* tell me what's shocking to her, and second? Excuse me if I'm not real impressed by your caretaking side. You want to masturbate to the Hallmark Channel—knock yourself out. But then don't question me about where I go or what I do to keep things on track—or make like I owe you an operational update. Ain't going to happen."

Jim dragged a hand through his hair. "One day, Adrian. Gimme one day."

"So you can do what? Get mani-pedis together and go to the mall? Fuck that—"

"I just need one day, and then I'm back. I promise."

The other angel cursed under his breath as he picked up his crystal dagger and tucked it into the small of his back.

"You have my word on it," Jim said roughly. "I'll be a hundred percent all in. I just need you to do something for me in the meantime—"

"Annnnnd the sonofabitch wants something. How perfect—"

"Adrian. Please."

Ad looked around like he was hoping to find some sanity somewhere. Finally, he muttered, "What do you need me to do?"

When Jim finished the ask, Adrian just stared at him.

After a long, tense moment, the angel said, "You owe me. We clear? I do this for you, you owe me."

Jim stuck out his palm. "On my honor."

Chapter
Twenty-four

It was harder to go back into the parking garage than she'd thought.

As Cait entered the facility and took her pink ticket, the gate rose and . . . that was about it. Her foot refused to leave the brakes and her SUV stayed right where it was, as if her Lexus were afraid of what was up there, too.

The flashbacks were intense enough to have her release the steering wheel and grip her thighs, her body bracing itself even though her doors were locked and it was daylight and there was no way whoever or whatever it had been was still—

Beep!

Her eyes shot to the rearview mirror. Behind her, a woman in a minivan was looking as stressed as anybody who no doubt had a carload of kids, too many appointments, and no privacy in the bathroom would be.

Cait hit the gas and began the ascent, giving herself all kinds of pep talk. But as she got closer and closer to the top floor, her body was flooded with *no*. Which was really pretty crazy. Again, it was broad daylight, and people were all over the place, getting in and out of cars. No isolation, no darkness.

"Nope. Not doing this."

Wrenching the wheel to the side, she rerouted, heading for the *exit* arrows that would ultimately take her down instead of up.

She had to use all her self-control to keep from punching the accelerator and going all Jeff Gordon on the escape.

At the bottom, she presented her ticket to the woman in the kiosk and began to explain to her adrenal gland that she was about to get out of here. Really. Like, for sure—

"Wait a minute," the ticket taker said. "Did you just come in? Or am I getting another misread?"

"I, ah—I forgot my phone. Have to go home."

The woman batted the air in front of her. "Oh, honey, I know all about that. You go through. There's a minimum of an hour, but we'll just pretend you were never here."

Amen to that. "Thank you so much. It means . . . a lot."

The ticket taker beamed like doing a good deed had made her day.

And didn't that make Cait feel like crap about lying—but was she really going to explain why she was panicking?

And what do you know, it looked like God Himself approved of her decision to leave her car on the street—twenty yards past the garage entrance, there was a vacant metered space. Backing the Lexus in, she grabbed her purse and checked her new hair in the mirror.

Wow. Even after a two-hour painting class and a breezy, slightly humid day? The stuff was hanging like a champ, the color glowing, the layers bringing out the natural curl.

As scrambled as she was inside, it seemed bizarre that her image was so collected.

Getting out, she locked up and found—bonus—that there were twenty-three minutes left on the meter—so she only had to put one dollar and seventy-five cents on her credit card.

"Once more with feeling," she said as she walked toward the Palace Theatre's sign.

As she went along, she fussed with her yoga pants and her loose J.Crew barn coat. Chances were good G.B. would be in something casual, right? No way they would make him practice in a tuxedo.

Crossing over that mosaic stretch in the pavement, she opened the door to the foyer. The first thing she smelled was floor cleaner, and over in the corner, there was a polisher plugged into an out-let, standing at attention as if ready to be called back into service.

"Careful," a man in a navy blue uniform said as he came out of the lobby. "Just finished waxing it."

"Thanks." She hiked up her purse on her shoulder. "Hey, I'm sorry to bother you. But I'm supposed to be meeting someone here? I'm a little late—"

"Yes, you are."

Cait turned. It was the receptionist from the night before, the one from the glass office who'd lost it all over G.B. Dressed in something short and tight, she was propping open the door of that staff-only corridor next to will-call—and the good news was, she didn't appear to be as angry as she had been, but she wasn't any sort of Suzy Sunshine, either.

Matter of fact, that expression of haughtiness and superiority rubbed Cait like barbed wire.

"Follow me," the woman said in a bored voice.

You know, you had to wonder why people did jobs they hated, Cait thought as she headed across the slippery floor.

Although in this economy, you took what you got, she sup-posed as she stepped through into the corridor.

"He's very busy, you know," the receptionist announced as she strode off like something was on fire down the hall. "G.B. is a *very* busy guy."

Then why did he ask me to come, Cait thought dryly. "I can imagine."

"He's the most talented one here. But then, he works so hard."

"Uh-huh."

By this time, they were already passing by the glass office, the receptionist's high heels making like a snare drum—to the point where you had to wonder how she stayed upright.

Thank God for flats. And the gym.

As they went deeper and deeper into the theater complex, things began to clutter the hallway, a controlled chaos of props, stray chairs, and lighting equipment taking up space as the corridor widened. Double doors began to crop up with signs like RE-HEARSAL I and MUSIC III mounted over them, and then a fleet of bulletin boards appeared, one every ten feet or so, their faces covered with schedules, notices, ads for take-out places.

Suddenly, the receptionist with the attitude disorder stopped short with no notice. As she pivoted on her stillies, she smiled with enough condescension to strip paint off a car door. "You can't go any farther—they're doing a read-through onstage. But I'll let him know you're here."

As she sauntered off, her chin was up, her body moving with a sinuous strut—like she was used to being stared at.

"Wow," Cait muttered as she leaned in and checked out the nearest bulletin board. "I can *so* see why they hired that for reception."

But at least how the woman behaved was her own issue. And with any luck, Cait would never have to see her again.

Lifting a production schedule out of the way, she eyed a flyer for a Chinese place, and then a B.C. comic strip that made her smile, and . . . a couple of business cards from a psychic down on Trade Street.

For no good reason, she thought of the vibe from the night before as she'd run for that elevator.

Funny, there had been two times in her life when she'd been as afraid as that. One had been a couple of summers ago, when she'd been waterskiing on Saratoga Lake and had gone outside the boat wake just as they were heading into a turn. Momentum being what it was, she had shot forward, her speed overtaking her skill in the work of a moment. When she'd lost her balance, the initial impact had been so violent, it had felt as though she'd crashed into pavement—and then things had gotten nasty. The skis had popped off her feet in a messy fashion, twisting her ankles, wrenching her in midair as she had bounced like a skipping stone across the water's surface.

The PFD had kept her from sinking when things had eventually slowed down, but she'd ended up facedown in the water. Stunned, in pain, unable to coordinate her arms or legs, she had opened her mouth for air and gotten nothing of the sort.

A friend had dived in at just that second and rolled her over in the nick of time.

The terror had come that night. Lying in a bed at that stuffy cabin she and Teresa had rented for the week, she had passed out from pain meds, discomfort, and exhaustion—only to wake up screaming in panic.

The dream had been that she was trapped on her stomach, and instead of help coming and flipping her over for air, she'd breathed in water until she was choking, drowning . . . dying.

Same sensation as she'd run from whoever had been chasing her last night.

And the other time she'd felt that scared? It had been much earlier, back when she'd been twelve. She'd been standing in a hospital corridor, waiting for news about her brother's condition. As things had gotten worse, the fear had been about reality setting in. No matter how bad the accident had seemed, she'd never thought they would lose him—and when that had been a possibility? True terror.

In both those situations, there had been a good reason to feel as she had. And yes, getting chased in a parking garage would also do it—but there had been more to the experience than that.

She had sensed evil last night. Her bones had recognized it, sure as her eyes could catch a flash of movement or her ears could pick up the sound of distant thunder.

She knew what she knew.

And she wished she had been able to see more. In her parents' lexicon, evil came in all guises—and she wasn't sure why, but she wanted to know what it had looked like. A man, tall or short, light or dark, slim or heavyset, armed or not . . . she just wanted to know.

Because in the absence of knowledge, her mind had been making up some pretty weird stuff.

Demon, for example. Although where that came from, she had no clue. Maybe it was her parents, yet again, talking in her head?

Cait reached up and pulled out the thumbtack that was holding the cards to the cork. Three fell free, fluttering to the floor, and when she picked them up, she stared at the purple print. YASEMIN OAKS. PALM READINGS, TAROT, DREAMSCAPING, PSYCHIC INSIGHT. Her logo was an open hand.

Cait put two back. The third she slipped into her purse—

"Hi!"

Spinning around as if she'd been caught stealing, she put her hand to her throat. "G.B., hi."

As he smiled at her, he looked really good in his jeans and his loose black shirt, his hair tied back, his shoes leather and long toed. Oh, and yup, same cologne—and just as delicious.

For a moment, she was a little starstruck, just as she'd been before, the idea that he was actually standing in front of her, talking to her, seeming strange and wonderful.

She shook herself. "Sorry, hello."

Wait, she'd already hi'd him.

As she floundered, he just kept smiling, like he was honestly glad she'd come. "You look great. Can I hug you?"

When he held his arms wide, she blinked for a second and then went in for a quick embrace. "I probably smell like turpentine."

"Not in the slightest. How was your class?" He pulled back. "Good?"

"Yeah, we're studying shadow, light sourcing, that kind of thing."

"Sounds fascinating."

She lifted a brow. "Are you being charming again?"

"Maybe. It comes easily with you." He nodded over his shoulder. "How'd you like a little tour on our way down to the break room? You've got to see the stage, it's incredible—and we're taking a breather from rehearsing."

"Now, that would be a treat."

Falling in beside him, she had to look up to meet his eyes, and from that angle, she was struck again by the thought that she'd seen him somewhere before. "I've been to a number of shows, but never behind the scenes."

G.B. casually put his arm around her. "Let me be your guide."

Nice gesture. Nice guy. Now, if only she could shut her mother's voice up in her head, she might stop feeling guilty and actually enjoy this.

No doubt she needed a shrink more than a tarot card reader.

More black curtains, now falling vertically in their path so they had to push them aside. And then a preamble open space that was filled with mile-high scaffolding, and huge background props, one of which was a townscape, the other a park scene.

"It's so vast," she murmured, looking way, way up to a ceiling she couldn't see. "Hey, is that what they call a catwalk over there?"

"Check you out with the theater lingo. Yup, that's where the lighting guys do their thing. And here's . . ."

He led the way around one last curtain, and then . . .

"Oh . . . my . . . God . . ." she whispered.

Stepping out onto the golden floorboards, she was astounded by the breadth of space before her, the expanse of the ceiling, the regal nature of it all: Five thousand red velvet seats rose up in three sections, the concentric rows moving away from the black orchestral pit like rings from a stone thrown in still water. Articulated plaster molding that was gold leafed ran up the side walls where the box seats were and across the balcony of the second-story seating area and all around the Greco-Roman murals that were painted on the walls. Red-carpeted aisles striped down toward the stage, and red velvet curtains hung next to all the exits. . . .

And far, far above, directly in the center, a chandelier the size of a house hung in the midst of a glorious painted scene of cherubs.

What an honor to perform here. To just stand here, as a matter of fact.

"When was this built?" she wondered aloud as she walked around a long table that was littered with scripts and pens and Starbucks coffee mugs.

"Late eighteen hundreds, I heard someone say."

"It's breathtaking from the audience . . . but like this? It's . . . awe inspiring."

G.B. wandered around, too, hands on his lean hips, eyes searching out into the space. "I'm so glad you think that, too. I feel it every time I get onstage here. It makes me want to be a Richard Burton kind of actor." He laughed. "I mean, the singing is great, but could you imagine doing Shakespeare from here?"

As he assumed an orator pose, she measured him. "I can totally see it for you."

"Really?" He turned to her. "I'm serious."

"So am I."

He smiled after a moment and came over to her, the sound of his hard-soled shoes rising up. "You know, they say this place is haunted."

"By who?"

"Are you scared of ghosts?" He rubbed her arms. "People talk about all kinds of suspicious noises and feelings of dread—"

Something in her face must have given her away, because he stopped abruptly. "What's wrong?"

Cait brushed off the concern. "Oh, I'm fine."

"No, you're not."

"Did you say something about a break room?"

As she went to walk away, he moved in front of her and stayed there. "Talk to me."

"It's nothing—I just, you know, I had . . . a strange thing happen to me last night." She pushed her hair back. "It's . . ." Crap. She might as well tell him. "The truth is, when I went to will-call after you left to go warm up? The ticket wasn't there—"

"What do you mean, there wasn't a—"

"—so I went home to wait—"

"What the hell—"

"No, don't get angry. I'm sure it was just an innocent mix-up. Anyway, when I came back so I could meet you at the end of the performance, I parked in the garage and . . . someone chased me, or something—"

The change in him was so abrupt and complete, she actually took a step back: Fury in his face contorted his features, making him look like someone who could go out and put a serious hurt on a person. But it wasn't directed at her, not at all.

"Are you okay?" he demanded.

"Yes. I wasn't hurt because I was able to get into an elevator and lock the doors. The police—"

"You had to hide? And you called the police! Jesus Christ, why didn't you tell me?"

"It all ended okay. I promise you."

G.B. broke off and paced around in a tight circle. "You were smart. But for fuck's sake, that never should have happened."

"Well, it's an iffy part of town."

"I'm talking about the ticket. I gave it to—" He stopped and blew out a curse. "I just . . . you should have been here, with me. Not out in the dark, getting mauled by God only knows who. Come here."

With a quick shift, he pulled her into his body and held her, dropping his head into her hair and running his hand up and down her back. "I should have been there to protect you."

"Breathe deeply, feel the breath going in and out of your nose, down the back of your throat, expanding your lungs. . . ."

Are. You. Fucking. Kidding. Me.

The demon Devina had her ass in the air, her hands and feet planted on a smelly purple mat, her hair and her double Ds in her face—and that seventy-pound Rubbermaid dumb bitch in the front of the class wanted her to *breathe*?

"Feel the strength in your body, but also look for the areas that can relax in the pose. Breathe. Let go in your stomach and . . ."

Areas of relaxation? Yeah, right. Her hamstrings felt like they were being stripped off her bones; she had so much blood in her head, her eyes were bulging; and her arms were trembling as they attempted to keep holding her in this insane, unnatural position.

Her earlobes were at ease.

Actually, only the left one was.

Downward dog? Shit, she should remember this when she had to work someone over in Hell. She'd rather have somebody come at her with a knife.

"And release into child's pose."

Thank fuck.

As Devina collapsed onto the mat and fell forward over her bent legs, she hated everything about the hot-yoga experience. The sweat. The cramping. The cloying stink—was that incense *really* necessary? Come on, this wasn't a Catholic church.

"And now we will have our relaxation. Please lie on your back and find a comfortable position for your arms. You may do arms out or down by your sides, or even over your head. Whatever you prefer."

At the moment, she would prefer her hands around that woman's throat, squeezing until the teacher turned cardiac-arrest blue.

"Breathe. Close your eyes. Focus on relaxing your toes . . . your feet . . . your . . ."

Screw you, lady.

In a show of rebellion, Devina kept her peepers open for the sole reason that she was tired of being bossed around by that pipe cleaner-like chick.

As that annoying, pseudo-soothing voice droned on, the vocabulary working its way up the body, Devina just hung out and waited for the BS to be over. Whatever. She could have left, but she was a perverse motherfucker and kind of enjoyed getting all riled up by a silly human she could kill on a whim.

Then again, she had something pleasant to turn her attention to.

She had spent the night in Jim Heron's arms.

Salt 'N' Pepa old-school said it right: *Whatta man, whatta man, whatta man, whatta mighty good man. . . .*

Now, it had sucked that she'd had to clothe herself in the skin of someone else—most particularly that stupid virgin—but the fact was, Devina was so used to being other people, it hadn't been any real barrier to the bliss. Besides, the idea that she had thwarted Jim's never-again had more than sustained her.

She'd wanted sex, of course—that wouldn't have rung true, however.

Not on their first night together.

The way she looked at it? It was an acting challenge. She'd had to reach deep and try to behave as that Barten thing would, all the while subtly, and inexorably, starting to seduce him. Big fun, and it had really put a spark in things—she could totally see why relationship experts touted role-play as a way to spice up a couple's love life.

This was just what the pair of them needed.

Plus, it gave her something to focus on as she was forced to follow the rules in the game—okay, well, mostly color within the lines of the war: She'd had to scare that artist last night in the parking garage—it was important to keep the woman headed in the direction she'd voluntarily gone in at the end of the evening.

Just a nudge. Nothing obvious.

And hey, demons were allowed to be in public places. It wasn't her fault that the woman freaked out and called the cops from a locked elevator, then bolted for home . . . and ended up in the arms of a very hot lover.

Okay, okay, fine, she'd also caused Jim's little "accident" in his truck.

Black cats were sometimes not really cats.

But come on, that had been personal, not anything to do with the larger fight between good and evil. She'd just been so bitched that he was all focused on and lovey-dovey supportive with the virgin that she hadn't been able to help herself—

The yoga instructor popped into her visual field, that clueless, perma-happy, I'm-regular-'cuz-I-eat-organic expression making Devina want to force-feed her Hershey bars until she died from hyperglycemia. "Relax your eyelids. Find your inner peace. Breathe . . ."

Devina closed her eyes just so she didn't do something that required a Shop-Vac to clean up—

Another interruption abruptly cut into her "relaxation" time—but it was not her phone going off or a tap on the shoulder or more cocksucking advice on the inhale/exhale thing.

Frowning, she sat up, and broke the horizontal covenant; the summoning was just such a surprise. Fortunately, the teacher picked that moment to call game-over, telling people to settle on their butts with their legs crossed, and do some sort of palm-togethering thing.

Devina waited through that bullshit, because she wanted to keep the male who had called out to her guessing for a little bit: A smart woman knew that men liked the chase, and that was the same whether they were human . . . or angel.

Finally the class broke up, people getting to their feet and chatting among themselves—probably about the buzz that came from mainlining smoothies made from cow flops and carrot juice.

Quelle delish.

Devina cut through them with the efficiency of a New Yorker

on a sidewalk, dodging around as she made for the wall of cubbies by the door of the studio. Everyone else had Merrells or sandals. She popped her Louboutins back on her bare feet and got the hell out of there.

When she slid into her Mercedes, she shut the door and was momentarily derailed by the lack of hood ornament. Even though the thing had been sacrificed for the best possible reason, her OCD blew up its absence into a national emergency.

"You called the dealership," she told herself. "You put the order in. Tuesday. You just have to make it to Tuesday. . . ."

She felt like she'd lost a leg—and only half of her knew that wasn't the case.

Then again, running at only fifty percent psychotic was an improvement. Before she'd started going to her therapist? She'd have either thrown the car out on the street, or she'd have gone to Caldwell Mercedes and forced them at gunpoint to remove someone else's thingy and put it on her own fucking hood.

See. Progress.

Starting up her engine, she hit the gas to get out of the lot before the exit was blocked either by beaters held together with Free Tibet bumper stickers or Priuses with clean-energy logos all over them. As she headed across town, the summoning signal remained strong, and that was good. It meant she'd have enough time for a proper cleanup.

Just another delay, letting him stew in his juices.

When she got to her HQ, she went down to the lower floor and breathed out a sigh of relief to find everything in its place again. Ditching the yoga pants and skin-tight sports top into the trash, she headed for her bathroom—and once again felt trapped between her desire for marble and a Jacuzzi and multiple showerheads . . . and the reality that she didn't trust anyone to work down here among her things.

Her rule was a simple one: Move in and stay put as long as she could.

Goddamn Jim. If only he hadn't found where she'd been hiding out before this.

Great water pressure in those pipes. And Carrara everywhere.

As it was, she was stuck with a relatively anemic spray, white clinical tile, and a urinal next to the sink.

No wonder she'd been so desperate for a hotel stay.

But the good news was, the water was hot, and the soap was her favorite from Fragonard—apricot and clementine. Getting out, she grabbed one of her Porthault towels and wound her hair up tight; then she wrapped a second one around her body.

Given her imminent get-together, she waltzed over to her wardrobe and chose carefully. Short, tight skirt from Louis Vuitton's resort collection. A Missoni blouse that was a second skin with plenty of downward draft. No hose, no bra, no panties. Same pair of Loubous she'd worn to yoga.

Devina laid everything out on her big bed, and then went to do hair and makeup at her vanity. She took her time . . . and still that summons hung on.

Must be important, and how delicious was that? About time she was paid some proper respect.

Dressed and ready to go, she went over to her mirror and stepped through. After a whirl of transportation, she stood at the base of her well, staring up at the viscous walls and the groaning, restless masses trapped within them.

Straightening her skirt and smoothing her hair, she went over to her stained and battered worktable . . . and called the angel Adrian down to her.

As he appeared before her, he was just as big as he had always been, his shoulders the kind of thing that offered plenty of acreage to claw at, his heavy arms as thick and muscled under his

T-shirt as a prizefighter's, his hips anchoring a cock that she knew well, and had missed.

The best part? He was icy-cold angry, his good eye and his milky one both narrowed and spitting out hatred, his jaw clenched, the veins in his neck standing out in sharp relief.

Ohhhhh, yeah. After a night of lying chastely with Jim, she was sexually frustrated in the extreme. This was just what she needed to tame the burn down.

"Why, hello," she drawled with a smile. "Pining for me again?"

Chapter Twenty-five

"This is . . . incredible."

Cait actually had to look over at the plastic box her sandwich had come in. "I mean, I really can't believe this came out of a vending machine and was—"

"Premade, right?" G.B. sat down across the little stainless-steel table and nodded. "It defies the laws of cold storage."

"I feel like it should be served in a fancy restaurant." She wiped her mouth with her paper napkin. "I didn't have a lot of hope, to be honest."

"I will never steer you wrong." G.B. peeled off the aluminum top of his. "I got the ham—what did you choose again?"

"Turkey. I didn't want to gamble with all the mayonnaise on the chicken salad—but after this? I probably would. I think this is real chutney in here." She turned her sandwich his way. "Really."

G.B. nodded as he bit into his own. "Almost all of the cast

went out to eat, but that's a little rich for my blood—besides, with this? Why bother." While chewing, he cracked open a little bag of Cape Cod potato chips. "Share these with me?"

Cait shook her head and put her hand in front of her mouth. "I watch my weight."

He rolled his eyes. "Come on. You're perfect."

"I don't know about that—and I'm not psycho or anything, just a little dusting around the edges, as I call it. No snacking, no extras like rolls or chips or cookies, and I'm careful on the alcohol and the soda. A little gym time and I do okay."

She was chattering on about nothing, mostly because she still felt awkward from that embrace onstage—for no good reason. He'd been so wonderful, hugging her close, doing that male thing that made you feel like someone had your back. And afterward? He'd made a real effort to be charming and a little silly, as if he knew she needed that to pull out of her mood—

Ah, hell . . . it wasn't about the embracing.

She was going out with Duke again tonight.

That was the problem.

"Is there a sketch pad in there?" he asked, nodding to the vacant chair next to her.

She glanced down at her big purse. "Yup. It may be a cliché, but I take one with me everywhere."

"Makes sense. I'm the same way—I have a lyric notebook. I keep it in my bag always—sleep with it, too. My friends who aren't in the biz think I'm crazy—I'm always taking it out, scribbling, toying with words."

"Been there, done that, except it's pictures for me. Sometimes I feel like I'm surrounded by accountants and lawyers—it's nice to be with someone who gets it."

"Simpatico," he said with a smile.

As they chatted along, they were alone in the square room,

sitting among the vending machines, a coffeemaker and a refrigerator with a PT STAFF ONLY (THIS MEANS YOU, CHUCK) sign on its door. The three other tables were empty, although the smell of fresh java and popcorn lingered in the air as if someone had used things very recently.

"So, being in *Rent*'s a pretty big deal," she said.

"Yeah, I mean, this isn't Broadway, but I'm happy to have steady work for about eight weeks. And it'll be the first time I'm onstage doing any acting along with the singing. I'm pretty pumped about that."

"How long do you rehearse for?"

"The next two weeks straight, till about six at night. Which is good, because I can keep my gig schedule." He finished off his sandwich and the chips. "I dunno, I'm getting tired of the multitasking, keeping all these balls in the air."

"I know what that feels like. Before I got my teaching position? I was working four different jobs as I submitted illustrations for projects, did my own artwork, and generally prayed that I'd be able to keep a roof over my head."

He eased back, his handsome face relaxed, his beautiful hands wiping themselves on a napkin. "So, you don't have parental help?"

Cait laughed. "Absolutely not. My mom and dad don't come from anything, and any extra money goes to the church."

"Religious types?"

"Like you read about—literally."

"So you're not close to them."

She wiped her own palms, and then tucked the wad of napkin into her empty, sandwich-shaped container. "Yes and no. I mean, they're still my parents, you know? So I love them. They're just hard to talk to about anything other than their beliefs—and they leave the country a lot to go on missionary trips. So that's kind of isolating. Plus there's some residual damage."

He frowned. "From what."

"Just all the rhetoric. It's in my head, and even though I'm an adult and I live a thousand miles away from them, sometimes their judgments are just . . . all I can hear. And it's not supportive stuff, if you get my drift."

"You seem like the sort of daughter anyone would be proud of."

Cait stared into his steady, kind eyes, and flushed at the compliment. Changing the subject, because she couldn't handle the approval, she said, "You're a good listener, anybody ever tell you that?"

"Maybe. But the fact that you think I am? Means something to me."

"We're back to the charm thing again, are we?"

G.B. winked at her. "Is it working?"

"Maybe." She glanced away. "What about you? What's your story?"

"Sad one, I'm afraid." At this, he gathered the trash and got up, crossing over and pitching the remnants of their lunch into a thigh-high trash bin. "No clue who my father was and Mom died in childbirth. I was raised in an orphanage, and I made it out of there with a high school diploma. After that? I went to college on a scholarship, and have worked at any opportunity that has come my way ever since."

"You've been on your own for a long time."

"Taught me a lot. And you know what they say: That which doesn't kill you gives you material for songs."

"Still, that must have been a hard way to grow up."

He shrugged and sat back down. "I'm an optimist, actually. And I believe in making destiny happen. You can't wait for the world to give you what you want, you've got to take it."

Cait tried to imagine what it would be like to have no family— talk about damage. Her mom and dad might have an agenda, but they did love her in their own ways.

For a moment, she thought of G.B. at the café, interacting with his fans, smiling and being so sincere about his gratitude. Lot of love coming at him in that situation.

Made sense that he'd want to fill a childhood void by performing.

"What?" he said with a smile. "You're looking at me funny."

"Sorry."

"Don't apologize . . . I like your eyes on me. Aw, look, you're a blusher." He put his arms on the table and leaned into them. "Be honest. Are you feeling sorry for me?"

"Not at all. But your life makes me respect you more."

And there was another angle to it. She shouldn't have been surprised to find that there was a real person behind the singer Teresa was so enamored of—but it had been hard not to put him on a pedestal because of his voice, and imagine that everything had been white-picket-fence for him. Funny, the disillusionment was not a bad thing, not at all. As he talked with her, sat with her, exchanged with her, he was becoming three-dimensional, something so much more than a handsome hypothetical with an awesome talent.

"Will you let me draw you," she blurted. As soon as she realized what she'd said, she waved her hand. "Sorry, that's just—"

"Yes," he said with a slow, intimate smile. "I would love that."

Cait reached into her purse without looking away from him, and took out her sketch pad.

"Don't move—wait, you're frowning."

"Oh, I was hoping—never mind. This is fine, too." As his smile came back, he relaxed again in the chair. "I can't wait to see how you see me."

Cait's pencil found her right hand as she flipped to a new page and started fiercely putting lead on paper. Fast strokes, darting across the white expanse, pulling his features out of the flat plane, sculpting his face and shoulders, his glorious hair, his compelling, intense eyes—

"G.B.! What the hell?" A man leaned into the room. "I've been looking for you for a half hour. You can't be late for this kind of stuff."

G.B. bolted out of his chair and glanced at his watch. "Oh, God, Dave, I'm so sorry—"

"Spare me, okay? Just get your ass up to Rehearsal Three, now. We've moved in there because they're installing new bulbs stage right and the noise is ridiculous."

As the guy took off, Cait flipped her sketchbook shut and fumbled to get it in her purse. "I'm so sorry."

"No, it's okay, he's tightly wound." And yet G.B. looked stressed, all that relaxation gone. "I probably should go. I had no idea that so much time had passed."

Cait got up, and in the process dumped half her purse out. "Damn it. No, no, I've got it—you'd better head off—I can find my way out."

"Are you sure?"

"Absolutely—"

As she looked up, he came in fast, and before she knew it, he'd planted a kiss on her mouth. Quick, soft, but the kind of thing that left no room to question where he wanted things to go: Friendship was not it.

Straightening, he said softly, "I'll call you tonight."

"Oh, okay, sure, thanks . . ."

And then he was gone, running off, his footfalls receding down the hall.

Left by herself, Cait looked around the room, as if the vending machine or maybe the refrigerator Chuck wasn't allowed in could give her advice, answers, strength.

After a dry spell that had lasted how long, two great guys appeared at once.

Well, one guy was great. The other was . . . a maelstrom.

Come to think of it, put the pair of them together, and you had the perfect man.

Nature, however, didn't work that way in this case. And neither did she. She couldn't do both; she just didn't have it in her.

The question was, who did she pick?

Chapter
Twenty-six

It had been a while since Adrian had been to the land down under—and no, not Australia. As he stared at the walls that stretched up indefinitely, his stomach turned, and he wished like hell he hadn't told Jim he'd keep Devina busy.

Naturally, she'd propped herself up on her worktable, like she wanted to force him to look over there.

"Well," she said in that deep, velvety voice of hers, "did you miss me?"

Glancing in the demon's direction, Adrian felt his hatred surge. She was sitting there all crossed legs and cleavage exposed, clearly enjoying the fact that he'd given her a metaphysical jingle. Hah. What he'd actually like to "give" her was a stab in the back—just like what she'd had one of her harpies do to Eddie.

"Not in the slightest," he heard himself answer.

"Aw, Adrian." She hopped off her perch and started walking over, all hip sway and then some. "Still bitter about your buddy?"

"No. What's done is done."

That pout of hers relented a little. "So phlegmatic. You aren't going to therapy by any chance, are you? I've found it's helped me tremendously."

"With what? Coming to terms with the fact that you're going to lose this game?"

She stopped about a foot away from him, and her no-bullshit voice came out. "Don't be so sure, angel. This round is going to go my way."

"Bet you said that about the other three you lost, didn't you." He leaned in toward her, even though it put extra stress on his bad leg. "Losing all those times must have come as a shocker."

"I've got two flags."

"Only one of which you've earned."

Now she smiled, her luscious lips peeling off her sharp white teeth. "Both are still mine." She pointed over to a stout oak door that had iron reinforcements all over it. "Cast your eyes on my decor."

Sure enough, over that exit, there were two of the game's flags, mounted on the jambs.

Man, that pissed him off.

"You're angry at Jim, aren't you," the demon drawled.

"No."

"Liar." Rising up on her tiptoes, she licked across his mouth, her tongue lingering on his flesh. "Isn't that why you've come? To get back at him?"

"No." If that was the case, he'd have left the other angel high and dry.

"Oh, really?" Her hands went to his chest, palms flattening on his pecs as her hips brushed the front of his. "I think you did."

His body revolted at the proximity, his skin prickling up, his shoulders tightening into steel cables, his gut twisting even more.

And all that got worse as he looked past her falsely beautiful face to that table.

Impossible not to remember what she'd done to him on it.

Abruptly, he wondered if Eddie hadn't been right. A long time ago, after Adrian had finally gotten free from down here, his best friend had warned him that that kind of abuse lingered not just in the mind and on emotional levels, but in the soul, in the bones, in the blood.

Ad had brushed all that off, of course, but now . . .

Staring at that table, he thought that Eddie might have been right.

"You know," Devina said as her hands traveled down, down, down his torso, "sleeping with me would destroy him. He's very jealous of me, possessive—it borders on stalkerish."

Adrian refocused on the demon's jet-black, glittering eyes. "What?"

"Jim's obsessed with me. Violently so. It's actually very sweet. And your best revenge is to fuck me. He'll never get over it—his best friend with his best girl. Come on, it's the stuff of movies, right?"

As her words sank in, Adrian's brows popped. Yeah, wowzer. He'd thought Devina was a lot of things over the aeons they'd been going around and around with each other, but he'd never felt as though she was out of her mind in the more conventional sense.

Like in Stacy-from–*Wayne's World* nutso.

Go fig.

"Did you say you were in therapy?" Adrian shook his head. "Does that also include medication or are you trying to go natural?"

"I don't believe in anti-depressants. I think they cloud the mind."

Riiiiiiiiiiiiiiiiiiight.

She eased back against him. "Now, where were we?"

You were channeling the role of cray-cray-never-was-girlfriend and I was negotiating with my stomach to make sure all that toast from breakfast stayed put.

Devina slid her palm between his legs, and Adrian flinched, his eyes clamping shut, his head turning away.

God, they had hit this corner before, her coming on to him, him going along with it, them having sex because . . . well, sometimes he liked to feel the dirtiness on the outside of himself. It was the only relief he'd ever gotten from the stench she'd infected him with on the inside.

She's in me, Jim. She's inside of me. . . .

Devina pressed that mouth of hers against the side of his throat as she rubbed him up and down, breasts pushing into his chest, long leg sneaking around the back of his own.

"Don't tell me that you don't want this," she breathed. "Because I know you do."

Adrian opened his mouth to tell her the fifteen different reasons he in fact did not—and then it dawned on him. Yes, he was numb and disgusted with himself and her . . . but in the past, that had never discouraged his cock. Now, though?

The phone was ringing and nobody was picking it up, so to speak.

He was utterly flaccid. Which was the definition of impotence, wasn't it.

Adrian glanced back over at that worktable and smiled. "You're right, Devina."

She let her head fall back and stared at him from under heavy, seductive lids. "I always am. So how about I get to work on you?"

"Okay. Yeah."

The demon dropped to her knees and pushed her hands up his thighs. "You're doing the right thing, Adrian."

As she reached for his fly and slowly undid his pants, he helped her out, pulling his muscle shirt up his abs, staring down as if he gave a shit about what she was doing to him.

When his jeans hit the floor, there was a moment of pause, as if she were surprised with all he didn't have to offer.

"I'm conflicted," he said. "About Jim."

"Ah . . ." She nuzzled his flaccid sex. "I can help with that."

As her wet mouth engulfed his lazy cock, Adrian just looked straight ahead. He felt the suction, the warmth, the sensation of her reaching under and stroking his balls . . . but it was no different than someone brushing against his forearm or patting him on the back.

Before he'd done that little swaperoo with Matthias? He'd been capable of getting hard at a moment's notice, even with Devina.

Now? Nada.

Devina retracted the suction, pulling back until his head popped out from between her red lips. As he just flopped back to a limp vertical, her brows dropped down like she was confronted with an anomaly of unimaginable proportions.

Adrian just shrugged to himself. Jim had asked him to keep the demon busy, and her trying to get him up was as good a time-passer as any. Rather amusing, actually—

A small voice in him, one that was nearly buried, pointed out that it wasn't amusing at all. That it was one more piece of shrapnel in him, another nail in a coffin that was nearly complete, thanks to her having killed Eddie.

Ad didn't care, though. He was dead whether he was up on the Earth dicking around with the war, or down here getting a blow job that got him nowhere.

Didn't matter.

"Suck harder," Adrian drawled as he gripped her head and thrust into her mouth. "Let me feel you on me."

The warehouse district in Caldwell was exactly that: warehouses. In a district.

No big revelation there.

And yet, as Jim slowed his Harley down in the middle of a long block, he saw the area through new eyes: Desolate, really, even though a lot of the facilities had been renovated and turned into pricey condos.

Killing the bike's engine, he twisted around. "You okay back there?"

Sissy nodded and dismounted, shucking her helmet and shaking out her hair. As she looked around, he studied her. Built long and thin, she hardly seemed the type who would prefer the cold wind in her face and nothing but an engine and two tires between her body and the road . . . but she had asked to take the hog.

And he had said yes.

Rising off the seat, he kicked out the stand and leaned the bike to the side.

"What are we doing here?" she asked as she glanced over at him.

Man, he hated being back on this street, in front of this particular building. "The entrance is around the corner."

As he led the way, he could feel her following him, and he found himself wanting to move her in beside him. Maybe put an arm around her shoulder or hold her hand—he just didn't want her to be alone in this, and shit knew that could happen even if you were with someone.

But he let that impulse go as they came up to a set of industrial-size doors.

Willing the things open, he held them wide so she could pass by and go up the short flight of stairs.

Suppose they could have just walked through. He really wanted to be a gentleman with her, though.

After going through the second set of security doors, he gave her a moment in the stark "lobby" to look around in case that jogged her memory.

"I don't think I've ever been here before, have I?" she said.

Devina probably hadn't brought her through the main entrance, no. "The cargo elevator's over here."

The lift was big enough to park a car in, and as he punched the button that had a "5" on it, he reminded himself that coming here had been his bright idea.

Jesus, he hoped he was doing the right thing.

Ding. Ding. Ding. Annnnnd . . .

Ding.

After he threw the manual release, the doors split wide at their midline, and the hall outside still carried the paint smell of new construction.

As was typical of these warehouse overhauls, the decor was deliberately rustic, the hall dark and gloomy as if on purpose, the brick walls still sporting their original, sloppy mortar job, the wooden floors burdened with the choppy, stained patina of heavy use.

Sissy moved forward, beelining for the nickel-plated aluminum door that let in to where the demon had previously kept her collection, her mirror, and herself.

Which explained why there were seven dead bolt locks on the thing.

Placing a hand on the portal, Sissy closed her eyes and leaned in until her forehead touched the metal.

"I can feel . . . something. . . ." She was frowning so hard, he caught the expression even from where he was standing.

"You don't have to go inside."

"Yes, I do."

With that, she gripped the handle, pushed down—and it opened, clearly because the last person here had fucked up and not locked things behind them when they'd left.

Empty. Space.

Last time he'd been here, it had looked like something out of a flea market. Shit had been crammed in everywhere: bureaus crowding the varnished floors, clocks covering the walls, the kitchen layered in knives. Now it was nothing but a bowling alley without lanes and pins.

Sissy's borrowed running shoes made no sound as she walked around, arms crossed, head down.

She ended up at the bathroom.

The door was open, the gray marble flooring the color of a thunderstorm, the white accents bright as snow. As she stepped across the threshold, his reflex was to grab her and bring her back.

Closing his eyes, Jim saw blood everywhere, flowing down her pale skin, coating her blond hair, turning the porcelain tub red.

"I remember. . . ."

Her voice was so quiet, it barely cut into his reliving the nightmare—but it was enough to snap him out of the replay. Walking over, his footsteps were not like hers: His combat boots sounded out loud and proud, and he wanted it that way. He wanted to disturb the stillness and the emptiness, wanted to break through reality and invade the past, changing it, altering its course, taking innocence back.

But of course, that wasn't going to happen.

As he closed in on that bathroom, he remembered the door, that fucking door that he'd opened and . . .

Pulling his brain back from that abyss, he wondered whether Devina had rented the loft? Owned it? The place didn't seem to be listed for resale, but it was empty.

Knowing her, she'd bought it before moving in and was determined to keep it. She hated losing things that were hers.

Now he was in the bathroom, too.

All the mess had been cleaned up as if it had never been, the milky light from the smoked windows across the way penetrating the space, pulling out soft shadows.

Sissy knelt down beside the tub. Running a hand up and down the porcelain, she shook her head. "Here . . . there was something here."

When he didn't reply, she twisted around and looked up at him. "Wasn't there."

Chapter
Twenty-seven

Up above the Earth, past the clouds and the sky, farther still away from the atmosphere, even more distant than the galaxy, the Milky Way, the universe . . . the archangel Albert was sitting down to tea in a grove not far from the Manse of Souls.

In truth, he was not hungry a'tall.

"Bertie, my dear friend, whate'er ails you?"

Looking up across the dainty sandwiches and the silver tea service, he met the archangel Byron's eyes. Behind rose-colored glasses, they were grave, and that was the saddest commentary on the status of the game. Even sadder, somehow, than the fact that there were only two flags flying on the castle's parapet, no longer three: Byron was the optimist among the four of them, always believing in a kind and just destiny for the quick and the dead . . . and the angels.

To have him aggrieved?

Bad. Very bad.

"Shall I serve the tea?" Bertie said by way of reply. "I shan't think we'll be joined."

After all, when he'd arrived initially and found only Byron seated, he had gone in search of the other two . . . Nigel, who was their leader; and Colin, who was their warrior. Alas, however, there had been no answer when he'd approached the closed flap of Nigel's beautiful silk tent, and likewise, Colin's camp by the river had been empty.

Now, in Colin's case, it was not unusual for him to disappear without commentary, but Nigel never departed without checking in. And he had not been inside the manse, either. Indeed, as Bertie had searched therein, he had found nothing located but the souls of the righteous passing a peaceful eternity within the protected walls.

Which was as it should be—but might ne'er be again if this war was lost.

He supposed it was possible that Nigel had gone to see the Maker. That would be the only reason he would break away without word—

"Bertie? I indicated yes, please?"

Refocusing, he found that the other archangel had his porcelain teacup held outward. "Oh, right, terribly sorry."

He picked up the silver pot and poured out a fragrant amber stream with practiced ease. Then he did the same for himself, accepting the sugar cubes when they were offered to him and declining the scones.

"Perhaps a sandwich, then?" Byron inquired.

Stirring with a silver spoon, Bertie glanced over the perfectly constructed deviled-ham squares and circular cucumber-and-cream-cheese delectables. There were tiny *petits fours*, too, and little pieces of fudge, and orange slices as well.

He could not eat any of it.

"When this started," he said quietly, "it never occurred to one that one's side might lose. One never considered that possibility."

"Yes." Byron added some milk out of a delicate pitcher. "I feel much the same."

In fact, Bertie tried to imagine an existence different from this and could not. His most enjoyable job was to be a gatekeeper, along with the others, to welcome the new arrivals and to help smooth the way for them—after all, Heaven could be a shock to those who had left the Earth conflicted or in grief, and further, even those who had been prepared to go could mourn the loss of their family, their friends, their life. Fortunately, any such strife ne'er lasted as soon as they understood that time here had no meaning, that moments and millennia were interchangeable in the manse—and thus they would be reunited in the blink of an eye, even if it took fifty years.

He loved his work. Interacting with the souls had brought out a dimension in him he had lacked, in spite of the fact that his role, out of the four of them, was to be the heart: Although he was not alive in the human sense, and never had been, he had found, over the ages, that he had embraced on a personal level humans' need for comfort and companionship, for love and security.

And that commiseration made any impending loss in the larger war so much more upsetting. He could not bear to lose his colleagues, his purpose, his home.

"I feel rather helpless," he murmured, as he looked over the undulating lawn.

Green, so very green, yet it was not a chromatic one-note. There were blades of every shade in the verdant carpet, from shamrock to emerald to chartreuse and sea foam. And in that sense, what was the very foundation of Heaven was like the souls below: different variations of the same thing making a glorious composite—

Far off in the distance, there was a flash of movement—and even though he could not see what it was quite yet, he knew precisely the cause.

Tarquin, his beloved Irish wolfhound, had gone off for a runabout, something the dear old boy did on a regular basis, sure as if he were watching his lean waistline: streaking over the ground, body stretched out long and lithe, tongue hanging out as he charged for the tea table, he was clearly enjoying his exercise.

It was only when the dog, which was not actually a dog, got closer, that it became obvious joy was not a part of the approach.

At the table, Tarquin skidded to a halt, his panting loud and frothy. He did not sniff around in hopes of a snack, however: He stood there meeting Bertie's eyes, sending out some kind of an urgent message.

Bertie put his teacup down and wiped his mouth. "What is it, darling one? Whatever is wrong?"

As Bertie cradled that massive head between his hands, Colin's voice intruded upon the scene.

"Nigel's gone."

Bertie wrenched around. "I beg your pardon?"

The other archangel came forward from out of the very air, and dearest fates, he looked absolutely wretched, his skin as pale as his white clothes, his dark hair ragged as a torn cloth. "He's not coming back."

Byron stiffened. "Do not say such a thing."

Oh, no, Bertie thought . . . no . . .

Colin's voice cracked. "He did it himself."

All the blood drained out of Bertie's head. "Surely you do not mean—"

Colin stared out over the landscape and yet his eyes focused on nothing. "I went to get him for tea, and I found him. So when

I say he's gone—it's not because he decided to go for a long walk. Now, if you will excuse me, I'm going to go get drunk."

"Colin," Bertie breathed. "Dearest fates upon us, no."

"Fates upon us. Yes, quite." The archangel put his palm out as both Bertie and Byron began to get to their feet. "No. No compassion. In fact, no response, please. I'm going to deal with this in my own way, thank you."

The archangel Colin turned away as if in a trance, and in contrast to his sudden appearance, he ambulated away in halting, uneven steps—stumbling and tripping now and again as he went down toward the river.

"No . . ." Byron moaned. "Surely this cannot be."

Bertie grabbed onto Tarquin's neck and held the great beast to him. No, this was not supposed to be how it all went. When they had begun this war, there had been . . . rules. There had been the understanding that Devina was the enemy. There had been the expectation of victory and peace e'er after.

Never, ever this.

Shifting his eyes over to the two flags on the parapet, he knew why, however.

"Whatever shall we do now," Byron whispered.

That was the question, of course. The war was going to rage on—it was just going to do so without Nigel . . . and Colin. For one without the other, when it came to that pair, meant that both were lost.

"This was not supposed to happen," Byron said. "I did not foresee this a'tall."

As tears welled in Bertie's eyes, he had to agree—

A cold warning trembled across his shoulders as he measured the stout walls of the castle, and the moat, and the drawbridge.

As much as he mourned his dearest friend, there was a larger worry, a far, far more emergent problem. One of Biblical proportions, as they might say upon the Earth.

"Byron." He rose out of his seat and took the collar of the great dog. "Byron, get upon your feet."

The other archangel lifted his distraught eyes. "Why?"

"Come hither." Bertie began to back away from the table, leading Tarquin with him. "Now."

"Bertie, whate'er is wrong with you—"

"We must needs get inside the castle, and lock it up tight." Bertie pivoted and started to walk faster, calling over his shoulder. "We are all that is left to protect them."

At that, there was a loud clanging noise, as if the archangel had burst up and caught the underside of the table with his legs.

Byron had clearly extrapolated to the same conclusion Bertie had: Assuming Colin had not misinterpreted whatever he had found in Nigel's tent, Nigel was well and truly unreachable now, and Colin not far behind. And that meant Heaven was weakened.

It had long been a fact that the souls were behind those fortifications for good reason. All it would take was an infiltration by Devina, and she wouldn't have to worry about the war's resolution.

She would determine that herself.

Bertie fell into a flat-out run, and Tarquin, as if sensing their predicament, loped alongside him, his gait growing longer and longer until he broke free and became the first of the three of them to cross the drawbridge.

Bertie was the second, and as his fine leather-soled shoes encountered the thick wooden boards, he looked overhead, praying that he didn't see shadows forming in the sky above. Skidding to a halt by the gear and cable system that would raise the planks, he was relieved to find Byron shooting across the moat at a dead run.

Together, he and the other archangel placed hands on the massive crank and threw their weight into a pumping rhythm as Tarquin splayed his massive forepaws and scrummed down, growling deep in his chest in warning as he backed up inside to allow the drawbridge to raise.

Devina had yet to arrive. If she had, her presence would have been sensed.

But Bertie knew she would come—and likely, soon. She and Nigel were required to meet on a regular basis with the Maker, and they were not allowed to forgo the sessions. If they did not attend? They were penalized.

The instant Nigel didn't appear at the scheduled time?

That canny demon would suspect something dire had happened, and it was in her nature to investigate the cause. And if she infiltrated the grounds? The manse was the only safe place to be—and even then, it had never truly been tested.

As the planks found home, locking in up top, Bertie went to one side, and Byron went to the other and together, they completed the final step: Tremendous forged iron bars thick as a torso slid across into deeply carved compartments in the twelve-foot-thick walls, hitting home with a resonant, echoing thud.

He couldn't remember the last time these precautions had been taken.

Collapsing back against the cool stone, all Bertie could think about were his dear friends—his family, indeed—stuck on the far side.

"God save them," he whispered.

Tarquin whimpered and nudged his hand. As he stroked that regal head, he said, "Darling one, we shall be safe herein."

At least until Devina tried to enter. Then? He did not know.

With a wave of despair, he looked over at Byron . . . and watched as the archangel slowly drew off his rose-colored glasses. His hands were trembling so badly, he dropped them.

Landing on the stone floor, the lenses shattered into countless pieces.

Chapter
Twenty-eight

As Sissy stared up at Jim from her crouch by the bathtub, his face was drawn and pale. And that answered her question, didn't it.

She turned back to the porcelain expanse and felt her stomach burn. "It must have happened here, then."

God, her voice sounded funny to her own ears.

It seemed so weird to think that something as traumatic as her own death could be lost in her head, the experience hidden like that furniture back at the old house, obscured even as the contours filled out the draping cloth of her amnesia—because she sensed she *had* been in here, in this loft, in this marble-floored room . . . in this tub.

But that was all she got.

Letting her weight fall back, she sat on her butt, drawing her knees up to her chest. Surely something would come forward if she stayed here long enough. Some image, the memory of a sound, a smell, a sensation . . . and that would unlock the door.

Or burn the sheets, as it were.

But all she got . . . was that fire in her gut. On the other hand, why wouldn't she be getting pissed off again.

"Looks like you're going to have to tell me anyway," she said. "The show part of this isn't working."

"Nothing?"

"No."

When Jim didn't say anything further, she looked up. He was no longer standing. Instead, he was against the wall by the door, sliding down slowly until he, too, was sitting on the hard marble. As he draped his arms on his knees and rubbed his face, she was struck by how visibly upset he was.

Under any other circumstances, she would have backed off. Especially in her old life. "Tell me."

There was a long pause before he replied. "I don't know how she brought you here. I don't know whether she stuffed you in a trunk or tied your arms and legs and threw you in the back of a van. I don't know if she had you in a trance, or drugged you, or incapacitated you in some way I can only guess at." Jim swallowed hard. "I know that you were sacrificed because you were a virgin, and it was to protect her mirror. I know that I found you here . . . and you were gone—"

Jim's voice broke at that point.

He cleared his throat, like he intended to go on. But nothing came out when he opened his mouth.

With a rough hand, he scrubbed his jaw.

Still nothing.

His inability to speak reached her on some deep level. This was a tough man, a hard man, and she knew without being told that he did not waste time with emotional stuff. And yet here he was. . . .

As he blinked hard, Sissy was drawn out of her own drama.

Reaching out, she put her hand on his forearm. "It wasn't your fault, you know. You were—"

"I should have gotten here sooner—"

"—not to blame for this—"

"—could have saved—"

"Stop it," she barked. "Listen to me. Not your fault. Not at all."

And then he began to weep.

Oh . . . my God, she thought. It was the last thing she expected.

And it was not like a girl would. Not with some high-pitched hysteria. He wept soundlessly, those huge shoulders quaking, his breath ragged, his face hidden behind his palms as if he didn't want her or anybody to see him like this.

"You were gone. . . ."

Sissy crab-walked over to sit beside him, but then didn't know what to say . . . do. "It's not your fault," she told him again roughly.

"I was too late. . . . You were already gone. Jesus Christ, you were . . . gone. And the truth is, ever since I found you, every time I close my eyes, every time I try to sleep, the image of you hanging over this goddamn, motherfucking tub tortures me."

Sissy reached out and pulled him to her. It was an asinine thing to do—he was twice her size, and anything but a boy. Except he fell against her sure as a rootless tree, landing in a sprawl that pushed her closer to the tub.

Cradling him in her arms, she felt rather than heard his sobs, and strangely, offering him comfort eased her. It made her seem . . . strong, and that was critical in the midst of this scene of her greatest powerlessness.

And she wasn't sure she needed to know any further details. She had been hoping that information would lead to some kind of understanding, even if it was painful. It did not, though. She was here where her death had taken place, and had some broad brushstrokes about the event—mainly Jim's reaction—and she wasn't any more grounded.

The only thing she felt was that anger deep inside her. Even as she embraced Jim, and honestly felt commiseration for his suffering, that fury burned.

Jim shifted his position, wrapping his arms around her, holding her in return.

Closing her eyes, Sissy tried to reach a place of peace. Or . . . resignation. Or . . . something.

She could not. But it was strange . . . being close to Jim like this?

Now, that was not weird. At all.

In fact, she became acutely aware of his body, his heft, his masculine scent. And that did bring something else out in her. She wasn't sure exactly what it was, but it was better than the anger, that was for sure.

A torturous slide show was playing in Jim's brain.

Well, not a show as in a series of images. There were only two. One of Sissy. The other of his mother.

One was in this bathroom. The other in a farmhouse kitchen. Both were heavily tinted in the color red, in the former case, in the tub, and in the latter, all over a linoleum floor.

He was not an emotional guy. Never had been—well, not since he'd been thirteen.

The event that had spawned that second slide, namely him finding his mother half dead and near-totally desecrated on their kitchen floor, had zipped him up but good. And he'd assumed that was a permanent thing . . . being here, though, reliving his part in Sissy's passing, feeling the horror and the rage at the waste of it all, along with his impotence as he tried and failed to save her . . . it cracked open his vault, busting through the layers of not-going-there-ever, splintering the wall he'd built up.

"Who?" Sissy said.

Jim pulled back and swiped his palms over his wet face. "What?"

"You said a name."

"Nah."

She nodded, her eyes locking on his. "Who was she?" When he didn't answer, she reached up and put her soft hand on his cheek. "Who did you lose? Other than me, who did you not get there in time for?"

"This isn't about my past—"

"Actually, I think it is. I always used to believe things happened for a reason. Maybe we came here . . . for you." As he started to shake his head, she cut him off. "This didn't get me what I was looking for. I don't feel any better. So at least . . . maybe we can help you."

Jim frowned. His mother's death had in fact been the first of the uglies in his life, the starting gun of his race to what he'd become in XOps. If that murder hadn't happened, would he have ended up in a different place?

Yes, he thought. Without that, he would have been a farmer out there in the Midwest, working the land, using his hands.

It was totally foreign to speak of it all, but for some reason, the words came and could not be denied. "We lived out on the plains. My mom and me. Alone. It was a small farm, surrounded by huge farms. So when these men broke into the house and . . . hurt her . . . nobody heard her scream. I came home and found her in the kitchen, she didn't have much time left. So much blood, the blood everywhere . . . God . . ." A choking sensation made it nearly impossible to go on, but somehow, he had to. "She told me to run—she whispered it. They were upstairs, taking what little we had. I wanted to stay with her, but she made me go. I ran out to the truck—I didn't have a license, I was too young, but I knew how to drive. I got in and floored the gas—I can remember looking in the rearview mirror and seeing the dust boiling up behind me on the road. Later, I came back. After all the police stuff was taken care of, I buried her myself, dug the hole in the pasture by the ridge. There was no one else to mourn her."

Sissy exhaled slowly, as if an echo of all his pain had gone through her chest, too.

"I can't imagine being out in the world alone," she said. "You must have been Chillie's age—when having a paper route is a stretch of responsibility. What did you do? Where did you go after . . ."

"The military."

"They don't take people that young, do they?"

He was not about to tell her that he'd been recruited into XOps because of the way he'd slaughtered the three men who'd killed his mother. Those murders had been so violent, they'd hit the national press—but he'd never been caught.

XOps had put it together, though. And they had come looking for him.

Sissy pushed her hair back. "You must have had a couple of years on your own."

"Well, eventually, they accepted me." After he'd been properly screened for sociopathic tendencies—and found to have enough to qualify him. And then he'd gotten through a form of "basic training" that was so brutal, people had been known not just to quit, but keel over dead from it.

"You and I have a lot in common," Sissy murmured. "Hell takes a lot of forms, doesn't it."

"You're too young to know that."

"Not young anymore."

He was beginning to really believe that.

"Do you want the rest of the story," he said gruffly. "Yours, that is."

"Yes."

Jim felt like he was sinking into quicksand again as he chose his words. They might as well finish this, though. "Devina came while we were here. My boys had to knock me out by force—they knew if they'd let me stay, I would have fought her and probably lost. It was early times for me—shit, it feels like a million years ago. But I did return. By then? She'd cleaned the place out. Everything was gone, even you." He rubbed his eyes like they hurt. "We found you later."

"Where?"

"The quarry."

Sissy frowned. "The one out by—"

"Yeah."

"Dear Lord . . ." she whispered. "My poor parents. My sister. My grandparents."

Her hand went to her stomach and she made an expression like she was nauseated. Couldn't blame her.

After a moment, she said, "When you were little, and you got punished . . . did you ever picture yourself at your own funeral? Because I did—I used to imagine that my mom and dad were in tears, regretting every 'meanie' they'd ever done to me. That was such a wrong thing for me to do."

She grimaced as she shifted around, and he was reminded they were on a cold, hard floor—except then she rubbed her belly as if it hurt.

"Are you okay?" he said. "You want to get out of here?"

"I feel like I have indigestion."

"Why wouldn't you."

Jim got to his feet and offered a hand. As she took it and he pulled her up, she grunted, and couldn't seem to straighten.

"Sissy?"

"My stomach . . ." She lifted the hem of his shirt, pulling it up— "Oh, God! What is that!"

He had no fucking clue, at first. But then, he knew: Across the flat, pale stretch of skin, there was a pattern in the flesh, a pattern that was glowing as if lit from within.

Devina had carved it there as part of the ritual.

"Get it off me. . . ." Sissy started rubbing. "Get it off me!"

Jim captured her hands and bent down. That red illumination was all wrong, he thought. It was emanating from within her. . . .

He carefully lowered the shirt back into place. "Let's get out of here. And then we'll see what we can do about it, okay?"

Sissy grabbed onto the shirt and held it in place, a look of stark terror distorting her beautiful features. "What if she's inside me?"

Jim shook his head, even as the back of his neck tightened. "Not possible."

And then he said the one thing that, later on, he would come to regret: "You're mine."

Chapter
Twenty-nine

Cait spent the afternoon counting down the hours.

After leaving her date with G.B., she went home, sat at her desk . . . and checked the time about every twenty minutes or so. She did get some work done, however, although it was the difference between walking at the side of the road and being in a car going sixty-five.

Forward motion, but only in a relative sense.

She and Duke were meeting at six, and so, after some tense negotiations with her Guilt-o-meter, she decided to give herself an hour to get ready—which was outrageous, but seemed necessary. And then considering she needed fifteen minutes to drive into town, she was therefore allowed to get up out of her chair at four forty-five.

Don't wear a bra.

Putting her pencil down, she had to close her eyes as her body responded—

Her phone went off next to her, ringing loud in her silent house. As she grabbed for it, her heart pounded. Please, please, let it not be Duke canceling . . .

Unknown phone number. "Hello?"

". . . Cait? . . ."

As the male voice sank in, she sat up in confusion. "Thom?"

"Hi." Her old college boyfriend cleared his throat as the greeting came out funny. "Sorry, hi."

"Well, ah, hi. How are you?" In her head she did the math. The last time she'd spoken with him had been about six months ago—and he'd been very sure that he and the girlfriend were pregnant. Three plus six equals nine.

"I'm good, thanks. And you?"

They were both stilted, but then, come on. They'd nearly gotten engaged—up until he'd cheated on her. And now he and the woman were pregnant—actually, had no doubt just had a healthy, beautiful boy or a girl.

"Good, good, thank you."

In the silence that followed, for some reason, Cait remembered exactly where she'd been sitting when he'd rung her phone for their previous call back in November. She'd been upstairs in her bedroom, ironing clothes, and she'd kept it together during the five- or six-minute conversation. Had also been honestly glad he was telling her in person before the news got out within their network of buddies.

After she'd hung up, though? She'd turned off the lights, gotten into bed, and cried for about six hours.

Next day she'd joined the nearest Bally Total Fitness.

"I just wanted you to know . . . that we had the baby. Early last night."

As she reclosed her eyes, her first thought was that she was thrilled she was meeting Duke in about an hour and a half. To hear this news without having her date to look forward to probably would have resulted in another day under the covers.

Her second? Was that, as before, he didn't come across as if he were gloating, or showing off his good fortune. No, Thom seemed almost apologetic, just as he had when he'd told her about the pregnancy—he was clearly trying to do the right thing in a difficult situation.

"I'm so happy for you." She couldn't bring herself to say the other woman's name. That hadn't changed even with Duke on the horizon. "I really, truly am."

"I wanted you to know before, well, everyone else does."

"What's his or her name?"

"We've named him Thomas, after me."

"That's great. You must be so excited."

"I am. I mean, this wasn't planned, but . . . sometimes life is like that, you know?"

Tell me about it, Thom. "Yes, I know. When's the wedding?"

Because surely he would marry the woman now.

"Not for a while. We have to get through the first couple months with him—well, Margot does. I'm working around the clock."

"Wall Street will do that to you."

"Sure does." Pause. "Are you okay?"

Cait bristled at that. What, like she'd been sitting around pining after him forever?

Okay, maybe that had been true for a little while. "You know what? I really am. I'm in a good place, work's fantastic, and my personal life is . . ." She didn't finish that part with any details. Seemed too much as if she were trying to prove something. ". . . going well."

The relief that came across the connection was palpable. "Oh, I'm so glad to hear that."

And you know, it was funny; she believed that was true for him. In this moment, sitting with the phone squeezed to her ear and the awkwardness on both sides making her want to end things quickly, she realized . . . Thom was a good guy.

"Can I ask you something?" she blurted.

"Anything. I mean that, Cait."

"When you met . . ." Okay, time to man up. For God's sake, at this point, the pair of them had been together longer than she and Thom had. ". . . Margot, was it a love-at-first-sight kind of thing? Like, an overwhelming, no-going-back free fall?"

She was, of course, thinking of Duke. Even though that probably didn't make a lot of sense. She barely knew the guy, after all.

Thom cleared his throat. "Are you sure you want me to answer that?"

"Yeah, I really am. Although maybe this is not the right time. You're probably still at the hospital, right?"

"No, no, it's okay. They're both sleeping, and the parents have all gone home for showers."

She could just picture him in some kind of white corridor, leaning a shoulder on the wall and crossing one loafer or wingtip so that it balanced on the toe.

Thom blew out a long breath. "I saw her in the library, across a distance . . . and I can't explain it. I just stopped dead, right where I was. It wasn't in my nature to have that kind of reaction, and still isn't—and just so you and I are clear? I walked away. I didn't talk to her, I didn't ask anyone about her, I didn't take a seat and stare at her for hours. I just turned right around and left."

He was correct—that sort of struck-dumb hadn't been typical of him. Thom had always been just like her: measured, careful, focused on studying rather than people.

In fact, their friends had always said they were the perfect couple, and when they'd broken up the spring of senior year, the split had been a major topic of conversation. Looking back now, she imagined it had been easier in some ways to be on her side of things, i.e., the victim, the one who had been deserted—although that certainly hadn't been a party. At least their social circle had pitied her, though, rather than gotten all snarky in her direction.

"It must have been a surprise for you," she said.

"It wasn't what I wanted. Not at all."

"When did it happen, you know, her and you?"

What a crazy time to be finally asking these questions. When he'd told her he'd found someone else, she hadn't wanted any details—just a cardboard box to pack up the things he'd left in her dorm room.

"A year later."

Cait recoiled. "You two dated for a year?"

"No. I saw her first a year, maybe a year and a half before I . . . you know. It was fall our junior year. Cait, I was going to marry you. I was committed to you. I wanted to be with you. The last thing I ever considered was that somebody else would get in the way. After I saw her, I stopped studying in the library. I left parties—do you remember that Super Bowl party at Rich's? The one where he got arrested afterward? I said I was sick—but it was because she was there. I didn't want to be anywhere around her."

Cait eased back in her chair. "God . . ."

"You were always working, Cait, especially our senior year—and that is not to put anything on you. That was the way we were. It's just . . . you were always so busy, and I was busy, and then one night . . . you went to visit your parents for Presidents' Day weekend because they were finally home for a little while? I was sitting in our quad, Teresa was out, Greg was gone . . . and I don't know what . . . exactly it was, but I got up and put my coat on, and I walked across campus at ten o'clock at night. I went to the library that night, and she was there. And that was . . . what happened. About two weeks after that was when I spoke with you. Margot and I had not been together by that time, but I knew where things were headed, I knew that . . . Christ, Cait, the last thing I ever wanted to do was hurt you."

"I believe that," she said hoarsely. "I do."

"And you know, the reason I called you before we announced, and why I'm calling you now? I've embarrassed you enough. I don't want you to ever be on the receiving end of unexpected news again—at least not that has to do with me. Even though it was how many years ago, I've never gotten over that whole thing with us, Cait. It was a blessing to meet Margot, but a curse, too. She's my other half, but I had to hurt . . . you."

As tears welled, it wasn't from grief. More from a sense that in reality, they had both hurt each other, in their own ways. And though she had never wished him ill per se, the idea that he hadn't waltzed away into the arms of some hot new love free and clear made her feel like it was more equitable, somehow.

"I'm really glad you called," she said. "I truly am."

Thom exhaled long and slow. "I've wanted to explain myself for a long time. But not from a self-serving point of view, more because I honestly still care about you. And I always will."

Cait smiled sadly, remembering how the two of them could spend hours studying side by side. They had been the perfect companions, and she'd been looking for stability back then. But was that true love?

Not like he'd found with Margot.

"You take care of yourself, Thom."

"You, too, Cait."

As she ended the call, she stared at her phone.

It was good to know he was as decent as she'd thought he was. He'd avoided his truth for a good year . . . and then it had just been his time, she supposed. And yes, the whole thing had been heartbreaking, the trauma of losing what she'd planned her life to be, that artificial structure she had created herself but called destiny, absolutely crushing. But she had always wondered whether or not he had been the man she'd assumed she knew.

He was.

The only thing that could have been worse? Learning that all along, through the course of their relationship, he had been nothing but a lie.

Plus, now that she had met Duke? She understood what Thom meant. Sometimes . . . you just crossed paths with someone irresistible, and depending on your circumstance? It could be devastating.

In her case? She was single, and that was a good thing. How would she have felt if she'd run into the likes of Duke . . . and been in a relationship?

On that note, Cait glanced at her clock. Four thirty-nine.

For most of her life, she would have forced herself to sit still for the remaining six minutes. Now? Screw that.

It was time to get ready.

Shutting down her workstation, she headed for the second floor, and it was as she threw on her shower and let all her clothes dump on the floor again that she realized . . . yes, in fact, she was probably going through exactly what had happened to Thom.

For years, she hadn't been prepared to cut him any slack. And when he'd called to say they were pregnant? She had turned to her diet and the gym to crush all the emotions that had come up.

But now? After talking to him downstairs?

A weight had been lifted off of her, and the relief she had been seeking in all kinds of other outlets settled through her, a balm that ushered in with it the sort of peace that had seemed impossible to achieve.

Interesting. She and her mom and dad disagreed about a lot. But if this was the forgiveness they advocated? It was freedom from your own pain.

And that was a very, very good thing.

Cait tried not to be on time. Unfortunately, old habits died hard, and she was three minutes early. After eyeing the Riverside Diner's parking lot, she decided to drive on by and waste some time going around the block for a while.

Six ten. That was her sweet spot. Not too early, not too late.

At the allotted moment in history—not that she was blowing this out of proportion or anything, she pulled her SUV into the parking area and found a spot. It was kind of a surprise to be so nervous as she looked around for his truck.

Not in the lot: From what she could see thanks to a combination of streetlights and the fading glow of the sunset's last gasp, there were ten or twelve vehicles and a couple of motorcycles. No trucks.

Maybe he was fashionably late, too.

Getting out and locking up, she headed for the entrance, her stomach doing that butterfly thing she'd heard about, but never experienced before. And like her brain didn't want to be left out of the flutter-party, all sorts of random nonsense were jumping through her head, none of the thoughts sticking, her skull like a child's bouncy castle filled with balls.

Pulling open the doors, she walked into a traditional fifties diner, red Naugahyde booths going down one side, a counter with stools across the aisle, a serving setup and flap doors into the kitchen behind that.

Duke wasn't in the booths, although several men looked up at her arrival and did a double take—something that had happened on campus today as well. Yup, blonds definitely got more attention, but she wasn't sure about the fun, especially if tonight's date ended up not happening. Which would be two evenings in a row. Although at least there was a good chance she wouldn't get chased into an elevator—

There he was.

Through the arches that led into the other dining room, he was at a booth by the back exit, facing out, staring right at her.

He didn't smile. Or wave. Or sit a little straighter.

But his burning eyes ate her up, the impact of that stare flushing away everything that was between them—the tables, the waitresses, the other patrons, the distance across a red carpeted floor.

It was just as it had been when they'd looked at each other in the café parking lot.

As Cait walked over to him, she found that her body moved differently, a sensual feeling infusing her legs and hips and breasts with a slow-boil heat that she wanted to turn up.

"Hi," she said, her voice deeper than usual.

"You look good." His eyes dipped down her. "Really good."

"Thanks. You, too." Although he could have been wearing a seventies lounge suit and she probably would have drooled over the polyester.

Sliding in opposite him, she took off her coat and was acutely aware of the way her breasts moved against the fine material of her blouse—and so was he. Now he changed positions, moving around as if impatient.

Or maybe uncomfortable thanks to an . . . um, yeah.

And that was totally hot.

Without further conversation, he extended his hand across

the tabletop, palm up, and in reply, she put hers on top of his immediately.

God, he was . . . extraordinary. Rugged. Handsome, but with an edge. And still every bit as muscular in that black T-shirt as he had been before. His dark hair was a little shorter than she remembered, as if he'd had it trimmed during the day—maybe for their date? And there was no five o'clock shadow shading that strong jaw of his. Which suggested he'd showered and shaved in preparation for her.

Which was a compliment, wasn't it.

As she stared at him across the table, she couldn't help but compare him to G.B. With the other man, she had been starstruck, yes—and there was a certain intensity there. But that experience was a curiously removed one, almost as if she were examining something that was exotic up close for the first time.

With Duke? He was just flat-out sexy, from those hooded eyes to his full lips to those shoulders—

"I waited all day for this," he said in a gravel-filled voice.

Cait flushed from head to foot. "Me, too—"

Like the echo from some distant world that had nothing to do with her or him, she heard a phone go off dimly. Might have been her own; she didn't care. In fact, a stampede could thunder through the diner and she doubted she would notice, or care.

God, she wanted him. Here. Now . . .

"Tell me something," he said.

"What?"

"Your name. I still don't know what it is."

Cait smiled and dropped her eyes. Guess she'd missed that. "It's Cait. As in Caitlyn."

"That's nice."

"Thank you."

Annnnnnd now back to the mutual staring.

In fact, they were still sitting like that, looking into each other's eyes, holding hands, when the waitress came over with menus. Neither of them acknowledged what was delivered, or made much of a response when they were asked what they wanted to drink.

"I'm not hungry," he said, "for food. How about you?"

Cait shook her head. And that was that.

They both exited the booth and, after he left a fiver as a tip, walked out of the restaurant.

Outside, the cool weather did nothing to clear her head. So when he pointed to a Victorian boathouse a couple hundred yards away and nodded his head as if asking a question?

"Yes," she said.

Closest shot at privacy they had: It was too early in the season for people to be walking around after dark, and she had to imagine there was a secluded place in there somewhere. Bottom line? She had no interest in futzing around with who followed who in what vehicle to God only knew where.

Even the short walk was going to take forever.

Which proved that in some situations, distance, like time, was relative.

Chapter Thirty

"Devina, you have me concerned."

As the demon sat on her therapist's couch, she fiddled with the horse-bit buckle on her Gucci bag. The office was totally not her—overstuffed cushions, mucky brown tones, shaggy throw rug, all kinds of beech wood mounted on stands like it was worth something. Two Kleenex boxes. For the weepers.

"Devina?"

Her therapist was sitting across a glass-topped table, her ample body draped as always in folds of flower-print fabric. Talk about somebody slipcovering themselves—Devina looked like shit in her real form, but she cured that with good flesh that was tailored well. This woman with the soft voice and perma-concerned expression? The muumuus were *not* a look.

Although how else could you cover all that?

Then again, it wasn't entirely her fault. As a human, all she had to choose from were clothes if she wanted to change her appearance. Well, that and plastic surgery, which could only do so much—

"Devina."

Oh, look, she was leaning forward and getting intense.

Devina focused on her purse again, thinking about how she and the therapist were such opposites. The woman might have been built like one of her throw pillows, but she was beautiful on the inside—beneath those layers of a slowing metabolism coupled with a sedentary job and probably some pharmacological estrogen, her soul glowed with the pure white light of goodness.

Devina was not that. Without her exterior lie?

As tears welled, she found it hard to speak past the lump in her throat. "I am . . . ugly."

"Can you tell me more?"

Goddamn, she was so upset, she wasn't even offended the therapist didn't offer an, "OMG, you are so not!"

"I don't know what I'm saying." Devina waved her hand around. "It's nothing important. Let's change the subject."

"I can respect how much you don't want to discuss this. But frequently, the things we don't want to talk about are the ones we truly need to resolve. It's the work that is necessary to come fully into ourselves. Perhaps you can share with me what triggered your feelings?"

An image of her on her knees in front of Adrian, sucking his flaccid cock, hit her like a ton of bricks.

Ripping open her bag, she began to count the thirteen identical lipsticks that she always had with her—

"Devina, can you stop that?" When she just shook her head, the therapist said, "Well, perhaps try to? Remember, OCD is at least partially a maladaptive system of self-preservation. It's rooted, in that regard, to the need to make ourselves feel safe in an unpredictable world—a world where people can let us down or hurt us, and where, with respect to things that are important to us, outcomes can be outside of our control. We hold on to objects and rituals more and more tightly, under the mistaken belief that it will make us more secure. But eventually, we get strangled by our coping mechanism."

"Are you going to make me throw out another tube of these?"

"As we've discussed, the solution is to increase our range of emotional function. Become more secure in our ability to withstand the slings and arrows of life. The first step in that journey is talking—and that's why you're here."

Great recap there, honey.

Devina glanced at the clock. Shit, they still had thirty-five minutes left. Thirty-four. Thirty—

"I'm ugly," she said again.

"That's never come up in our sessions before."

Well, she'd never failed in making a guy come before.

As Devina pushed her hair back, the thought of what her real stuff looked like made her want to weep outright—what locks she did have were stringy and attached to rotting flesh. And the rest of her was just as bad. Without this stolen suit of Sexy Bitch? Yeah, sure, she'd get a lot of attention walking through a hotel lobby or into a restaurant, but it'd be because people were assuming the zombie apocalypse had actually happened.

"I met up with an old lover." Devina shook her head. "And not old as in geriatric—this man and I have history. Serious history."

"You've never discussed your personal life."

Well, when you were a demon fighting with the forces of good for dominion over the world—and you were seeking help from a human? You used a lot of euphemisms.

Another example of clothing something for palatability.

And actually, she had talked a lot about her and Jim: their

struggles, their triumphs. All in the context of a made-up scenario about business, of course—but the therapist had a point: Devina had left a lot of the bump-and-grind out.

This didn't concern her and Jim, however.

"He's a force of nature, this former lover of mine." She smoothed her Prabal Gurung skirt. "We've had an acrimonious course—you could say we see the world from completely different perspectives. But the attraction has always been very strong."

"How long have you known him?"

Oh, God, centuries. "All my adult life. Our paths keep crossing. He called me today and wanted to see me—and I couldn't say no. We ended up . . . becoming intimate."

"And was that a satisfying experience for you?"

"No." Devina dropped her head into her palms. "I am totally humiliated."

She had never, in her immortal life, had a guy—

"Why? Devina?"

"He was . . . unable to perform."

"Well, most men have that challenge on occasion. It's not uncommon—"

"It's *never* happened to me before."

"So you're blaming yourself."

"No offense, but there wasn't anyone else with him." Devina rubbed her temples. "I tried for hours. It was so awful—and I know that he wanted to be with me. He urged me to keep going, and I did. But . . . nothing."

In a fit of desperation, she'd ended up ditching her clothes and laying herself out on her table, taking care of herself in front of him. Most men orgasmed all over themselves when she did that, and Adrian's eyes had never left her. And still . . .

"He never got hard." For shit's sake, she wished she could get those images out of her brain. "It was a nightmare."

"And again, I say, it sounds to me as if you're blaming yourself."

"If I'd been more attractive, or if I'd only have—"

"Has it never occurred to you that there could be a medical reason for the issue?"

"There hasn't been in the past."

"Things change. People can develop conditions that make sex difficult, or go on medications that complicate arousal."

Unfortunately, this was one of the corners she and her therapist occasionally came to, where the reality didn't fit the fake construction: Immortals like Adrian didn't need Cialis or Viagra; they didn't roll over one morning with circulatory problems or go on enough antidepressants to deflate their dicks. It was one of the perks of not living under the burden of an expiration date.

"Devina, you wouldn't expect a case of diabetes to be cured by a seductive glance, would you? Of course not. So it could well be the same here. Perhaps, no matter what you or he wanted or did, intercourse would have been impossible."

There were a lot of times when the woman's advice was spot-on. This was not one of them, unfortunately.

"Did you talk with him about what happened and how it made you feel?"

"No." Devina shook her head. "He had to go, and I dressed and followed him out. Then we spent some time together."

They'd ended up back on Earth, at a Target, of all things. She'd followed him around as he'd picked out clothes from the young women's racks, hideous little things that were made with all the sophistication and skill of an eight-year-old's paper airplanes.

She'd guessed that they were for darling Sissy—which was the only reason Devina hadn't pulled rank and dragged him over to Saks. The worse that girl looked, the better.

Actually, on the humiliation scale, it was hard to know what ranked worse—all that flaccid, or the shopping excursion from hell. And it was strange—the closest Devina had ever come to being cock-whipped was when she was with Jim. But Adrian's lack of response had been so upsetting, she hadn't known what to do with herself. She'd been brought to heel like a dog, walking around those pinwheels full of cheap clothes behind him, docile as a retriever.

After that? He was hungry—so they'd gone to TGIFriday's in Lucas Square.

She hadn't even been able to enjoy the agog stares of the other patrons when she'd walked in with all her couture.

The potato skins with bacon hadn't been half-bad, though. And the fudge brownie had lifted her spirits a little, although that hadn't lasted past the sugar buzz.

Sitting across from each other, they hadn't talked much, but what was there to be said? Being enemies was a fun thing, except when it wasn't.

"You know, Devina, it's possible he's blaming himself in an equally erroneous fashion."

"I doubt it. He'd seemed fine, actually." Which was one more ass slapper. That Adrian hadn't been bothered one way or the other had been an insult. You'd think he'd have the grace to be even slightly affected.

He'd come to her for the sex, after all.

"Are you going to see him again?"

Devina shrugged. "Undoubtedly I will." She smoothed her short skirt again. "I'm not sure I want to though. Not in a big hurry to relive all of that."

"You know, Devina, I have to ask. Is there anything else that's going on for you right now? Sometimes our reactions are compounded by . . ."

As the woman droned on, an image of Jim Heron looking at

Sissy with possession in his eyes came to mind. Talk about your stingers. And maybe the therapist had a point. Adrian was second in line at this point on her Metaphysical Fuckable List—and having a bad experience with him would have mattered so much less if the angel at the top hadn't been so enamored of someone else.

Set a bad stage, as it were.

". . . sorry you're being challenged like this, but it presents an opportunity to develop new coping skills. I imagine you're feeling very triggered?"

As a matter of fact, she was. The compulsive need to perform an extensive review of her collection, the whole thing, was trembling on the edge of her consciousness, about to become an earthquake that took over every thought or feeling or priority.

"My suggestion," the therapist interjected, "is to do something that makes you feel beautiful, instead. Maybe it's journaling about all your positive attributes, your accomplishments, your successes. Perhaps it's meeting up with a friend and having a nice meal. A yoga class."

Ha. Been there, done that. And it had made her want to commit murder—no doubt not the direction that the therapist was going in.

"I want you to think in terms of self-affirming things. It is important for you to reach out beyond the compulsions—to find solace and purpose within yourself and your support system. Be creative. Have fun with it. But above all, know that the more you stretch yourself to explore your feelings, tolerating the bad ones and discovering that they too shall pass, the stronger and better off you will be. You can do this, Devina. I have faith in you."

Devina looked across at the woman. Given that her therapist wore a cross around her thick neck, one could extrapolate the irony if she knew that she'd just tried to inspire a demon.

Surprise!

And, you know, Devina was almost tempted to drop her slip-cover, just to see the reaction—and to give some credibility to her statements about how hideous she really was. But what stopped her was all the dead-serious in the woman's face. The therapist honestly believed everything she was saying, and that was kind of touching.

"So I just leave here. . . ." Devina cleared her throat. "And . . ."

"Anything that keeps you from acting on a ritual. The best thing to do, especially as denying the urges becomes more uncomfortable, is to go about your life. Focus on self-affirmation, and activities that give you a sense of mastery. Anything that will root you in all of the strength you possess. You can do this."

"Be creative. Have fun with it, huh?"

As the therapist nodded like a bobblehead doll, all Devina could think of was, God, she'd rather go back to Target.

Chapter Thirty-one

"It's after hours. The door's locked."

As Cait jogged the boathouse's combination lock, the disappointment she was feeling was obvious in her voice. But come on, of course the facility was still going to be mostly off-limits in late April.

"Here." Duke stepped into the light thrown by the fixture overhead. "Let me take a look at it."

"It's totally locked."

Damn it. Where could they go now? There was nothing else around, really—not unless they wanted to be picked up on public-obscenity charges. It looked like they were going to have to go back and get their cars—

Click. Creak.

Hello, wide-open.

Duke motioned the way in gallantly.

"How did you . . ."

"I work for the city during the day. This is an officially owned

Caldwell property, and gee, what do you know, I have the master combination to all the locks."

"You are incredible."

Those lids dropped low again. "You haven't seen anything yet."

In an instant, Cait was totally aroused, and as she brushed past him, she deliberately let her shoulder move across his chest. He hadn't bothered to bring a coat, and his invincibility with the weather made her wonder if he couldn't lift cars, stop bullets with his teeth, leap buildings in a—

Okay, now she was being ridiculous.

Inside, it was dark as night, the illumination from the lights along the roofline no match for the grime-covered windows. The only thing that registered was the sound of the water clapping under the cribs—a good reminder to watch where you were going so you didn't fall in—

"Ouch!"

Or run into something.

"Are you okay?" he said right behind her.

"Yes, I hit a . . ."

Well, she wasn't too sure what the thing was, but hard-as-a-rock certainly covered it. Reaching out, she found the sharp vertical edge that had caught her right in the shin, and then a long, widening rail—ah, yes, a canoe, she thought as she felt around.

"Come here," Duke growled, spinning her around. "You can hang on to me."

Cait needed no other invitation. She went right against his powerful body, arms rising up so she could grab the back of his neck and bring his mouth to hers. Their lips met in a clash of flesh, the sexual need exploding between them, everything going even more desperate than it had the night before: She was only dimly aware of him kicking the door shut. And after that, nothing mattered but what they were doing.

Duke's hands were rough as they ripped the bottom of her shirt free from her skirt, and then his broad palms were on her breasts.

"Oh, yeah, that's what I want," he bit out before melding his lips to her own again.

The kissing was utterly delicious, the slide of velvet on velvet as intoxicating as the way he was caressing her—but he broke up the dueling of their tongues and pulled back all too soon. Fortunately, the relocation of that mouth of his was so not a problem, considering where he went next.

Duke beelined for what he had bared, and as warm, wet suction found her nipple, Cait closed her eyes and went limp in his powerful grip. As he licked and teased at her, his strong arms gathered her up off the dock, and held her aloft.

Unlike her, he knew exactly where to go: A moment later, she was laid down on a soft pile of boat cushions.

"This okay?" he asked.

"Lay me on asphalt, concrete, wherever. Just come with me."

"Oh, I will. You can bet your life on that one."

His mouth was back on hers a split second later, his tongue entering her mouth, penetrating her as one of his knees pushed in between her legs and then his hips thrust against her—he was utterly erect, his arousal pushing into her core, the barriers of their clothes frustrating to the point of pain.

As she dug her nails into his upper arms, her scrambled brain incapable of figuring out zippers and button flies, she was out of her mind and totally aware at the same time: He tasted of fresh coffee, and smelled of some kind of woodsy cologne, and as she clawed at one of his shoulders, his body was like a steel cable.

Just as she had remembered.

As he shoved her jacket aside and pushed up her shirt even further, his pelvis surged against her, finding a rhythm that would be oh, so much more effective if someone, anyone just got his pants down to his thighs. Taking the initiative, she shifted her hands downward, her only clear thought that she'd rip things in half if she had to—

Duke positively purred as she rubbed against his arousal, her hands sloppy as she popped the first of what proved to be, yup, just her luck, a button fly.

"I have what we need," he grunted as he pushed himself off of her to help.

Yes, you certainly do, she thought as he shucked what covered him and exposed his—

She nearly laughed. So much for that whole cold-shrinks thing.

And then she was all business. She gripped his girth—

"Oh . . . fucking hell, I need this."

His words devolved into nothing but guttural syllables as she stroked up and down his shaft. He even fell against her, as if his arms had lost their strength.

"Wait, wait." He grabbed her hand and squeezed, stilling her. "I'm going to come if you keep that up."

"I thought that was the point." As her eyes had adjusted, she could make out part of his harsh face in the dimness. "Or have I misread this?"

Wow, she actually sounded kind of tantalizing. Go her.

And clearly, it worked—he kissed her hard, and then groaned, "Inside of you. I want you to feel me orgasm."

Rearing up over her, he reached into his back pocket and took out a foil square. Biting through the wrapper, just as he had the night before, he rolled the condom onto himself as she swept off her panties.

She all but yanked him back down.

This time, he was the one who joined them, the blunt head of his erection pushing into her, guided by his steady hand—and then there was a thrust, a deep one. But there was no pain. Her body was more than ready—all she felt was that incredible stretching and sense of fullness.

As Duke dropped his head into her neck, she smoothed down to the small of his back and arched under him so that they were linked even more fully. With perfect synchronicity, they began to move together, the surging penetrations increasing in power and tempo.

No way to kiss. Too fast and furious.

This was going to be over so soon, too soon, but she had no self control—

"Oh, God," she shouted.

The release shattered through her, sending her flying even though her corporeal form never left the Earth. And Duke was only a moment behind her, his hips jackhammering into her and then freezing as he locked in against her core.

Deep inside of her, just as he'd told her, his arousal kicked, the spasming cueing off another orgasm for her.

Cait was panting hard in the aftermath, and as he collapsed on top of her, she loved the weight of him—and the fact that he had wanted this as much as she had.

"I thought about this all night," he said into her ear. "All night . . . I had the fever for you."

As she laughed, she was surprised by the sound—it was like something from a movie, uttered by the siren in the film, not the sensible neighbor/friend/homely girl who was second fiddle.

It wasn't anything she had ever heard come out of her mouth before.

But she hadn't had sex like that before, either.

"Did you," she drawled as she subtly arched, creating friction in all the right places.

Nuzzling at her throat, Duke gave her a soft bite. "You like that I couldn't sleep?"

"Yes."

"Do you want to know what I did to myself? To pass the time?" Now he was the one drawling, his voice slow and lazy. "Answer me."

"Yes," she breathed.

He began to move inside of her again. "I sleep naked, you know."

"Oh, God," she moaned.

"And I couldn't keep my hands to myself."

Cait squeezed her eyes together as her body jerked under his, images of him lying on a bed, head kicked back in ecstasy as he pleasured himself to thoughts of her, making her pant again.

"Come for me, Cait," he commanded.

And she did.

Duke orgasmed for the second time within minutes of his first release, his cock having a seemingly endless appetite for the undone, half-naked woman underneath him.

The sounds she was making were driving him as crazy as the feel of her was, her sex holding his cock tight as a fist, her flesh hot and wet as he drove into her again and again, riding out both of their releases for as long as he could.

But he couldn't keep taking chances like this. Condoms were a one-use-only kind of thing, and he wanted to take care of her in the right manner.

As was his way, he didn't waste any time—as soon as he wasn't seeing double from clenching his jaw, he reached between them and held the condom in place as he withdrew. Yup, twice in a row was not safe—and with the way he was feeling? Give him another minute and a half and he was going to be tempted to go for number three.

He was *so* not interested in stopping—and he had another Trojan, but goddamn it, he was too impatient for that.

Dropping his head, he found one of her nipples and ran his tongue around it as he adjusted his position, his knees moving off the boat cushions and finding the decking. Handling Cait harder than he would have liked, he shuffled her around as he kept kissing his way down her body—and like she'd read his mind and wanted exactly what he did, her knees fell wide, her thighs parting as she arched up for his mouth.

Gripping the insides of her legs, he swept his palms upward until he reached her heat with his fingertips. Stroking her, he watched from above as she writhed on the cushions, the luscious planes and angles of her body contorting in the shadows, the fact that she wasn't completely naked making everything seem even hotter.

When he couldn't stand the teasing for a second longer, he covered her core with his mouth, sucking at her as he reached up and palmed her breasts. From a distance, he heard her call his name, but all sound was filtered through the prism of an almost unholy need to possess her, to get inside of her, to clothe himself in all this heat of hers.

Her slick flesh was so smooth against his tongue as he licked at her and then penetrated her, dipping deep inside of her. And because he wanted her to orgasm for him again, he rubbed his thumb in circles at the top of her sex, urging her up to and over that awesome cliff.

She came against his face.

And he fucking loved it.

So much so, he didn't stop. He drove her harder, giving her another one as he put a hand down to his cock and squeezed hard, pumping up and back.

He said her name against her flesh as he ejaculated—

A loud clapping sound went off behind them, and he instantly came back online with reality, jacking up from between her thighs and wrenching around as he put a hand on her lower belly to hold her in place.

Just the door.

In his haste to get on her, he hadn't bothered to check that it had re-latched itself, and the wind had blown things wide and then sucked them shut.

"It's okay," he told her. "I got this."

Wiping his mouth and jaw with his hand, he stalked over and closed the panels properly. It was time to go, though. He didn't care about getting caught, but he was willing to bet she did.

"That scared me," she said as he came back over.

She had pulled down her shirt and was bent in half, obviously tugging her panties back into place. As she straightened and got to her feet, he thought her re-dressing should have counted as a crime.

"Next time," he heard himself say, "I want to fuck you in a bed."

Chapter
Thirty-two

Wash your hands, G.B. told himself. Just wash your frickin' hands.

This is going to be fine.

As he stood over the sink in the basement of the Palace Theatre, his heart was going a million miles a minute. But at least his vision had cleared and he could see the industrial faucet in front of him, and the deep-bellied sink, and the bald bulb that hung from a chain over his head.

"Wash . . . your . . . hands."

He'd taken the heavy-duty gloves he'd used off . . . but he still felt like he had to clean himself.

He closed his eyes, but that was not a good idea. Not for his brain and not for his balance. As he opened them again, he was at least able to stop himself from listing to one side. The images in his mind? They persisted, raw and with sound and smell.

As he rubbed his soapy palms together, he looked for something else to clean them with even though there was nothing on them, some kind of heavy-duty—

Bleach. There was bleach in a dusty bottle under the sink, along with some other chemicals.

The Clorox burned as he poured it on both his hands, first the left, and then the right. The stench was horrible, but this part of the theater's vast basement complex wasn't exactly a flower shop—which was a good thing.

Not a lot of foot traffic.

"Just pull it together," he said. "You need to pull it together."

He shut off the water with his elbows and went to rub his hands dry on his—oh, shit. His shirt.

He stripped himself and wadded up the cotton, shoving it into the three-inch-wide space between the sink and the battered cupboard. He'd have to come back for it; he had other things to worry about now—but at least he had a clean button-down in his backpack.

The next thing he washed was his face, his neck, his chest. And hit all that shit with bleach, too.

When he was finally done, a quick check of his watch reassured him that other than housekeeping staff, he was likely totally alone.

Walking around the cramped space, he brushed cobwebs out of the way, but was thankful for them. Along with the heavy layer of dust on the countertops and the seventies labels on the supplies on the shelves, it seemed reasonable to assume no one had been anywhere near here recently.

Well, except for him and Jennifer. And she'd stayed out in the hall.

She wasn't going anywhere. Anymore.

"Shit, shit, shit."

Focus. He needed to fucking focus—God, he hated when he got like this. All scattered and weird in the head—

"Hello."

G.B. let out a bark as he wheeled around. Standing in the doorway, looking like twelve million dollars, was that brunette, the one who had come and visited him the night before last.

"I'm glad I found you," she said in that seductive voice of hers.

"How did you know I was down here?"

Had she seen—

The woman waved a manicured hand, batting away the question. "Someone upstairs saw you. They said you were with a woman—I hope I'm not interrupting."

From out of nowhere, the self-preservation that had always rescued him came to the forefront, zipping him up tight.

"I'm not sure where she went." He felt himself smiling. "What can I do for you?"

The woman walked into the squalid room, her perfume covering up the sting of the bleach and the musty odor of the damp concrete walls.

"I've been thinking about you," she murmured.

"Have you?" He snagged an old cloth and wiped his hands, wishing the thing was clean. "That's lucky for me."

She looked around the utility room. "What are you doing down here? Half naked?"

"I was looking for some old props. I ended up with paint all over my hands—and my shirt."

"Messy, messy. But you took care of it, didn't you."

Something in the tone of her voice made his eyes narrow. For a split second, he could have sworn knowledge seemed to glow in her stare.

"Did the bleach help?" She sniffed the air. "I can smell it. You know, clean hands are so important."

What the . . . fuck?

"Actually, I've been thinking about you, too," he said, taking control of the conversation. "And what you told me."

"That's why I've come. I believe some things should be done face-to-face."

"So you've listened to my demo?"

"Yes, I have." She took a step forward.

"And?"

As she took another step toward him, he stayed put and let her close the distance. He was aware that there was plenty down the darkened hall that he couldn't have her or anyone else see, and so he needed her out of here—fast.

"I love it."

"Do you?" He deliberately let his eyes drift down to her spectacular breasts. "That means a lot."

An A & R Vice President at RCA loved his demo? Shit, the fact that she was smoking hot was for once secondary. "Let's go upstairs and talk—"

The woman cut him off. "I like it down here. It's gritty and raw."

The light above the sink flickered.

"I find that surprising," he demurred. "Given the way you dress."

Last time he'd seen the kind of stuff she was wearing, he'd been in a taxi heading down Madison Avenue, looking at window displays.

She licked those cherry-red lips of hers. "I believe in sampling—the work, that is."

"Do you." Shit. Bad timing. "Well, you've heard my—"

"You are your own product. You write and perform your own songs. Very unusual these days." Leaning in, she smoothed his bare chest. "Very special."

Not the time or place.

G.B. took her wrist gently and removed her palm. "I'm flattered."

Her left eye twitched a little. But then she smiled in a sharp way. "You should be. It's not every singer that I show an interest in."

"Are you looking to sign me?"

"Maybe." There was a silence. "I have to sample the goods first."

Gone was the seduction—now it was a demand, and the math was very clear: Either he banged her here, or any conversation about his future was going right into the shitter. And she was legit. He'd gone to the Internet and looked her up.

Devina D'Angelo.

If timing was everything, he couldn't figure out what his destiny was supposed to be. The opportunity he'd waited his whole adult life for had shown up—at exactly the perfectly wrong moment.

"I like to sample the goods," she said for a third time, putting her hand back on his pec. "And afterward, maybe we can find you a clean shirt."

Again, there seemed to be some kind of knowledge behind her black eyes. But he was probably just being paranoid.

After a moment, he felt his head nod. "Okay . . . yeah. Sounds good."

Chapter
Thirty-three

"These are all for me?"

As Sissy leaned into the huge white-and-red Target bag, she was astounded. It was like a bathtub full of yoga pants, and shirts, and sweatshirts—even bras and underwear and socks. And there was another load, this one with books, magazines, bath towels, toothbrushes, and toothpaste.

She sat back in the kitchen chair. "Thank you—this is incredible."

Adrian, Jim's roommate, colleague, fellow angel, whatever, looked over as he shut the refrigerator. "And I brought a couple of dinners home with me. Some loaded potato skins or something—and ribs. Also a steak."

Across the way, she sensed Jim looking at her and she glanced over. He was leaning against the doorjamb, arms crossed over his chest, eyes heavy-lidded.

For a moment, she pictured him on the floor of that bathroom, weeping. Difficult to ever imagine that had happened—right now, between his hard body and impregnable expression, he seemed bulletproof.

After leaving the warehouse, they had driven out to the quarry because she'd had to see if anything came to her. No luck. But they had spent a long time out there, just sitting side by side, waiting for the sun to go down. The cloud cover had been spotty to the west, and as the rays had broken through, the peaches and pinks in the horizon had nearly been too bright to look at.

She had stared into them until her eyes had run with tears from the burning.

In a lot of ways, that was the end of her journey. There were no more places to go, no other veins of memory to mine, nothing left to investigate.

As Jim checked his watch for the second time, she said, "You're leaving, aren't you."

One of his dark blond brows lifted like he was surprised to have been called out. "I have to go."

Adrian eased down into a chair with a grunt and nodded at her. "You and I are going to stay here."

So the pair of them had had a talk while she'd been in the ladies' room.

"How long will you be gone?" she asked.

"Just going to chat with the boss." Jim shrugged. "Depends on how it goes."

"I am tired." At least, she thought she was. Shouldn't she be?

There was a long, awkward pause, as if Jim didn't want to take off to wherever he was going. To fill the time, she glanced back and forth between the two men, realizing only Jim had a halo: No glow around Adrian's head.

"Take care of her," Jim said gruffly before he turned and walked off.

Closing her eyes, she listened to his footfalls fade, and wondered if it wasn't a lie . . . if instead, he wasn't walking off into the horizon, just as the sun had.

For some reason, that panicked her.

"Tell me there's a TV in this place," she said roughly. "And cable."

The man, angel, whatever, shook his head. "Sorry. No dice. Jim's got a laptop, but there's no hot spot here, no modem."

Great.

"Can I ask you something," she blurted, not expecting any kind of—

"Yeah, sure."

Well, that was a change of pace. Unless he assumed she just wanted to inquire about the weather? "You were injured in a fight, right?"

"Nah, the limp and the cane are an artistic choice."

Shoot. She didn't want to offend him. "I'm sorry, I didn't mean to—"

He pointed to his chest. "Asshole. You gotta know that about me. When I'm in a good mood, it's fun for me, when I'm like this, it's more of a reflex. So yeah, ask whatever you want—just don't take my answers all that seriously."

"Well, are you an angel?"

"Most of the time, yeah."

"So why don't you have a halo? Is Jim something special and that's why he can heal himself and you can't?"

"Halo?" Adrian frowned. "I don't know about that one, but yup, Jim was chosen by both sides to do this final war. Both the good guys and that bad bitch had to agree on him. And as for my shit? Long story—but these things aren't ever 'healable.'"

"I'm so sorry." She shifted in her chair. "What do you mean, final war?"

"Evidently the Creator is as bored of life as the rest of us are. He set this thing up—seven souls, seven rounds. Jim's job is on the field, trying to make the people choose the right path. And if he doesn't prevail? It's gonna get really fucking hot around here."

Sissy wrapped her arms about herself. "Hell's actually not all that warm . . ."

Adrian winced. "Sorry. I'd forgotten that you . . . yeah, sorry."

As a shiver laddered up her spine and settled in her nape, she knew she had to change the subject. "It's okay . . . so, ah, what did Jim do before this?"

"Carpentry. Before that, he killed people for a living." As her eyes bulged, Adrian shrugged. "Look, if you want sugar-coating, you'd better read one of those mags I bought you. I'm not good at it."

"Killed people as in how?"

He leveled a stare at her. "Put a bullet in their brains. Poisoned them. Threw them off buildings—do you need a picture book?"

When she stuttered, he rubbed his face. "Sorry, I'm really not good at this, am I?"

"No, it's all right, I just—"

"It was for the U.S. government, I guess. That whole thing with him never mattered much to me. But his old boss was one of the souls in the war—actually he was in two rounds. We lost the first, but won the second with good ol' Matthias. And I don't hate the guy, actually."

"How many more rounds are there?"

"We're even at two to two with three to go at this point. And that's what I've been working on while Jim's been . . ."

As the angel let the sentence drift, Sissy sighed. "I've been in the way, huh."

"I think he's back on track now. No harm, no foul—yet. Assuming Nigel doesn't castrate him when he gets up there."

"Nigel?"

"Head of everything."

"Ah. So how are the souls chosen?"

"By the Maker and Nigel and Devina. We aren't told shit down here. Every round, the issue is who the hell is in play. Kinda hard for Jim to intercede at the crossroads and influence them if he doesn't know who they are. Again, we win or lose depending on the decision the soul makes, or the actions he or she does or doesn't commit. First to four wins? Takes the prize."

"Who knows about this . . . war?"

"Not the world at large, if that's what you're getting at. They won't know until the end—well, actually, only if we lose. If there are minions crawling the Earth, people are going to get a clue pretty fucking fast. Otherwise, it's going to just be business as usual."

Answers. *Finally*, she was getting some lay of the land.

"Will you tell me how I fit into all this?" She reached across the Target bags and put her hand on his forearm. "Please."

When all he did was curse under his breath, she rushed to fill the silence. "Jim took me to the demon's place today."

"You went to Hell? What the f—"

"No, the warehouse district, where she used to live, I guess? You know, where Jim found me in that bathroom?"

The angel shook his head and went back to rubbing his face, like maybe he didn't like what he was seeing in his mind. "Fucking Devina."

"He said something about a mirror." She covered her belly with her arms. "That I was killed . . . and marked to protect her mirror?"

"Her mirror's how she gets to Hell. It's the key to the lock down there, and if she loses that ugly old thing, she's separated forever."

"It's like something out of an evil fairy tale, then."

"That's one way of looking at it."

"But she only had me for a couple of weeks, right? That's how long Jim said I was dead."

"Well, technically you're still dead, honey. But yeah."

Sissy looked around the kitchen, noticing absently that someone had scrubbed the walls while she and Jim had been out. Once grungy and faded, the yellow was brightening up.

"So how many others like me have been sacrificed?" she asked in a dull voice.

Adrian groaned as he adjusted his position. "Time immemorial, right? She's existed that long—so I don't know. It's my understanding that the seal on the door lasts until it's broken by a third party. She can go in and out as many times as she wants to, but, like, when Jim went into that bathroom door, he broke it. I also think whenever she moves, she needs another sacrifice—new door and all that."

"There must be others like me down there, then."

"Yeah."

That anger started to curl in her gut again, the burning getting stoked once more. Reaching down, she lifted her shirt up and looked underneath.

She expected to find the glowing in her skin, but there was none, no markings, either. Maybe she'd imagined what she'd seen in that loft?

Tugging things back into place, she met the eyes of the angel.

"You got another question?" he prompted.

"The ones like me, trapped down there?" she said quietly. "Is there any way of getting them out?"

⊢━━━⊣

The drawbridge was up.

That was the first thing Jim noticed as he arrived in Heaven.

Actually, no, that was the second. The real number one was that his summons was not answered and he'd had to force himself up here.

Hadn't been aware he could do that until he'd found himself back-flatting on Heaven's lawn.

Getting to his feet, he brushed off his ass and frowned at the abandoned tea table. Hard to believe those four natty bastards would have walked away from it like that, leaving half-filled cups and itty-bitty sandwiches all over the place.

Something had happened.

"Nigel!" As his shout faded, he turned toward the fortified castle walls. "Colin!"

Nothing. Not even that huge wolfhound bounding over to him.

With few other options, he started hoofing it around the perimeter, hoping to run into someone. He'd gone about a fifty yards when he saw Nigel's colorful tent setup off in the distance, gleaming in the strangely diffused light. Breaking into a jog, he beat feet in its direction.

"Anyone home?" he barked as he got within range of the draped entrance. "Nigel? You in?"

He called out a couple more times. Lost his patience with the whole polite thing.

Welcome back, Ali Baba, he thought as he drew the fabric aside.

Just as before, jeweled colors glowed from every corner, the fine silks and satins hanging in folds that caught the golden light of many candles. The furniture was all antique and very fancy, the place looking like something out of an Old English excursion to the Middle East.

"Nigel?"

At first, the flash of silver on the floor seemed like nothing but the glare of candlelight playing tricks on his eyes. But as he refocused on it, he realized there was . . . a thin puddle of the shit? Right at the base of one of the curtain falls. It looked as if someone had melted down a sterling tea set right on the Oriental rug—

That was when he smelled the flowers.

Breathing in, his nose hummed with a bouquet of freshly cut blooms.

And then he heard a faint, rhythmic sound.

Drip, drip, drip . . .

As dread clawed its way into the center of his chest, he approached slowly, and watched from a distance as his hand reached out and grabbed hold of a ruby-colored curtain.

Even before he pulled the thing back, he knew what he was going to see.

"Oh . . . fuck . . . *no*."

On the far side, lying in an uncharacteristically messy sprawl on a chaise longue, Nigel was at once perfectly alive and completely gone: unmoving, with no breath in his chest or expression to his face, he was nonetheless the picture of health, a blush to his smooth cheeks, his skin retaining that glow he had had during his version of "life."

There was a crystal knife sticking straight out of his sternum, his own hand still locked on its grip, his eyes fixed on some far-off point.

That silver blood was everywhere on the floor, and the dripping was more of it falling into the biggest of the puddles, the one directly under the body.

Jim backed out into the main space, letting go of the drape. The thing did not return to its former place, however, getting bogged down in the archangel's blood, the doorway, such as it was, remaining open so that he could still see his "boss."

Something hit him in the back of the legs. A chair by an inlaid desk.

Jim let himself fall down into the cane seat. Staring at the game changer ahead of him, he was dumbfounded to the point of not being able to breathe.

His choices had caused this; he knew that without a doubt. And that was bad. But the real kicker? He couldn't say, even if he'd known this was going to be the result, that he would have done anything differently when it came to Sissy.

He just really fucking wished that he hadn't had to trade one for the other. Yeah, he'd gotten the girl out, but the cost had been so much higher than he'd thought.

And now he knew precisely why the drawbridge had been up.

Heaven was not as secure as it used to be, was it.

Chapter
Thirty-four

What was the saying? Once more with feeling . . . !

Cait leaned back as her plate of food arrived. Oh, yeeeeeahhh, cheeseburger with French fries. Nothing like a little red meat after what she and—

She glanced up as her cheeks got hot. Across the same table they'd been seated at before "things" had happened down at the boathouse, Duke was doing as she was—making way for about a thousand calories of burger goodness.

His had been without the cheese, though.

"Ketchup?" he asked, in that deep gravel voice of his.

After she nodded, he passed the Heinz, but didn't release it as she took hold of the bottle. When she looked up into his half-lidded eyes, he deliberately licked his lips.

Damn. That man was going to be the death of her. He totally was.

Cait's hands shook, but not from shyness, as she put her top bun aside and did the duty with the jar, banging it on the bottom to get enough out.

"Would you like my fries?" she asked as she put the thing down.

"Maybe. You're not going to eat them?"

"This burger alone is going to put me over the edge."

"Gotta keep your strength up."

Yeah. Wow. The way he said those words? It was like his mouth was against her throat and his body back on top of hers. In fact, every shift of his shoulders and blink of his eyes, all the syllables he spoke as well as the silences he kept, everything about him was a seductive reminder of where they had been . . . and where they would go again.

They were still not finished.

She did want to talk to him, though. Get to know this man who rocked her world and yet was still mostly a stranger.

"So . . . do you have a lot of family in town?" she said between bites.

"No. You?"

"My parents are out west. Middle of the country, actually." Pause. "They're missionaries. They leave the country a lot." Another pause. "I went to college here—at Union. And stayed on because I got a job teaching. I'm an artist. An illustrator."

She gave him the opportunity to pick up on the Union thing. When he didn't, she said, "Where did you go to college?"

"Would it bother you if I hadn't?"

She frowned, but then thought, maybe he'd dropped out and didn't want to tell her? "No."

He studied her for a time. "You know, I believe that."

"College doesn't automatically mean you're smart, or going to be more successful. For a lot of people, it's just four years of keggers and tailgates."

"Not a bad way to pass the time."

"True. But working your way into your twenties isn't so bad, either."

He wiped his mouth with his napkin. "Is that what you think I did?"

"You could settle the issue by just telling me."

"Maybe the mystery is working in my favor."

"You do *not* need any help, trust me."

There was another pause, and then he smiled a little. "That so?"

"Don't ask me to draw you a picture," she muttered.

"You're an artist, after all."

"Not that kind."

"Pity."

When the conversation died out again, she pushed her plate away. She loved being with him; it was undeniable. But that was in the horizontal sense. With both of them vertical? She was less sure—although come on, first dates were always a little rocky.

Right?

"I went to Union, too," he said gruffly.

As she looked up, he was focused on his fries, examining each one before making his choice and dragging it through a little pool of ketchup.

"What year?" she asked. When he answered, she shook her head. "That was just before my time, but we were almost there together. What did you major in?"

"I was premed."

"Really?" Because she didn't want him to know she had, in fact, Googled him.

"Surprise, huh. But I didn't follow up on it, as you can tell."

"Why not?"

"Things change."

Their waitress appeared at the table. "You finished already, ma'am?"

"Yes, thank you," Cait said. "Unless you'd like my fries?"

"Nah, I'm good." He pushed his own mostly full plate away as well. "And I'm done, too. Love a cup of coffee and a piece of apple pie, though. You want dessert?"

Cait shook her head. "No, thanks. But the coffee's a great idea."

"Bring two spoons." Duke handed his plate up and over. "In case she gets curious for a bite."

The waitress lingered a little, looking at Duke as if she herself might like a serving of him.

Okay, wow. For the first time in her life, Cait actually considered snarling at somebody.

"When can I see you again?" Duke said as soon as they were alone.

Cait crossed her arms and rested them on the table's edge. From the corner of her eye, she measured a couple sitting at a table across the way. The pair of them were talking with animation, laughing, smiling, holding hands from time to time.

"Is that a no?" Duke prompted.

Jerking herself to attention, she cleared her throat and felt a little lonely for some reason. "Ah . . ."

"Look, I'm not much of a talker. I'm sorry."

Part of her, the weak part, wanted to say or do anything that increased the likelihood of their being together again. Which, she supposed, would just mean putting the awkwardness aside and agreeing to meet tomorrow night—as well as stopping any attempt to turn this into something other than incredible, mind-blowing sex.

But she didn't take the easy route out. "Is it lack of interest or lack of practice?"

He was quiet long enough for their coffee and his pie and two spoons to be brought over, along with the check.

As the waitress put the slip of paper facedown, she said in a husky voice, "It's been my pleasure to serve you."

Or had she said "service"?

"You're welcome," Cait said sharply.

Little Miss Double Entendre got flustered at that point. Which was kind of satisfying, actually. As was the way the woman beat feet out of Dodge.

"It's not lack of interest." Duke cut into his pie. "Not at all. I have contact with a lot of people, just not in a conversating kind of way."

"You don't have any roommates?"

"No one permanent, at any rate."

She tried not to think of how many of them were like that waitress—failed. Also attempted not to dwell on the fact that he didn't seem to be looking for anything long term. But come on, what could she expect given the way they'd carried on?

"With my jobs?" he continued. "Not a lot of talking's necessary. On one, I use chain saws and shovels in the warm months, snowplows and salt in the cold. The other? Yeah, I shut people up for a living."

Forcing her mood out of the picture—because come on, they were both grown-ups—she refocused. "Maybe it'll help if I ask questions." When he shrugged, she took that as a yes. "What changed? When you decided to get out of college, that is?"

He took a sip of his coffee and stared at its black surface. "I just lost interest."

She didn't buy the simplicity for a second—

"There's no story there, Cait. It was years ago, and I was a different person. You ready to leave?"

He clearly was. He took out his wallet and pulled two twenties free.

"Ah, yes, of course." She pushed her untouched mug out of range, got her bag and her coat, and stood up. "Thanks for dinner."

"You need help with your coat?"

"No, thanks."

He led the way out, holding the two doors open for her, one after the other. The night was still clear and coolish, and she could smell dirt, the sure sign that winter was over.

Small stones under their soles crackled as they made their way across the parking lot to her car.

Keys. She should take out her—no, wait, she had a smart key now, thanks to Lexus.

At her driver's-side door, she gripped the handle, and automatically the lock popped open.

Oh, God, she didn't want things to end this way. The awkward silence now, the stilted conversation back in the diner.

Abruptly, she thought of G.B.—things had been so easy with him—

"I'm bad at this," Duke said roughly. "Really bad."

As she looked up, a car pulling out highlighted his face in the darkness. Behind his shadowed eyes, she could sense pain, the deep, abiding kind.

"You can trust me," she whispered, reaching up and touching his face. "You really can."

He turned in and kissed her palm. "Thank you." Except then he cursed. "The problem is, I don't know what this is between you and me. And I have a feeling I'm no more comfortable with dating than you are with a string of one-night stands."

"Do we have to make choices tonight?"

"You'll see me again?"

Something about the way he asked touched her. Maybe it was because he seemed so unsure of the answer. "Yes. I will."

His mouth came down on hers, brushing lightly once. Twice. And again. "Good. Tomorrow night. Can I pick you up?"

"Yes." She wrapped her arms around him and eased against his body. "I live at two fifteen Greenly Drive. Do you need to write that down?"

"No more than I did your number." As one of his hands threaded into her hair, his lids lowered. "Give me a little more before I go."

They were still kissing ten minutes later. And it took her another five to actually get into the car.

"I'm going to think about you all night," he said just before he shut her door.

Oh, God, and what would he do to pass all those empty hours, she wondered with a flare of heat.

"Don't keep your hands to yourself," she heard herself say.

"Don't worry, I won't." He shut her door. "Drive safe."

Stepping back, he gave her a wave and then walked off to one of the motorcycles that was parked by the side of the diner. Thanks to the neon glow from the signage, she got to watch him throw a leg over, jump the engine, and skid out, tearing off into the night with a roar.

She didn't remember the ride home.

Because in spite of the uncertainty of things, she was floating.

Chapter
Thirty-five

As Adrian looked at Sissy across the kitchen table, he wasn't thinking about the question she'd just asked about innocents in Hell. But his brain was, in fact, far, far south, down below, back with Devina.

Talk about a truly bizarre way of wasting a day. He'd done a lot of things on the sliding scale of sex, but watching a demon desperately try to give him a hard-on? New territory. And considering how flustered Devina had become? Shit, he should have volunteered for impotence decades ago.

Denial was that demon's self-destruct button.

And then she'd followed him around Target, and gone to a fucking restaurant that had had screaming kids in it.

He was practically glowing from the satisfaction.

"So is it possible?" Sissy prompted.

"I'm sorry?"

"Well, assuming there are more like me down there, can we get them out?"

"Oh, shit, I don't know." He pushed a hand through his hair. "To be honest, I've never given it any thought. Maybe Eddie would know."

"Who's Eddie?"

Okay, yup, that still hurt like a bitch. "A friend. He knows everything about the game."

"Would he talk to you about it? Or maybe me?"

"Probably not." Eddie wasn't talking to anybody anytime soon. "Listen, if I were in your shoes, I'd just hang here. Everything's going to be over one way or the other very soon."

The hard expression that came over the girl's face made him realize that "woman" covered her description much better. "That's kind of pointless, though, isn't it. What if the only way to save them is to get them out now?"

"But why? So they can watch the destruction of the world? Besides, if we do win, I imagine they'll be free anyway."

"Do you know that for certain?"

"No. But there are other issues. Devina doesn't let go of things easily." For fuck's sake, he would still be down there if she had her way. "You have to pry her possessions away from her."

"That's not my problem. It's hers."

Adrian felt his brows go up. "Let me get this straight. You've been in her wall, you know what it's like—and you'd risk ending up there forever for a bunch of people you don't know." He leaned in. "Because don't kid yourself. Devina released you, but you're the only one I've ever seen who's gotten out. If she gets a chance, she'll chain you again in a heartbeat—and it's hard to imagine a better way of guaranteeing that than to fuck around with her shit."

As he resettled into his chair, he couldn't believe what had just come out of his mouth. If he wanted Jim's head back in the game? Maybe having Sissy self-destruct would be the perfect way to do it—that angel would blame the demon, not this woman with the noble ideas, and would undoubtedly go on a rampage.

He should have kept his piehole closed.

"It's not like I've got anything here," she said. "And I'd rather go out doing something than sitting around like a piece of furniture, waiting for my fate to be delivered on my head."

"I thought you and Jim were together."

"*What?*"

Adrian hadn't expected to be off on that one. Clearly he was. "Guess I was wrong."

Sissy shook her head. "No, yeah, totally wrong. He's just . . . he took care of me, that's all."

And apparently "took care of" did not mean "banged all night long while we were in his bedroom alone."

Adrian found himself rubbing his face again. "Sorry. I read things wrong."

"Jim would never do anything like that . . . with me . . . um . . . ever. Me, neither. I'm not . . . um, yeah."

From the blush that hit her puss to the way she fidgeted in her chair, she was obviously not comfortable with the subject, but it wasn't like he was inclined to push it anyway.

Adrian got to his feet. "Listen, my advice to you is to stay out of as much of this as you can. You've already been compromised, and you've got a measure of freedom now—that's as much restitution as anyone can expect in this fucked-up world." He looked at the clock over the stove, not really expecting it to be operational—but hey, check it. The thing was working for once. "I gotta crash. Tomorrow the focus needs to be back on the war."

Limping out, he paused in the doorway and glanced over his

shoulder. Sissy was sitting still as an inanimate object, surrounded by the messy surplus he and Devina had chosen for her. Except for that long blond hair, she seemed ancient, the old-fashioned appliances and worn floor new and fresh compared to her aura.

Adrian kept going, pulling himself up the stairs by the balustrade, rounding the half landing by the grandfather clock slowly, taking a breather before tackling the last dozen steps up to the second-story foyer.

He didn't go to his bedroom.

As he made his way to the attic door and flipped the light switch at the bottom of the steep rise, his left leg was really lagging, and the scent of flowers depressed him to the point that he nearly decided to sleep on the stairwell.

He was getting tired of the constant refrain of, If only Eddie were here. . . .

Unfortunately, he didn't think it was ever going to be any less apropos than it was right now.

The angel had left his cane behind.

As Sissy got up and started to fold her new clothes neatly, she spied it leaning against the counter by the stove.

It wasn't as if she didn't see Adrian's point. When she had been in Hell, the only thing she had prayed for was getting out. Now that that had been granted, it seemed like a criminal lack of self-preservation to want to run any risks with herself.

But if Jim had thought that way, she'd still be down there.

I thought you and Jim were together.

Oh, God, had he really said that? Thought that?

Jim was the savior for a lot of people. Getting her out of there had been part of his job description—right?

Remembering the sight of him by that bathtub, she thought, Well, it might have been a little more personal than that. But things ended there between them.

Right . . . ?

With the clothes back in the bags, she picked up her load and headed out—only to snag the cane as she passed by, tucking it under her arm.

As she walked through the house, she wondered where Jim was, what he was doing, whether he was fighting or going a diplomatic route in whatever conflict he found.

Probably not diplomacy.

Up in her room, she was surprised to find that when she opened the drawers, a waft of lavender rose up into her nose. The liner paper was bright and fresh as the day it must have been laid down, the flower pattern winding its violet and green way all around the fragrant sheets. With quick efficiency, she filled the dresser, shut everything up tight . . . reopened things and picked out a pair of yoga pants and a loose T-shirt.

Adrian had not been too far off base on her size. Both were baggy, but they were a better fit than Jim's gigantic clothes by a mile.

She had no idea where the laundry was in the house, but for all she knew, they washed things in the sink and hung them to dry—

Sissy froze.

Above the bureau, there was an old mirror hanging on the wall, its glass wrinkly, like the ones that had been in her grandmother's house. And as she met her own eyes in its uneven surface, her reflection was at once stunning and entirely unremarkable—it wasn't as if her features had changed, or her hair was another color.

There was something way different, however.

Glowing around the crown of her head, like a diadem of subtle candlelight, was a halo.

Just like the one Jim had.

Reaching up, she patted at it and felt nothing, no barrier or resistance. It was there, though. The mirror might have been an antique, but it worked just fine—

Creaking overhead brought her eyes to the ceiling. Someone was walking around up there, the footfalls uneven—either because the path was obstructed or . . .

Grabbing the angel's cane, she rushed out. She wasn't sure where the way up was, but she was damn well going to find it.

So many doors. Into bedrooms. Another sitting room. Bathrooms. She kept going, passing by the main staircase, and finding much of the same on the other side—

Down at the far end, light glowed around the jambs of a shut door, and she knew before going over and opening it that there would be a set of stairs going up.

"Adrian?" she called out.

Abruptly the lights flickered, browning briefly as if from a power surge—and it nearly dissuaded her from going up. When they stayed on, however, she decided to ascend.

"Adrian . . . ?"

Breathing in, she smelled the most amazing bouquet of flowers, the scent a complex, multilayering of fragrance that put to shame those liner papers big-time. And then she heard chanting, soft, repetitive, insistent.

She tiptoed up the rest of the way, peering around the rough-cut balustrade at the top.

The flames of black candles waved lazily in invisible currents, bathing the attic from rafter to floorboard in soft, warm light. Cedar blanket chests and antique Louis Vuitton traveling trunks cast shadows, while hanging rods of old clothes appeared to move in the fluctuating illumination. Cobwebs hung in gossamer strings, undulating as if by the breath of ghosts, and the wind whistled through cracks somewhere.

But none of that really registered.

Halfway down the expanse, Adrian was sitting cross-legged, and rocking back and forth with his eyes closed. Stretched out before him, on a bed of mismatched blankets, was what she guessed had to be a body. A white sheet covered the person from head to toe, nothing showing of what was underneath.

The mourning was obvious in the tenor of the song, the painful tension in Adrian's face—

The angel stopped abruptly, his head ripping around to her.

"I—I'm sorry," she said, holding out his cane. "You left this downstairs. I thought . . . you might need it."

There was a good distance between them, twenty feet or so, but she saw the tears on his cheeks before he swept them away with a brisk hand.

"Leave it there," Adrian answered in a voice that cracked.

"Who is that?" she asked.

"None of your business."

"Is it your brother?" A man like that wasn't going to be upset over just anybody, and that certainly wasn't a woman under there. Way too big. "Is it?"

Adrian turned back to the shroud. "Close enough."

"I'm sorry for your loss."

"So am I."

Sissy was careful with his cane, laying it on top of one of the chests and making sure it didn't roll off. It seemed like the only way she could take care of him.

"Did she take him from you?" she asked.

No reason to specify the "she."

"Yeah, she did."

As Sissy stared across what seemed like miles as opposed to yards, she found the tableau of loss painful to look at. This was what her family was living through, her mom and her dad, her sister . . . her friends, her roommates and teachers at Union, her old teammates.

All because of that demon.

How many? she wondered. How many lived with the aftermath of what she had done?

She remembered Jim sitting in that bathroom, weeping by the tub.

"Was he an angel, too?" she asked gruffly.

"More like a saint." Adrian reached out and tugged at the sheet, smoothing the tiniest wrinkle. "Eddie was the very best of all of us. That was why she killed him."

"When did this happen?"

"No more than a week ago." Adrian rubbed his face again. "I was right beside him, I should have heard or seen . . . something. It just happened so fast."

"I need to help." As his head came back around, Sissy crossed her arms over her chest. "Whatever it takes to get her, I need in on it."

The angel stared at her for the longest time. Then he returned to his friend. "I'm getting an idea why Jim thinks you're special."

"Wha . . . ?" She couldn't have heard that right.

"And if you want to go after Devina? You want to ingest that poison and maybe die again from it?" He nodded. "That's your right. I won't stop you."

Sissy exhaled. "Thank you."

"Not something you should be grateful for, honey. Now . . . if you don't mind?"

"Your cane's right here." She laid a hand on it even though he wasn't looking. "Right here."

"Thanks."

Sissy whispered her way down the steep stairwell and closed the door silently. Then she tiptoed back to her own room.

Inside her skin, she was not quiet, however.

Her anger was roaring.

Chapter
Thirty-six

Jim left Nigel where the archangel lay. Not like the guy needed to go anywhere—and Devina couldn't touch him now that he was gone.

Back at the tea table, he stared at the four empty seats and knew he was getting nowhere wasting time up here. And yet he couldn't seem to leave, his feelings a complex interplay of guilt, mourning, and anger—

What the fuck?

Far across the lawn, off in the distance, a cloud had gathered close to the ground, something the size of a car or truck. At first it seemed as though it was smoke, but then as it started to move, he realized it was made up of countless—

A swarm.

It was a swarm of what seemed to be black wasps.

And it began to head his way, rushing forward in an accelerating wave pattern, surging with coordinated menace.

Jim bolted, heading for the moat. Thighs pumping, arms up, he ran the shit out of the grass, great strides taking him to the water source—

He didn't make it.

The impact was like getting pelted with cobblestones all over the back of his body, and then he was engulfed, the stings blanketing him, assaulting him from every angle while he was dragged back from the water that might have saved him. He swung his arms like a crazy man, trying to bat the attack away, but there were so many of them. . . .

He was spun around and elevated, the pricking pain fuzzing out his brain and dulling his response as his feet left the ground. And then there was a great suction, the pull so violent he felt as though his skin was going to go with it.

The swarm left him on a oner, peeling free just as fast as it had attacked.

Coalescing, it became Colin, the archangel. And the fury in his face was epic.

With a roar so loud it registered as agony in the ears, Colin attacked—and it was so not the same as being hit by that cop at the accident scene.

This was a semi-trailer truck knocking him down—and then beating the ever-living shit out of him, fists making contact with his face, his upper body, his gut. Pain stalled his brain, but instinct from a lifetime of fighting brought his arms up over his head. Trying to curl over on his side, he did his best to protect his internal organs—

The first stab penetrated his right shoulder. The second was too close to his carotid for comfort.

The insane bastard had a crystal knife.

And Jim was not going to make it through this.

"What the fuck are you doing?" he yelled.

"You killed him!" the Englishman spat. "You fucker! You self-ish motherfuck—"

Jim tried to capture that thrashing wrist, but there was blood flowing now, splashing all over the place, making any grip he could get slip free. The angel was completely out of control, the force of the stabbing increasing with every downward strike as opposed to easing off as energy ebbed.

In the midst of the flapping of his clothes, and the flashing of that clear blade, and the grunting hatred of his killer, he heard something else. . . .

Barking?

Just as Jim was about to lose consciousness, he turned his head. There, no more than four feet away, Dog was going apeshit.

Unfortunately, Colin didn't appear to hear any of it.

Which was how Jim finally saw the face of God.

Chapter
Thirty-seven

This time, Cait put her clothes away properly. Washed off her makeup and moisturized. Brushed and flossed and clipped her fingernails.

She was tired, but wired, as she and Teresa had called it in college.

Eventually, there was only so much pre-bed primping a girl could do before it was time to get under the sheets and commence the great ceiling stare-off.

God, what a night.

And it was interesting. No matter what happened in the future between them, Duke had taught her something significant. While she was with him down at the boathouse, she had lost track of everything for a little bit—and not just in terms of her work on the book or her classes or her bills. That internal monologue of criticism had actually shut up for once, and its absence had been more instructive than its commentary. She had simply existed in the moment when they'd been together, pulled free from her upbringing for a long breath of air . . . and it had been marvelous.

Of course, the tape that played in her head had come back online, especially during the awkwardness at the diner. But at least that transient experience had proved she could turn it off.

She needed to do that more often, preferably not with anyone else's help. . . .

It was entirely possible that that freedom was what "living" really meant.

Could it be that the vocabulary of a day or a night, what she did, where she went, who she was with, what color her hair or clothes were, was not the dispositive thing, not what would get her what she was after? Rather, it was her own internal approach to it all that made the difference.

Duh, she thought.

She just hadn't put it together until now.

And she did have Duke to thank for the revelation, even though he had no clue what he'd given her aside from the best sex she'd ever had.

Staring across her room, images of him were as vivid and three-dimensional as the moments that inspired her memories, and it didn't take long before she was out of bed, and going for her closet. Sometimes the only way to calm her brain down was to draw whatever was in it.

And reliving those eyes, that mouth, the jaw, she had touched? No big sacrifice.

Turning the overhead light on, she found the big bag she used during the day slumped in its cubby, sure as if it were asleep. Rummaging through the Altoids, tissue packs, sunscreen, sunglasses, old-fashioned address book, recent copy of *Arts Magazine*, hard pencil case, she found . . .

That her sketchbook wasn't in there.

Where the hell had she left it?

A quick trip downstairs proved that it wasn't in the kitchen, and she even went out into her car and checked under the seats.

On one level, it shouldn't have been a big deal. There hadn't been anything in it other than rough sketches, outlines, doodles, and notes on current projects, but the content wasn't the issue. Something of hers was out in the world on its little lonesome, unprotected—she felt as though she'd left her SUV unlocked downtown after dark.

Heading back to her bedroom, she shook her head. Maybe she needed to get a dog to reprioritize things properly.

Or . . . a child.

Her steps faltered and she stopped halfway to the second floor. She couldn't possibly have just thought that. Nope. She wasn't having children—that had never been part of her goals. Ever.

And okay, if she had had that passing brain spasm? It was clearly the result of the hormone overload she'd been enjoying for the last forty-eight hours.

She was *not* the maternal type. That had been something true as a bedrock ever since she'd had a mature thought about anything.

In fact, that resolution had been part of the reason Thom's call so many months ago had hit her so hard: He had always agreed with her. No kids—it made life simpler and less expensive. Nicer and more tidy. They were going to be two professionals living in a home with white carpets and lots of glass.

The spic-and-span version of a picket fence.

Cait restarted her ascent, her mind churning. Having sex on boat cushions in a semi-private place was not "nice," and neither was what she'd done the night before at that club on the floor. And making out by her parked car in the cold because she didn't want to leave the man she'd just made love with was definitely not "tidy."

And yet here she was, counting down the hours until she could become undone all over again.

Maybe the last six months at the gym and the various other self-improvements had been a case of laying a new kind of groundwork for her life. And if you went by the truism that timing was everything . . . a Duke, not a Thom, was what she needed.

It was entirely possible that nice-and-tidy wasn't what she was after anymore.

Her phone started to ring just as she was resettling against her pillows. With a lunge, she all but cleared her bedside table to get at the thing, a smile breaking out not just over her face, but deep within her chest. "Hello?"

Talk about perfect timing . . .

"Hey, Cait."

She sat upright in a rush. "G.B. Oh, hi."

"Were you expecting someone else?"

Yes. "No. Not really."

Crap.

"Sorry to call so late. But I've left you two messages, and when you didn't get back to me, I got worried—you know, after what happened to you in the parking garage."

"Oh, yeah, no. I mean, I'm fine." She pushed her hair back and pulled the lapels of her PJ top closer. "I just didn't get your voice mails."

It hadn't even dawned on her to check her phone.

"Hot date or something?" As Cait struggled to answer that one, he cursed softly. "I'm sorry. It's been a horrifically long day, and I'm probably over-reacting. I'm just glad you're okay."

"I'm fine. Home safe, as a matter of fact." She frowned. "What went wrong today?"

"Everything, but I didn't call to bitch to you, honest. I really was concerned."

"That's kind of you—except now I'm the one who's worried."

There was a pause. "It's good to hear your voice, how about that?"

"Did rehearsals not go well?"

"The director was being a dick, 'scuse my French. And there was some weird stuff with other staff people. The good news is, tomorrow is a new day, and—"

A beep cut in. Someone else was calling.

"Hey, G.B., give me a sec—hold on." She hit *hold call and answer*. "Hello?"

"Tell me you made it home all right."

Cait closed her eyes at the sound of that deep, husky voice. "I did."

"What are you wearing?"

"Cotton PJs."

"Are you going to make me beg for you to take them off?"

Cait bit her lip, eyes closing as her head fell back. "No . . ."

Her body was instantly ready again, needing that connection it had found with this man on her phone—

"Shit—I mean, crap. Hold on, Duke?"

"Yeah."

She clicked over to G.B. and felt like throwing up. "Hey, I've got to take this."

"Okay . . . but are you sure you're all right? You sound funny."

"No, I'm fine. Honest."

"You want to do lunch again at the theater tomorrow? That was a great break in my day, and I have a feeling I'm going to need the company."

"Yes, sure. That sounds good—I'll see you at one?"

"Noon's better, if that's okay with you? Or do you have class."

"No, that works fine."

"Great. It's a date. See you then."

As he ended the call on his side, she stared across the room and wondered if she'd done the right thing. She couldn't keep stringing him along if she wasn't really interested. But . . . she didn't know where things were going with Duke, did she? And if the two of them didn't work out, maybe something could develop with G.B. over time. She just didn't know.

One thing was clear. If she clicked back over to Duke, she knew exactly what was going to happen.

Pushing the complicated mix of emotions to the side, she re-opened the connection, thinking, Shoot, she just couldn't say no.

"Duke?" she breathed. "You still there?"

"You think I'd go anywhere?" His voice dropped even lower. "Now be a good girl . . . and get naked for me."

Oh, God, she loved it when he talked like that.

Cait put the phone aside and swept everything off. As her PJs fell to the floor, she pushed herself down under the covers, the warmth and weight a pitiful substitute for his body.

The second she picked up her cell again, he said, "Touch yourself. Pretend it's my hand, my mouth. . . ." A groan replaced the words—which told her exactly what he was doing on his end. "I need more. . . ."

She did what he asked, and as she undulated, the soft cotton sheets were rough against her tight nipples.

". . . want to be in you . . ."

Cait could barely hear what he was saying as she jacked further into the pillows and her body contorted, the orgasm rolling through her, heightened by the memories of where they had gone before . . . and the anticipation that there was more to come.

Literally.

As Duke growled, she could picture him with his teeth

clenched, his head also kicking back, that incredible, hard body surging as he came into his own fist.

"More," he said, almost as soon as he'd finished orgasming. "I want more of you . . ."

Insatiable had never been so satisfying.

And it was the perfect ending to a perfect evening.

After God only knew how many more rounds, he said, "I might be done tonight, but I'm still not finished with you."

"Is that a promise?" she drawled.

"Hand over my heart, ready to die."

As she got ready for the inevitable good-bye, she was stunned to find she wanted to say, "I love you"—not because she'd thought about it, but because it seemed so natural.

And wasn't that a cold dose of reality.

"Good night, Duke," she whispered instead.

"Sleep well. Or not. And if it's the latter, dream of me."

"Always."

Hanging up and turning out her light, she feared that was true. If she had thought Thom had done a number on her? What Duke could do was much worse. . . .

Or better, God willing.

Chapter
Thirty-eight

Jim went back to Earth in a daze. Maybe it was from blood loss but more likely it was the fact that whatever you believed about God, however you worshipped, ignored, or otherwise approached Him or Her, nobody was prepared to meet the Creator face-to-face.

The impact of that persona had been an orgasm on top of death throes draped in a free fall punctuated by a bone-shattering, hot asphalt, buck-stops-here slam.

Even Colin had felt it, and that had been the only thing that could have made the archangel stop—well, short of Jim bleeding out entirely.

And as for a description of the Maker? No words, no syllables, not even memory that was still short-term could bring it forth. The only thing Jim kept coming back to was that the Bible was right in one respect—the Divine was so much greater than man, Mount Everest to a molehill, the Atlantic to a fishbowl, the cold of space compared to that of an ice cube. And even those comparisons failed.

Then there was what had happened afterward . . . and Jim still didn't know what to make of that.

Back at the house, standing at the base of the stairs, he didn't know how in the hell he was going to make it up to the second floor, much less over to the bathroom to clean his sorry ass up—

The grandfather clock started to chime, that gonging stabbing right into his skull.

But at least the annoyance at the goddamn thing got him going. He refused to keep count, however—although when he finally got on its level, he shot it a glare and a half.

As he arrived up at the foyer, he stared down the hall toward Sissy's room. He wanted to go in there, lift her covers, slide in next to her and hold her. It seemed right to reconnect—for fuck's sake, he felt like he'd been gone forever.

Then again, nearly being dead again would do that to a guy.

Maybe that sense of an eternity passing was what Hell had been like for her? A blip on Earth, but forever in the mind and the soul.

With any luck, she'd be sleeping, so he decided it was better to leave her alone. Inside the bathroom, he cranked the hot water on, and was barely undressed when steam started to boil up out of the curtain.

Frowning, he reached inside. "Shit!"

Hot, very hot. As if the water heater had suddenly decided to start working properly for the first time since they'd moved in.

Miracles, miracles.

Readjusting the mix of H and C faucets, he got under the spray and cursed again—nothing like being reminded that he had two or three fairly major stab wounds that were still open. Sluicing the water back into his hair, he tilted his head and let the warmth run down his shoulders and torso. His body was beaten to shit, sore in every place that counted, but the good news, if there was any, was that in his previous life it would have taken him weeks in the hospital and months of rehab to get back on track.

Now a matter of hours would do it.

But he could be killed. Colin's attack proved it. So did Nigel's demise.

Man, out of all the deaths he thought he'd have on his conscience, that archangel's was not one. And there was no doubting that Nigel may have put the dagger in his own chest, but Jim's hand had been on the grip, too.

Out of the shower. Wrapped in a towel. Heading for his room with his bloodied clothes hanging from his arms like they were his internal organs.

Before shutting himself into the darkness, he stared in the direction of Sissy's room again. God, he just wanted to go there, knock on the door, have her tell him to come in. And then, without a lot of talk, he could lie next to her and hold her body for a little while.

They would both sleep.

That was all he wanted, just rest, peace, a time to recharge. Because the message from the Maker had been clear: The war was going to continue regardless of the loss.

"Fucking hell."

He'd never liked Nigel. He'd been frustrated with the guy's need to follow the rules, and incensed by that superior English manner. But he hadn't wanted the archangel dead—and oh, crap, Colin? File that under Fucking Batshit Pissed. Plus, there was no way of knowing where the other two archangels had been, and if they were half as angry as Nigel's buddy? Jim might as well turn himself over to Devina now, before they ripped him limb from limb.

He passed through into his room and ditched the clothes right by the door. He'd burn them tomorrow—and yes, he was going to tell Adrian what was going on. He was also going to get an update from the guy as to where they stood with the soul.

Time to move on.

One of the lessons he had learned long ago was that you couldn't go back. History was the only immutable thing anyone, mortals and immortals alike, had—and even that changed depending on what you knew of actual events at any given time. He couldn't go back and fix what Nigel had decided to do. He could only go forward.

Man, he needed—

"Jim?"

The sound of Sissy's voice stopped his body, but sped up his heart. "Sissy . . . ?"

"I thought I would wait up for you. I fell asleep."

He could just imagine what she looked like lying against his pillows, sitting up a little, eyes drowsy, hair slightly tangled.

"Can I join you?" he asked hoarsely.

"What happened? What's wrong?"

When there was a rustling and something hit the floor, he said, "No, don't bother turning on the light."

He didn't want her to see what kind of shape he was in. Maybe by morning . . . yeah, by morning, he would look back to normal.

More important, he would *be* back to normal: All roads led to Devina. Sissy and her family's suffering. Nigel's. Colin's. Adrian's. Those various dominoes had each fallen, thanks to one flick of the demon's manicured finger.

She had to lose the war—stipulated. But that was not enough. She needed the kind of agony she forced others to feel—and that was only going to happen if he took away the one thing that mattered to her.

Her precious collection of crap.

One way or the other, before the end of the war, he was going to find the shit and torch it. Then she would know what it felt like to be on the receiving end of the pain she dished out.

Eye for an eye. And after that? He was going to beat her at this game and wish her one final fuck-off before she was dusted.

"So can I?" he said.

"You don't sound right—I mean, yes, please."

If he'd been a gentleman, he would have put some clothes on. . . .

And what do you know, even as exhausted as he was, he went over and drew on some sweats and a muscle shirt before he got anywhere near the bed.

Stretching out took some effort, but then Sissy curled in against him.

Warm and soft, smelling like flowers from the shampoo and soap Adrian had gotten her. Heavenly woman . . .

"What did you say?" she whispered.

Shit. "Nothing." He cleared his throat. "I'm glad you came in here."

"Me, too."

As her arm sneaked around his waist, it was with the gentlest of movements, as if she knew he was hurting. Or maybe that was her way.

It was so strange, he thought, but lying next to her, he felt like he was home. And after having been transient and unconnected for so long, the powerful peace was a shock and a weakness, but in this quiet darkness, it was also right—

Sissy moved even closer, and as she repositioned herself, her breast brushed up against his side, its soft cushion making him draw in a swift breath.

"Jim?" she said, her voice right next to his ear. "Are you okay?"

He moved his lower body further back. "Yeah."

"You sound like you're in pain."

When he didn't reply, she inhaled deeply, as if frustrated—and that breast moved again, stroking him, whatever thin shirt she was wearing no barrier at all.

He was very sure she did not have a bra on.

"Jim, you know what I've learned? Talking helps."

Oh, God, she might as well be stretching him on a rack: His sex was waking up down below, in spite of the condition he was in, and the arousal felt like a torturous betrayal of her. Unfortunately, it wasn't like he could stop the powerful urge to roll on top of her and take her beautiful face carefully in his rough, scarred hands, and—

"My boss died today."

As Sissy stiffened, he thought, yup, the image of Nigel lying in a pool of silver blood wiped out his erection completely. And he hated that he was using the suicide to cure this kind of problem, but that wasn't the only reason he'd brought up the nightmare. He did want to talk about it. With her.

"I don't want to freak you out," he muttered. "And you know, someday I'm going to have good news to tell you. Promise."

Sissy sat up. "What happened?"

"I don't know. I went up there to meet with him and . . . yeah, the place was shut up tight, no one was around, and when I went looking, I found him. Dead."

"Jesus . . . Christ."

"That was my reaction, too." No reason to go into his feeling responsible for it. Sissy was tied up inextricably in all that, and God knew he was carrying around enough guilt for the both of them. "I'm a strategic thinker—and I never saw anything like that coming."

"What about Colin . . . ?"

Something niggled in the back of his brain. But then he shook off the sensation.

He also had no intention of going into the attack. "Not doing well. At all."

Sissy eased back down beside him, somehow ending up mostly on his chest. And though it made his stab wounds ache, he was not going to ask her to move.

Instead, as her straight hair fell onto him, tickling his upper arm, he sneaked a stroke of it . . . and one was not enough. In fact, as he played with the silky, blunt-cut ends, he found himself wanting to do it for the rest of his unnatural life.

"And I was right about Dog," he murmured.

"In what way?"

He shook his head, a wave of exhaustion coming over him, sapping his strength completely. "I'm really glad you were here when I walked in."

Sissy put herself into the crook of his arm, and it was so goddamn right, the pair of them alone in a darkness that was not threatening, comforting each other.

Talk about virgins . . . "I've never done this before," he heard himself say.

"Done what?"

"Lay like this with a woman."

"What do you usually do—" She stopped short. "Never mind, don't answer that."

"It's different with you."

As Sissy stiffened again, he thought, Okay, time to shut up now. "Sorry."

It was a long while before she shook her head against his biceps. "No, it's okay. And I'm sorry about your boss."

"Me, too. And thanks."

"Death is never expected, is it. Even when you know it's coming . . . it's always a surprise."

"Especially like that."

"What do you mean?"

Jim closed his eyes against the darkness. "He killed himself."

Lying beside Jim, clothed in the guise of his precious little girlfriend, Devina felt her heart skip a beat—again.

For a moment, all she could do was blink, reality receding as shock became the dominant emotion she felt—everything else left her, her aggression, her frustration, sexual and otherwise, her anger, her anxiety . . . the normal mix bleeding out like a color photograph left in the sun.

Nigel, gone.

It was unfathomable. The pair of them had been battling for so long, that ridiculous archangel had become a permanent stone in her stiletto, endlessly irritating, forcing her to limp when she'd rather run, wearing a hole in her flesh.

The only way she was going to get rid of him was by winning the war. That was the sole scenario under which his absence was supposed to happen.

At least, that had been her assumption.

The idea that he had committed suicide?

Fuck, fuck fuck—she needed to . . . go count lipsticks. Hangers in her closet. Shoes. Handbags. Maybe rifle through her drawers and make sure her lingerie was organized correctly by color.

She hated change, she really did.

"I shouldn't have said anything."

She shook herself back to attention. "Oh, no . . . I'm glad you did."

Okay, Devina, you need to think this through.

Focus on the positive—she had to listen to her therapist's advice and focus on the positive. And there was some good news in all this: Just as there were four compass points, there had always been four guardians in Heaven, all with complementary virtues and abilities. You had to wonder, with one of them gone, did the table become three-legged, and therefore radically less stable?

Worth finding out . . . and exploiting.

What if she could get into the Manse of Souls?

An intense vibration of need hit her even harder than the shock had. Talk about a collection to be mined . . . for all her existence, that had always been her ultimate goal—to possess the souls of the "good" who were, by the Maker's very design, destined to be out of her reach. The idea that she might be able to get up there and take them all? It was the supernova of shopping expeditions, like going to Saks Fifth Avenue with a U-Haul and a Centurion AmEx.

Just back the fucking truck up and load the shit.

She'd assumed that the war was the sole way to get that prize. In fact, that possibility had been the only reason to risk what she already had and accept the Maker's challenge. Taking the chance of losing what had taken her millennia to obtain? Not going to happen . . . except if the prize was the Powerball of possessions.

That had been worth it . . .

Goddamn it, she'd had wanted to be the one to kill Nigel.

But instead, he had flamed out—and in the process, created a loophole that could have given her what she'd been after without her having to put her own collection on the table for the taking.

Fucking hell.

In fact, she'd never have guessed that there were any weakness in that psyche of his, a set of loose panels that she could have unscrewed even further, or a series of cracks in his foundation that she could have put a crowbar in and forced ever wider. She would have exploited anything like that if she'd known it was there—but he'd always seemed such a worthy opponent, custom-tailored to counter her at every turn.

Like the Maker had planned it that way.

The only opponent better than Nigel?

Jim Heron—

Wait a minute.

As Devina's mind worked over the implications, a cold wash of dread ran all over her. Without Nigel in the picture? The implications of the war had just gotten even more dire.

Abruptly, a striking fear rang through her, the kind of thing she had never felt before. "I hope you don't ever leave me. I don't know what I would do without you."

"Shh. Come here, lie back down."

As Jim reached out and tried to draw her to him again, Devina could feel her disguise slipping, the image of Sissy Barten falling away, her features assuming their true cast of rotting flesh, all that beautiful blond hair shriveling back into her scalp.

"I have to go—"

"Sissy? What's wrong?"

"I—I'm sorry, I have to go—I'm sorry."

Devina leaped out of the bed and scrambled across the floor, the raw bones exposed on the bottoms of her feet making it impossible to find purchase on the hardwood.

"Sissy . . . ?"

The fact that he was calling some other woman's name out as she ran struck her as cruel—especially as she slammed face-first into her ugly reality again.

Just as she got to the door, she realized that as soon as she let any light in, he was going to know who she really was. Fortunately, the house's electricity was iffy on a good night, as she had learned.

Work of a moment to blow the bulb out in the hallway.

He was still yelling that god-awful name as she raced down the stairs, a running corpse dressed in one of his button-downs, her lie and her vulnerability exposed. Too scattered to spirit away, she was forced to comply with the laws of physics and gravity and actually pull open the front door.

I'm a strategic thinker, but I did not see this one coming.

As the demon burst out into the night, she was in horrified agreement. She was a strategist, too . . . and even still, it had never dawned on her that Nigel would do what he did—and in the process, doom Jim and her forever.

It was in the rules, those fucking rules the Maker had set out back in the beginning. Such a small little procedural notation . . . one that neither she nor Nigel had paid any attention to.

But oh, God, Jim and she could never be together at the end of the war now.

There was a footnote in the rules that said if either she or Nigel were killed or "died" in the line of duty, Jim would take their place—and another savior chosen. It had seemed like such a strange provision to make, although she had supposed at the time it was there so that no one decided to target the opposition on a personal level. It also detailed a line of succession so that the war could continue to a natural conclusion, as well as sanctions if either side took such a drastic step.

But Nigel had taken his own life, so there was no way to punish him.

And she was willing to bet the archangel had done it specifically to come between Jim and her—an ultimate fuck-you.

Because that archangel had razzed her about her feelings for the savior during their meetings with the Maker. And Nigel had always been a stickler for the letter of the law, so to speak.

No happily ever after for her and Jim now—whether she lost or she won.

This wasn't supposed to happen. She wasn't supposed to lose him—she was either going to win, and they were going to rule the

Heavens and Earth together . . . or she'd lose, and he would choose to immolate himself with her, going up into flames like something out of Shakespeare because he couldn't fathom an existence without her.

Driven by a horrible agony, Devina ran out into the road and crossed to the other side, not tracking where she was going, chased even though she was alone.

Goddamn therapist. Oh, sure, it was just great to form attachments to things other than things. Just fucking wonderful.

This was *such* a terrific help.

Chapter
Thirty-nine

As the sun came up, Adrian was sitting at the kitchen table, drinking coffee that did not taste as good as the stuff Sissy had made the morning before. With any luck she'd come down again, take pity on his sorry ass, and hook him up. If not? He might have to go the Egg McMuffin route.

He really didn't like this waiting, though, and not just because he was hungry—and the coffee really did suck.

Shifting around and trying to get that bum leg quiet, he was stiffer than he usually was. Then again, he'd had to stay on his feet while he'd been down below with Devina yesterday, and the effects of all that vertical were still with him.

Man, that demon could follow through when she wanted something.

Tenacity like a parasite. Natch.

He'd really enjoyed humiliating her—watching her work so

hard and get nowhere? Short of killing her, which he couldn't do without her precious mirror, it had been utterly satisfying.

Better than a fuckload of orgasms he wouldn't have wanted anyway.

"What's up, man."

Ad looked over his shoulder and cursed. "I was hoping you were Sissy. We need breakfast and she's a hell of a cook."

As Jim wandered in, he was walking stiffly, too, which was a surprise. All the grim on his face was not, however.

For some reason, Ad thought of the guy staring at Sissy: It was the only time he'd ever seen the savior look alive. And not as in pissed off.

They were both dead men walking in a lot of ways.

"What happened to you last night?" Ad asked.

"We gotta talk."

Something in that voice made Ad straighten in his chair, even though his hip didn't appreciate the added stress. "What."

Jim took his own goddamn time getting some of that watery coffee. And he waited until he was seated across the table to drop his bomb: "Nigel's gone."

Ad frowned. No way he'd heard that right. "Gone as in 'taking a breather from the game'? As in, 'off to the tailors'? Or . . ."

"He's *gone*."

An icy-cold mantle settled across Ad's shoulders. "Disappeared, you mean."

"No." Jim shook out a cigarette from a pack of Reds and lit it with his Bic. "I found him dead in his tent last night."

Ad's jaw unhinged, and he let his mouth fall open. "You can't . . . no, that's not . . ."

Jim answered without words, just staring right into his face.

"Give me one of those," Ad muttered, holding out his palm.

"You don't smoke."

"This morning I do."

Jim popped a brow, but shared, pushing over his cigs and his lighter. And Ad made like the guy, putting a cancer stick between his teeth, bringing flame to tip, breathing in.

The sense of suffocation was not remotely pleasurable. The buzz that came shortly after the inhale? Not bad.

"I was with that demon all day long," Ad said, shaking his head. "How did Devina—"

"Nigel's hand was on the hilt."

Ad felt his eyes bulge. "*He* did it?"

"Far as I can tell."

Adrian shook his head again. "Colin. Oh, shit, Colin did you see him?"

"We traded some words, yeah." Jim rubbed his chest and grimaced. "He had some sharp points to make."

Adrian scrubbed his face. He'd never particularly cared one way or the other about those archangels. At their worst, they were obstacles to work around. At best, they were so busy with their tea and crumpets, they stayed out of his way.

Well, except for that one time. At band camp.

But after losing Eddie? He felt for Colin. Best unkept secret in the universe, those two archangels had been. So that must hurt.

"This fucking war."

"Amen to that," Jim said, leaning back and tapping his ash into the sink.

Being immortal, Ad had never thought much about dying in the conventional "game over" sense. Lately? It was on his mind constantly—no doubt thanks to bunking in with Eddie.

Hard to lose your other half.

On that note . . . "Everything okay with Sissy?" As Jim glanced up in surprise, Adrian rolled his eyes. "Look, it's still none of my business what you do with her. But . . . she's okay. She's a good girl, that one—what."

"Ahhh, that's just a big fat one-eighty for you. As recently as yesterday morning, you were ready to clock me about her."

Adrian took another inhale and then stared at his cigarette's tip, because it was easier than looking at the savior. "I don't know, I guess I don't really blame you for trying to find a safe haven in all this. Just be careful. No foundation is sturdy in this game."

Jim studiously avoided all that. "Thanks for buying those clothes for her. What do I owe you?"

"It came to two hundred and eighty-seven bucks. But Devina put it on her credit card, so I think we should consider them gifts."

"You went *shopping* with her?"

"You told me to keep her busy, and she likes clothes. Whatever. The sex shit doesn't work anymore for me—although I have to say, it was amusing as fuck to watch her try to get me up."

Jim winced. "I'm sorry."

"What for? I've had to do worse down there. Her masturbating for hours was a vacay compared to the other shit. Just think, if I'd had a video camera, I could have Kim Kardashian'd her."

As they fell into a silence, he knew they were both thinking about that worktable of hers. Eddie was the only one out of the three of them who hadn't been down there in that capacity. He'd also never been with Devina in the conventional sense, either.

Another reason he should have been the last of them to go.

"So Sissy's been doing a great job with this place," Ad murmured.

Jim looked over again. "What do you mean?"

"You know, cleaning it up? Shit's looking much better since she's moved in."

"Last time I saw, she was trying to burn it down."

"Excuse me?"

"Long story. The transition's just been rough."

Ad nodded. "Nothing's easy in this, is it."

"So, are you going to tell me where we are? I'm ready to get back to work."

Ad got up and went to the sink, dousing his cig, the habit still not doing it for him. Turning around, he wondered where to start. "Colin said he could only go part of the way with the intel."

"Whatever we got, we can run with."

"That's what I told him . . ."

Across town, as the angels commiserated and Jim got his update, Cait was sitting at her desk, brushing a tear from her cheek. Clearing her throat, she prayed she didn't completely crumble. "I'm sorry, what was that, Mrs. Barten? The connection is bad."

Untrue. She was having trouble keeping her cell phone against her ear.

"Yes, of course," she said into the thing. "Yes. Absolutely . . ."

Even though she never wrote on drawing paper, she slid a fresh sheet over. And even though she never wrote with drawing pencils, she made sure she had all the details down.

"I'm honored." She wiped away another tear. "Yes, I have some stands I know exactly what we need. You can count on me. See you then. Yes . . . God willing."

As she ended the call, she got up slowly and went into the kitchen. Everything was tidy as always, not even dishes drying in the rack—because she had to put them away before she left the kitchen or she couldn't sit still at her desk.

She'd had some kind of destination. But abruptly, she found herself walking around on her linoleum, making a tight little circle, eyes lighting on the hand towels that were neatly hanging off the handle of the oven, and the napkins on the table in their rack, and the two place mats she had out even though she always ate alone. If she opened any of the cupboards? Soup cans and boxes of low-fat crackers and jars of pickles were lined up by type. Same in her refrigerator, the skim milk never mixing with the yogurt or the butter or the veggies.

The first line against chaos. And to think she'd always assumed the anal retentiveness would help, a kind of talisman against the whirlpool of life, a way of taming the hard edges of fate.

Wasn't doing anything for her at the moment. Not about her heading to see G.B. at noontime to tell him she was kind of in a relationship with someone else. Not with the desperate anticipation she had for nightfall.

Certainly not at all with what she was about to do.

"Shit."

Bracing herself, she went over to the door that led down into the cellar. It took her a moment before she could turn the knob and pull the panels open and reach forward to flick the light switch. As the fixture came on, the rough wooden steps were illuminated, as was the dark gray concrete floor below. The scent that rose to her nose was both earthy from the fifties-era concrete walls, and sweet from her fabric softener sheets.

Long trip down. A kind of forever to reach the bottom.

She didn't head over to her washing machine and ironing board. She went in the opposite direction, to the sealed plastic tubs that held her Christmas decorations and lights, and her Halloween things, and that sleeping bag she'd only used once or twice.

It was past all that that she kept her artwork on shelves, her tubes of drawings and flat boxes of paintings and so much more ordered chronologically by medium.

The things she had taken out of Sissy's locker at school were right where she'd put them. Cait had had to move some of her own pastels onto the floor to make room, something she had never felt comfortable doing before—especially not in the spring, when the rains came and leaks happened.

But as important as her things were, Sissy's were so much more so.

The hands that had made them were gone forever.

It took Cait a couple of trips to carry the folios and the box up to her kitchen table. And after a moment, she thought better about the placement and moved them away from the window. Maybe she should have left them downstairs? It wasn't like she was going to forget to bring them to the funeral at St. Patrick's.

Staring at it all, she stepped back in time, reversing the mental DVD of her life until she was once again twelve and living under the same roof with her parents. After her brother had died, she had been the one to pack up his things: Her mother and father had disappeared within days of the burial, going off on the first of all those mission trips, her grandmother moving in to take care of her.

She'd like her grandmother just fine, but it had felt like both she and Charlie had been deserted. And that sense had intensified when her parents had called a week later and said that they were bringing home a preacher who needed a place to stay for a month. In that small house, where else were they going to put the guy but Charlie's room?

It had seemed an insult to let some stranger sleep in her brother's bed or use his bureau and his closet, all while his clothes and car magazines and CDs were all over the place.

Using her own allowance money, she'd bought U-Haul boxes, and put everything in the attic . . . and when she had moved out east, she had taken it with her.

For all their pontificating, her parents had never really talked to her about the loss. Plenty of generic praying advice, yes, and she had to admit, the cynic in her aside, she had done some of that on her own. Still did. But she could have used some more conventional support in the form of talking, hugs, understanding, compassion.

Then again, her brother had always been her family.

It was weird, weird, weird to be thinking of all of this right now. But another funeral of another young life lost too early was likely to bring up things that were unresolved—

The knocking on her door was probably the FedEx man delivering the supply of pencils she'd ordered last week.

Wiping her cheeks on a just-in-case, she took out her scrunchie and re-pulled her hair back as she went for the door.

Not FedEx, although the box had been left on her front stoop.

Teresa was dressed in a pale blue business suit that did absolutely nothing for her coloring, and she was pissed, hands on her hips, glare on her face. "You never call, you never write. You *suck*. Now let me in—I have forty-five minutes before I have to be back to the office, and you're going to tell me *everything*."

Her oldest and dearest pushed past her, marching into the kitchen and sitting down next to all the artwork.

"So." Teresa crossed her arms over her chest and tapped her high-heeled shoe. "What's happening—"

Cait burst into tears.

"Oh, shit." Teresa jumped up and went in for the hug. "I'm such an ass. Are you okay? What's wrong? If he hurt you, I'll screw his reputation twelve ways to Sunday on the Internet. And key his car. And do some other stuff that you won't want to know about beforehand, but will certainly read of in the *CCJ*."

Cait held on tight. It was a while before she could say anything intelligent—but that was the thing with true friends.

They didn't necessarily need to hear the details of where you were . . . to be there for you.

Another one?

As Duke walked into the Shed and heard his name get called out, he eyed the guy standing by the muni truck he himself had been assigned to for the shift. Man, he couldn't remember the last time he'd had two subs in three days working with him. Maybe they'd fired the first? Turned out that one had had a bad limp, and though the city of Caldwell didn't discriminate, it was hard to be a laborer if you couldn't even stand up for any period of time.

"So are you Duke Phillips?" the man asked.

"Yeah. You with me for the day?" he muttered as he walked over with the keys.

"Yup."

"Well, I drive." Duke unlocked the doors and got in. "And set the route."

"No problem."

"We're going to be ripping out a hedgerow," Duke said, as they shut their doors and he started the engine. "After that, we've got inventory to do."

"What's that?"

Duke drove them out of the garage and into the sunlight. He'd come in at eleven, and was grateful for the extra hour of work. With any luck, he'd be back to full-time in another week or ten days.

"We drive through parks and cemeteries and make up a work list for the spring cleanup. If the projects are approved, we get more hours."

"Can I smoke in here?"

"Doesn't bother me." At least he wouldn't get a contact high, like he did at home with Rolly's pot. "Crack a window, though, so I don't have to hear about it."

As Duke's phone went off, he took the thing out. Checked the screen. Closed his eyes for a split second and then bumped the call.

It was Nicole. Wanting to talk about the kid, no doubt.

Man, the last thing he wanted to hear was that there was more trouble at school. That Nicole was taking a second go at having Duke talk to him. That that quicksand of madness was trying to suck him in again.

He set the terms between the three of them. No one else.

Besides, he had enough on his plate.

"Bad call?" the guy beside him asked.

Duke let the question slide. He was not interested in getting familiar with the fathead in the passenger seat—and he was certainly not going to let the stranger into his biz. Hell, he didn't allow that with people he knew.

Fortunately, there was no more talking as he took them into town, the rural miles and then the suburban blocks getting eaten up fast.

"So, I know you," the guy said as they hit some traffic going into the thick of downtown.

Duke glanced across the seat. Nope, he didn't recognize his one-shift partner. But that didn't mean the man hadn't been in line at the Iron Mask or something—although that hardly counted as "knowing."

"No, you don't."

"Yeah, I do." The man flicked the tip off his Marlboro out of the window crack and put the dead butt in his jacket pocket. "I know that you're going to face a crossroads soon, and you're going to have to make a choice. I'm here to help you do the right thing."

What the fuck?

Duke hit the brakes to stop at a red light, and turned to face Mr. Chatty. Time to set the ground rules before this became the longest workday of his life. "You and I have six hours where we are required to be . . . together . . . in . . . this . . ."

Duke let the screw-you wind down into silence as he met the man's eyes. Strange eyes. Strange color.

Just like the other "worker" he'd been paired with.

Abruptly, a cotton-wool feeling came over him—talk about your contact highs. It was a little like what he'd felt when he was around his star boarder for too long while Rolly was toking up— but it was so much more than that.

"Here's what we're going to do," the man said. "In another block and a half, you're going to turn right and take us down to the river. We're going to parallel-park and take a walk in the park so the GPS on this truck reports that we've done our job. But we're not going to be digging out any bushes. You're going to tell me where you're at—we're almost out of time and I need to be up to speed quick."

Duke blinked. And then his phone started ringing again.

He took it out slowly. As he saw who was calling, he looked back at the man. With a feeling of total unreality, he heard himself say, "Do you know . . . a woman with brunette hair?"

As that psychic crackpot from Trade Street went into Duke's voice mail, it was somehow not a surprise that the man beside him nodded slowly.

"Yeah, I do. And we need to keep you away from her."

Somewhere deep in his marrow, Duke knew that this was what he'd been waiting his whole adult life for. He'd always had some sense that things were not normal for him, no matter how much he tried to pretend otherwise—and that was the reason he'd gone to that psychic for all those years.

It was also the "why" behind his nightmares, the ones he told nobody about.

Duke's phone let out a beep, notifying him that a new message had been left for him.

Through the fog that had settled into his brain, he watched his thumb move over the smooth screen, calling the voice mail up . . . and then he put the cell up to his ear.

"Duke, this is Yasemin Oaks—you must come see me. At the very least, I need to speak with you urgently. The dreams are getting more intense—you are in danger—please, Duke, I'm warning you. Blood is going to flow and—"

"The light's green," the man next to him announced. "Hit the gas and take us down to the river. It's time, Duke. We've got shit to take care of."

For some strange reason, Duke thought of Cait. Beautiful Cait.

"I don't know you," he said roughly.

"You don't have to. But you need to trust me."

Snap out of it, he told himself. This is all bullcrap.

"Not going to happen," he heard himself say.

Abruptly, he put his phone away. Pushed his foot down on the accelerator. And was ready to go anywhere except over to the water—just to establish who was in charge.

After a moment, he glanced over at the other man. The son of a bitch was sitting in the passenger seat, jaw set like he knew exactly how this was going to play out.

Duke cursed under his breath. Yeah, no way he was telling this guy anything . . . and yet he couldn't ignore the sense of foreboding that was dogging him. Besides, he'd wanted to end this shit for so long, even as he was knee-deep in it right now. The trouble was, old habits, like bitter resentments, died hard.

"You don't have much of a choice," the man said. "You need me if you want to come out of this in one piece."

One piece? Duke thought. *Hah. I'm already broken.*

"You're going to tell me everything, Duke. You have to."

Chapter Forty

As Cait parallel-parked on Trade Street, no more than a block away from the Palace Theatre, she frowned and leaned into the windshield. It wasn't because she was lost this time, though. As opposed to when she'd been trying to find the hair salon a couple of nights ago, she had no confusion as to the theater's location.

The issue was the police.

There were six or seven Caldwell Police Department vehicles parked in front of the Palace, and about half a dozen uniformed officers milling around outside the main entrance.

Getting out into the sunshine, she pulled her light coat in tighter and slung her bag over her shoulder. She had to wait for a stream of traffic to go by, but eventually there was a break in the cars and she jaywalked across.

Probably not the smartest thing to do in front of a cop convention, but it sure seemed like the unis had bigger fish to fry than her.

As she approached the knot of officers, several of them turned to her.

"Hi," she said, blinking in the glare of their badges. "I'm here to meet a friend for lunch?"

The tallest one, an African-American guy with a voice that suggested you really did not mess with him, spoke up. "Who would that be?"

"G. B. Holde? He's a singer—he's here rehearsing for *Rent?*"

"You're meeting him for what?"

Abruptly, they were all focused on her, measuring her, no doubt taking mental pictures and notes. "Lunch? We were going to have a sandwich together?"

"Is this a regular thing?"

"Um, no. We made the date—er, you know, the time—last night?"

"Do you know him well?"

"Why are you here? What's happened?"

"What's your name, ma'am?"

"Cait. Caitlyn Douglass?" Maybe they were violating her rights, she didn't know. But she had nothing to hide. "Is he okay?"

"We can't let you inside, ma'am, I'm sorry. This is a crime scene."

Cait felt the blood leave her face. "Who died?"

"A young female."

Which meant G.B. was okay—and yet the intel was not any kind of relief. "Oh . . . God." Was it a case of Sissy all over again? Or . . . "I was chased in the parking lot the other night. You don't suppose this had anything to do with—"

"When was that, ma'am?"

Even more police officers clustered around her as she told them all what had happened to her. And then an exhausted man in a loose suit came out of the theater's glass doors.

"Detective?" someone called out. "We got a female over here."

A man with dark hair and a way-too-early-in-the-day five o'clock shadow walked across the mosaic stretch and put his hand out. "Detective de la Cruz. How you doing?"

Shaking his hand, she instantly felt comfortable with him. "Hi."

"You've got quite a crowd here." He nodded at his colleagues. "They're nosy—and paid to be that way. Me, too. So you mind telling me what's going on with you?"

In quick, clear terms, she explained everything that had happened to her the other night, and as she talked, he scribbled in a little spiral notebook.

"Well, I'm sorry you were chased like that." He put his notebook away. "Any follow-up on the perpetrator?"

"No. I haven't called, and no one's been in touch."

"I'll check back at the station and let you know one way or the other. As for your lunch, I'm sorry, but we can't let you in. Everybody who's working in the theater is being questioned by my team. As for this . . ." He took the notepad out again and flipped the cover open. "This G.B. guy? Is that the man you were going to meet?"

"Yes."

"Yeah, he's going to be busy for a while."

She frowned. "Detective, can you tell me anything about what's going on?"

"I'm sorry, I can't. But you'll hear about it tonight on the news," he said dryly as a van with a satellite dish on its roof pulled up across the street. "However, if you want me to get a message to G.B., I'd be happy to carry it in."

"I just want him to know I came . . . and that I hope he's okay."

Which was stupid. Someone had died. Nothing was okay.

After she got back to her car, she started her engine and pulled out of her spot. She didn't have any idea where she was going, although she did text G.B. at a stoplight, just in case the detective got busy or forgot.

With any luck, he would volunteer an update.

Hitting another stoplight, she made a random turn. And another. And even more, until she realized she was literally going nowhere. Pulling over, she found herself in Caldwell's financial district, the thicket of skyscrapers blocking out the light, the pedestrians all in gray and black like shadows of real people.

She really needed to just go home, she thought—even as she put the car in park and sat back in her seat.

Man, one thing that sucked as you got older was that you had so many more associations with things. A couple of years ago, she might have gone to that theater, heard that someone she didn't know had been killed, and probably only had a moment's pause. Now? After Sissy Barten's brutal murder, she was stuck in a domino effect that took her right back to that hospital, when her brother had been taken off the ventilator.

He should have been wearing a helmet. Goddamn him, he knew he wasn't supposed to skateboard without a helmet.

But teenagers were clueless enough to believe their skulls were stronger than concrete.

That had been the transformative part for her, she realized. If he'd only been properly prepared, he would have been okay—he would have survived the impact.

That had been the basis of the fixation on order for her: the idea that if you just made sure you were always neat and prepared, you'd be safe. If you put on a helmet, you would never be injured. If you always wore your seat belt, and got regular checkups, and flossed and brushed, and never, ever took a step without first considering what kind of padding and safety equipment you needed . . .

She thought of Thom: If you stuck with nice guys who you

weren't really passionate about, you wouldn't have to worry about getting your heart broken.

"Yeah, right," she muttered to herself. That had happened anyway. And curiously . . . it had been okay. It *was* okay.

And didn't that make her think about the differences between G.B. and Duke.

She had known that she was going to have to make a choice at some point. She had not expected to have that decision come to her here and now, as she sat in her car at the side of the road, swarms of business types walking by, taxis shooting up and down the street, distant sirens suggesting that crises were all around.

She had tried the safe option once before and the outcome had been what it was—and in fact, crash helmets only helped in certain kinds of accidents . . . and even neat freaks who relied on order to protect themselves got chased in garages and scared shitless.

Hell, for all she knew, whatever woman had been killed at the theater had had a color-coded closet, too.

There was no protection from injury, disillusionment, disappointment.

God, what a depressing thought. And yet it was liberating, too.

She knew who she wanted.

At least . . . she thought she did.

The knock on her window made her shout in alarm.

"Ma'am?" It was a meter maid, her voice buffered by the closed windows. "I'm going to have to ticket you if you don't get moving."

"Sorry," Cait said, trying to remember where the gearshift was. "I'll leave right now. Thanks."

Getting back into the flow of traffic, she felt a strange dread come over her, as if her destiny was somehow threatened. But . . . that was just crazy.

Wasn't it?

At the next stoplight, she dragged her bag over and searched through it . . . and as she found what she was looking for, she couldn't believe she was thinking about calling that psychic, the one whose business card she'd taken from the corkboard at the theater.

Focusing on the address, she mentally mapped out a route. She'd never been to anyone like that before, and had no idea what to expect—or what she could possibly get out of it.

The only thing she was sure of was that a kind of . . . crossroads . . . seemed to have appeared before her, and she wanted some sort of confirmation that the direction she intended to go in was the correct one.

Couldn't hurt, right.

Hitting the gas, she got lost in images of the two men, anxiety sharpening the pictures to an almost painful degree. . . .

When Cait's car stopped again, she was barely aware of having hit the brakes. And . . . wait a minute, this was not the grungier end of Trade Street. In fact, it was . . .

Where the hell was she?

Too much grass to be downtown.

She was about to pull a U-ey when she saw the stray dog. Small, low to the ground, and scruffy as a floor mop, it was seated on the broad stretch of lawn and staring right at her.

Cait got out. "You okay there, boy?"

Somehow she knew it was a boy. No collar, though. Poor thing.

As it lifted its forepaw, she was compelled to go around the front of her car—and that was when the place she'd arrived at came into her consciousness.

Not the psychic's, no. Try church and steeple.

It was St. Patrick's Cathedral, the grande dame of all Christian houses of worship in Caldwell, the one with the Gothic spires, and all the saints, and the stained glass that looked like jewels.

Where Sissy Barten's funeral was going to occur.

How had she ended up here?

She turned back to see the dog, but he was gone. "Where are you?"

Cait looked all around, pivoting in a circle—he'd disappeared, though.

Following a long moment, and for no good reason she could think of, her feet decided to take the term *walkway* to heart, pulling a one-after-another that brought her up to a side entrance. As she reached out to open the door, and found the heavy weight obliging, she labeled the impulse that carried her over the threshold under "preparation for Sissy's event."

There was no other purpose for her to come here. In fact, she hadn't been in a church since she'd moved to Caldwell—unless she'd gone home and been dragged to services. And she certainly wasn't Catholic, all that regal tradition antithetical to the pine-floored, white-washed, garden-flowers-on-the-altar simplicity she was used to, and had revolted against.

Inside, she had to close her eyes and take a deep breath. Oh, wow, did that smell good—incense and old wood and beeswax.

She was in a side vestibule, as it turned out, and as she walked across the polished stone floor, her footsteps echoed forward into the vast expanse of the nave. Stone block walls rose to seemingly incalculable heights, the buttresses flying like the wings of angels at every juncture, depictions of holy men and women marking the corners and the straightaways, different chapels running down the longest length from the incredible entrance to the beautiful altar.

So many pews, stretching out on both sides of the bloodred aisle—and she pictured them filled with people, grown-ups and children, grandparents and teenagers. All the stages of life—

"Hello."

Cait nearly lost her footing on the slick marble. "Oh! I'm sorry."

An old man dressed in a mucky green janitor suit smiled as he put his mop back in his rolling bucket. "Don't apologize. You're welcome here."

"I'm not Catholic." She winced. "I mean—"

"It doesn't matter. Everyone's welcome here."

She cleared her throat. "Well, I didn't come to worship. I don't go to church anymore. Ah, actually, I'm . . . I'm bringing some paintings that Sissy Barten did? You know, for her funeral? I thought it would make sense to check out things beforehand?"

"Oh, of course." He moved his pail out of the way. "Her family has been really involved here over the years—there're going to be a lot of people. I think you should plan on setting it all up in the narthex. That way there's enough space so her work can be seen well. Come this way."

As he started to walk away from the altar, she paused and looked back at the crucified Jesus on the cross that was the focal point of the entire building.

"Are you coming?" he said gently. "Or would you like a moment here?"

"Oh, no. I'm fine." Except she didn't turn around. Didn't move. "I'm not Catholic."

"You don't have to be." When she still hesitated, he dropped his voice. "You know, the truth is, it's all the same."

"I'm sorry?"

He leaned in and put his hand on her arm—and oh, God, the moment the contact was made, she felt suffused by something she'd never come close to before . . . grace, she supposed her parents would have called it, that transcendental glow that supposedly came with revelation.

But he was just a janitor. . . .

"It's all the same. No matter the vocabulary, it's all the same." He patted her. "I have to head to the office for a minute. I'll come back in a bit and show you where to go."

"I'm okay."

"I know you are. Sit down and soak it all in. I'll return soon."

Left alone, she told her feet to get moving again. Instead, she ended up doing what he said . . . sitting down, putting her hands in her lap, and staring up, past the pews in front of her, to the majesty and the power before her.

In the kind silence that surrounded her, Cait discovered she was really glad she'd come here. Even if she hadn't meant to.

Who knew what the psychic would have told her. But she never did find out.

Destiny, she would discover, took care of itself.

Chapter Forty-one

Up in the attic, Sissy stood behind Adrian—who was not looking at her. Or refusing to look at her was more like it. Fine. She was just going to keep talking to his back as he sat cross-legged in front of that shrouded figure.

"Except you must know more, right? There has to be more." She passed an eye over the deceased, and felt a stab of guilt. But whatever, she needed the help and he was the only one around. Jim had left without a goodbye, or an I'll-be-back-when—so it was just her and Adrian.

And her frustration.

She threw her hands up. "I'd go to the Internet, but you can't trust anything on it. And like the Caldwell Public Library is going to cover this?"

She could also wait and go to Jim—except for the fact that one, the guy didn't seem to know as much as Adrian; and two, she had the sense he wanted to keep her out of the war.

Whereas she was ready to get into it.

Adrian rubbed his jaw—like it was either that or start scream-ing. "You are a pain in my ass. No offense."

She wanted to come closer. Didn't dare. "I've got to forge my own way here. I have no choice—and if that means pissing you off, that's the way it is."

"If I were angry, you'd know it. Terminally annoyed is more accurate."

"Please. Just point me in the right direction. I'll take things from there."

He laughed in a short burst. "Funny you say it like that."

"Why?"

The angel glanced over his shoulder. "You're not going to give up on this, are you."

"Nope."

With a curse, Adrian leaned to the side and got his cane. Grimacing as he stood up, he leveled his stare on her. "Okay, fine. But, first off, I don't know if I can find it. I make no prom-ises."

"What's 'it'?"

"What you're looking for. And . . ." He shoved his forefinger in her face. "You damage it in any way, and I'm going to take the shit out of your hide. I don't care if you're a girl or not. Are we clear?"

She put her hand out. "Deal."

The guy rolled his eyes. But he did shake on it.

Then he led her down to the second floor. Down to the first. Through the back door. Out toward the garage.

Talk about your lean-to's—even though the long, thin build-ing had a roof and three walls, it was listing like Adrian did when he walked, looking as if the only thing keeping it standing were the thick vines that grew up on its sides. And although there were four rolling doors, it appeared as though only two of them worked: The other pair on the far end had two-by-fours nailed kitty-corner all over the front of them.

Adrian bent over and locked a grip on the first door, heaving his considerable strength into it. The high-pitched screech of metal on metal made her cover her ears as he pulled the weight up ancient tracks, disappearing the chipped, paint-flaking panels into the darkness.

"You stay out here."

He vanished into the shadows, and then she heard a flick-flick . . . flick-flick . . . and a lot more cursing.

Evidently the lights were out.

"Can you get me a flashlight," he said. "There's one in the— ow! Fuck me!"

"Explorer?"

"Yeah."

"I think I need the keys—" Before she finished speaking, a set came flying out of the garage. Catching them, she said, "Hey, are you okay?"

"Fine and fucking dandy—it's just a goddamn mess in here."

Figuring she had a matter of nanoseconds before he lost his patience completely and told her to screw off, she jogged over to the SUV and beelined for the glove compartment. A quick click, and she had a beam that was strong enough to blind her even in the daylight. Perfect.

Back at the garage, she shined it inside. "Wooooow . . ."

And she thought the attic was full of adventures. Turned out the garage was an open single bay stuffed full of an incalculable amount of lawn equipment and carpentry machines and automobiles that must have come from the fifties. There were a number of new additions, however—three dust-free duffel bags were clustered around Adrian's feet.

Buttressing himself on that cane, he got down on his knees and unzipped the first of them. Out came . . . a huge leather coat. A couple pairs of jeans. Combat boots. Shirts. Each item was set aside with care on the concrete.

Eddie's things.

Sissy was tempted to step away and give Adrian some privacy, but he needed the light. And maybe the company.

He was talking: "Such a good little packer, he was. I used to think it was a waste of fucking time. When we moved, though . . . I did it like he would have. Folded everything. Put the shit in by category."

Sissy blinked back tears as she wondered how her family was going to do things differently in the future. She didn't want her survivors changing themselves as a way to remember her . . . but she probably would have done the same thing.

"I'm sure he appreciated it," she whispered.

"He's dead. He'll never know."

"Are you certain about that?"

The angel's hands stilled for a heartbeat. "Dunno." He moved to the next bag. "Maybe it's in this one. I know I packed the goddamn thing—ah . . . got it."

Awkwardly moving around, he held his forearm up against the flashlight. "You can turn that off."

"Sorry." *Click.*

Adrian grunted as he got to his feet and walked out into the sunshine. "Here. This is all I got to offer you."

It was a book, an ancient book that was thick as a tree trunk.

Tucking the flashlight under her arm, she accepted the thing with trembling hands. The cover was so old, she couldn't even tell what color the leather was—something between red and black and gray and brown. And there had been some kind of embossing and maybe some gold leaf, but most of that was worn smooth and worn off.

"What is this?" she said, gingerly opening the tone.

Inhaling deeply, she smelled flowers, the kind that were up in the attic, and as she scanned the title page, she had a vague impression of Latin words.

Thank God her father had made her study that in high school.

"I have no clue." Adrian looked away, to the rooftop of the mansion. "It's where he went whenever he got that look in his eye—the one that meant he was worried he was coming up with the wrong answer. He hated that."

Sissy frowned as she realized that Adrian was in serious pain. He had one hand on the small of his back, and was arching to the side as if trying to pop something into place.

It had been hard for him to be on his knees like that.

"Hold this for a sec," she said, returning the book to him.

Walking around him, she turned on the flashlight and entered the garage. Laying the beam down by her feet, she crouched by the open duffels.

One by one, she put the things he had taken out back where they had been, making sure that the categories were preserved. When she was finished, she zipped up the two bags and shuffled them into their original position.

As she exited, she got up on her tiptoes and pulled down the door, batting away the leaves that hung off the bottom, and the spider that tried to land on her hand.

Back by his side, she took the book from him again. "Thanks."

When she went to turn away, his hand landed on her shoulder. Looking up at him, she found it physically painful to see him struggle for words.

She put her hand over his. "You're welcome."

Taking care of someone's dead was just as important as taking care of their living.

When Jim got home, it was about two seconds after five p.m. Thanks to Angel Airlines, he didn't have to worry about a commute—and good thing. He was coming back and checking in only long enough to make sure that Sissy and Ad were hanging out okay. Then he had to go back to tailing Duke Phillips.

Opening the front door—

"What the . . ." Inhaling again, he nearly groaned. Onions sautéing with spices. Something meat, too. And fresh bread?

As he shut himself in, he faltered again. Talk about a woman's touch . . . even though the light was fading in the sky, everything was so much brighter inside the house, the lamps shining as if the bulbs and silk shades had all been cleaned. The rugs were more colorful, too, like someone had vacuumed everywhere—and the floors. Jesus Christ, the floors were gleaming.

Glancing up the stairs, he was astounded to find that the carpet runner wasn't actually brown . . . it was a deep garnet red. And the carved balustrade was glowing from having been polished. And the walls? The paper that had been gradually peeling free and dropping down was reaffixed, the pattern itself resurrected from aged obscurity, the subtle vines and blooms showing once again.

Jim headed back to the kitchen, and was gob smacked to find Adrian in an apron, sitting at the kitchen table, cutting green beans with a crystal dagger like he was performing heart surgery.

"Like this?" the angel was saying intently.

Sissy pivoted away from a steaming pot. "Perfect. Yeah, just nip the ends."

Ad nodded and went back to work.

The fact that neither of them noticed him was a little galling. But he couldn't really be jealous of Adrian—who, at last glance, had only grudgingly accepted her presence. Right?

Then again, six hours later, how times had changed. They were best frickin' buddies, evidently.

Jim cleared his throat. "Smells good."

Sissy jumped enough to drop her spoon, but Adrian just glanced up, and then returned to his job.

"You want to eat with us?" she said as she smoothed her hair. "We're going to be ready in thirty minutes?"

He could wait that long. "Yeah. Please."

Feeling like he was back in his mama's house, he went to the sink and washed his hands. Hey, check it, he could actually see out the window into the backyard for the first time. And as he rinsed off, he noticed that the stainless-steel sink was shiny as new. So were the pans that were sitting in a pile in the rack.

Jim took his time drying things on a clean dishrag, lingering just behind Sissy. Her hair had been pulled back into a messy knot, held in place by a big barrette. At her nape, tiny curls had formed, and he had an almost irresistible urge to touch them, wrap them around his finger . . . and the impulses didn't stop there. He wanted to wrap his height around her from behind and plant a lingering kiss on the side of her throat.

Wheeling away, he took a seat across from Ad and watched the guy make a pile of cut green beans in a white enameled pot full of water.

"So how did today go?" Ad asked.

"Stayed tight with the guy. There's bad juju all over him—frankly, it's a hot mess. I just wanted to come home and see . . ."

Adrian finished things for him. "Me, of course. And I'm really touched—you're so awesome like that. You bring me chocolates? Flowers?"

Just as Jim was about to fuck-off the guy, the other angel said softly, "I got her. You don't have to worry."

Jim cocked a brow. But, man, that did decrease his stress. It was one thing asking his roommate to play bodyguard, another to have him volunteer for it.

"Thanks."

"No problem."

Dinner was on about a half an hour later, just as promised, and Jim wished the meal had been hours late. As Sissy worked in the kitchen, his eyes were glued to her, watching her move around, or tuck a strand of hair behind her ear, or pull up the loose sweats she was wearing over and over again.

He'd never spent much time with women, and he certainly wasn't into that flighty, giggly, everything-pink bullshit that some of them seemed determined to define themselves by. Still, he was very certain that few of the fairer sex pulled together a meal for two hungry men with the confidence and poise and results that Sissy did—and he found himself loving that about her.

Maybe there was a point to that man/stomach connection.

When she finally sat down, she put her hands out, palms up.

"Prayer," she ordered as both he and Adrian stared at her in confusion.

"Ah . . ."

"Er . . ."

"Prayer." She rapped her knuckles on the table.

Both he and Adrian complied, the three of them forming a triangle, the links shockingly strong.

She bowed her head and talked so fast that he couldn't understand the words. Didn't matter, though. In the midst of the war, and the deaths, and the sense that time was running out . . . an easing came over Jim, relaxing his breathing and his shoulders, reminding him of days long past—the good ones, the ones he hadn't thought of in so many years.

The ones that he was shocked to find were still with him.

And what do you know—the beef stew?

Delicious.

Chapter
Forty-two

"Are you kidding me? I thought this one was going to last."

As Duke stepped back from his door and let Rolly in, he should have known better, but come on—one day? That was all the woman had lasted with the guy?

Then again . . .

Rolly shrugged as he threw his backpack down. "Dude, I swear, I thought she was something special." He went over to the refrigerator and opened things up. "Oh, man, there's nothing to eat."

"And this is a surprise?"

"You never have food in here."

"Like I always tell you, you want a cook and turndown service, go to your mother's."

"No way, she's too demanding."

Well, maybe there was still hope, Duke thought as he shut the front door and tightened the bath towel that was around his waist. Maybe the woman would rethink things.

Rolly's ass hit the sofa cushions and he sighed like the two parties had been separated for a year. "You know, you could get cable out here."

"And encourage you to stay longer?"

"You loooooooove me," the guy called out as Duke went into the bedroom.

"Not really."

Duke went over to his closet and opened the louvered doors. Not much in there. But it wasn't like he had any occasions to wear suits.

In the end, he pulled on his newest pair of jeans, a black muscle shirt, and his black leather jacket—in other words, his work uniform.

Pausing in front of the mirror over the simple pine bureau in the corner, he met his own eyes and thought of his newest buddy at work.

The pair of them had gone down by the river and done their thing, and then hit two of the six parks they had to go through. Duke had the unmistakable impression that the quiet bastard was waiting him out, watching, biding time.

Not his problem.

Returning to the main space of the house, he loomed over the sofa, where Rolly had stretched out and was snoring already.

Fuck it. He was going to focus on the positive of having the guy back—it was like a free ADT system. Because if anyone broke in here, Rolly would call.

Surely the idiot would call.

Duke shut things up tight as he left, and while he walked over to his ride, he shook his head at the beater Rolly had been driving around since they'd been at Union. The stoner had gotten it new—from his very proud parents back in the days when they'd thought he'd amount to something.

Those times had passed. The thing was going on a wing and a prayer, the paint on the hood faded, the bumpers uneven from various impacts, one wheel sporting a mismatched rim because there hadn't been money to get the proper replacement. And yet Rolly was happy enough with it.

Always would be.

Which was sad, and kind of nice, too.

Getting behind the wheel of his truck, Duke refused to let himself think too much about where he was going and why. The emotions were too complex for him to process—and maybe he didn't like the directions they were pulling him in.

He had started this thing with Cait to get in the way of that singer with the fake-ass, sensitive, Mr. Nice Guy act.

Now, though, that goal seemed very secondary.

And that was terrifying. The woman was supposed to be a lay, nothing more. That was not how things were trending, though—and he had no clue how to handle it all.

Life had already taught him that love was a dangerous fallacy, and women, as with all people, were incredibly fickle. Like he needed to relearn all that?

Yet it was with a singular fixation that he drove into Caldwell, peeling off the Northway when he got to a residential area full of small houses and little neighborhood shops. The address Cait had given him was not one he was familiar with, but then, this was where young families lived—and he'd never been a part of one of those.

Counting the numbers down, he pulled over in front of a white clapboard with clipped bushes, a tended-to lawn and a detached garage out in back. Her SUV, the Lexus, was parked off to the side.

For some reason, he couldn't get out, and he passed the time staring at her house. There were two windows upstairs, one of which had a light on in it. Downstairs, there was a broad bay to balance the offset front door, and plenty of illumination, including a glowing fixture right over the entrance.

Kind of like a postcard, and yeah, he could have called this. Cait struck him as the sort of person who'd have a tidy home.

He nearly kept going.

Gripping the steering wheel, he thought . . . this was wrong. Not his larger purpose, no. But this part of it, the part with her.

Cursing, he glared out at the road ahead of him. "Goddamn it."

Man, this inner conflict bullshit was *not* part of the plan. This hesitation, this sense that he was doing a nasty on the way to getting back at G.B. should *not* be his problem.

Collateral damage happened. And she was an adult, capable of making her own decisions—and it wasn't like he'd coerced her into the sex. Far from it.

"Shit."

Forcing his hand forward, he turned off the engine and got out because he didn't know what else to do with himself. The instant he faced the house, however, a surge went through him and clarified things, reminding him that there was another dimension in play in all this.

God, the sex.

He hadn't expected it to get so out of control. When he'd seen her behind that café, he'd felt the attraction then at the club, he'd followed through on it. But he'd assumed those hard-core orgasms had been because of the satisfaction to be had in taking something G.B. wanted. At the boathouse last night, however, he'd begun to think there was more to it than that.

And now, as he walked up and pushed the doorbell, he was sure of it.

He wanted to see her naked this time; take her on something soft like a bed so he didn't have to worry about bruising her; do her from behind and then with her straddling him.

The extent to which he needed the sex was a warning—

The door opened—and oh, shit, there she was. And for a split second, the impact of her in that loose navy blue dress flushed his brain, his senses overriding his thought processes entirely.

"Hi," she said roughly.

As her hand went up and fiddled with the collar, she seemed off.

Frowning, he looked behind her, but there didn't seem to be anyone else in the house. Maybe that was the problem?

"You okay with this?" he asked. "We can go somewhere public if you'd rather."

After all, she'd only met him a matter of days ago—

"No. I want you here. As long as you . . . you know, you're all right with it?"

In lieu of an answer, he stepped forward, took hold of her, and kissed the breath out of her. He just wanted to have her against him, and only intended for a quick reconnect—but of course, once he got his hands on her, that went right out the window. With her breasts against his chest, and her mouth under his, his body got hungry.

Starved, was more like it.

Fucking hell, her lips were so soft against his, and the way she yielded to him, her spine arching into him, made him want to lay her out right on the floor and—

Duke pulled away and shut the door so they didn't give her neighbors a show. And as he paused to stare down at her, the fact that she was breathing hard and looking up at him as if he were already naked in her eyes?

Just where he wanted her.

"Hi," he drawled, brushing back some of her blond hair. "Miss me?"

The smile on her face made his sternum ache. "Yes, I did."

"I smell dinner?"

"Lasagna. Just homemade—I didn't know whether you would . . ." As she let that fade, she put her hand on his face, shaking her head. "God, every time I see you . . ."

"What."

"I just forget what you look like. Until you're in front of me."

"Good or bad."

For a moment, her expression changed as if she were taken somewhere else in her head. But then she shook things and seemed to refocus. "Good, very good."

Duke did some touching of his own, running his fingertips down her neck. "Do you think we'll make it through dinner this time?"

Man, he was amazing, Cait thought as she absorbed the sight and feel of her lover. To think her memories seemed vivid? They so didn't compare to the real thing.

Wait, he'd asked her a question, hadn't he.

Something about making it to dinner?

"I don't know," she said slowly as erotic flashbacks made her feel dizzy. Still, talking like civilized people for half an hour was probably a good short-term goal. Then they could . . . "Ah, let me show you around—not that there's much to show."

That awkwardness, the discordant, off kilter stuff that she'd felt at the diner after the boathouse hookup, came back—and made her wonder about having him to her home.

He was, after all, still a stranger, technically.

Too late now, though.

Before she got a chance to lead any kind of tour, Duke glanced over her head with a remote expression. "Nice place. But I like the looks of its owner even more."

"You haven't seen anything." She flushed. "I mean, of my home."

He shrugged. "This place could be the Taj Mahal and I'd think the same thing."

She pivoted away so the blush that hit her face wasn't quite so obvious. At least the sexual connection was still alive and well between them. "So . . . this is the living room."

She stopped the narration there or she was liable to point out such exotic features as the couch, the TV, the lamp on the side table . . . the frickin' rug.

"And I work in here."

Moving onward to the porch, she pulled a Vanna White, turning in a circle and feeling like an idiot. But at least she didn't have to apologize for the shape things were in. She'd spent the last two hours cleaning everything from floor to attic—although that had been more because she was nervous than any sort of mess.

"Great light in here," he murmured, putting his hands in his pockets and wandering over to the display of pages on the tables.

As he inspected each drawing, Cait crossed her arms over her chest and shifted her weight back and forth. The sight of this tall, broad man in black clothes standing over her work made her feel like she was in a funhouse, everything going wonky on her. He was not at all like Thom . . . or G.B. No, he was latent power and raw sex, a bonfire upright in a pair of black combat boots.

She wanted him.

Holy hell, she couldn't wait to get her hands on him again.

"What's this?" he asked, pointing without touching.

She walked over, smoothing her loose skirt and feeling her panty hose ride up. She'd worn a bra tonight—because she'd wanted him to take it off her with his teeth—but the reality was, she wished she didn't have any makeup on, and was in sweats.

Long day. Very long.

She still hadn't heard from G.B. And the time she'd spent in that church was lingering with her, hanging like a weight around her neck for no valid reason she could think of.

It was really good to see Duke, though. Just his presence reprioritized things, at least for the next couple of hours: There was nothing she could do right now about G.B. or Sissy's funeral, and that was true whether or not she was alone. And what she and this man were likely to get up to? What a way to pass the night.

"It's a book I'm working on," she said, kicking herself back to attention.

"Nice dog."

"I love Labs—I grew up with one. Are you a dog person?"

"Never had pets." He continued to go down her storyboarding table, taking his time—and that made her feel a little more comfortable. Maybe they'd have things to talk about after all. "Did you always know you wanted to be an artist?"

Cait shrugged. "I just was one. Kind of like someone who's good with math or science—I came out this way."

"These are really good."

"I teach, too."

"Where?"

"At Union, actually." As he glanced over his shoulder, she shrugged. "I didn't get very far, did I."

"You went from student to professor." He turned back to her work. "That's a hell of a distance."

There was a strange note in his voice, but before she could follow up, the buzzer went off in the kitchen.

"'Scuse me."

She could feel his eyes tracking her as she headed for the lasagna, and that itch to get him good and naked nearly made her derail the whole save-dinner-from-burning thing: After all, there was a couch in her living room with plenty of leg room—and that was a huge step up from boat cushions or linoleum.

Grabbing an oven mitt, she popped open the stove and leaned back so she didn't melt her eye makeup off.

"Oh, thank you, Jesus," she whispered as she took the pan out.

"That looks perfect," he said next to her.

The sound of his voice made her jump, but she recovered quick. "I'm not much of a cook."

"That would be a lie."

As she put the lasagna on a mat on the table she'd set, she did a quick survey. Yup, everything was in place—

"Wine. I forgot to offer you wine."

"I'll get it. Have a seat."

"It's just the bottle over there on the counter."

She picked the chair in the corner so she could watch him, and yup, that was a good plan. First thing he did was take off his jacket and hang it on the pegs by her back door—those arms. Dear Lord, those arms. And then luckily, he had to turn away to open that Italian red: As he took the old-fashioned uncorker-thingy and screwed it down into the bottle's head, the bunching and releasing of his biceps and triceps made her thank God for the necessity of manual labor. And his back was just as spectacular, the expanse of his shoulders flaring out wide on top before his torso narrowed in tight at his hips.

And his . . . lower assets . . . were sheer perfection in those jeans.

Bruce Springsteen's ancient album cover had a case of the middle-aged sags compared to Duke.

As he came over with the bottle, she picked up the spatula she'd laid out and got busy cutting squares through the melted mozzarella.

"You want some, too, yes?" he said.

"Please."

As they served each other, she felt a little more relaxed. And then when he took a bite and was all about the *mmmmmmmmm?* She might as well have been Julia frickin' Child.

"I'm glad you like it," she said, sipping her wine. "I—oh, no, I put out *hors d'oeuvres* and forgot."

Just another example of her game. Yup. Real player over here.

He glanced over at the crackers and cheese by the toaster. "I'm a main-event kind of guy."

As his eyes swung back, they traveled down her body—and she had to rearrange herself in the chair. "Especially with you," he tacked on.

In spite of the fact that it had taken her an hour to make the dinner and forty minutes to cook it, she was suddenly ready to push her plate away and finish the tour of the second floor in her bed.

"Can I admit to something embarrassing?" she blurted.

He cocked a brow. "This is really Stouffer's?"

She shook her head. "No. I honestly did make it."

"It would have been okay if you hadn't. You don't need to impress me like that."

Cait dropped her eyes to her plate. "You're sweet."

"Not really. So what's your 'something'?"

"You're the first man to set foot in this house." As his head whipped up, she put her palm out. "No, no, it's not weird or anything. I mean, of course, there've been workmen. Like the electrician when I—never mind. You're just the first one I've, you know, invited in. For . . . a date."

Duke lowered his fork and wiped his mouth with his napkin.

"Sorry," she said slowly. "Did I cross a boundary or something?"

"No."

Liar, she thought as she pushed at her food. Damn it, she should have just kept things light and easy. Except that wasn't really her. Gym body or not, she wasn't into casual sex and it was hard to pretend she was.

"I'm . . ." When he didn't finish, she grimaced and wanted a do-over, starting at the front door. Or at least when she'd come in here to tackle the lasagna.

"I'll be honest, too, then." He wiped his mouth a second time, as if he needed something to do with his hands. "I don't deserve the honor."

The statement was factual, and he didn't dwell on it—he just went back to eating.

"Why do you say that?" she asked.

He shrugged, and then nodded at her plate. "You don't like this?"

"Why?" she repeated.

It was a while before he answered. "As you know, I didn't graduate from Union. Looking around your house, I'm guessing that the men you usually go for finish things."

Again, he clearly wasn't in search of sympathy, or subtly manipulating her into an ego stroke: His voice was as level as if he had been discussing the weather.

As she thought of Thom and his career in finance, Duke cocked a brow at her. "Am I wrong?"

"I don't have a long list of men."

"Also not a surprise." He took another bite and chewed. "And let me guess—you almost got married at some point, but it didn't work out."

"Maybe."

"So that's a yes."

"It was a long time ago."

"College was, it's true."

"Wait, why did you drop out?"

He glanced at the pan. "Mind if I have some more?"

"Not at all." What she would like even more? For him to answer a question easily. "What about you? Did you ever marry?"

His harsh laugh was reply enough. "Nope. Not in the cards for me, as it turned out."

"Sounds like I'm not the only one who almost made it to the altar."

He paused with his seconds halfway to his plate. "You're very smart, you know that."

For some reason, the comment made her feel more beautiful than any other compliment he could have given her. "Well, the blond's just hair color, actually."

He hesitated again, his eyes narrowing. "Really?"

"I'd just gotten it done the night I met you, actually."

When he seemed nonplussed, she frowned. "Why are you looking at me like that?"

Chapter Forty-three

Sitting cross-legged on her bed, Sissy had the book Adrian had given her on top of a pillow in her lap. Even with all the lights on, and her eyes being excellent, she was getting a tension headache from frowning at the tiny, faded writing.

Her Latin was so not good enough for this.

Leaning back against her headboard, she cursed softly.

"That bad, huh?"

Turning toward the open door, she saw Adrian standing there with a bag of Chips Ahoy!

He jogged the sealed cookies. "Want a little sin?"

"Yes. Please."

As he limped in, she wished she knew how he'd been hurt. What had happened exactly. But she had a feeling that was seriously off-limits.

Sitting down at the foot of her bed, he did the deed of opening things up, and then offered the chocolate-chip cookies to her. She took four.

"You know," Adrian said between bites of his own, "Eddie always did say that thing read like stereo instructions."

"It's nearly incomprehensible—and it's totally discombobulated . . . like stream-of-consciousness stuff. No organization, just a series of random riffs."

"Well, what have you got so far?"

"Can you people really do spells?"

"Jim can, yup. I'm okay at it. Eddie was better than I am—he used to tell me I had ADHD and that was the root of my problem. You need to focus properly."

"Can you do one for me now?"

"Like I'm a trick pony?"

"Come on. I need a break, and I'm honestly curious."

Adrian popped another cookie into his mouth. Then he held out a palm. Frowning in concentration, he made a waving motion with his free hand over it.

"Presto!"

She leaned in. "What did you do?"

"I made nothing appear. Just like magic."

Sissy started to laugh. "You're a freak."

"Too right. And an idiot. I should have brought up the milk."

She looked down at the book again and got serious. "Tell me more about the mirror." When he didn't reply, she glanced back up at him. "Please."

"You hit me with this even after I hooked you up with the Ahoys?"

Except he stretched out across the end of her bed, propping his head up on his hand. He kept munching away, somehow not getting cookie crumbs all over the place.

"The mirror, the mirror . . ." He shook his head. "It's the ugliest fucking thing you've ever seen. Old and decaying, just like her."

"Whenever I've seen the demon, she's been young and beautiful."

"Just another of her lies." He rubbed an eyebrow with his thumb. "Like I said, the thing with her is, she needs that portal. She loses the mirror? She's stuck on this plane, at least from what Eddie always told me. Now, you'd assume the easiest thing to do would be to break it, but if you do? You get sucked into the shards and you ain't never coming out. The key would be to get control of the POS. Take it out of her possession and make it so she can't get access to it. Logically, that's the only set of chains you're ever going to put on her."

"You found me in that bathroom." She put her hand across her abdomen. "To protect . . ."

"Yeah."

"Why didn't you take the mirror with you when you left?"

Adrian blew out a curse. "Jim had flipped the fuck out when he saw you, and because he'd tripped her spell, she was coming back at a dead run. It was a choice between keeping the savior from attacking and probably getting shanked . . . or taking the mirror. We chose him."

"So she's killed someone else to replace me."

The angel cleared his throat. "Yeah." Abruptly, he reached out and put his hand on her knee. "Hey, hey . . . you need to stop thinking about all that. That's not your biz."

"If Jim felt that way, I'd still be in Hell."

"Doesn't mean you have to be a hero up here." He took out another cookie. "Or down there."

Sissy was quiet a long time. And then she heard herself say, "She hurt him."

"Excuse me?"

"I saw Jim. . . ." It was so hard to put it into words, and she didn't know why she was bringing it up now. "She hurt him. Her . . . people hurt him. Bad."

When Adrian didn't reply, she glanced up. His face was set in stone, no expression to be found within the composite of his features. And that was when she knew . . . he'd had the same abuse done to him.

"Sissy, do me a favor?"

"What?"

"Don't tell him you saw that, okay? It'll kill him."

"That woman needs to be stopped," Sissy said darkly.

"That's what Jim's trying to do."

Sissy was silent for a time. "There's another thing I've been wondering. How did he get me out?"

"He traded a win for you."

As those simple words sunk in, Sissy felt her head go a little fuzzy. "I'm sorry . . . he did what?"

As Duke traced Cait's blond hair with his eyes, a feeling of dread hit him hard. You don't suppose . . . oh, come on, there was no reason to be paranoid.

"I thought it was natural," he heard himself say.

"You don't like brunettes?"

"Ah, no, that's not it." He shook his head, thinking, Enough with that psychic. "The blond looks good on you."

"Thanks."

As she picked up her fork and started to eat once more, he tried to forget Yasemin Oaks' warning, the strange men sitting shotgun with him, the sense of foreboding that was killing his otherwise healthy appetite. He should be talking to Cait, pulling a little uncomplicated chatter out of his ass, pretending that he was focused on normal things . . .

"God, this is so awkward again," she said. But then she looked up in a flash, as if she hadn't meant to speak out loud. "I'm sorry— I didn't mean—"

"No, I know what you're saying." He pushed his hand through his hair. "I just . . . I want you to know that no matter what happens . . . I want to be here. With you."

He held her stare with his own, and was surprised to find that regardless of the intentions he'd started out with? That was the God's honest. Sitting in this neat little kitchen, in her neat little house, eating her perfectly cooked lasagna? There was nowhere else he'd rather be—and not because he was making a revenge fantasy real.

And for some crazy fucking reason, he seemed to want her to know that.

He broke the eye contact first. "I haven't . . ." He cleared his throat forcefully, and thought that he really should shut the hell up. "I don't feel things anymore, you know? I don't . . . well, I haven't had emotions like this in forever."

"Emotions like what?" she whispered.

Duke rubbed the center of his chest, and skirted the question. "You want to know the irony? I was going to be a cardiologist. I was always fascinated by hearts, how they work, why they work. Didn't get that far, of course. But that was my plan."

"What really happened?" She reached over and put her hand on his forearm. "You can tell me."

Well, my brother found out that I was in love with a woman, and he seduced her and left her pregnant . . . and it fucked with my head so bad, I've never gotten over it. Especially because I knew him all along—I knew what he was capable of. And I've been waiting for years to get back at him. . . .

Duke looked across the table at Cait, and finished the thought: *You were the way I was going to do it.*

For the longest time, he'd been watching G.B. from a distance, checking up on him from the sidelines, monitoring that career of his. And his fraternal twin had proven to have nothing in common with Duke, except for one thing—he never, ever dated anybody seriously. There had been casual hooks, yeah. Things that happened in bars or clubs or behind the scenes. But the bastard had never once invited a woman to see him sing or perform, a specific woman, a woman who was a quality female like this one.

Duke had known the instant Cait had shown up at the Palace Theatre why she was there—G.B.'s fans always came in pairs, besties doubling or tripling up to ogle him and hear him spout shit that was the polar opposite of the person he really was.

Cait, on the other hand, had been there alone, and sure enough, there to meet up with him at his request.

She'd had to be someone special to him to break G.B.'s pattern, and it was not a surprise that both he and his brother were attracted to her—hell, any man with half a brain would be. So Duke had known instantly what to do—yeah, sure, it wouldn't be even close to what had been done to him, but then, G.B. had always had a much, much thinner skin.

Less was required to have the same effect—

Abruptly, Duke started shaking his head, and before he knew what he was doing, he got to his feet. "I have to go. I'm sorry. I can't stay."

As Cait blanched, he knew he really had to leave. She deserved so much better than all this—even though she wanted him, too, his motives hadn't been clean at the beginning, and for some reason, that seemed to taint everything about his presence here tonight.

"I—"

He cut her off. "This is just a bad idea. I came here for—shit, nothing that you're going to want or merit."

She looked at the dinner she'd so carefully prepared for them—and he felt worse than he had in a very, very long time.

"I'm sorry," he said. "I really am."

As she put her napkin down and got out of her chair, she straightened the pretty dress she had put on for him. "Okay. And things are awkward, I know. I just . . ."

"It's not you—"

"Oh, my God, that line." She actually smiled a little. "I never thought it would be used on me."

Duke stepped into her and touched her face. Goddamn, she was so lovely, and as he paused to soak everything in, he knew he was doing the right thing. The beef with his brother was nasty, evil stuff, and nothing this woman needed to get sucked into—he was still going to take his losses out of that asshole's hide; he was just going to find another way.

Duke dropped his arm. "I don't want this to end."

She frowned. "It doesn't have to."

"Yes, it does."

Cait took hold of his hands. "Listen, I know you say you're not good at relationships—and I get that. But I'm willing to give it time if you are."

"Cait—"

"I'm serious. I'm no better at this than you. I haven't even been on a date in years. After Thom left me for someone else, I've just been working and doing all the 'right' things. I've also been living half a life. I got a wake-up call about six months ago, and I just decided I had to stop putting things off, I had to get out there. I think you're the same."

"You don't know me."

"So give me a chance to. I'm not going to beg you to stay—that's up to you. What I am saying is that I'd like the chance to find out where this is going. If that's not something you're comfortable with, then you know where the door is—but I think you're making a huge mistake."

In the tense silence that followed, Duke was astonished to find himself agreeing with her—even though it was probably a bad idea. As much as he hated to admit it, she had woken him up, and he didn't want to go back to the shadows—but at the same time? The stakes were high.

He'd already lived through a loss like this once. . . .

And then he realized, the solution to everything might be easier and more honest than he thought.

Taking Cait's face in his hands, he tilted her head back and stared into her eyes.

"Are you seeing anyone else?" he demanded.

The answer to that question was the only thing that mattered tonight.

Chapter
Forty-four

As Cait looked up at Duke, she was astounded at how still he had become, as if her answer was the only thing in the world that mattered to him. And right now, that vulnerability was the most attractive thing about him.

It was also what made her mind up once and for all. G.B. was a wonderful man, a truly sensitive and kind soul—and she enjoyed his company. But it was not anything close to what she felt with Duke, and she has to fully commit to whatever relationship they had together or there was no chance of things going anywhere.

Live now. Take a chance.

Safety was only a step away from suffocation.

"No, I'm not seeing anybody," she answered him. "You're the only one I'm interested in—"

At that moment, her cell phone began to ring by her purse, the vibration rattling it across the counter.

"That's good," Duke said roughly. "That's what I want. Oh, God, that's what I need—"

His lips found hers, crushing her mouth as strong arms tightened around her. His body was exactly as she remembered it, rock-hard and dominating, and as she fit her curves to his power, her breasts felt heavy and a burn lit up in her core.

This was what they both needed.

When he finally lifted his head, he said in a voice full of gravel, "I want you on a bed. Now."

Cait nodded and took his hand, leading him through the living room and up the shallow stairs. As they ascended, he filled the stairwell just as he had her office—and the same was true when they got into her bedroom. Everything seemed to shrink in, the walls and the ceiling pulling closer together.

But she didn't have a lot of time to think about that.

They came together without words, bodies meeting by her bed, her dress and hose disappearing fast to the floor. Before she knew it, Duke had stretched her out in her bra and panties and was covering her with his weight just as she wanted him to. As he kissed her some more, her hands dug into his hair and she writhed under him . . . especially as he slowly worked his way down to her breasts, his mouth lingering on her skin as if he liked the taste of her. With quick finesse, the front release of her bra was triggered, the cups slipping free of her sensitive breasts, his broad palms replacing them for a moment.

And then he found her nipples with his lips.

As he licked and sucked at her, one of his hands kept going, drifting over her hip to her upper thigh, moving in between her legs—

Arching up against his mouth, she felt the first stabbing precursor of an orgasm blow through her sex, and he must have known it, because he groaned in response.

"I gotta get you naked," he growled, rising up as he hooked his thumbs on the fragile side strings of her panties.

Watching him pull them off her made her feel voluptuous even though she really wasn't—

"Oh, yeah," he groaned, his eyes glowing with heat as the last bit of her body was exposed to him.

Focusing on her core, he licked his mouth in anticipation.

"Let me see you," he said as he parted her legs.

Before he went down on her, though, she stopped him. Sitting up, she put a hand on his chest. "Wait, wait—fair is fair. I get you unclothed, too."

With hands that shook from impatience, she yanked the bottom of his muscle shirt out of his waistband and dragged the thing up his—

Holy . . . crap. First time she had seen this real estate up close and naked—and boy was it worth the eye-time. His torso might as well have been carved, the muscles bulging at his pecs and flexing across his abdomen. There was no fat on him, and no hair to obscure the incredible expanse.

"You are . . . unbelievable," she said.

"Enough about me." He bent down to kiss her neck. "Now, where was I—"

"Nope." She held him off again. "Too many pants left on you."

Shifting the dynamic, she assumed the job of directing things by tugging on his arm, urging him to lie flat. But, as strong as he was, he wasn't going horizontal on the bed unless he decided to—

Well, what do you know, he accepted her lead, angling down and putting his head on her pillows, his long length dangling his boots off the foot of the bed. He took care of those combats himself, bringing each leg up, hands ripping the laces free. And as soon as he'd kicked them off onto the carpet, she took over, straddling his thighs, going for that button fly.

His half-lidded eyes stared up at her as she released his incredible arousal. "You sure you want to waste time getting those jeans off?" he drawled.

He had a point. She could do what she wanted with him just like this.

Slipping her hands onto his erection, she relished the way he torqued, that incredible body contracting all over, his white teeth clamping down on his lower lip as he hissed in a lungful of air.

Standing his arousal up, she led with her tongue, drawing a circle over the blunt head. And then she sucked him in, filling her mouth with all that erection. Now it was his hands tightening in her hair, his hips rolling upward as his head arched back, his breathing getting labored.

"Oh, fuuuuuuuuuuuck . . ."

There was something totally intoxicating about having him undone, thanks to what she was doing to his sex. And that was even before she found a rhythm with her hands and her lips.

"Oh, Jesus—fuck . . . "

Without warning, he shot upright, dragging her off of him. His hands were rough as he tilted her face and took her mouth with a hot, hungry kiss.

"You're going to be the death of me," he said.

"Why? Because I like the way you feel in my mouth—"

That growl came back, vibrating against her lips as he flipped her onto her back and mounted her.

"Drawer," she said, reaching out to her bedside table.

He was quick and efficient with the condom, and then he was between her legs, making room for himself. As he angled his arousal against her, he slowed down and looked in her eyes.

And that was when she feared . . . she could fall in love with him.

⊢———⊣

Downstairs, directly below the pair of frickin' lovebirds, Jim was sitting on the living room couch, his legs stretched out, his arms crossed over his chest, his lids low—but not because he was tired.

Duke had not given shit up during the day . . . and except for a roommate who appeared to have a pot problem, and this nice woman he was taking care of upstairs? There didn't seem to be anything dramatic going on with the guy.

Further, Devina wasn't lurking around this house. No minions, either.

And Adrian had just texted to let him know that Sissy was reading in her bed, and the angel was counting the lint in his navel.

Too quiet. Waaaaay too quiet, considering they were what, seventy-two hours into this round? Or had it been four days? He didn't fucking know.

Frankly, he could have used a good fight. Maybe something with a lot of hand-to-hand.

He hated having time to think—with every blink of his eyes, he saw Nigel on that chaise longue, that silver blood everywhere, those eyes staring up sightless of whatever happened to be above Heaven. And then there was Colin.

Jim knew what that white rage felt like—and looked like. Adrian had felt it, too, when Eddie had been killed. Jim himself had known it after his mother had been taken from him.

Less stability was exactly what they did not need—

Sitting up, he twisted around to the front door.

"Speak of the devil," he muttered as he got up and walked through the locked panels.

Devina was standing out on the lawn, right underneath the streetlamp, the glow around her an unholy one, rather than anything thrown by that light. She was dressed in skintight black jeans and a tight black top that was low-cut enough to flash the lacy cups of her bloodred bra—no coat to warm her against the chill, but then, she was a reptile like that. As usual, her heels were tall enough to make it look like she was standing on her tiptoes, and her hair was all curled around her shoulders.

So yup, SOP all around. Except there was one thing that was completely and totally off: no bravado. No swagger. No anger. She was as quiet and still as a dagger left on a table.

"Out for a stroll," he said dryly.

"You got anything you want to tell me?"

"How much time you got."

Down at the end of the street, a car turned in, its headlights flashing brightly on the approach. Neither one of them was visible to the human eye, though, so there was no slowdown, no gawking at the bombshell "woman" in the pool of illumination.

Luckily for the contingency of humans, they just sped right by, getting out of range.

"Nothing?" she prompted.

Jim narrowed his eyes. "Not that you'd want to hear."

"I know about Nigel."

No reaction. He refused to show any reaction at all. Maybe the Maker had told her? "Do you."

"That puts them at a disadvantage, you know." She waited as if expecting something, anything to come back at her. "They're vulnerable."

"'They' as in who?"

"Don't be a fucking asshole, Jim."

He shrugged, but she did have a point. The pair of them were kind of beyond any coy routine. "And you're telling me this because . . . ?"

"I thought you'd want to know. Assuming you don't already."

"No offense, Devina, but I find it impossible to believe you're trying to help me."

"Everything's changed now."

"Because Nigel bit it? I'm not sure he's that important, frankly—but the point's moot."

She shook her head. "You don't get it, Jim. You're the one they're going to have replace him."

Years of training and experience were the only reason his expression didn't change. But shit, that had certainly never dawned on him.

"Not in my job description," he drawled, like he didn't give a shit.

"Wait for it. Whether or not you win the war—"

"*When* I win it—"

"That's your future now, Jim, and you're not going to have a choice. You're going to be conscripted."

"Oh, come on, Devina, you're so full of shit—"

"How do you think those four got their jobs? You think they were born up there? Don't be naive, Jim. Your fate's been sealed."

He stared at her for a long time, connecting the dots and not liking the map that came into focus. "And you're telling me this why?"

Even though he knew. He just wanted to see if she'd admit it.

Devina's voice was the most level he'd ever heard it: "You need to think long and hard about where you're at. You're going to be in a jail for eternity. You're going to be Nigel."

"And you really think I'm going to believe you. About anything."

It was satisfying to see her wince as the barb hit home. "I knew you were going to say that," she whispered thinly. Except then she seemed to recover. "But that doesn't change what is fact. There is a way out, however."

"And what's that?"

There was a long pause. "We quit. You and I refuse to play the game anymore."

Chapter Forty-five

As Duke drove into his woman again and again, his body was on the best kind of autopilot, no thoughts contaminating the sex, no emotions clouding the purity of the pleasure. The tight hold on his cock was transmuted through every inch of him, each thrust and retreat echoing outward under his skin, everything magnified.

It had never been like this with anyone for him. Not even Nicole back in the old days—

The orgasm slammed into him, locking his hips tight into the cradle of Cait's pelvis, the rhythmic pulses of her own release milking him, making his head spin. Collapsing against her, he turned his face into her sweet, soft neck and breathed heavily.

So impatient for her. Every time it seemed like it was the first. And he was still hungry.

But they weren't taking the chance with doing a double again.

Reaching between them, he held on to the base of the condom as he slowly retracted.

"Where's your bathroom?" He had paid no attention to anything when they'd come up.

"Over there."

Rolling off, he went in the direction she was pointing, going through a narrow doorway, locating the light switch by patting the wall. His eyes blinked hard as he was momentarily blinded, but then he took care of things, flushing what they'd used, cupping his hands under some cold water and taking a drink.

It was not a surprise that everything had its place, all the towels hanging precisely on the rail of the sliding shower door, the single toothbrush standing up straight in its holder, no brushes or makeup cluttering the counter around the sink.

As he straightened and wiped his mouth off, he met his stare in the mirror.

The unmistakable conviction that he was walking the same path he had before dogged him. G.B. was a seductive son of a bitch . . . but she wanted Duke. She really did—

Hadn't Nicole been the same, though?

"Shut up," he told himself. "Just shut the fuck up."

"Are you okay?" Cait called out from the bedroom.

He hit the switch like he could turn off his thoughts, too. And as he walked back out, he hung tight to the way she had just been with him.

As if to prove a point to himself, he returned to her with a vengence, fusing his flesh with hers, finding her mouth in the dimness, licking his way inside of her. He was instantly hard again, his body raring to go.

Totally out of his mind, he took her from behind this time,

maneuvering her onto her side, moving in tight on her. Easing her top leg up, he swept his palm down her smooth skin, grabbing hold behind her knee. Then he pushed inside, his erection finding her entrance like it knew exactly where to go.

So smooth, so hot, even deeper, even better.

Sweeping her hair aside, he bit at her shoulder, nipping at her, before twisting her head around so he could kiss her—but only for a short time. The rhythm got fast quickly, making it impossible to sustain the contact.

When she called out his name? He nearly came. The only thing that stopped him was that he wanted to concentrate on the feel of her release. He wanted to know that he'd given that to her, that he was that close to the heart of her, that he alone was able to do that for her.

Cait's fingernails bit into his side, and the flares of pain nearly pitched him over the edge— except then she went stiff underneath him, and he surged in deep and held still. Closing his eyes, he became acutely aware of everything about her, especially the way her hips moved against him, creating the friction, working herself.

Just as she was slowing down, he knew it was his turn and he burrowed his arms around her so he could dig—

"Shit!"

He withdrew so fast, he nearly flipped off the bed.

"Duke? What—"

"No condom." He rubbed his face. "No condom, damn it, I'm sorry."

"Did you—"

"No, no, I didn't come." But talk about not having any game head going. "Thank God."

She sat up and brushed her hair back. "Wow."

"I'm clean—I never do stuff like this." And wouldn't that be more convincing if the mistake itself hadn't just happened. "I lost my damn mind."

"It takes two."

"My responsibility." As he flopped onto his back, he could feel his balls already protesting—and that was going to get worse. "I'm sorry. Shit."

His cock lay hard, hot, and aching up on his belly, but that was not going to happen—

Her gentle hand landed on his hip, and he jumped.

"You didn't lie about that, did you," she whispered.

"What?"

"You didn't . . . you know."

Lifting his head, he looked down his own body. "No." He stopped her before she could make contact. "And it's okay."

She frowned. "Are you trying to punish yourself?"

"Seems right to. You don't want to have my kid, trust me."

"You stopped in time, Duke. It's okay."

He could tell by the way she slid in beside him that she wanted to help him out, but the burn of denial felt right, felt appropriate.

A small balance of the scales for him not having taken care of her properly.

"Duke, please let me—"

"No, I'm good." He kissed the top of her head. "Don't worry about me."

"Excuse me?" Jim demanded. Surely he couldn't have just heard his psychotic enemy suggest that he was going to be the new Nigel . . . and that that could be avoided only if they pulled out, so to speak.

Whatever. One thing he was certain of? He absolutely, positively was not going to step into the spats that Nigel had always worn—that was *not* going to happen. She had to be wrong. Had to be . . .

Except the demon didn't budge, meeting him square in the eye. "You and I quit."

He laughed in a hard rush. "You've said some fucked-up things, Devina, but this tops 'em all. Congratulations."

"The game can't exist without us. If you refuse to play—"

"Then you're going to win the next two rounds and it's game over. You don't honestly think I'd fall for that?"

"But I refuse to play, too. It's over."

Jim crossed his arms over his chest. This whole savior thing had not been presented to him as a choice: Either man up, or your mother is going to be lost to Hell forever. What other option had he had? So, yeah, not a lot of decision-making there for him. And accordingly, it had never dawned on him that he might simply be able to . . . stop.

Provided Devina did as well.

In which case, nobody won—or lost.

"They'll just find someone else," he said, aware that that was a question. "To fill both our shoes."

"Wrong. There is nobody else like me. I am a sole creation, unique to the Maker's vision. Well, I am now that my predecessor's dead."

He could certainly see how one of her was enough for the universe. "This is not up to us."

"Bullshit. The Maker may have created everything, but He gave us free will. You think He ordained Nigel to do what he did? Hell, no. Nigel chose that path—and if anything, his actions prove my point. We have choices in this, too."

"Not on this level. Not with what you're talking about."

"That is the weakest thought you've ever had."

"Maybe. But I could still win this, and then I'm rid of you."

"No, under the rules, you get to be Nigel for the rest of your unnatural life. You mean to tell me you're going to be satisfied eating crumpets and babysitting for that castle up there? You'll lose your fucking mind."

Jim paced around, shaking his head. "You'll excuse me if I don't take all this at face value. You aren't exactly known for an altruistic nature."

"This whole war is a fucking waste of time. It's nothing but a contest for His amusement, and I have no intention of being a trick pony for Him anymore—if you also are willing to stand down."

They stared at each other for a long moment. The takeaway, Jim supposed, was that even with the win they'd bartered for, she wasn't sure she could come out on top. Therefore, this plan was her strategy for winning it all: Get Jim to flake out . . . and then take everything because of a forfeiture.

Thinking that she was coming at this in any way but for her sole benefit would be like expecting a rattler not to use its fangs.

"I can't trust you," he said evenly.

She jutted forward on those heels of hers. "And I already know your word is for shit—or do I need to remind you that you lied to my face. The difference here is, I've never given you a vow to break."

"There's always room for Jell-O, sweetheart."

"Try me."

"Couldn't we start with something easier, like you borrowing a fiver from me?"

"Joke all you want. But I'm right about all this—and do the math. It's mutually assured destruction, so the playing field is leveled."

"Yeah, but come on. Assuming that you're not fucking me completely, and I really don't believe that for a heartbeat, do you honestly think if we go to the Maker and hit Him with this, that He'll be all, 'Whatever, you guys,' do you? Not going to happen."

"Won't be the first time He's hated His creation, I'll tell you that. And what is He going to do? Make me act if I don't want to?"

"But according to you, if Nigel's dead, my fate's sealed—so technically, I'm out of the game already."

"Not if you quit, Jim. Not if you stop playing right here and now." When he fell silent, she nodded. "You think about it, and then you call me."

Jim expected her to sidle in for a kiss. Instead, she just gave him another long look . . . and then she was gone into the night.

Left alone, he turned back to the house, where he had to imagine there was a round two or three going on.

She hadn't even tried to get to the soul in play. And she'd shown up without minions, without some sex ploy, with nothing but her charming self, and a bright idea—not her usual MO. But come on, he wasn't going to be a fool.

Yeah . . . the only rationale that made any sense was that she'd decided she really couldn't win this. Except . . . they were even, now, and she was arrogant—so he wasn't sure he could buy that. Then again . . . they were two-two only because he'd given her one of the rounds.

Jim wandered slowly back into the house, passing through the door again, sitting back down on the sofa.

She had a point about the free will thing. Choice had always been part of the human experience, for good and bad. Did that apply to angels and demons, too?

It had never dawned on him that he could opt out of this bullshit.

And Devina was right.

He did *not* want to be Nigel when he grew up.

The question was, how could he independently verify all of it. And how much time did he have before the Maker came a-knockin' . . . and Jim ended up with a "promotion" he didn't want?

Chapter
Forty-six

Cait was back in the Palace Theatre's parking garage.

She was once again on that ramp that ran down between levels, walking fast, hearing the footsteps of someone behind her.

Panic got her going even quicker as she shot out to the lower lineup of cars and broke into a full-on bolt. Dragging her purse in front of her, she dug into it for her phone—

A gun. This time she had a gun.

Instead of her cell, she took out something mean and black. It was loaded, although she didn't know how she knew that, and as she gripped the weapon, her palm fit perfectly, sure as if the thing had been made for her.

In the manner of dreams, she kept running, heading for the doors of the elevator that seemed to be ten miles off in the distance and staying that way. And in her wake, her attacker was getting tighter on her, closing in—

In the blink of an eye, she was at the vertical pair of buttons, one arrow up, one down. She jabbed at both with her left hand, craning around, waiting for whatever it was to come out of the shadows.

The ceiling lights were extinguishing one by one, tracking the figure, always a step ahead so she couldn't see who it was.

Punching the buttons—she was punching the buttons as those illuminating fixtures went dark and death came for her.

The doors were not opening. This time she was locked out of her escape.

Spinning around, she slammed her back against the elevator's closed entrance and put the gun up at chest height.

"No!" she screamed. "Stop!"

Whoever it was just kept coming. For an eternity, she stood braced for death's approach, time slowing to a crawl even as her heart fluttered in her chest and her blood boiled with terror.

"Noooo!"

Losing control, she pulled the trigger over and over again, shooting at whatever was coming at her, the popping sounds echoing all around, the recoil vibrating up her forearms and into her shoulders. The more she squeezed off rounds, the faster her attacker seemed to come—

The lights directly over her head were the only ones that stayed on. So she finally saw what she was firing at.

Her scream was louder than the gun—

"Cait! Cait, wake up!"

Someone was in her face, holding her arms, getting in the way.

Stuck between reality and the nightmare, she pushed against a solid weight, trying to get away, panic overtaking higher reasoning.

"Cait!" The voice, the deep male voice, chipped a crack in her fear. "Easy, there—it was a nightmare, whatever it was—just a dream, *Cait*."

She froze, everything except for her breathing going still. ". . . I was going to die. . . ."

"Come here . . . lie on me, come here."

Duke. It was Duke with her in the bed, and the instant she made that connection, she collapsed into his bare chest, his arms wrapping around her and holding her tight.

"Shh, you're okay. I got you."

The shivering came next, her whole body quaking. "Thank God you're here," she said roughly. "Oh, God . . ."

If she'd woken up alone?

"You're all right."

"It was awful . . . it was so real—I was back in that parking garage, getting chased—"

"What parking garage?"

As she told him what had happened to her, she felt him stiffen underneath her, his powerful body tightening up as if he were prepared to go out into Caldwell and find whoever it had been—and kill them.

"Except, in the dream, I had a gun, I was shooting—but at the last moment, it . . ." She covered her face with her hands and felt like throwing up. "It was a horrible corpse attacking me, a rotting half skeleton with glowing black eyes—it was so *real*. . . ."

Gradually, thanks to him stroking her back with his broad hand, she calmed down.

"I wish you'd told me about that sooner," he said, after she finally sighed and relaxed.

"The police haven't found anyone."

"Bad part of town, that theater district."

"I know."

In the silence that followed, she thought of G.B.

She propped her chin on Duke's chest. "Just so we're really clear. I'm not seeing him anymore."

"The singer?"

"Yes. I'm going to call him tomorrow."

"So he doesn't know about this. Between you and me."

"He will, though."

Duke tucked a strand of hair behind her ear. After a while, he said, "Good. I'm a one-woman kind of man." He leaned up and kissed her. "Well, when it comes to you, that is. And as for what went down in that garage? I wish I'd been there to help you."

Funny, that was just what G.B. had said. Then again, there was a commonality to the protective instinct in men, wasn't there.

Duke frowned. "It was just before you came and saw me at the club, wasn't it." When she nodded, he cursed. "Great. I jump you like an animal—"

"I wanted it, remember." She traced his jaw with her finger-tips, feeling the stubble of his five-o'clock shadow—or five a.m., or whatever the hell time it was. "I debated going to see you for the longest time."

"Yeah?"

Boy, it was so much easier to talk to him like this, lying close in her bed, the soft light from the hall glowing over the planes of his face.

"As I told you, it's been a long time for me."

Duke pulled her in for another kiss and then rolled her onto her side. "Was it worth the gamble?"

"And the wait."

With slow, lazy strokes, he licked his way into her mouth, and it was funny how it no longer felt so strange to put her arms around the back of his neck and feel his pecs on her naked breasts. This was natural; this coming together was like breathing, neces-sary and easy.

Parting her thighs, she welcomed him in close, and this time they both went for the drawer, making sure that a condom was in place before things got too far.

Thank God he'd caught that mistake when he had. Although that punishment thing had seemed a little unnecessary.

Slow, loving, and tender.

As he entered her, she sighed and wrapped her legs around the backs of his thighs, giving herself up to the communion. He moved like a wave on top of her, the pleasure building slowly, cresting into a shimmering climax that went through her and lingered, her body tingling, a pleasant sense of falling overtaking her.

And then his orgasm followed, his hips tightening, his breath hitching in. As he worked himself in and out of her, she ran her hands up and down his surging back, the smooth skin and tight muscles undulating under her palms.

"I'm glad you're here," she whispered when he finally fell still.

"Me, too—"

A flash from outside sent a fresh source of light into the room, illuminating them both.

"What the hell?" he said looking around.

"Was that lightning?"

"Not this time of the year, it isn't," he said grimly as he withdrew . . . and got out of bed.

Chapter
Forty-seven

Jim was not leaving the pair of them unprotected. As he stood with his hands on the outside of the woman's cute little house, he passed some energy from his core into the structure itself, the transfer creating a brief flare of light . . . along with a protective barrier that would warn him if the demon, or any of her types, crossed its threshold. It would also inform him if that man or woman took off as well.

He was so over sleeping on her couch, however. It was five a.m., well, nearly six, actually, and he wanted to go home to catch an hour of sleep, have a shower, food up. The truth was, he was dizzy from lack of rest and nutrition, and as much as he was committed to this round of the war, his years at XOps had told him that he was a danger to himself and others if he got as worn-out as he was.

Not that he would necessarily have been sleeping at home.

Goddamn Devina. Just when he thought she'd nailed him for the last time? She popped a new and different kind of shit.

Unbelievable, he thought for the hundredth time as he removed his palms from the clapboard and stepped back.

To his eyes, there was a light field all around the home, starting at the ground line and rising up past the first and second floors to run over the hip roof.

Tight as a tick.

Ghosting home, he walked up the front steps of the mansion and reached for the door. As he pulled it open, no squeaks . . . and no creaks as he went down to the kitchen and cracked the refrigerator. Lots of food, now, and he ate the remnants of that beef stew Sissy had cooked cold and standing up.

The stuff was really good even under those circumstances.

His next move was to go up and hit the shower. Funny, the water tasted different as he opened his mouth under the spray—it used to be copper and dirt; now it was like it came from some kind of spring, a sparkling clean rush that danced over his tongue and down his throat.

Hard to believe that Sissy had managed to scrub up the inside of the pipes, too, but he'd take it.

Stepping out from the water, he wrapped a towel around his hips, picked up his clothes and went into the hall. It was impossible not to think of her down even farther, past those closed doors, lying in between her sheets.

He wanted her in his bed. But he was willing to bet his left nut that he wasn't going to be lucky two nights in a row—not when he was getting back this late.

Cursing, he pushed his way into his room, dumped his duds on the dirty pile, and draped the towel on a hook on the back of the door. Then he walked barefooted across—

"You're home."

His steps faltered as he closed his eyes in relief and gratitude. "You're here."

"Where else would I be?"

The world went for a little spin, the pitch-black room whirling around him. "Lemme get some sweats on. Hold up."

Throwing a hand out, he navigated his way across to the clean pile and bent down—

Click.

As light blinded him, he jacked upright and went for his cock, covering it with both hands. "Clothes—need clothes."

Fuck him, he thought as he glanced over. Sissy was sitting up in the bedding, blond hair tangled, cheeks pink like she was a little warm from having been curled up. The white T-shirt she had on was entirely modest . . . except when the letch part of him began to speculate what was under it.

She seemed totally shocked as she looked at him. "I figured you . . . couldn't . . . see. . . ."

While her voice drifted, he could feel her eyes on his body—and she was looking at just about everything he had. "Let me get dressed first," he told her roughly.

But she didn't move, and that meant he couldn't: She'd caught him on the side view, so if he dropped his hands to pick up his sweats, he was either going to flash her his ass, or give her a lateral full monty.

Which, considering how he was hung? Would still give her a hell of an eyeful.

"Sissy, look away, would you."

God, it was impossible not to remember the last time he'd said those words to her . . . down below, after Devina had worked him over and the remnants of the abuse were all over him.

Don't look at me!

Now he was ordering that for a different reason: He still had her best interests at heart, one hundred percent. The problem was, his body wasn't connecting all that well to his brain at the moment.

Because he had the horrible conviction that she might, possibly, like what she saw.

She certainly wasn't screeching away in horror. In fact, it seemed as though she were—

"You're beautiful," she whispered.

Jim closed his eyes. Prayed for self-control. "Listen, you need to—"

"Let me see you. . . ." She cleared her throat. "Please, just let me . . ."

"Sissy, it's not going to happen. We can't—I can't. . . ." Such a load of horseshit that was. His cock was starting to wake up, and fully operational was so not what this situation needed. "Listen, you need to go back to your room. Or I've got to go—"

"I got cheated, Jim. I was taken too soon—don't make me spend an eternity wondering what it's like."

For the second time in however many hours, he found himself thinking, She couldn't possibly have just said that to me.

The groan that rattled up through his chest was an expletive if he'd ever heard one.

"Why do you think I've come in here every night?" He could hear the sheets shifting on the bed as if she were sitting up even further. "I'm hoping . . . praying . . . that you'll . . ."

His breath was starting to get harsh, his body getting waaauuuy tar ahead of him—and the reaction was as strong as it was quick. Which suggested something he really hated to look at too closely: Yeah, he'd gotten her out to save her. But he also wanted her.

Now, to be fair, the latter had been a very recent development. It hadn't started until he'd gotten a sense of how much she'd aged down below—he'd never been into chippies before, and he sure as hell wasn't starting now.

She was a woman, though. After all she'd been through, she was a child no longer.

"Are you going to make me say it?" Her voice grew small. "Jim?"

"Don't ask me this. For the love of God, don't ask me this."

"Why, Jim?"

He really wished she'd stop using his name. "I can't . . . it's not right."

"Why?"

Releasing one of his hands, he scrubbed his face. "You know why."

"Are you in love with someone else?"

Strange question. "No."

"Do you . . . want me? Jim?"

More rustling, and Jesus, he could just imagine the sheets falling down to her hips, pooling around her waist. Except in his OMG fantasy, she wasn't wearing anything more than he was, and her breasts were—

"You're going to kill me," he moaned.

"That's not what I want to do right now."

"Sissy—"

"Who else can I go to? Who else is there? If not you . . . then who?"

Well, now, put like that? It made him want to castrate the balance of the male population in Caldwell. Make that New York State as a whole . . . or maybe the eastern seaboard.

Do not look over at her, he told himself. You look at her once and you're—

The sound of her crying softly brought his head around. Oh, fuck him. She'd put her face in her hands and was trying to keep her dignity as much as she could.

"You don't want me," Jim heard himself say. "Not really. You just think you do."

At that, she dropped the shield of her palms. "Don't tell me what I feel or think. You don't know me like that."

"I know from stress." Christ, did he ever. "I know a *shitload* about wartime stress, and you and I may be sitting in this house without bombs falling on our heads—but make no mistake. This situation we're in is hard-core—and if you don't have a serious case of PTSD after what you've just been through? I'm the fucking Easter bunny."

"What does that have to do with—"

"People do not make good decisions when they're under extreme pressure. When they're in our shoes, people do *not* do the right thing."

"But what if it is the right thing." She met his gaze head-on. "Who are you to say it isn't?"

"I'm the other half of it. And I know more about this than you do."

"Because I'm a virgin."

"Because you have never been to war. And I've lived in it for twenty years."

"So then you know . . . sometimes people don't come home."

Well, hell. He kind of wished she wasn't as smart as she was.

Moving fast, he yanked on some sweats and discreetly folded his erection up flat, tying the thing down with a savage yank. Then he pulled on a muscle shirt and went over to the bed. Sitting beside her, he reached out and tucked some of her straight hair behind her ear.

"I'm sorry." He dropped his hand. "But I have to do the right thing by you. I can't live with myself otherwise."

Her gaze clung to his. "Then just kiss me. Just kiss me and I'll go. It's the only thing I'll ever ask of you."

He started to shake his head, but as her eyes glossed over with tears, she broke him in half.

"Don't cry," he said in a voice that cracked.

She had been cheated out of so much.

"Look at me." When she didn't, he took her chin and tilted her face to his. "You're the one who's beautiful. . . ."

He trailed off at that point, because come on, it wasn't like he could make her promises of first loves, and true loves, and a marriage with babies. She wasn't going to get any of that.

"Close your eyes," he said roughly.

If he had to meet her stare, he was going to lose his nerve—because something told him this was going to be as much of a revelation for her as it was for him. And in that, he wasn't sporting the big head. It was impossible to believe that this was her first kiss, but he was willing to bet its implications were very, very different.

Holy shit, was he going to do this?

Just the kiss, though. That much he was rock solid on.

Jim leaned in, focusing on her perfectly formed lips. Oh, God, he wanted this badly—but even as the thought crossed his mind, he tore it up. This was for her, and his body was going to have to hang the fuck back.

Sissy did just as she was told, locking those lids down . . . but she was ready for what was coming. Her mouth parted as he leaned in and—

The knock on his door was as welcome as a clawhammer through the back of his skull.

And then a voice said, "Jim? You okay?"

Sissy's voice.

Jim ripped away so fast, he jumped half across the room without hitting the floor—and as he flew, he watched the vision of Sissy on the bed morph into Devina, brunette waves replacing blond lengths, black shark eyes emerging from blue, huge breasts pushing out the front of that shirt.

"Jesus Christ!" he barked.

"Well," the demon muttered dryly, "you can't blame a girl for trying."

"Jim?" Sissy asked again through the closed door.

On that note, Devina up and left in a puff of black smoke.

Out in the hall, Sissy wondered what she was doing bothering the man.

She'd gotten up to keep reading through that giant book Adrian had given her, thinking she'd have some coffee first and then sit in the parlor while the sun came up. After all, staying in her bed and staring at the ceiling hadn't been all that productive for the five hours she'd done it for—so she'd figured, what the heck, might as well try to get something done.

As she'd passed by Jim's room, though, she'd heard him talking to himself, the heavy door muffling the words.

She'd been so worried about him, out there alone, doing God only knew what.

And maybe . . . she'd missed him.

She'd not been sure what to do with that one. Or entirely clear why she'd felt compelled to knock and say his name—

The door whipped open, and for a split second, she wondered why Jim had stuck his finger in a light socket—if his eyes were any wider, he'd have been staring out of the top of his head.

"Are you okay?" she said, taking a step back.

His stare flipped around her face.

"What . . . why are you looking at me like that?"

"I, ah . . . I . . ."

For a split second, he focused on her mouth, locking on her lips—then he shook his head and cursed.

"Was there someone in there with you?" she said, trying not

to look past him. Trying not to feel . . . something . . . about that possibility.

It had never occurred to her that he might have some kind of a personal life.

"No." His voice was hoarse. "I'm alone."

"No offense, you don't look right." He looked . . . good, though.

Not that she should be thinking about anything like that . . . still, he'd had a shower and smelled like clean soap, and he was an incredibly handsome man . . . what with the dark blond hair and all that muscle and—

Oh, God, she was totally thinking like that.

"You're up early," he muttered, ducking back into his room and pacing around like he had energy to work off or something.

She peered in, even though it was none of her business.

The bed was messy, the sheets tangled up—but the pillows were arranged at the base of the headboard, a pair on each side— and both had the imprints of heads on them.

Had he been sleeping with someone in here?

Tucking her arms around her chest, she thought, Wow, just when she'd thought things couldn't get any weirder. Because she really shouldn't care one way or another.

But she did.

Over at the bureau, he braced his hands and leaned into his heavy arms, dropping his head.

"Jim?" When he didn't reply, she said, "You're scaring me."

"Sorry, just been a long night."

"What's happening in this round?"

"Nothing much."

How that equated to a long night, she wasn't sure. Then again, he probably hated the waiting. And yet . . . waiting wouldn't cause some to look like he did when he'd opened the door.

"So you can't sleep?" he said as he stared at the floor.

"No." She frowned. "Is there something I can do to help?"

"Thanks, but I'm great."

"Really."

He straightened and turned his back to her. Then he seemed to be rearranging something on himself. When he pivoted around again, he was more in control.

"You want breakfast?" he said abruptly.

"Ah, sure. Maybe I'll cook, though?" Given the fact that there hadn't been any food in the house until she'd come here, you had to assume that he and Adrian weren't chef-types.

"Great idea. Come on, I gotta get away from this room."

Why, she thought. And she almost asked—but the expression on his face as he walked by her shut that idea down pretty quick.

As they headed for the stairs together, tension flared between them and made her twitchy.

"Did I do something wrong?" she blurted. Maybe Adrian had told him about the book?

Jim stopped with his hand on the banister. After a long moment, he looked over his shoulder, and said quietly, "I owe you an apology."

She recoiled. "For what?"

"It's too long a story."

"It's five thirty a.m. How much more time do you need?"

"Look, I just want you to know that . . ." He cursed. "I don't know what I'm saying here."

With that, he kept going, hitting the stairs, leaving her with nothing but an unsettled feeling that she was, once again, in the dark.

Chapter Forty-eight

"I should go."

Okay, those were the three saddest words in the English language as far as Cait was concerned. But Duke had a point. It was six o'clock, and she had to guess it was, in fact, time for him to go home.

They were both lying on their sides with their heads on her pillows, facing each other with the sheets tucked in around their warm bodies. It had been a long, long time since she'd shared a moment like this, a night like this. Such a reminder of why people put up with the stresses of relationships—this communion was about so much more than what they had physically shared.

"When am I coming back?" he demanded.

She had to smile. It was not in his nature to sugarcoat things, or beat around the bush—and it was curiously relaxing to always know where she stood with him. "When do you want to?"

"Tonight."

Her response was to lean in and kiss him. "Sounds perfect—oh, wait."

"What?"

"Ah . . . I have a funeral to go to today. Not sure what kind of mood I'll be in."

He frowned, and stroked her hair back. "Anyone close to you?"

"A student of mine. She died . . . unexpectedly." Yeah, 'cause you didn't exactly schedule getting abducted and murdered. "It's going to be really emotional."

"Shit. He or she must have been really young."

"She. And she was nineteen. It's a tragedy. You may have read about it in the paper—Sissy Barten?"

"I'm not really up on the news. But I am sorry."

"So young to have lost her life. It's just . . . I don't want to get morbid or anything, but it's a huge reminder of how easily people's destinies can get off-track through no fault of their own. I mean, she was in a good college and keeping her nose clean. She worked hard and was crazy talented—everything was going so well for her. And then one night she goes on a random errand, and it all ends. I don't know how to make sense of it, and I can't imagine what her family's going through. Life is just so short."

Duke was quiet for a while. "You're right."

"Anyway, I don't know how I'm going to be. Maybe tomorrow night?"

He shook his head. "I take you as you come. If you don't want to see anybody, that's one thing. But if you're feeling like you've got to front for me? Not necessary."

"Thanks." She smiled at him. "Why don't we play it by ear and see how I do? Would that be okay?"

"Yup."

"You are . . . pretty wonderful, you know that?"

"Not really, but if you think so? All that matters."

At that, he kissed her the way he always did, taking over, own-ing her in some indescribable way. But then he was getting out of bed, his naked body gleaming in the light from the hall—

Shoot, the man dressed with disarming efficiency.

She could have used a longer show.

And maybe he was right. After the funeral, maybe getting to-gether was a good idea, a way of taking her mind off things . . .

All too soon he was standing at the foot of her bed, looming with that body of his, dressed in what she'd taken off of him.

"Can I make you coffee on my way out?" he said.

"I think I might go back to sleep."

"Oh, man, did I keep you up last night?"

"You don't sound very sorry about it."

He came around and ducked down. "That's because I'm not."

The kiss was a lingering one, telling her more than words could how much he had valued the night before . . . and however many nights might be coming for them in the future.

"This is the first time in a long time . . ." She hesitated.

"What?"

"I just . . . I haven't really been looking forward to the future." As it dawned on her how that could be taken, she rushed ahead. "Wait, wait, not that I'm thinking anything nutty—I swear. It's . . . I don't know. I love my jobs and my life, I really do. I just haven't been excited about anything for a long while."

Duke stared into her eyes for the longest time. "Me neither."

By nine a.m., the sun was rarin' to go, rising up over the tree line and throwing out the kind of BTUs that suggested winter was well fucked, and summer not just a hypothetical.

Having pulled into work, Duke parked his truck where he al-ways did in the lot beside the Shed—but instead of getting out and moving along to clock in, he just stared through the chain-link fence at that great, rising fireball.

With a slow, deliberate circle, he ran his hand around the steering wheel, even though he wasn't just in park, his engine was off: nowhere to go, but driving anyway.

After he'd left Cait's, he'd gone home, and found Rolly out cold, but breathing on the sofa. At that point, he'd listened to a message from his supervisor, left sometime the night before, and discovered he was pulling a full shift in the morning—good news. And then Alex Hess had texted him that she was putting him back on the schedule at the Iron Mask next week—better news.

Ordinarily, he hated free time.

Although . . . with Cait on the horizon? Wasn't so sure about that anymore. Especially because nights were when they were likely to see each other.

How much had she slept in? he wondered.

God, how long had it been since he'd thought like that? Since Nicole.

Yeah, and you know how that worked out, a part of him bitched.

"Shut it."

When his brain didn't cough up anything else, he smiled harshly. Nice change of pace—you argue with yourself and some-times you could really get through to the other guy.

. . . *it's a huge reminder of how easily people's destinies can get off-track* . . .

Fuck. That one sentence had been banging around his head since he'd pulled away from the curb in front of his woman's house. Over and over. To the point where it was driving him batshit.

Taking his phone out, he put in the password, went into his voice mails, and just looked at the list. Nicole's newest had been the third he'd received while he'd been at Cait's, and unlike the other two, he'd listened to what she'd left a number of times.

As he stared at his phone, he thought, See, this was why you stayed in your comfort zone. You started making a connection with someone, your ice got broken . . . and then you started doing stupid fucking shit.

He probably would have been okay if Cait hadn't brought up that student of hers. For some reason, that was hammering in his head, too.

"I'm losing my mind," he said as he looked out of his truck's windshield again. "Losing it . . ."

As with his attraction to Cait, he couldn't exactly explain why things were so different for him all of a sudden. Well, not completely different. He was still focused on payback when it came to his brother. But it seemed as if some other hand was on his steering wheel, turning him this way. That way. In a circle.

Refocusing on his phone, he watched from what felt like the distance of a mile as his thumb hit . . . *call back*.

Just as the ringing started, he caught a flash of movement out of the corner of his eye. It was the blond-haired man who had tailed him yesterday, stepping out from behind another parked truck. With all the nonchalance of someone who held most of the cards, he put a cigarette between his teeth and flicked a Bic, leaning into the flame.

As he exhaled, he lifted his hand in a wave.

"Hello?" came the response through the phone.

Hang up, Duke ordered himself. Hang the fuck up—you don't want to do this. . . .

"Hello," he heard himself say.

Chapter Forty-nine

"So you can understand why we're curious about where you were."

As the question came at G.B., he kept his cool, smiling at the detective who was sitting across the interrogation table from him.

First thing this morning, he'd gotten the call to come down to the Caldwell Police Department, and of course he'd complied. He wasn't stupid.

And he'd watched enough episodes of *The First 48* to know how to act.

"You're just doing your job," G.B. said with a casual shrug. "But I don't have anything else to tell you."

Detective . . . what was his name? de la Truz? . . . smiled back. "Well, you could explain why you didn't think to mention that you and Jennifer Espie had been in a relationship."

G.B. linked his hands in his lap and was careful to hold eye contact steadily. "That's because we weren't."

"If you want to mince words, fine. But you didn't tell us you two were sleeping together."

"It wasn't a regular thing, Detective. Come on, I'm so busy with work, I have no personal life. She and I have some friends in common, and yeah, sure, we hooked up a couple of times, but it wasn't anything serious. I just didn't think it was relevant."

"The girl was murdered in the theater you both work in, and you didn't consider the idea that disclosing your past relations might be a good idea?"

"What can I say. I'm a singer, not a lawyer."

The guy flipped through his little notebook. "I hear you're an actor, too."

"*Rent*'s my first musical."

Brown eyes lifted. "The director says you're a natural."

"That's really cool of him."

"He says you're able to summon emotion on a dime."

"Well, that's part of the gig, isn't it?"

De la Whoever smiled again. "Yeah. It is. Which brings me to another question I have. One of the promoters for that jazz concert you sang backup in . . . what was that singer's name? Millicent?"

"Millicent Jayson."

"Yeah, that's the one. Anyway, the promoter said before you went onstage that night, he saw you and Jennifer arguing in her office. You know, the one with all the glass?"

G.B. had expected this. "She was upset with me."

"And why was that?"

"Like I told you, we didn't have a regular thing going. She wanted that, though. And she got all up in my face."

"About what?"

G.B. made a show of rubbing his jaw. "I had a woman come to see me that night, someone I was actually interested in. I asked management if I could use one of the comp tickets they'd reserved for VIPs—you know, if they had any left. They did, and Jennifer was supposed to leave it at will-call for my date. She was also supposed to get me backstage clearance. When I came to get the tags for backstage, she just went off on me."

"Cait Douglass, right?"

Okay, it was a little surprise that they had that name. "Yeah, that's her. The woman I invited, that is."

"She was also supposed to meet you for lunch yesterday."

"Yeah, she and I were going to grab a quick sandwich down in the break room. Obviously, because of what happened . . . we didn't, yeah, you know."

How in the hell did—

The detective pursued the fight angle for some time, prodding, prompting, clearly trying to trip things up. But G.B. just stayed on message and on tone—calm, cool, helpful and collected.

Eventually, the guy shut that notebook. "Well, there's only one other thing I've got for you, then."

"Fire away."

"Why were you down in the basement the night Jennifer was killed?"

G.B. frowned. "I'm sorry?"

"I don't know if you're aware of this, but security cameras were installed about a month ago. The crime in that part of town has been rising, and the owners of the theater became concerned about break-ins. The stairwells are all monitored now. We have tape of you coming up the back about ten p.m."

Fuck . . . him.

Wait a minute.

G.B. smiled and shrugged again. "I went down to do vocal exercises."

"Excuse me?"

"I'm assuming you've been down in that hall, right?"

"Yes. I have."

Because that was where the body had been, duh. Not that G.B. let on about that—after all, one of the easiest ways to incriminate yourself was to cop to details not provided to you.

"Well, then you know that it extends forever, like, almost from one end of the theater complex to the other. Naturally, it has the best acoustics in the building. I went down there to practice scales—the echoing is incredible; you can practically do a barbershop quartet with yourself."

The detective's eyes narrowed. "No one has reported hearing any singing that night."

"But that's the point. If you close the fire door at the base of the stairs, the sound isn't going to carry."

"You expect me to believe that you went down there to yodel on the same night that girl was murdered, and no one saw you or heard you singing."

"Look, straight up? This production of *Rent* could be my big break. Yeah, Caldwell is a regional market, but I had to beat out fifty guys my age with my vocal range for this fucking part. The director is a prick—everyone knows it—but he's also got a national reputation. If I don't hit those notes? He's going to throw me out and fill the part with somebody else." He leaned. "And you actually think I *wouldn't* be practicing late at night to get it right?"

"Well. You've got answers for everything, haven't you."

"I'm just telling the truth. Do with it what you will." G.B. checked his watch. "Listen, I'm sorry to say this, but I have to go to a job in about a half hour."

"Where you working at?"

"It's a funeral. Maybe you know the girl? She was murdered a little while ago—Sissy Barten?"

The detective pushed a hand through his short-cropped hair. "Yeah. I know who she is."

"You find out who did that yet?"

"Yup."

"Good. I'm glad to hear it." G.B. looked down. "Her family asked me to sing. I guess they'd heard me at her graduation from high school the year before—a friend of a friend got in touch with me, and like I was going to say no? It was horrible what happened to her."

"What happened to Jennifer Espie was pretty horrible, too."

"How was she killed, by the way?"

"That's another thing I've been thinking about. May I see your hands?"

"Sure." G.B. stretched them out palms down, then palms up.

There was nothing on them. But then, he used that pair of workman's gloves, the kind that were rated for handling chemicals. Thick gloves, very thick—and they'd run up his forearms.

They were in the Hudson River now.

"Do you want to take samples or something?" he asked.

"Interesting idea to bring up. You watch a lot of CSI, by any chance?"

"No," he lied.

"Jennifer was killed in a violent way."

Yup. He'd walked down with her and taken her all the way around to the back exit, the one that was triple-locked, had no windows anywhere near it, and was practically in the next zip code from anyplace anyone usually was. The gloves had been in his back pockets, one jammed in each side, and she hadn't even balked at the fact that he'd had them with him. He'd turned out the light, and talked to her until she'd given in to him; then he'd pivoted her around like he was going to fuck her from behind. . . .

And slammed her face-first into the wall. *Boom!* Splash! Blood everywhere. And then he'd done it again, and again, and again. . . .

Messy, very messy.

But he'd had to get it all out. In situations like that, when he'd done things just like that before, he'd always found that the violence was a purging—and the further he went with it, the cleaner he felt afterward.

When she was no longer twitching on the floor, he'd caught his breath, and had to start thinking. Yeah, he'd remembered to bring the gloves, but kind of like a session of really good sex, he tended to be a little spacey for a while afterward.

Next move was to get the fuck out of there—and clean the fuck up. That was how he'd ended up in that workroom . . . where the brunette had come to him.

The sex had been awesome, actually. What he was hoping, though, was that she had headed out of town right afterward—and that Jennifer's murder didn't go further than the local press.

What he really didn't need was her connecting any dots for the CPD. And finding him with no shirt on in a room full of bleach fumes the night that some chick was killed in the basement?

"Would you let me?"

"I'm sorry?" he said, refocusing.

"Take samples from under your nails?"

"Sure. Absolutely."

The detective knocked on the table and stood up. "This won't take long. We'll get you out fast so you can be at that funeral."

"Thanks—and if you need anything else, just holler."

"Oh, I will." At the door, the detective paused. "You've got quite a following here in Caldie."

"I'm just trying to make it, like anybody else."

The man nodded. "If you decide to go out of town, or out of state, give me a call, will you?"

G.B. forced his brows to frown. "Am I a suspect or something?"

"Just consider it a courtesy at this point, okay?"

With that, G.B. was left alone in the bald little room. As his heart rate increased, his first instinct was to jump up and pace around, but he knew better. There were cameras in the corners.

Cameras that caught everything—

"Well . . . what do you know," he whispered to himself, a kind of awe coming over him.

He was going to get away with this, after all. In spite of those stairwell cameras that he hadn't known about—and which should have been as big a problem as that brunette for him.

Fate, however, had smiled upon him, hadn't it. When he'd been in that workroom, before the brunette had come and found him? He remembered the lights flickering—and he was willing to bet his life on the fact that there had been some data loss associated with the power surge. Because this detective with the sharp eyes would have led with any record of G.B. and Jennifer going down those stairs together.

Which they had done right before he'd killed her.

Yeah, no "courtesy" for an out-of-town trip if the cops had that kind of evidence—he'd be in fucking custody.

Something had definitely happened to that security camera in the stairwell.

And thank God.

It was without a doubt his savior in all this, he thought with a smile.

Chapter
Fifty

So many people, Cait thought as she looked around the narthex of St. Patrick's Cathedral.

For the past two hours, she had stood on the periphery, watching the ceaseless tide of mourners funnel in. She hadn't been to many of these kinds of services, fortunately—but she knew enough to recognize the shift in demographics: The younger the person in the casket, the larger and more diverse the crowd. When the elders passed on, usually there was only what older friends were left, with the few young being those of close familial relationship.

Not in Sissy Barten's case.

There were people of all ages—children, teenagers, lot of college students, some of whom Cait recognized and hugged. There were young families and middle-aged people, and then the older spectrum as well.

Almost all of them stopped by and looked at Sissy's drawings and paintings, as if using the work as a conduit to connect themselves with her.

No open casket, or so Cait had been told—and she was glad for that. This was hard enough without having to see Sissy—and maybe that made Cait a wimp . . . but she'd read the *CCJ* articles on the nature of the killing. Gruesome. Very gruesome.

"Thank you so much for this."

Cait jumped and turned around. Sissy's mother was right at her elbow, the woman looking about a hundred years old.

"For what—oh, bringing her art?" Cait shook her head. "It's my privilege to."

"Will you join us for the burial? At Pine Grove?"

"Of course. Absolutely."

"My husband would like to leave all of this in place and then collect it after we're finished at the cemetery, if it's okay with you? We'll take the art home."

"I have some portfolios that you can use and keep—they'll make sure everything is protected."

"Thank you." The woman reached out and took Cait's hand, giving it a squeeze. "You were her favorite professor. She spoke of you constantly."

Cait's eyes flooded with tears. "Thank you for telling me that—she was a tremendously talented person, and so wonderful to be around. I'm just . . . terribly sorry."

"We are too."

The pair of them hugged, holding on to each other for a moment that lasted an eternity. And then someone came up to talk to Mrs. Barten, and Cait stepped out of the way to dab at her eyes.

So hard. This was just so damned hard.

Peering to the side, she looked through an old pane of glass into the body of the church. Down the long nave, the pews that had been empty when she'd been here the day before were stuffed with people, heads turning this way and that as they chatted with the folks around them. Even out here, she could hear the chatter, the occasional coughs, the shuffling of countless feet, the creaking of old wood as more seats were taken.

Staring down that vast aisle, she found herself locking on the altar again, and as she focused on the figure of Jesus upon the cross, and the incredible stained-glass windows all around the statue, she thought of her parents.

True believers. They had made the commitment to their religion with their hearts, minds, and souls, their faith transforming the complex mixture of mythology and history of the Bible into a living, breathing dictate for everything they did.

She'd resented them for it, but had never thought any deeper than that about her feelings . . . or theirs. But standing in the front of the church, having stared at all those grief-stricken faces, she wondered for the first time if maybe her mother and father's mission to bring relief and guidance to people like these wasn't somehow a good thing.

Take out the "maybe." In fact, they had told her countless times how they just wanted to help—that was what drove them.

Cait hadn't listened. She'd been too hurt to try to see anything from their point of view. Now, though . . . if she'd had a way to do anything to improve this sad occasion, if there was anything she could say or do to bring forward any help . . . she'd do it—

"Cait?"

Cait recoiled as her name was—"G.B.?"

"Hi. This is a surprise."

As he leaned in for a hug, she wrapped her arms around him. "What are you doing here?" What, like she was a gatekeeper or something? "I mean, I didn't expect to see you here. Did you know Sissy?"

He pulled back and shook his head. "The family asked me to come and sing."

"Oh, that's so nice of you."

He did as she had, leaning to the side and searching the crowd on the far side of the glass. "Lot of people."

"I've been thinking the same thing."

Her eyes went over him quickly. His long hair was pulled back and tied at the base of his neck, his suit and tie black, his button-down white. His shoes were polished, and he smelled like he was fresh from the shower.

He looked as good as he always did.

His blue eyes swung back around to her. "I got your message yesterday. I've been meaning to call you."

"Oh, listen, with what happened at the theater, I can imagine things have gotten complicated."

"They even called me down to the station for questioning." As her eyes bugged, he shook his head. "They're doing it to everyone. It's crazy—but you know, someone's dead and they have to find out who killed her."

Another funeral, Cait thought. For another family, another segment of the community.

"Are you all right?" she asked.

"I'm fine. It's just been an exhausting twenty-four hours."

"I can't even imagine. Listen, I haven't read the paper or been online since it happened—who was she?"

"Nobody important." He winced. "What I mean is—"

"No, I know what you meant. And good Lord, if there's anything I can do to help, let me know."

He smiled at her. "You're the best—and I'm going to take you up on that."

Instantly, a shaft of guilt went through her. But come on, now was not the time to tell him that they were on friends-only status. Or to focus on anything but Sissy and her family.

"Where are you sitting?" he asked, nodding to the church proper.

"In the back somewhere. I'm going to the burial, too."

"So am I. You want to ride over together?"

She nodded. "Yes, please. That would be great."

He kissed her cheek and then walked off, going through the double doors, and striding forward to the front—where he talked to a couple of men who were wearing robes.

She probably should find a place to sit. They'd be starting soon.

Just as she passed over the threshold, something along the far left caught her eye. It was the janitor she'd seen the day before, still dressed in his mucky green overalls. He was looking right at her, his old face wearing such sorrow on it, it seemed as though he knew Sissy personally, too.

He lifted his hand in a wave, and after Cait returned the greeting, the janitor turned away, walking along the far edge of the pews, staring over the assembled masses as if mourning along with them. And then he did the strangest thing. At the front of the church, he slid in beside a young girl who was maybe fourteen or so—who had long straight blond hair just as Sissy had.

Had to be Sissy's sister.

Guess he was a personal friend of the family's.

"Excuse us," someone said from behind her.

"Oh, sorry." Cait moved aside so that a woman with a stroller could get by.

When Cait glanced up again . . . the janitor was gone.

"Are you sure you want to do this?"

Sissy only half heard the words, and what did register was filtered through some kind of echo-chamber effect, the syllables repeating endlessly, overlapping one another until she wasn't sure exactly what had been spoken.

Standing on the lawn of the great cathedral, she felt like the ghost she was, the few stragglers who were arriving for her funeral not noticing her presence—or that of the angel who stood beside her.

She had debated whether to come or not. When Chillie had pitched the newspaper on the front porch this morning, she'd had no intention of reading it—but when she'd unwrapped the thing, she'd seen her own picture below the fold.

And learned the when and where of her own funeral.

Adrian had insisted on coming with her, and she'd been glad, actually. The ride on his Harley had done a lot to clear her head—although all that improvement had gone right into the crapper as soon as they'd pulled up to the church she'd gone to most every Sunday of her life. And then she'd started to recognize the people who were coming up the broad walkway to the front entrance: Her old babysitter with her husband and her baby in a stroller. Her choir teacher from elementary school. The people who lived across the street.

She'd thought that seeing her parents and her sister would be the worst part. And that was probably the truth—so how much harder was this going to get?

"I want to go in," she said. Except her feet didn't move.

"Here." A huge forearm butted into her peripheral vision. "I'll walk with you."

Sissy ended up holding on to the angel's huge biceps for dear life as the two of them entered through the open doors.

"My pictures . . ." she whispered, looking around.

About a dozen pieces of her art were mounted on easels in a semi-circle around the foyer, the pastels and ink drawings and oil paintings all ones she had done as part of her art major.

"Oh, my God, I remember doing this last fall." Walking over, she stood in front of a depiction of the Caldwell bridges that she'd painted in the rust-colored hues of autumn. She'd completed it right on the shores of the Hudson, had sat there in the sunshine for two hours with the canvas and her palette and a conviction that life lasted forever—and wasn't that a good thing.

A sudden flare of organ music suggested the service was about to get started.

Pressing on, she overrode a strange terror and walked through the narthex's double doors into the body of the church. Everything was just as she remembered, which was a shock of sorts. Regardless of what the calendar said, she was still convinced she had been gone for centuries.

From that moment on, autopilot took over, some inner metronome driving her footsteps forward, left, right, left, right. When she got to the front, and saw her parents and her sister, she stopped.

"Here, take this," Adrian said gruffly.

As a red do-rag was pressed into her hands, she wondered why she needed it—but that was when she found out she was crying: Tears were streaming down her face, falling to the floor of the church.

"You can go sit down if you like."

Sissy wheeled around, expecting to see some late arrival hustling for a seat and the person at the end of the nearest pew moving aside to accommodate them. Instead, it was a janitor she didn't recognize, an old guy in a dark green jumpsuit.

And he was looking directly at her.

"Go on, there's a seat over there for you."

"How can you see me?" she blurted.

"Because you're here," he answered gently, like that was self-evident. "Go on now, and sit."

She looked over to where he was pointing, and immediately shook her head. "Oh, no, I couldn't—"

"It's there for you, Sissy. Sit."

The chair he wanted her to use was the gold leafed one that was set between the Virgin Mary's side chapel and that of John the Baptist. Raised up on a pedestal, it had a red velvet cushion, and filligreed woodwork, and was the closest she'd ever gotten to any kind of throne.

Ever since she was a young girl, she had always wanted to sit down in it—even if just for a heartbeat. But of course, there had always been a wide satin ribbon tied across that seat, a clear warning to all that it was a work of art, not something functional.

Certainly not for a little girl. Or a big one, at that.

Today there was no ribbon tied between the curling arms.

"It is for you."

The janitor put his hand on her shoulder, and instantly the most incredible sense of calm came over her, every painful nuance of this dissipating . . . replaced by a profound sense of love for all the people who had come for her and her family.

So much love, forming the foundation of the agony within the congregation, but also providing the only uplift that was available.

Following the janitor, Sissy went over and stepped up onto the platform. As organ music crescendoed, she sat in the chair, placing her hands gently on the golden arms. And it was strange, in a way . . . this felt proper, not foreign.

Turning to look at the janitor—

He was gone, as if he'd never been . . . nowhere in the crowd, not walking away down an aisle, not standing off to the side. It was as if he had just disappeared into thin air—and yet, Adrian was nodding his head as if he approved of something someone was saying to him.

Looking away from the angel, she focused on the altar, and it was at that moment that the organ let out another powerful surge of harmony . . . and a guy she vaguely recognized, who had a ponytail and was wearing a black suit, walked out from behind the velvet curtains.

Her only other thought, as he began to sing strong and true . . . was that he had a halo, too.

Chapter
Fifty-one

Duke was so done with the silent-type peanut gallery that was riding shotgun next to him. The son of a bitch just sat there in the passenger seat, lighting up every once in a while, as they went from park to park.

All without saying a fucking word.

Ah, hell, it could be worse, Duke supposed. Someone with a chatty streak would have done his nut totally in.

"Last one," he said, talking mostly to himself.

Pulling in between the cast-iron gates of Pine Grove Cemetery, he checked the clock on the dash: three thirty. Good.

The guy next to him finally showed a reaction, sitting up in his seat and frowning. "Hey, you mind if we go right here at this lane?"

"No difference to me. We have to case the entire place."

Following the winding road, Duke looked over the headstones without seeing them. Instead, he was focused on the cedar trees and the maples, the oaks and the pines, looking for downed limbs, or branches that were hanging half-dead. The cemetery had been bleeding money for the last five years, and on the brink of ruin—at least until the city had stepped in and taken over the heavy-lifting maintenance.

And there was an internal logic to that Robin Hood routine: Rumor had it the mayor's mother was buried somewhere on the grounds—no way he was going to let things go into the shitter on his watch in office.

So, yeah, muni workers were now responsible for snow re-moval and large projects, with the mowing left to a skeleton crew of groundsmen.

Whatever. More hours for him, which he—

He knew even before they got close what burial was happening . . . Cait's Lexus was among the row of cars parked off to the side of the lane.

Long, long, long line of vehicles.

Duke drove past them and intended to keep going—except then he saw someone he recognized. And no, it wasn't his woman that got his attention. It was the motherfucker standing next to her.

He hit the brakes.

"What the hell are they doing here?" he heard his wingman say.

Funny, he was thinking that very thing.

The two of them got out of the truck at the same time.

The burial had obviously just concluded, people breaking off into little somber groups and talking quietly as they dispersed into the sunlight.

It was with a sense of utter unreality that Duke watched from across the way as Cait's blond head turned to a man who had long, dark hair pulled back from a face that belonged on a maga-zine cover. The pair of them went over to a group of three who were standing directly over the grave, and after a suitable period of hugging, they turned away and began walking in the direction of her car.

Duke stepped forward before he was aware of moving. And then he was walking a path to intercept them.

Cait saw him first, and her expression changed instantly, recognition replacing her sadness. "Duke! Hi," she called out with a wave.

Look at me, Duke thought. Look at me, you son of a bitch.

His brother's eyes swung around, and it was so satisfying to watch the bastard's whole body tighten up as if he'd been slapped. There was also a moment of confusion as he watched Cait rush forward, her arms out and ready for an embrace.

As she came up to him, Duke was more than happy to oblige, pulling her against him, staring over her head at his godforsaken brother.

A flash of epic fury made G.B. seem downright ugly, but of course he covered it up fast. He'd always been good at that. Very few knew what he was really like.

"I didn't expect to see you here," Cait said against Duke's pecs.

He bent down and kissed her, right on the mouth. "Just doing my job. You okay?"

"It's been rough. I didn't expect it to be this hard."

G.B. walked right up, his eyes burning, his face as relaxed as ever. "Hi."

Duke smiled with his teeth. "Hey."

Cait frowned. "You two know each other?"

"Yes, we do." G.B. put his hand out. "How are you?"

The only reason Duke shook the goddamn thing was that he didn't want Cait involved any further in what was going on between them. She'd made her choice, and it was the right one—and that was the extent of her entanglement.

Also, as soon as he could, he was going to tell her everything—he'd already decided that over the course of the day. But not here, at the frickin' cemetery, two minutes after she'd buried her student.

G.B. smiled like the motherfucker he was. "So, Cait, can you take me back to my car? I have to go to rehearsals."

She stepped away. "Oh, yes, of course." She glanced at G.B. "Will you give us a moment?"

Yeah, G.B., run along there, asshole, would you.

Only Duke knew exactly how pissed off the guy had to be as he nodded like nothing was doing and sauntered away.

Cait turned to him and rubbed his arms. "I'm glad to see you."

"Me, too. Lucky coincidence."

"Listen, if it's okay with you, I'd like to go home and finish my work tonight. With everything that's been going on, I'm worried about getting behind, and the deadline is coming soon. If I press through, I can get it all wrapped up, and then . . ."

"Yeah. Absolutely. You just call me, okay? I'm around."

"Perfect. Thank you." She lifted up on her tiptoes and kissed him briefly. "See you very soon?"

"You got me, lady." He tucked some of that hair behind her ear. "Anytime you want me."

He watched her walk off toward her car, pausing to let a minivan by before crossing the lane.

When she left, G.B. was in her passenger seat.

Across the distance that separated him from his brother, Duke could feel the hatred like an ice pick going into the side of his head—and for a moment, he nearly shouted after her.

But his brother was a shit, not a killer.

And this was quite a moment, wasn't it. Without meaning to, it looked as though Duke had won the game he'd taken himself out of.

As Cait drove them back to wherever they'd been, Duke couldn't imagine the conversation. At least G.B. had nothing on him, though; he'd always kept his nose clean. What was the guy going to do? Tell her how Duke had been with a woman and G.B. had come along and knocked her up and left her and the kid high and dry?

Yeah, that would reflect well on the SOB.

So strange . . . G.B. had been full of hate since the day they'd been born, almost as if there had been a set amount of morality that had had to be split between the pair of them—and Duke had gotten the largest balance by far of however much there was.

And it wasn't like he himself was a rabid Good Samaritan or some shit.

Look what he'd been willing to do to Cait.

Until he'd come to his senses, that is.

Jim strode across the lane toward the grave site. As he closed in, he was cursing himself. Of course Sissy would want to be at her own funeral—and he should have been the one to take her. He hadn't known when it was though . . . and the criminal thing? He hadn't thought to find out.

Most of the people who'd come were wandering off, but not Sissy or her family. The grave was a square hole cut in the earth, a yawning mouth set to claim the remains in the coffin. Sissy's mom and dad and sister were on one side . . . Sissy on the other. And whereas her family were looking down; she was staring at them.

Adrian, who was off to the side, gave a nod.

"How's she doing?" Jim asked as he came up to the guy.

Dumb fucking question.

Adrian shrugged. "She's amazing. That's how she's doing."

"Oh." Jim cleared his throat. "Yeah. Good."

Talk about inappropriate. He wasn't actually chaffing at his buddy over here because the bastard had taken the girl to her *funeral.*

Wow. Classy.

With tangible sorrow, her parents put their arms around their remaining daughter and the trio turned away, leaving Sissy behind.

"Gimme me a minute, would ya?" Jim asked.

Not waiting for an answer, he went over to Sissy. "Hey, there."

She jumped as if surprised. "Oh, hi."

Instantly, he recognized that something was off with her. But come on, like this was happy times? "How you feeling?"

"Good. You know, fine. Okay. I'm all right."

He wanted to put his arms around her and pull her into his chest. He wanted his body to be what she held on to as she struggled to find her footing. He wanted to be the guy she turned to when she needed something, anything.

Instead, they just stood side by side, as her eyes clung to her mother, father and sister. The emotion in her face was so powerful, it was like a tangible object, something with heft and substance and a handle to grab onto.

God knew she was going to be carrying that shit around with her for a very, very long time.

Just as he was about to tell her how sorry he was, she shook her head and met his eyes. "So, how's work?"

Bizarre thing to ask about, considering what she was going through, but maybe she needed the distraction?

"Good. Fine. You know."

Guess two could play at that game.

She nodded over at the tall, dark-haired man Jim had been tailing for the past twenty-four hours. "Is he the soul?"

"Yeah."

"Oh."

"Listen, Sissy, I can . . ." Do what? Take some more time off? Not going to happen. Devina might not have shown up here, but she was, as always, a busy little bitch.

You can't blame a girl for trying.

God, he couldn't believe she'd somehow infiltrated the spell around the mansion. And crap, he needed to tell Adrian what had happened. It was just so damned embarrassing. He had, however, redoubled the protection at the house. Maybe it had weakened because he'd had his head up his ass—

". . . was he an angel, too?"

He shook himself back to attention. "I'm sorry?"

"The other guy? Who's with my old teacher over there?"

Jim pivoted. "I'm so not following this. What?"

"Over by the Lexus. That singer with the ponytail. He's got a halo, too—but everyone can see him."

About twenty-five yards off, a blond-haired woman was getting into an SUV with a man who was tall and had long black hair. Neither one appeared to be particularly happy, but there was certainly no glow or anything around either of their heads.

"I'm not sure what you're talking about," Jim said gently. Damn it, he wanted to go home with her—

"The guy has a halo, like you and me."

Cranking his head back around, Jim frowned. "Halo?"

Sissy rolled her eyes and made a little circle around her skull. "Can't you see mine?"

"No. There's nothing there."

"Oh. Well, I see them. And you've got one, too."

Sure, fine, whatever. "Listen, I hate to do this, but I've got to go."

Duke Phillips was looking around as if searching for him, and if Jim didn't make an appearance in the next nanosecond or two, the guy was going to be convinced he was losing his mind—not a good thing, considering Jim had been getting fucking nowhere with this soul yet.

"It's okay, you do you." Sissy glanced back at Adrian. "I think he and I are going for a drive. I need to clear my head. I feel . . . really weird . . . right now."

Jim ground his teeth. "Okay. Yeah, sure. I get it. I'll check in later, all right?"

"Sure."

She was the one who turned away, and she did not look back as she went over to his buddy. On Adrian's side? As she approached, the angel's face had a softness to it that Jim had never seen before.

Great. Just fucking wonderful.

Chapter Fifty-two

"I was going to tell you sooner."

Cait put the brakes on as she came up to one of the cemetery's fleet of stop signs. Glancing over, she did not feel good about wherever G.B. was at in his head. He was staring out the side window, chin propped up on the knuckles of his hand, eyes narrowed coldly.

It was a reminder of how she didn't really know him.

"But honestly," she continued, unsure whether he was listening, "I didn't know where things were going."

Hitting the gas again, she tried to remember how to get out of the cemetery. She wasn't so hot with directions on a good day, and this had not been a good day. Left?

Why the hell not.

Turning the wheel, she felt the graves press in on her, a chill frisking the back of her neck.

"I'm sorry," he said abruptly. "I just . . . I would have liked a chance to see what you and I could be together. That's all."

He didn't look at her. Just kept staring off into space.

"It's complicated," he tacked on.

"I haven't handled this well." She cursed under her breath. "It was so weird—I met both of you on the same night."

And it was odd to think they seemed to know each other a little—what were the chances? Then again, Caldwell was a small city—not as close-knit as a town, sure, but it wasn't a Manhattan or Chicago, either.

He rubbed his eyes. "This has just been a really strange couple of days."

"I'm so sorry I've added to the difficulty."

He didn't say much else on the way back to St. Patrick's, and though she hated to admit it, it was a relief to pull up next to the front door and put the SUV in park so he could get out.

Turning to him, she wondered what to say.

"Cait, I've got to tell you something—"

A phone went off, and the ringing was not hers. With a soft curse, G.B. shoved a hand into his suit coat, and as he looked at the number, he seemed annoyed.

"Hold on, I gotta take this." He put the thing up to his ear. "Hello? Yeah, hey, Detective, how are you? You were? I didn't see you during the service. Oh, yeah, thanks." There was a silence. "I have rehearsals today—I'm actually in trouble because I've been gone for so long this afternoon. Okay. Fine. Yeah, I'll come over again. Right now? All right, gimme a minute to get downtown."

When he hung up, he shook his head. "The police want to talk to me some more."

Boy, this day kept getting better for him, didn't it. "That's awful."

"Yeah, it is. Listen, I've got to go, but can we—"

"Absolutely. Just give me a call whenever you're free." The last thing she wanted to do was make him feel like he was an afterthought. "I'm going to be working at home tonight, finishing up the book."

"Okay. Thanks."

He got out as if he were distracted, but come on. The police were on his phone about a murder. How could he not be thinking about something other than his dating status?

G.B. walked off in a hurry, crossing the road and getting into an older-model BMW. As he tore off, he didn't glance at her as he passed by, but she sure as hell got a good look at him—and that chill went up her neck again.

The expression on his face was positively volcanic. He was furious, his profile shockingly ugly.

Shaking her head, Cait got out, walked up to the cathedral's grand entrance and pulled open the heavy doors. Inside the foyer, Sissy's art was still on display, and as Cait went over to start packing things up, the sound of her heels on the marble floor echoed loudly.

Funny, the space hadn't seemed so large with all the people in it. Empty now, the narthex appeared as big as a football stadium.

She'd left the portfolios in the coatroom, and it took her no time at all to load up the artwork carefully and leave it out in the open. Reaching into her bag, she went for her sketchbook, intending to rip free a page and write a quick note—

Damn it, she'd lost the thing, remember?

How was she going to—

"I'll let her parents know where it is."

Wheeling around, she found that janitor standing right in front of the double doors that opened to the pews and the altar.

"Oh, thank you. I don't want Sissy's things to get lost."

"Don't worry. I won't let anything happen to them." He nodded to the easels. "May I help you carry these out?"

"I can do it. But thanks."

The old man helped her anyway, allowing her to make only one trip.

As she closed her SUV's hatch, she turned to the man and felt the oddest urge to hug him. But that wouldn't have been appropriate.

"May I give you a piece of advice?" he said, smiling in a way that made his eyes nearly disappear under their burden of wrinkles.

"Please."

"Talk it out."

"I'm sorry?"

"You need to talk it out. If you do that, everything will be all right—eventually. If you don't, you're going to miss the life you want."

Poor old guy. Clearly dementia was setting in.

Not wanting to upset him, she patted his arm. "Okay, I promise. I'll do that."

Getting into her car, she gave him a last wave and took off, heading for home. She'd gone about three blocks when she figured out where her sketch pad was.

"Son of a gun," she muttered.

And she might as well go back and get it.

Rerouting didn't require a huge time suck, and she kept to the surface roads as she went toward downtown. Closing in on the thick of the city, she was relieved to find that the traffic was light; then again, it wasn't quite the tail end of the workday yet, rush hour still about an hour off.

Her parking space, the one nearly across from the Palace, was open again, and she parked smoothly and locked up. Waiting for a break in the flow of cars, she jogged across and hoped that her luck with janitors continued.

Nope. She was able to get into the public foyer, but the lobby was locked and empty. Going over to will-call, she peered in. No-body was in the office—

The staff-only door opened wide and she turned. A police officer was coming out, and he paused to look behind himself like he was waiting for a colleague.

"Excuse me," she said to the guy. "May I go down to the office? I think I left something here the day before yesterday and I want to see if anyone picked it up."

"Do you know where you're going?"

"Just through this hall."

"Okay, g'head."

She walked fast down the corridor, passing by some other cops, probably the ones the uni at the door was waiting for. As she went along, it was ironic that she was yet again looking for a lost-and-found box. Maybe she'd have more luck than when she'd been on the search for her gold earring.

Coming around the corner, she straightened her skirt as she approached the glass office. She was not looking forward to going rounds with that receptionist again, but who else was she going to ask?

It turned out that the reception space was empty, but as she tried the glass door, she was able to pull things open. "Hello?"

The desk was orderly, the computer screen displaying a slowly rotating Palace logo, the phone ringing quietly.

"Hello . . . ?"

There were clearly more offices in the back, a rear hallway going off in two directions, but she didn't want to intrude—

Her foot hit something unexpected, her balance instantly going haywire as she tripped forward. Catching herself on the corner of the desk, she looked down. A cardboard box filled with personal effects was on the floor: Aluminum travel mug. Plant. Picture of—

Frowning, Cait knelt down. Without touching anything, she

got close enough to see the image of two young women standing side by side on a beach, their arms around each other's shoulders. The one on the right was . . .

An odd foreboding brought her head up and around to the empty chair behind the desk.

"Can I help you?"

Cait jumped up. A man had come in, an exhausted, half-bald, used-to-be-good-looking man in wrinkled clothes.

"I—ah, I'm sorry to bother you. I was looking for the receptionist?"

He recoiled like she'd slapped him. "You didn't hear?"

Before she asked . . . before he answered her . . . she knew who had been killed. "No, no, I haven't . . ."

"Jenny's dead." He marched past her. "So unless you're applying for the position, I can't do anything for you."

And that was that. He disappeared down the inner hall, a door slamming shut a moment later.

Cait didn't stick around. Trying to find her sketchbook was such a low priority compared to what was going on here.

At least it was a relatively new one. The only thing in it . . . had been those sketches of G.B.

By the time G.B. got out of his second round of questioning, he had reverted back to his old ways, the ones he worked so hard to hide, the ones that had gotten him into trouble before.

Unfortunately, his submersion into himself so complete, he was having trouble seeing what was ahead of him.

Fury, as great and wide a divide as it had always been, owned him.

Getting into his car, he grasped the steering wheel and tried to focus. He could feel a plan developing in his head, and he had enough sense to know that it wasn't a good one. It wasn't clean. It wasn't tight.

And he was in enough trouble already with the whole Jennifer thing. But he couldn't . . . concentrate . . . on . . . anything else—

As his phone rang, he fumbled with the thing, dropping the cell in his lap as he took it out of his inside pocket. He answered without checking, without thinking—

"Hello, G.B." Female voice. Low. Seductive. "What are you doing, G.B.?"

The sound of the brunette he'd fucked in that basement workroom pierced through the veil of his emotions, the fog of his anger, the clouds of his past.

"I've been thinking about you."

As she spoke, he thought that he should say something back to her to let her know he was actually on the line—but she seemed to be already aware of that.

"What are you going to do about all this, G.B.?" she asked.

"About what?" he mumbled.

"What are you going to decide to do?"

God, how did she know? Because he *was* torn, the urge to act warring with the sense that it was in his best interest to let this shit with Cait go.

But his brother was in the way. His fucking goody-two-shoes *brother* was getting her. And he just couldn't let that happen.

The shit with that whole Nicole thing had been for fun. But he actually *liked* Cait.

"You know she cheated on you."

"Who . . ." he asked.

"That blond you like so much. She fucked your brother last night."

He frowned. "How . . . how do you—"

"You *know* she did. You saw him kiss her at the grave site. You think that happens between two people who are just friends? Don't be naive."

G.B. brought up a hand and started to rub his forehead, back and forth, back and forth, as if he were sanding the skin off. He had always hated Duke. Had come out of the womb detesting the guy. And yeah, sure, it had never been logical, but some things were so strong that you didn't need to understand them. They just . . . were.

It was like he had a demon inside of him, and sometimes the evil needed to get out before it ate G.B. alive.

Like with Jennifer in the theater basement. A switch got flipped and . . . everything else disappeared except the malignancy—and keeping that inside? Impossible.

Man, one of the single biggest satisfactions in his life had been taking Duke's boring-ass girlfriend away from him— seducing her right out from under his brother's nose. God, so fucking pathetic—the pair of them had been so "in love," parading around that college campus arm in arm, full of dreams. But there had been fractures in the relationship to exploit—Darling Nikki, as the song went, hadn't been quite the nicey-nice girl Duke had believed she was. What a skank. And she hadn't been on the pill—so when G.B. had poked holes in the condoms before he used them? Not long before she was nauseous every morning and then—oopsie! She'd had to tell her BF she'd cheated on him.

When Duke had found out, his first stop had been G.B.'s apartment—and the guy had beaten him so badly, he'd needed dental implants afterward. But it was so worth it—and the payback had lasted for years.

Was going to last at least until the kid was eighteen, right?

"G.B., I think you need to do something about all this."

Coming back to the present, he shook his head. The brunette was right. So fucking right.

"Go to the mall, G.B. Turn your car on, and go to the mall. The food court, G.B. Go there, and find your path. I'll be waiting for you at the end—and I've got a lifetime contract to offer you."

He blinked, thinking that was a strange way of putting things. "What . . . ?"

"I'm offering you what you've always wanted, what you sing about—I'm prepared to give you eternal life."

"In the public eye?"

"You will be surrounded forever, G.B.—I'll take care of everything. I'll take care of you. Go to the mall, right now—think of this as your audition. Pass? And you're in like Flynn."

"I need to go to rehearsals."

"Like I said, I'll take care of it all."

"I don't understand how you—"

"You're boring me, and wasting time. Stop with the questions. Start with the actions."

The call was ended and he looked down at his phone. Man, those A & R people really did have a lot of pull, didn't they.

Before he was conscious of making a decision, he found himself driving, his hands and feet doing all the right things as he made turns and accelerated down straightaways and slowed down for other traffic.

The Caldwell Galleria Mall was a huge, sprawling expanse of stores that was surrounded by a Ford Motor Company production plant's worth of parking lots. He hadn't been there in years, but he remembered, back from his orphanage era, being brought here around Christmastime . . . paraded around the red and green window displays . . . unable to buy anything because he'd never had any money.

Which was what happened when you didn't know who your father was and you killed your mother in childbirth.

He and that fraternal twin of his had had such a great start, hadn't they.

The food court was around the far side, and he found a parking space that was pretty close to the doors. Walking like a zombie, he zeroed in on the entrance, passing by the smokers who were standing around the trash bins, and the mothers pushing infants around in strollers, and the next generation of bar sluts with their prepubescent legs showing under postage-stamp skirts.

Something told him to tuck his ponytail in under his jacket, and hunch his shoulders while keeping his head down. He didn't want any attention on himself, and sure as shit, there were probably fans here somewhere.

He entered through the side push doors, not the revolving center one, and hung back. There was quite a distance between him and the teeming trough area, a Kay Jewelers store, a RadioShack, and a Brookstone separating him from the stalls of high-calorie junk food. For a moment, his head cleared enough for him to wonder what the fuck he was doing considering rehearsal was no doubt waiting for him, but then, off to the right, he saw a pair of dark heads going along. One was about two feet shorter than the other, the boy who walked next to the man looking sullen, the man who was beside the boy wearing a hard expression.

G.B. inhaled, a strange feeling in his chest making him want to cough.

The brunette on the phone had been right. Seeing those two together?

Certainly laid a path out for him, nice and clean.

Dipping his hand into that inner jacket pocket again, he got a hold of his phone.

His heart rate skyrocketed as he thought about dialing. For some reason, he had the sense that the decision he was about to make was going to affect so much more than just the situation with Duke. And not in a good way.

Turn away, he told himself. Just stop this.

After all, why the fuck did he care about Cait and his brother? He was on the verge of getting noticed, about to finally make it. . . .

No, you aren't, an inner voice pointed out. They're going to get you for that murder.

He blinked and thought about the follow-up by good ol' Detective de la Cruz, as it had turned out the guy was called.

They'd found something, hadn't they.

"Goddamn it," G.B. muttered. He should have stopped that shit with Jennifer. And he should be stopping this.

But come on, if he was going to go out, it might as well be with a bang . . . right?

The brunette had a point. He knew just what to do.

Chapter
Fifty-three

Cait sat back at her drafting table and inspected the second-to-last drawing of the book. The puppy, who had gotten himself in trouble trying to hide his bone, was being scolded by his owner, the little five-year-old boy telling him he had to be careful down by the river so he didn't drown.

Which was the point of the whole series: It wasn't so much what life did to us, but what we tried to do to keep life from happening that caused most of our problems.

I.e., don't get so worried about keeping your things safe that you end up putting them on a raft that floats away from you.

She knew what the next page said, and she could feel herself easing up, sure as if she were the little chocolate Lab: She was a happily-ever-after person at heart, and as always, the puppy re-united with his bone made her feel like everything had been worth it.

She was just taking the drawing over to her display table when her phone rang. Jogging over to get it, she hoped it was Duke checking in. Maybe she was up to having him come over, after all.

"Hello?" she said.

"Hey."

Cait caught her disappointment before it came out in her voice. "Oh, G.B., hi."

"Listen . . . I've got to tell you something."

The sound of his voice was all wrong, the words tight and awkward, nothing like the smooth cadence he usually sported.

"Are you okay?"

"I'm really sorry to do this."

He certainly sounded like it. "G.B., what's—"

"Did Duke ever tell you about his family?"

She frowned. "He said he didn't have any."

"That's a lie, Cait." There was a long pause. "I'm his brother."

Cait backed up blindly, putting out a hand for her work chair. When she ran into it, she sat down—more like fell down.

"I'm sorry. I . . ." Had she heard that right?

He certainly hadn't stuttered—

Oh, crap, she thought. That was why, back in the beginning, she'd kept thinking she'd seen Duke somewhere before: He and G.B. *did* look alike. They weren't identical, but they were close, very close. Why hadn't the similarity occurred to her before now?

"Oh . . . God."

"There's more, though." G.B. cursed. "There's so much more he hasn't told you. Look, you don't have to be with me, that's not why I'm calling. But I like you, I honestly like you, and I know for certain you do not belong with him."

With a sense that the world was spinning around her, she held on to the corner of her desk. Dimly, she noticed that in the background of the connection, there was a lot of chattering, as if he were in a public place.

"Cait, I want you to come out and see something. You deserve to know the truth—he's not who you think he is."

Abruptly, she thought of all those silences she and Duke had shared. She'd assumed that what he'd said was true—that he wasn't good at talking. It sure as hell fit his macho, tough-guy persona. But had there been another reason?

"Cait, just see for yourself. Then you can make up your own mind. Come now, though, I don't know how much longer he's going to be here."

After G.B. gave her a location and she'd hung up, she found that she couldn't breathe. But she was clear on one thing. As memories from that nightmare with Thom began to replay in her mind, the need to have some solid footing, even if it hurt, drove her to get her purse, go out to her SUV, and head over to where G.B. had told her to meet him.

Fifteen minutes later, she pulled up to the Caldwell Galleria, and she almost forgot to lock up the Lexus as she strode over to the entryway of the food court. Going in through the revolving center doors, she looked around, expecting to see G.B., or Duke, or somebody.

There were a lot of people, but none she recognized.

Walking down past a display of pearl necklaces and engagement rings, she kept going, oily scents of stir-fry, French fries, and doughnut holes making her absently wonder how many calories she was breathing in. Where was—

Cait stopped dead.

About fifty tables were set up in the center of it all, red and yellow plastic trays full of logo'd food covering the tiny tops, all kinds of teenagers and parents and little kids stuffing their faces. And in the midst of them?

Duke.

And he wasn't alone. He was sitting across from a carbon copy of himself, the young boy showing all the promise of the same height and strength of his father.

It was Duke's son.

That was the only explanation.

Didn't have any family here, huh.

Her first impulse was to march over and get into his face—but she wasn't going to do that in front of the child. Nope. Duke had more than earned a lashing, but his son did not deserve to see any of that.

Spinning around, Cait slammed face-first into a twelve-foot-tall biker, the bearded guy catching her in the nick of time, or she would have landed on her face.

"You okay there, lady?" he asked in a Southern baritone.

"Yes, yes, I'm sorry, yes, please, thank you."

Scrambling out of the mall, she rushed into the fresh air, and quickly located the trash bins on either side of the entrance . . . because there was a good chance she was going to throw up the leftover lasagna she'd had when she'd gotten home from the funeral.

"Oh . . . God . . ."

Abruptly, she thought of her last conversation with Thom, the one that had revealed a truth that made things easier, not harder, to live with.

This shit with Duke in there?

It was so much worse than Thom falling in love with the woman he would later spend the rest of his life with. That had hurt, yes, but at least that particular ex of hers had proven to be the good guy she'd always believed him to be.

No family, she thought bitterly as she went out to her car. Duke must have a very different definition of the word.

Getting in, she slammed the door and gripped the wheel, and blinked hard—although whether that was from hurt or anger, she didn't know. Wrapping her arms around her stomach, she couldn't believe she'd invited that liar over to her house . . . welcomed him into her bed . . . woken up next to him just this morning with all kinds of delusions of intimacy. . . .

Snagging her phone from her bag, she went into recent calls and hit the one that was at the top.

G.B. answered on the second ring. "Are you okay?"

"I don't think so . . . actually, no, I'm really, totally not."

"Cait—" His voice broke. "Cait, I'm really sorry. If I'd known you were seeing him, I would have told you. He's evil . . . he's an evil guy."

Holding the phone up to her ear, she didn't fully focus on the parking lot in front of her, or the sun that was just about to set behind the JCPenney up ahead, or the couple who were walking hand in hand in front of her.

"G.B., I need to know something," she said in a dull tone.

"Anything."

"I need to know where he lives."

She was absolutely going to confront him, but it was going to be in person, not over the phone. She wanted the satisfaction of seeing his reaction when he found out that he'd been caught in his lies.

"Where am I . . . where . . . am I . . ."

As Cait heard the words leave her lips, she thought . . . God, she'd said the same thing the night this had all started. Instead of being in search of a hair salon, though, she was out in the boonies, driving along rural roads that were not marked, in search of a farm.

Didn't exactly narrow things in this kind of neighborhood—

Cait slammed on the brakes, the Lexus grabbing onto the pavement and stopping just before a turnoff that had a mailbox reading, RR 1924, next to it.

Swallowing hard, she wondered if she was really going to go through with this—namely, wait for Duke to get home and confront him in person.

The decision was made once and for all as she thought of G.B.'s expression when Duke had come out of nowhere at the grave site. G.B. had been shocked not just because she'd been seeing someone else—but rather because he'd known what it meant; he'd known the man she'd been fooled by.

Someone capable of lying about whether or not he had a kid? A brother who was alive and well?

Nothing was out of bounds.

She turned in and started down the dirt path, going past acres of shorn cornfields that would no doubt imminently be turned over for planting season. The farmhouse that first appeared was quite large, a brick construction of sturdy, ageless style. She went by it, as she'd been told to do, and kept on the road, eventually coming up to a squat ranch that had a decade-old car parked off to one side and a picnic table underneath a pine tree on the other.

Stopping right in front, she got out and looked around. Then she marched up to the windowless door and knocked.

Heart pounding, she had no idea who was going to answer the—

The stench of pot smoke that greeted her was enough to make her cough. And sure enough, as she looked past the skinny, happy-looking guy between the jambs, she saw two different bongs, a plastic bag full of weed, and enough lighters to start a bonfire on a pitted coffee table.

Annnnnnnnnnnnnd he did drugs.

What a fucking winner.

"Hi," the man said. "Are you Cathy?"

Like he'd expected someone by that name.

"No." Anger sharpened her tone. "Does Duke Phillips live here?"

"Yup, this is his place and I'm his roommate—what can I do you for?"

Lies, drugs, and a roomie.

You know what, she thought. This was bullcrap. Duke didn't deserve some confrontation. The best thing she could do, the only thing she *should* do, was take care of herself.

Cait just shook her head. "Nothing, actually."

As she pivoted away, he said, "You here to see Duke? He's due home any minute. You want to wait? I've got some cold pizza."

"No, thank you."

"Who should I tell him was here?"

"Nobody. I just took a wrong turn, but I'm going to fix that."

Cait went back for her SUV, and was rather proud of herself. No tears. No sobbing. No hysterics.

She did, however, feel like the stupidest woman alive—

"Wait! Hold on!"

She closed her eyes as she put her hand on her door. "Yes?"

The guy came loping over. "Seriously. You came here to see Duke, right? I mean, no one comes out here without a reason."

Cait cocked a brow. "Actually, fine. You can tell him that the joke's up. His brother told me all about him, and I've just come from the mall, where I saw Duke with his son. So he's not to call or come by to see me ever again." She opened her door and hopped into her seat. "Oh, and you can throw in a 'fuck off' in there somewhere while you're at it."

As she started her engine, the pothead backed off with his palms up, like he was afraid she might mow him down in her bid to get back to civilization.

Clearly, he hadn't smoked out all his brain cells.

Chapter
Fifty-four

When Duke pulled his truck up in front of the Appaloosa Way condo, he put things in park, but didn't cut the engine.

Nicole had been entirely too grateful when he'd called her on the way home from work and offered to take the kid out for a mall crawl and a talking-to. And maybe because of that, he didn't want to go inside even though she wasn't due home from her shift for another couple of hours.

Some lines, he didn't want to cross.

Others . . . might be okay.

He looked across the seat. The boy was sitting there like a bump on a log, lanky arms linked across his pigeon chest, his long hair in his face.

"So do we understand each other," Duke said grimly.

"What," came the grousing response. "Like you takin' me out for a burger's gonna make me—"

Duke reached across and clamped a hard hand on the kid's shoulder. As Tony's wide eyes swung to his, he dropped his voice. "You're gonna stop bullying that kid, are we clear? I hear anything more about you picking on him? The next visit will not be about an early fucking dinner."

Tony narrowed his eyes. "I can do what I—"

"Not while I'm around, you can't."

"You're not my father!"

"Well, there's no one else stepping up, so it looks like you're stuck with me." Duke put his face in close. "No more. Do you hear me—whatever the hell is wrong in your own life, you do *not* take it out on some poor son of a bitch in your class."

The kid's momentary flash-in-the-pan aggression didn't last in the face of a grown man getting up in his grille. But Duke wanted this to be about more than ripping Tony a new one.

He sat back. "Look, I know I haven't been around much, but I was wondering if maybe you and me, we could start getting together. My night job doesn't start until late, and you're just fucking around here in the afternoon. No reason we shouldn't kick some hours together."

Wow. Parental figure of the year over here, dropping the f-bomb. Whatever. He'd never done this before.

After a period of silence, Tony glanced over. Looked away. Looked back.

The suspicion and mistrust were a ball buster, they really were. But like the kid hadn't earned the right to be cautious?

"You're a bouncer, right?" Tony asked.

"Yeah."

"Do you beat people up at work?"

"Only when they deserve it."

"Cool . . ."

"Not really. Dealing with stupid, drunk people is no way to make a living." Duke shook his head. "I wanted to be a doctor, actually. Now, *that* is cool."

"Why aren't you one?"

Because your mother and I were . . .

Fuck that. "I quit college."

"Why?"

"I was a pussy." Yeeeeeeah, he probably shouldn't be using that kind of language around the kid, but the truth was the truth. "I didn't even apply to medical school. I pulled out two credits shy of what I needed to graduate. Biggest mistake I ever made."

His head had been too fucked to keep going, although in retrospect, he knew that was more about the evil that his brother was than anything he'd felt for Nicole: The concept that he'd shared a womb with someone capable of such casual cruelty had crippled him, shut him down . . . essentially infected him.

A chance meeting with Cait seemed to be turning that around, though.

And now he was going to try doing the same to Tony.

Trickle-down wasn't just about economics.

"Monday," he said. "Five p.m. Be in your gym shorts with a towel and a bottle of water on you. We're going to go play basketball. Deal?"

Tony narrowed those eyes again. But after a moment, he nodded. "Okay."

Duke nodded back. And stayed around to watch the kid walk to the door and disappear inside.

Before he could even put his truck in drive again, his phone went off—for the third time. Answering the call, he barked, "Rolly, what the *hell* is your problem?"

"You had a visitor."

Duke rolled his eyes. "Oh, for fuck's sake, do *not* tell me you're dropping acid again. The last time, you were convinced Bob Barker was staging an intervention."

"Okay, that was just a bad trip."

"Yeah, because you didn't listen to Mr. Price Is Right and put up your damn bong—"

"It was a woman. She was talking all weird, something about your brother? And, um . . ."

A blast of cold fear cleared his head and then some. "What. Rolly, what did she say?"

"Something about seeing you with your son?"

Duke exhaled in a rush, a swift pain hitting him in the gut sure as if he'd been kicked by a steel-toed boot. "When did she come by?"

"'Bout an hour ago? That's why I've been calling you. You never have visitors, and she looked pretty upset—"

"I gotta go. Bye."

Stomping on the accelerator, he skidded out as he turned around and flashed down to the exit of the development.

"Jesus fucking Christ," he bit out as he called a number he'd never expected to dial.

Five rings later, like the phone's owner wasn't in any goddamn hurry, a voice drawled, "Helllllllo."

"You fucking asshole."

"I'm sorry, who is this?" G.B. mocked.

"You know exactly who it is. What the fuck are you doing?"

"God, how rude are you, my dearest, darling, long-lost brother? We don't speak for how many years, and you don't even ask how I'm doing before you—"

"Do not try to play me. I know what you are, and I know what you're capable of." He'd just evidently forgotten that—why the *hell* hadn't it dawned on him that his brother was a liar, too? "Leave Cait out of this."

"Oh, but see, I can't do that. You were the one who brought her into it."

"You don't even know her!"

"And neither do you—or should I say, neither will you. Duke, you've just got to understand something—you can't keep women from me. Didn't work with Nicole, not going to work with this new one."

Duke's hand cranked down so hard on his cell that it let out a long beep, like it was going into cardiac arrest. "Listen to me. You stay the fuck away from her—"

"Not your call. And do yourself a favor. Don't try to win her back—you don't have a chance."

"We'll see about that."

He hung up the phone and then threw the thing at the dash. Slamming his hands into the wheel, he clenched his teeth around the scream in his throat. He knew better than to try to talk to his brother—back in the early days, he'd given that enough shots to last twelve lifetimes.

No talking. No reasoning.

The only thing he could potentially work with was Cait.

"*Shit!*"

Steaming across town, he pulled into her neighborhood going Nascar fast, but slowed down—because running over some kid or somebody's dog over was not going to help the situation. And as he came up to her house, he was sorely relieved to see her car in the driveway.

Now, if he could just get her to answer the door.

Jumping out of his truck, he jogged up to the front entrance. Just as he was about to push the doorbell, he frowned and looked over his shoulder.

He could have sworn someone was standing right behind him. The presence wasn't aggressive, though. Quite the contrary; it was almost like, after all these years of going it alone . . . he'd picked up a guardian angel or something.

Whatever, he thought as he punched the bell's button.

"Please answer the door," he prayed as he hit the thing again.

Cait was sitting at her desk, getting nothing done, when she heard a *ding-dong* go off at the front of her house.

She checked her phone. No calls. But she had a feeling who it was. The question was then . . . what did she do about it.

Ding-donnnnng.

Getting up, she brought her bottle of water with her for no other reason than she wanted something for her hands to do. And as she closed in on the door, she thought, Well, she had wanted to see his face when she told him what she thought of him . . .

Now was her chance.

Opening the way up, she stood strong and stared right into Duke's face. "You really think there's anything you can say that I want to hear right now?"

"Can we do this inside?"

"No, here is good. You're not going to be here long."

"Cait, I swear—"

She held up her palm. "Wrong approach. Any vow you give me? Isn't worth a dime."

He cursed and paced back and forth on her stoop. "Cait, you've got to understand my brother—"

"This isn't about him. It's about you."

"It's all about him! He's evil, Cait, I swear to it—he's—"

"Evil? What do you call lying about the fact that you have a son?"

"Tony's not mine. He's G.B.'s."

Cait opened her mouth. Closed it. Felt a pounding in her temples that suggested very soon, maybe in the next ten minutes, she was going to need to lie down in a dark room for several hours.

"You know what," she said slowly. "I think it would be best if I don't see either one of you again. Please just get in your truck and go—I've got enough to worry about in this life. I don't need this drama."

Stepping back, she was about to close the door on him when he caught the thing and held it wide. "Just let me explain. You don't have to do anything but listen, and if at the end of it, you still think I'm full of shit? Throw me out. Hell, I'll throw myself out. But, Cait, please. Don't let him do this to me again."

She frowned, thinking that was a weird phrasing.

Oddly, she remembered the janitor.

Talk it out. You need to talk it out.

"Please, Cait." God, there was such anguish in that voice of his. "Just hear me out."

After a long moment, she inched back enough to let him through. Closing the door, she went over to the bay window that faced the street and sat with one hip on its ledge. She didn't want him getting any ideas that either one of them was going to get comfortable.

Duke walked around her little living room, dragging his hand through his hair, shaking his head, looking like he was about to explode from some inner conflict. Whatever. She wasn't going to prompt him or make this easy on him in any way: As the light drained fully out of the sky, and the lamps that were on in the room became the only source of illumination, she just sat and watched him suffer.

Kind of gratifying, considering how she'd felt since she'd been to that goddamn mall.

"When you asked me whether or not I had family," he said abruptly, "I told you I didn't, because short of sharing some DNA with G.B.? He and I are strangers—and I want to keep it that way. I *need* to keep it that way." He closed his eyes and cursed. "We grew up at Our Lady's, and he started killing things then—"

Cait felt her eyes bug.

"G.B. exhibited all the classic signs of serious pathology. Setting fires, stealing, wetting his bed, setting traps for other kids. He was removed from the place and sent to a juvie facility by the time he was ten, and he never forgave me for the fact that I was the one they kept. He hated me—although, honestly, he hated everyone and everything, it seemed. After he left? I didn't see him for years. But eventually, he found me at Union. Didn't know it, though. I had no clue where he'd been or what he'd become."

He stopped and looked at her. "I was dating a woman, had been for a while. It was my senior year and I had all kinds of plans, you know, med school—she was going to go, too. We were all about the future. But you know, premed? Hard major. And I wanted to be ahead of everyone else. I was busy busting my ass in the library—while my brother, who'd been watching me, tracking my patterns, infiltrating my life . . . was starting to talk to her. He's a great one for cover-ups—a liar right out of the history books. And he got through to her, in ways I couldn't."

Cait blinked, the plausibility of the story increasing a little with every word he spoke—even though she wished it didn't.

"He, ah, well, let's just say he started sleeping with her behind my back. I found out about it all because she got pregnant. And I'm sure Tony's not my son as I hadn't been with her for two months before that because—to be honest, because I was focused on my work and not her." He cursed again. "I spent a lot of time blaming myself, thinking that if I'd paid more attention to the relationship, maybe it wouldn't have happened—but ultimately, I believe G.B. would have gotten through. He wanted to ruin me that badly. And he did—and it worked. I left school, shut down, backed out of everything. It was incredibly successful, and what he'd set out to do to me." He dragged that hand back into his hair. "I can't explain why the whole thing castrated me like it did. I just . . . the world didn't feel safe at all, anymore. And I guess I figured, fuck it and fuck everybody. I'm out."

As shades of her own story filled in the picture he was painting . . . she felt a commiseration she hadn't expected, and probably should have fought.

The trouble was, his affect was spot on, the confusion, the pain, the anger . . . everything she knew from having walked that path herself ringing true.

And yet . . . G.B. had seemed equally credible—

From out of nowhere, she thought of the way that man had looked behind the wheel of his car as he'd driven off from St. Patrick's.

That expression . . . what if it revealed who he really was?

"I don't know what to say," she blurted.

"I told you, all you need to do is listen." Duke sat on the couch, and braced his elbows on his knees, his eyes nothing but straight-shooter as he stared up at her. "And here's the part I'm not proud of—well, actually, I'm not proud of a lot, but this . . . this is the part that involves you. When I saw you at that café? I knew you'd been to see him—you had that . . . hypnotized look on your face as you walked out. See, our roles got reversed after the Nicole thing. I started to track him at that point—and I went there that night to . . . I don't know. I was pissed off because I'd just covered the child support he was supposed to be paying for, like, the hundredth month in a row. But when you looked at me, and I got out . . . there was something between you and me. Later, I went to that theater hoping that you were just there to hear him sing, but then you said he'd asked you to meet him."

"So you wanted to see me because he wanted me, too."

His eyes didn't blink, didn't move . . . didn't lie. "That's right. I asked you to the Iron Mask because I wanted to take something he wanted—but Cait, that didn't last. Listen, I swear on . . . well, I don't have anything of any value to swear on . . . but everything changed for me. I've been head fucked over the whole thing between you and me, because I knew things had started wrong, and I didn't know how to tell you. It just never occurred to me that he'd get to you before I could, to be honest. He hasn't shown any interest in me since what happened with Nicole."

Cait looked down at her Poland Spring bottle. Picked the corner of the label. Chewed on her lip.

For some reason, the image of G.B. and that receptionist fighting together dogged her. The woman had been viciously mad, out of her mind, totally rude—and G.B. had handled it so smoothly, like he seemed to handle everything.

But then behind that wheel of his car, his face . . . that beautiful, handsome face . . . had been so twisted.

Which was the real one? That was the question.

She cleared her throat. "This is a lot to take in."

"I know. I've had to live with it all my life, and I still can't understand it. Not fully." He laughed harshly. "You want to know how weird it is? I've been going to a psychic for years, down on Trade Street. None of this seems real, so I thought maybe someone who deals in the unreal could help . . . protect me or some shit. I don't know."

"Has it worked?"

"No. She's just been calling me nonstop about a dream she's been having about some brunette."

Cait touched her hair. "What kind of dream?"

"She just wants me to stay away from—" He stopped. "But listen, you're a blond now, right. Although honestly, if she was talking about you? She was probably right. You don't need this shit."

Duke got to his feet and went to the door. As he turned and looked across at her, he was grave. "I've said my piece, and I'm really glad you heard me out. You don't ever have to see me again— but I just want to ask you for one thing. If he shows up at your door, if he calls or texts you, if he writes you a song and wants to sing it to you, get the fuck away from him as fast as you can. Please. I beg of you, don't have anything to do with him."

Cait measured every single thing about Duke for the longest time. "Did you hear about the girl who died at the theater?" she murmured.

"I'm sorry?"

Cait shrugged and got down from the window's ledge. "There was a murder—I guess it was two nights ago? Downtown at the Palace Theatre, where he's been rehearsing. I didn't think about it at the time, but he told me the police are on him about it. You don't suppose . . ."

Duke marched over and took her shoulders gently in his hands. "Cait. Let me be perfectly clear about this. My brother is capable of absolutely anything. If you know of or saw something that leads you to believe he might have a grudge against that girl? Or some kind of beef? Call the police and tell them. Immediately. And like I said, for the love of God, don't ever let him into your house. Promise me."

She looked up at him. Damn, what a story. But sometimes even the implausible was true.

That was the basis of all fiction, right?

When he turned away again, she reached out and caught him.

The hug was meant to be quick, nothing but a brief, spontaneous contact. But the instant his arms went around her, she didn't want to let go so fast. Dear Lord, he was still big, and hard, but the fact that he'd done nothing but talk to her for the last ten minutes was the best part of him.

She wasn't just jumping back into anything, though. Too much, this had all been too much—and she was totally confused.

After a moment, she pushed herself away. "I won't."

"I'm sorry?" Duke said.

"Let him in. I'm not going to do that."

Duke brushed her cheek.

This time, when he went to leave, she let him go.

The soft sound of the door shutting was the loneliest thing she'd ever heard, and as she went over and sat where he had, her orderly little house and her orderly little life pressed in on her.

She had never expected something like this to be where she ended up at the end of her year of transformation—thinner, with better hair . . . but still very much alone.

Then again, destiny didn't come with an à la carte menu of options. You couldn't pick and choose where you went—not in any meaningful sense, at least.

Listening to the mournful tick-tock of the clock on her mantel, she collapsed back into the chair and closed her eyes.

No crying, though.

This was just a broken heart. It was not something like what Sissy Barten's family was going through—and in a time like this, she'd do well to remember that things could be much, much worse.

At least she hadn't ended up like that poor girl at the theater . . .

Chapter Fifty-five

Jim was standing in the darkness, watching from the corner of the living room as Duke unloaded big-time to the woman he'd been sleeping with. And as Jim listened, the sense that he'd been cuckolded for the second time penetrated his brain and made it hum.

Oh . . . fuck . . .

He'd gotten the wrong goddamn soul again, hadn't he.

Ducking free of the room, he stepped through the back door, got out his phone, and hit up Adrian.

The angel answered on the first ring. "What's up?"

Jim rubbed his aching eyes. "When you went to see Colin, back in the beginning of this—you asked him who the soul was, right?"

"Yeah. And he told me it was that Duke Phillips guy."

Jim shook his head wearily. "I don't think that's it. I don't know . . . what exactly did Colin say?"

"Look, Jim, seriously? All I was interested in was the intel—"

"I think we've been tracking the wrong guy here."

"Impossible. Under what scenario would Colin be incented to lie?"

"Just what did he tell you?"

"I don't remember—I asked him who it was, we went back and forth because he didn't want to tell me. Blah, blah, blah—and then he said . . ." There was a long pause. "Oh, shit."

Exactly, Jim thought, closing his lids. "What."

"He said he couldn't go all the way. He could only get me half-way there—I took that to mean that all he could do was ID the guy, and he couldn't help in the field." There was a pause. "Exactly what the hell's going on where you are?"

Jim looked through the windows into that living room, where Duke and his lady friend were hugging it out.

"They're brothers," Jim said. "And I'm pretty sure Duke's nothing but the triggering agent. The other one. . . the evil one's the soul."

"I'm coming right now—"

"No! You can't leave Sissy alone."

"Then I'll bring her with me."

"*Never*. She is not a part of this—are we clear? Stay the fuck home—"

"Fuck you, Jim—"

"Devina got into our house, okay? She got into my room, and not just once, but several times."

There was a looooooooooong pause. "What the fuck? When? Why didn't you tell me?"

"I couldn't find a moment."

"You didn't think it might be important enough to pull me aside? Like, for a split second?"

"I didn't know until this morning when I almost fucked her, okay?"

"Oh, *shit*."

"That just about covers it—"

Abruptly, Jim stopped talking and turned around. Sure enough, standing right behind him, the demon had made an appearance. "Ad, I got company. Stay where you are."

As he ended the call, Devina didn't smile. Didn't oil on up to him and start stroking his cock. She just stood apart and stared at him—and that was the scary thing. He much preferred her unstable and flying off the handle.

"So, have you thought about my suggestion," she asked after a moment.

"No."

"Liar."

Jim quickly did the math. He was willing to bet his left nut that the crossroads was happening right here, right now, whether it was here in this house or somewhere else. And if he was right, and Duke was not the soul, then he'd had no time to try to influence that other brother—and there wasn't going to be any.

This was the consequence Nigel had been so upset about. This was the culmination of Jim's decision to focus on Sissy. This was the payment for the distraction he'd entertained.

Damn it. He'd really fucked this round up, hadn't he—and there was no going back.

So he had two choices. Either he tried to find Duke's evil half somewhere in the city, and pray like hell that he could talk some sense into a guy he knew nothing about. Or . . .

"Let's go," he said.

Her perfectly arched brows rose. "Where?"

"Anywhere."

"To do what?" Now she trailed a delicate hand along the tops of her breasts. "Are you going to fuck me?"

"No. But I'll talk about the future."

"We can do that here," she muttered with a bored tone.

"No." Because if he couldn't influence the soul in these last few minutes, the least he could do was make sure she didn't, either. He had no idea what she'd done in this round, but —

"You want me away from this house, don't you," she drawled.

"You were the one who brought up that bright idea about quitting."

She laughed with an edge. "Jim, you know me well enough by now that I'm a lot of things—but never, ever stupid. You want me somewhere else? That's only happening one way."

In the pause that followed, he thought of Sissy. And as she came into his mind, the black hole in the center of his chest became filled with a ringing, nearly crippling, pain.

The demon took a step forward. "You and I can both leave here together. But only if it's to do what I want."

From out of nowhere, a full-body flush of total-nasty hit him hard. Which was a new one: In all the course of his life in XOps, he'd never had a problem with any kind of torture. He'd been subjected to it once or twice, and hadn't dwelled on the shit. And the same had been true in this war with Devina. Whatever she'd done to him, and what he'd done with her out of hatred—none of it had stuck in his head for even a moment after they'd parted.

This, however, was going to kill him. If he went with her now, if he did what he knew she was going to ask of him, he was going to die a little on the inside.

Funny, he hadn't been aware of being alive.

Sissy had brought that to him, however. She had opened him up—and that was why this was going to be the hardest thing he'd ever done.

"Where," he heard himself say.

"I think the Freidmont Hotel. Yes, I'll get a suite there, and I think that would be perfect for what I have in mind." There was a long silence between them. "So are we leaving. Or perhaps you would like to have me here?"

Yes, he had made a mistake in overfocusing on Sissy in the beginning. Yes, it had caused terrible, unforeseen consequences. And yes, to make amends . . . this was what he had to do.

"Fine," he said.

Now the demon truly smiled, her red lips parting, her eyes lighting with an unholy joy. "You first, angel mine."

***

What. The. Fuck.

From G.B.'s position across the street and down a couple of houses from where he'd followed Cait to earlier in the night, he couldn't believe what the fuck he was looking at. Duke had come to her front door and she'd been all pissy and shit—fine, good. But now, inside the house, spotlit in that front window, she was hugging him like that?

"You gotta be kidding me," he muttered.

Maybe Duke's powers of persuasion had improved with age. And that was going to prove to be very unfortunate for Cait Douglass.

Moments later, his cocksucking brother got into that big-ass truck of his and took off.

Goddamn it, G.B. hadn't wanted it to go down like this. But if there was even a chance Cait was going to take that fucker back? Well, he was going to have to once again create a situation where Duke had to live with a reality he couldn't bear.

G.B. had been thrown out with the trash, forced to go and get roughed up at that juvenile detention center for fucking years. Meanwhile, golden boy had gotten to go to high school, and get a scholarship to college, and have that girl of his. Guess the first payback hadn't been hard-core enough, though—otherwise, the guy would have stayed clear of anyone G.B. had been seeing.

He was happy to raise the stakes.

With a resigned shrug, he reached into the black bag he'd brought with him on a just-in-case. Taking out another pair of black industrial gloves—because they'd worked so well with Jennifer—he pulled them up his forearms and got out of his car. He had a knife with him, holstered at the small of his back, invisible under his loose coat. With a black baseball cap on, and the black trousers he'd worn to the funeral, he was a walking shadow as he crossed the pavement, being careful to stay out of the pools of light cast by the streetlamps.

He sidled around to the back of her house, keeping flush with the clapboards, grateful that she wasn't much of a gardener and hadn't put bushes everywhere around the foundation. In the back, there was a glass-enclosed porch with no doors . . . but he found a rear entry on her porch.

Locked.

Cupping his hands, he leaned into the nearest window. The kitchen was simple and neat . . . and he could see through to the living room. She was leaning back in a chair, head resting on the cushions, a bottle of water in one hand.

Was she asleep? That would certainly make things easier.

A little farther on, he found a storm door, but that, too, was secured. So was the door into the garage.

Damn it. If he had to break in, this was probably going to get messy before he wanted it to.

Heading around the rest of the house, he was all the way to the front again when he frowned and ducked over to the main entrance. There was no possible way—

The handle turned beautifully. Which meant there was probably a dead bolt—

The door opened in total silence.

And there she was. Eyes closed, breathing evenly, looking for all intents and purposes like she'd passed out.

He shut the door before some change in scent or temperature or draft alerted her.

Unlike Cait, he was careful to turn the bolt.

Moving slowly, soundlessly, he walked close to the walls, assuming that the floorboards were less likely to creak that way. He went past her and kept going, making a fat circle so that he could come up directly from behind her.

He didn't kneel or anything. He needed to be free to jump when it came to that—

Cait lifted a hand and rubbed her nose; then sighed as she resettled her arm on the chair. "Damn it," she whispered.

Reaching forward with his gloved hand, G.B. touched her blond hair, stroking the ends. Great hair. It had been what he'd first noticed about her back at the café.

Wasn't it weird that that chance meeting had brought them to this?

"Wake up, Cait," he said loud and clearly. "Time to play."

With that, he turned off the lamp next to her.

Chapter Fifty-six

The sound of a man's voice directly in her ear jerked Cait to attention, a surge of terror throwing her upright as the room went dark—

Rough hands locked on her hair, digging in, latching on, yanking her so violently to the side that her body flipped off her feet and she slammed face-first into the hard wooden planks of the floor.

Momentarily stunned, she watched in the dimness as a pair of nice black shoes came into her wonky vision.

G.B.'s voice was even. Almost bored. "I can't believe you fell for his sob story, I mean, really—I thought you were smarter than that."

He grabbed her head with both hands and dragged her back up, holding her with such vicious strength, she was convinced he was going to snap her neck.

As she struggled, he kissed the exposed column of her throat, running his tongue up to her ear. "But I guess you're a typical dumb blond. Kind of a shame, I actually liked you."

With that, he threw her into the wall headfirst, the impact enough to knock her framed diploma off its mounting. The glass shattered, and she stepped in it, pieces cutting through the socks she was wearing.

"I even killed for you." He banged her again into the Sheetrock. "I mean, I wouldn't have wasted time on that Jennifer thing—but she almost got you hurt. She ditched that ticket and you were terrorized in that garage. Remember?"

He grabbed on again and cranked her head back to meet her in the eye—and that was when she knew true terror: He was totally placid, his face almost pleasant.

"Remember?" he repeated, retightening his grip on her hair. "Sort of ironic, isn't it—given how this is going to play out."

She braced herself for another vertical impact, but he had other ideas. He ripped her back to the floor and pinned her facedown. As he mounted her from behind, his weight settling on her lower body, she cried out—

The knife was about six inches long, and had a blade that was cared for so well, it gleamed white in the distant light of her office.

"No more of that yelling. Don't want to wake the neighbors."

"You're not going . . ." She couldn't breathe.

"To get away with this? Of course I am. You'd be surprised what I've gotten away with in the past."

"You're . . ."

"Just stop, I know what I'm doing, okay?" At that, one hand locked on the back of her neck to keep her in place, and the other started working on her clothes.

Tears speared into her eyes, terror making her tremble all over.

Not like this, oh, dear God . . . but she couldn't move, and wasn't going to try screaming again in fear of—

A thunderous noise broke through the pounding horror in her blood, and she wasn't the only one who heard it; she could feel G.B. freeze above her. A moment later, it was repeated . . . and a third time, and a—

The explosion that came next was something she knew, if she lived through this, that she would never, ever forget. It was unholy, a roar that was loud and deadly as a wild animal's attack call.

An instant later, the weight on top of her was gone, and even as close to fainting as she was, she took advantage of it, wrenching herself up and shoving herself backward.

"Duke!" she screamed.

Duke's much larger body had taken G.B. down, the pair of them rolling around.

"He has a knife!" she yelled.

Like either one of them was listening? Scrambling to her feet, she wanted to help, needed to—

Fuck the phone and 911. What she required was upstairs, in her bedroom.

As the pair of them struggled for control of the weapon, she ran for the staircase, skidding in her now-bloody socks, ricocheting off the walls, scampering to the second floor. And even though it was totally dark up there, she found her bedside table in a second.

Her handgun was one she was licensed to carry and had been trained to use. But all of that had been on a hypothetical. It had never occurred to her that she might have to use the nine-millimeter autoloader.

She all but fell down the stairs.

Pulling herself around the base of the balustrade, she entered her living room with the weapon up at shoulder height and the safety off.

All hell had broken loose, her furniture busted up, more pictures down from the walls, the lamp knocked over.

They were up on their feet again, a hideous waltz happening as they circled around and around. Duke had control of G.B.'s arm, his superior strength on the verge of winning out, but he'd been stabbed, blood dripping off his elbow and from a wound in his side.

For a split second, she thought . . . yes, they truly did look like brothers. Nearly twins, as a matter of fact.

Then she leveled the gun at the two of them. "Drop the knife," she said in a voice that didn't sound like her own.

Both of the brothers looked toward her, identical pairs of blue eyes locking on the barrel of her gun.

Later, she would realize that Duke really did love her. Because for a split second, his concern for her distracted him and his focus was lost . . . and that was all it took.

G.B. pulled a second knife out from God only knew where and plunged it right into his gut.

"No!" she screamed.

Everything went into slow motion at that point. Duke dropped to his knees, clutching his abdomen, curling over. Above him, G.B. threw the knife up over his head, his eyes rapt, his body strung in an arc—

Pop! Pop! POPPOPPOPPOPPOP!

Cait started knocking off rounds, the bullets firing cleanly out of her well-oiled gun, one after another after another . . . driving G.B. back, the impacts jerking him like a puppet. And as he went, so she followed, discharging the entire clip as she walked with him.

Just as she had done in that dream she'd had early in the morning.

When she was finally finished, he was falling backward, his

feet tripping over themselves, his expression one of utter and complete shock, as if this was not at all what he'd had in mind.

He hit one of the glass windows of her office in the center of its large pane, and his weight and trajectory were too much for the fragile barrier to hold: he broke it as he finally fell back completely, his limp body shattering the expanse in a spectacular display of light and sound.

But she didn't give a shit about him.

Whirling around, she all but fell on Duke. "Oh, God, please don't die, please don't . . ."

With a groan, he pitched to the side, and she could tell he was struggling to focus. "Duke, I'm going to call nine-one-one, just hold on."

As she went for the phone on her desk, he captured her arm with a burst of strength that didn't last. "Cait . . . ? Are you there?"

Oh, shit. "Yes, I'm right here."

"I'm not going to live through this, Cait."

"No, you are! You're going to—"

"I love you," he said as he started cough. When blood appeared on his lips, she nearly screamed again. "I want you to—"

"I love you, too!" Oh, God, she meant that. With all her heart and her soul, even though she barely knew him, and even though—

"Just be with me as I go, okay? Just . . . stay with me. . . ."

"No! You fight it! Goddamn it, you fight and stick around until the—"

Fast, everything was going so fast now, as if time felt it needed to catch up from the slowdown that had just occurred. She needed to stop this—oh, God, how did this happen—how did—

As her mind threatened to hamster itself into immobility, Duke's voice reached her through the delirium.

"Cait, are you still there?" His eyes were moving around, but they were unfocused—and there was more blood, everywhere. "Cait?"

Pull it together. She was going to pull it together. Right. Fucking. Now.

As her brain came back on, there was only one thing she wanted more than to give him his dying wish. And that was to save his life. Which was not going to happen if she stood by and let him continue to hemorrhage on her living room floor.

For the second time, she tried to break away from him . . . and this time, he couldn't hold on to her.

Chapter Fifty-seven

"More coffee?"

When Adrian didn't answer, Sissy got up from the kitchen table and took his mug with her. As she poured out what was left in the pot, steam rose up and tickled her nose. Funny, the old pot seemed to be getting the stuff hotter by the hour, instead of the other way around.

"It's so late," she said, looking at the clock for the thousandth time.

She'd tried reading more of that book he'd given her. Had flipped through the magazines in that Target bag. Had even resorted to reading the newspaper, something she'd always assumed only parents did.

"How much longer can this go on . . . ?" she wondered out loud.

She couldn't believe she was still asking that as dawn closed in—and there still had been no word from Jim. No sign of him. No anything at all.

For a while, she'd assumed Adrian was just better at this waiting thing than she was. But then she'd realized he'd fallen asleep sitting up, his battered body somehow knowing enough to keep him propped upright at the kitchen table.

"I'm just going to go to the bathroom," she said to him in his repose. "I'll be right back."

After all, that coffee she'd been drinking all night had to go someplace.

As she headed out, her companion didn't show any reaction to her excusing herself, and that was okay. If she couldn't get any rest, he might as well have the benefit of it. And at least someone in the household would be perky enough to deal with whatever might come home.

Striding down the hall, and into the parlor, she shut herself in the formal guest bath. There were another nine or so to choose from, but she didn't want to go upstairs, and the other two on this level weren't as pretty.

She liked the flowered silk wallpaper, so sue her.

After taking care of business, she went to the sink and cranked on the gold handle. So strange. Every time she came in here, the fixtures seemed to get shinier, the mirror losing even more of the black pits that had marred its wavy surface, the crystal sconces coming back to life.

It was almost as if the house were de-aging.

But of course, that wasn't possible.

After drying her hands on a towel that was softer than it had been when she'd used it at midnight, some six hours before, she walked out toward the—

A flash of reflected light appeared across the marble floor for a moment . . . before disappearing as if it had never been.

Frowning, she changed directions and walked to the front part of the house. The door was closed, as it should be—so it couldn't have been from someone—like, oh, say, Jim—coming home. Besides, he walked through those kinds of things normally, didn't he.

Just as she was about to go back toward the kitchen, she heard the subtlest creaking above her head.

Someone was going up the stairs.

Rushing around in her stocking feet, she was about to bound up two at a time, but instead she stopped. Collected herself. Proceeded in a silent way.

As she passed the grandfather clock, it began to chime, its incessant droning pissing her off—as if the thing were making the noise in hopes of giving her away.

When she got to the top, she was just in time to see the hall bathroom door shut and hear the shower come on.

So it was him.

Fine. She would wait out here.

The second-story sitting area had an arrangement similar to the one in the parlor, sofas and love seats placed with care around an Oriental rug, little side tables supporting lamps and small objects made of stone as well as coasters for drinks consumed long, long ago.

Funny, her grandmother had had a collection of those carved rocks, too. Sissy had particularly liked the ones that were cut and polished to be fruit—green grapes made of jade, purple ones made of amethyst, apples and pears from various shades of quartz.

As the shower droned on, the grandfather clock eventually got over itself and fell silent, and she got bored with pacing around, so she sat down in the far corner.

Not long thereafter, the water cut off.

And Jim came out into the light with nothing but a towel on.

Surging to her feet, she went to say his name—

Something stopped her. Well, actually, it was him: He looked absolutely hollowed out, a shell of the man she knew, and yet that wasn't it. No . . . there was something else—

His mouth was swollen, but not like he'd gotten punched. Just red and puffy. And there were scratches on his bare chest and his arms.

Made by fingernails.

And he wasn't just exhausted; he was spent.

Sissy didn't know a lot about sex—well, the mechanics, sure, but it wasn't like she'd personally gone much past second base or anything. And it hadn't been because she was a prude. She'd just never found a boy who seemed worth the risks of pregnancy—had never been so flipping turned on that she'd let booze or romantic delusions go to her head.

She knew enough, though, to be one hundred percent sure that that man had spent most of the night having had it.

And the confirmation? Not that she needed it?

As he walked on to his room, he flashed his back: Which was covered in a shockly huge black-and-white tattoo of the Grim Reaper. And there were scratches on both the ink and the flesh, as if someone had been hanging on to him as he—

"Are you kidding me," she demanded.

He stopped dead in his tracks. But instead of turning around, he just dropped his head, as if he were too tired to hold it up anymore.

"I thought you were supposed to be fighting the war." She went over to him, getting right in front of his well-used body. "But that's not what you did all night, was it."

"Sissy . . . you don't understand."

"Oh, please, like you're going to hit me with another 'Stay out of it, this is all toooooo complicated for you, little girl'? Do you honestly think I don't know what the walk of shame looks like?

Christ, I saw it all the time in my dorm. I just never thought I'd associate it with you."

He pushed a hand through his wet hair and finally met her in the eye. "I'm going to bed now."

"Okay, great. So I guess Adrian and I'll just go find the soul—"

"We lost the round, okay? We lost."

Sissy stopped breathing for a moment. Then that anger deep inside of her flared. "Because you were fucking around with some woman, right?"

"As a matter of fact . . . that's exactly the case."

"Some savior you are. God, you're *pathetic*, you know that."

As Sissy pivoted on her heel, Jim watched her walk off. It was probably for the best. No, definitely for the best.

She was right; he had spent the night fucking. And when the round concluded itself? He'd been with Devina when she'd gotten the signal. Naturally, she'd insisted he come down to Hell with her to get her flag, and he'd gone because, once again, the only virtue she had was that she couldn't be in two places at once.

As long as she was with him? She wasn't with Sissy and Adrian and Eddie.

And with the way things were right now, that was the best he could hope for . . . the only thing he could expect to go his way.

So he'd sat down there and witnessed the soul arrive, a black shadow streaming the length of the well, entering the viscous wall, a fresh scream pealing out as the damned realized that death had not freed him at all.

In fact, he was trapped forever. Tortured forever. Not life everlasting . . . more like life never-ending.

And then he'd watched as Devina had taken a guitar string, a gold earring shaped like a shell, and an old Rolex watch out of her pocket.

"Just more to add to my collection," she'd said with a self-satisfied smile.

After that? No more reason to stay. And even the demon had been yawning like she'd needed some rest . . .

The slam of Sissy's door went through Jim like a bolt of lightning, his legs nearly going out from under him. The weakness wasn't simply because he was physically exhausted. Spiritually, he was coming to realize, he was dying inside.

If Devina was a parasite, as Eddie had said, and she entered through a wound in the soul . . . he knew he was making the infection in him worse every time he saw her, anytime he was with her. But even knowing that, he would have done no differently tonight.

Sacrifices were to be made. Had to be.

For some reason, he thought of the night he had spent sitting outside of Sissy's room like a dog.

That was the closest he was ever going to be to her.

And that hurt more than anything else.

Shutting himself in his room, he went over and got in his bed. The lights were off, and even though the daylight was coming soon, the room was dark because of the velvet drapes that were thick enough to keep a vampire safe from even July sunlight.

Within hours the cycle of the war would start again, another soul ready to be conquered or lost. And assuming the Maker didn't come and recruit him into Nigel's vacated seat at the tea table, Jim was now down one, the momentum of the war having shifted dramatically in the opposite direction.

Somehow, by some miracle, he needed to find the strength to fight again, at least until he learned whether Devina had spoken the truth . . . or had lied as usual.

He had no idea where the focus and drive were going to come from.

His tank was truly empty.

So maybe Devina was, for once, right. For the first time in his life, he saw the value of quitting. He sure as shit wasn't doing anyone any good with the way things stood now.

Closing his eyes, he let his body take over, the need for sleep canceling everything out, erasing even the fact that Sissy was pissed off down the hall, and Adrian was somewhere in the house no doubt aching from the sacrifices he himself had made, and Eddie was still lying in state, smelling as beautiful as a spring meadow.

He was a blank slate as he was claimed by a black void, his last conscious thought that he knew why Nigel had done what he had.

And he didn't blame the archangel one bit.

Chapter
Fifty-eight

"Okay, I think that's all I need."

As Detective de la Cruz, the one Cait had met outside the Palace Theatre, closed his little booklet, Cait winced and went to rub her eyes.

"Ow." Yeah, not touching much of her puss would be a good idea. If she remembered correctly, she had a dozen stitches in it.

"Can I get the nurse for you?" the man asked, concern on his tired face.

"No, I'm fine." She pulled the white hospital sheets up higher on herself. "Just have to remember not to . . ."

Make any contact with anything on her body, whatsoever.

He gently touched her shoulder, being careful not to get in the way of her IV. "I'm going to put in my report that it was justifiable homicide, Ms. Douglass. I don't think this incident is going to go to a grand jury, I really don't. The D.A. and I have worked together for a long time and there's a lot of trust between us. If you hadn't killed him, he'd have finished the attack on you. Guaranteed."

"Thank you, Detective. I've never . . . I never thought something like this would happen to me."

"You survived. And you're going to get through this. It's going to take time, but . . . you'll come out of it."

She could feel tears coming again, but God, she'd cried enough for ten years. "Thanks."

"Call me if there's anything I can do for you, okay? And I'll e-mail you a list of counselors that have experience with this stuff. They can really help on the flipside. Trust me."

He smiled at her, and then walked out, shutting the door quietly behind himself. Turning her head to the window across her private room, she stared at the gathering sun, and listened to the beeping behind her, and the hushed voices at the nursing station outside, and the bustle in the hall of people coming and going.

She hurt all over, her body aching in places she hadn't even known she had. And she wished, more than anything, that she had someone to call, somebody who could come and tell her, even though she wouldn't have believed it, that everything was going to be all right.

She'd decided not to get in touch with her parents. Not yet. Even if they were in the country, she wouldn't have wanted them to come rushing east with their manic prayers and Bible verses. She wasn't as angry with them as she'd always been, but she wasn't up to all that, either. And she couldn't call Teresa. God, no . . . she'd shot the woman's favorite singer dead, for godsakes.

Then again, knowing her old roommate? The fact that G.B. had turned out to be a homicidal maniac was going to change her opinion pretty damn fast.

For all Cait knew, she was going to be hero in the woman's eyes when they saw each other next: Teresa liked Dirty Harry movies even more than she liked heavy metal from the Reagan decade—

Some kind of shouting lit off out in the hall, and suddenly, all the normally quiet sounds went total-chaos, people yelling, running, the focus getting louder and louder as if a hurricane were closing in on her room—

Her door opened, some big shape pushing it wide.

"Duke!" She sat up so fast, her stomach nearly revolted from the pain. "Oh, my God! Duke, what are you—"

"Sir, I have to ask you to go back to your—"

"You were just operated on, sir, you need to—"

"Mr. Phillips! Please at least sit down—"

In spite of the fact that he was white as a ghost and weaving like a drunk and surrounded by hysterical medical staff, Duke ignored the drama, shuffling in with his hospital johnny and his compression stockings, leaning on his IV pole for support.

"Hi," he said in a hoarse voice.

Cait burst into tears and broke out laughing at the same time, a total emotional overload taking her in both directions until all she could do was reach out to him.

"There room for two up on that thing?" he said with a grunt, still ignoring the swarm of people in scrubs and name tags.

"For you, yes." She wiped her face but didn't get far clearing her eyesight. And she continued to laugh and cry as she pushed herself over.

It was a hard thing to watch, him stretching out. Clearly he was in tremendous pain, his body moving like an old man's, his coloring becoming worse—if that was possible.

But then he shoved away the hands that grabbed for him.

"What. You wanted me to sit down, I did you one better. Now, leave me the hell alone."

Well, looked like her bouncer was prepared to start swinging if he had to—and no one needed that, did they.

"Give us a minute," she said to everyone. "He'll leave as soon as we get a chance to talk, okay? I promise. Please."

Lot of grumbling. Some threats to call various doctors as well as security if Mr. Phillips wasn't in his own room in another five minutes. But they did leave.

When the door eased shut, she touched his face, reassuring herself that he was real. "I thought I'd lost you."

"I'm too stubborn to die like that."

"I'm so glad . . . to see you."

Even though his hand was shaking, probably because he had all the blood pressure of a deflated balloon, he brought her in for a kiss

His lips were still soft. And his eyes were still blue. And his skin was still warm.

"I thought I was going to lose me, too," he admitted.

"It killed me to leave you. But I had to get the phone."

"You saved my life."

Her brows went down. "Oh, I don't know—"

He silenced her by putting his forefinger up on her mouth. "You did."

"Does that mean you owe me some huge debt?"

"Yeah."

"Good." She had to smile, even though the gash on her cheek stung. "Will you take me on another date. When my face is back to normal?"

"You're as beautiful as ever. To me . . . you'll always be beautiful." As he kissed her again, she believed him. Completely. "And I will take you on that date."

Laying his head down next to hers, he stared at her for the longest time. "You gave me my freedom, too."

So funny. She had wanted to get out there and live . . . talk about being careful of what you wished for. And yet she couldn't think of anything better than having this man next to her. The detective was right: It was going to take a long, long time to get over something like this, and there was a good possibility she was never going to be the same.

But she had Duke. And the sense that neither of them was going anywhere else for the rest of their days . . . and nights.

For some reason, she thought of the janitor in that church. Thank God she had listened to him and heard Duke out, letting him talk. "I want you to know something."

"What?" he said.

"I really feel like this was supposed to happen. This whole . . . crazy thing. I just . . . you know, it was all supposed to go down exactly as it did."

"Funny, I was just thinking the same thing." He smiled even as his eyes fluttered shut. And then in a sleepy voice, like his body had been unwilling to rest until it was beside hers again, he said, "Love you . . . Cait Douglass. Love you with all my heart."

Cait stroked his hair, and imagined him drifting off. . . .

"I think I want to go back to college," he said suddenly, even though his eyes were still closed and she could have sworn he'd fallen asleep. "I want to finish. Maybe apply to medical school. Think it's time to be respectable."

"We could drive to Union together if our classes match up."

He smiled again. "It's another date."

Long road to recovery, she thought as she continued to stroke him. But yup, she had the unequivocal sense that they were going to do it together . . . that they were going to do a lot of things together.

Abruptly, she pictured herself behind the wheel of her car, squinting into the darkness, lost and trying to find her destination.

Where am I . . . where am I. . . .

Shutting her own eyes, she snuggled into Duke and knew she'd finally gotten where she'd wanted to be. With him, she was home.

Forever more.